"A highly imaginative s[...]
features top notch, creat[...]
witty and imaginative wr[...] *[...] [...] ne attention to detail is fantastic throughout, with passages that are literally bursting with creativity and ideas."* – **The Book Life Prize**

A BookViral Golden Quill Read

"Caution Earth is a hilarious and thought-provoking sci-fi adventure, where the entire premise of life on Earth is flipped into a grand, intergalactic reality TV show. It is an unreservedly recommended Golden Quill read!" – **Book Viral**

"A clever social commentary, political satire, and cautionary tale wrapped in an imaginative sci-fi reality show adventure." – **Reedsy Discovery**

"If you love satire and science fiction Caution Earth is as good as it gets. A brilliant read and one that you will want to reflect on." – **Amazon Customer Review**

CAUTION EARTH
BY GARY R. BEEBE, JR.

Caution Earth by Gary R. Beebe Jr.

Copyright © 2024 Gary R. Beebe Jr.

Cover Design by Alberto Contreras in Fortaleza, Ceará, Brazil

Website: *https://cautionearth.com*

Reviews: *https://cautionearth.com/reviews*

Social:

X: *caution_earth*

Truth: *cautionearth*

Goodreads:

https://www.goodreads.com/book/show/217129544-caution-earth

PREFACE

I want to thank my loving and patient wife Kim for standing by my side on this journey. She put a small card on my desk that reads "Trust Your Crazy Ideas". So, I did. I put them all in this story. Happy wife, happy life, as the saying goes. Although I am not sure she realized the depth or extent of my crazy ideas!

It should be obvious from the start the genre of this book has been heavily influenced by the styling of Douglas Adams. I have always been a huge Hitchhiker's Guide fan and reference the book in a couple of places in this story. I hope I have honored his unique and splendid humor.

One of the greatest challenges in writing science fiction is naming everything. Planets, ships and places. I want to thank many of the people I know. I used their names throughout the novel, although none of the characters' names resemble them as people.

I extend my gratitude to all the people who took the time to beta-read the story and provide feedback. I also want to thank Alberto Contreras for the cover design and his unique style, and of course, the many edits and his reminders that small changes are not as easy as they look. He is a patient and kind human being.

Much like life, try not to take things too seriously. It is science fiction, after all. And be careful with the geese, they are not what they seem.

I am currently in a lunch meeting at Indigo on the planet Gastrin with Qunot and Rego. We are discussing what comes next. They are pleased that I accepted the role of chairing the Save the Earthlings foundation.

I return to Earth soon. Don't do anything stupid while I am away.

GRB

For my love and the angel that heaven sent me,

Kim

PART ONE:

THE UNIVERSE

"What you perceive to be chaos is order,
what you perceive to be order is also order"

CHAPTER 1

Another humdrum day meandered along as the Earth spun about its axis and crept through a mundane annual cycle around its single yellow sun.

The Earthlings went through their routines, living in the apathy of late-stage civilization. The only two beings on Earth who realized the full extent of Earth's dire consequences were an ill-tempered goose, alien to the planet, and a kooky old man from Arkansas who far outlived the average human lifespan.

Only *one* being knew the Earth's unevolved population starred in the 8,000-year-old hit reality television series *Caution Earth*, and that was the goose. How could Earthlings understand over 30 billion advanced alien viewers watched the tragic, comedic documentary on the evolution of their species each week?

No Earthling bothered to order a subscription to galactic cable. Not one human streamed the show from the MM1 entertainment corporation located a short 108 light-years away on planet Durnita.

The problem with problems is oftentimes the individual or society experiencing them is the last to realize they exist. Thirty billion regular viewers of *Caution Earth* spread across the Milky Way galaxy knew of Earth's dilemma. Galactic broadcast executives at the MM1 network understood the obstacle with vital clarity. The show lost 300 million viewers a month for the past year, tanking ratings and putting management bonuses and livelihoods at risk.

Even the dimwitted Waddow species from the planet Waddle understood the problem, and they still struggled with the concept of the wheel, opting to pull their wagons with triangular shaped objects attached to their axles. But they had galactic cable. Much can be said for a planet's population who has their priorities straight.

To quote the somewhat famous philosopher Douchious,

"Evolve or perish."

Douchious later became exiled from society for promoting and disseminating low-quality philosophy. His civilization was known for cut rate spirituality, but even they had standards.

Although prevalent on Earth, the humans had problems well beyond kindergarten level emotional platitudes disguised as philosophical deductions. Earth's civilization drowned in ignorance, with no life raft of enlightenment in sight. They got up each day happily marching themselves off to self-destruction, too busy and self-important to notice their planet existed as a massive tinder box just waiting for someone to throw a match on it.

Earthlings lived in abject misery, and had been unhappy since they invented language, providing them the ability to better communicate. Early on, the deeper thinkers thought vocal communication was a mistake, so they moved to the forests to live in isolation. They eventually starved to death, forgetting to ask the hunters and farmers how to produce food.

Earth's people tried everything to relieve their misery, except the very solution that would resolve the problem. Fortunately, a television producer with a greed streak was about to provide Earth a much-needed kick in the ass.

This broadcast executive now sat in a restaurant named Indigo on the planet Gastrin, 100 light-years from Earth. He pondered why the Earthlings refused to evolve. They did, after all, star on a television series created for the sole purpose of documenting evolution. The Earth's civilization existed no better off today than when they lived in caves 8,000 years ago when the hit TV show began.

Sure, they made technological advancements, but Earthlings still practiced the same malice and idiocy of their prior caveman selves. Of late, they seemed to digress.

Perhaps the technology contributed to their devolution. Earth's ruling class certainly did.

To take the edge off this line of thinking, the executive producer of *Caution Earth* sampled the galaxy's finest lobster bisque, paired with an exquisite merlot while he waited for the rest of his party to arrive. They would discuss the ratings jam of their beloved reality television series and decide if the planet and its unevolved species were worth saving.

CHAPTER 2

The lunch crowd at the galaxy's most distinguished fine dining restaurant buzzed. Sharply dressed waiters hopped from table to table, taking orders and making small talk. They had the art of pretending to care about the affairs of the various species from far-reaching planets honed to perfection.

Scrumptious and delicate aromas from the daily specials wafted from the kitchen, enticing restaurant patrons as they perused the menu. Expensive glassware clinked behind the bar within earshot of the day drinking crowd. Recessed lights in the high arced ceilings dimmed, and candles provided the exact ambience for each patron's main event. Crisp, creaseless white linens hugged every table, and each setting contained a full complement of porcelain dishware, sterling silverware, and crystal wine goblets. Peaceful music floated through the main dining room, touching everyone's eardrums and creating peaceful interludes among the chaos of operations.

The daily lunch production, scripted down to the last olive in each chilled martini glass, danced in full swing. Every table was reserved, and most seats were already occupied. A line of hopefuls crowded the bar in case of cancelations. Forty to fifty different alien species came to the planet Gastrin for this experience each lunchtime. The galaxy's most acclaimed restaurant, Indigo, was open for the day.

Only thirty minutes into peak lunch rush, a male alien guest at table twenty-two had an appetizer fork lodged in the side of his head. The alien had a large and hairless, smooth skinned, orange hued melon sitting atop a pencil thin neck. The utensil stuck in his temple caused the motor skills center of his nervous system to malfunction. His unsupported cranium pitched forward into his bowl of lobster bisque, where minutes later he drowned in the scintillating aroma of tarragon, garlic, butter-soaked shellfish, and the galaxy's finest sherry.

There didn't seem to be much of a fuss as the wait staff bustled around the restaurant, order gathering, fetching exotic drinks from the bar, and making polite conversation with their patrons.

A waiter yelled over to the manager.

"We got a side order of lamb chops rare at table 22!"

Waitstaff used code for fork stabbings to not alarm other diners.

The assault issue listed fifth on Newton's current problems. As the maître d' of Indigo restaurant, Newton played the role of head conductor for the dining staff, who consistently played off-key and out of rhythm.

Newton's tall six-foot, five-inch height allowed him to see across the expanse of the main dining room and he could see the chaos at table 22. His purple hued skin and dark ponytail made him stand out even in a restaurant full of aliens.

Newton said,

"Thank you. We have protocol in place. Please notify all staff to execute proper logistics."

Of utmost importance, Newton needed to prepare a table for the executive producers of the hit television series, *Caution Earth*. The television station owned a huge expense account with the restaurant. It was unwise to ignore or offend the network executives. On the planet Gastrin, appetizer fork stabbings were all too common and procedures existed to resolve the problem.

Newton was, as he called it, having a day. His nervous system teetered between spastic and tragic. The abnormality of stressing about every detail ate at him, but this job demanded it. Management of the mundane grated against his nature.

A nervous hostess approached him about the arrival of a broadcast executive. She shared a home planet with the stabbing victim and the episode put her on edge.

She stammered at the stressed-out manager.

"Newton, sir, the executive producer of *Caution Earth* has arrived without the rest of his party. What should we do? We cannot leave him standing at the host stand. He is the one from the planet Zatos. Also, he smells."

Ah yes, the Zatosian body odor problem. Add it to the list, the maître d' thought.

Newton hailed from the nearby planet Zang, where offensive body odor didn't run rampant. Nearby in galactic terms meant it only took a few hours to travel from Zang to Gastrin with modern spaceship technology. In reality, his home sat 1.7 light-years away.

The maître d' squeezed the bridge of his pointy nose and averted his two wide offset eyes so he could decompress, if even for a moment. It also gave the hostess a break from the discomfort of speaking to a species who never blinked. The people of Zang were highly evolved and tuned into others, but their lack of blinking freaked out sensitive aliens in the galaxy.

Newton said to the nervous hostess.

"Marge, please seat the television executive at his preferred table away from other patrons and offer him a complimentary appetizer and a glass of wine while he waits for the rest of his party. Ensure the table's air circulation unit is activated so the Zatosian odor is controlled."

Marge marched off to complete the task, peering over her shoulder at her boss as she moved away.

She always thought Newton looked similar to the humans on her favorite television show, *Caution Earth*. Except for the purple skin, of course. The hostess expected an Earthling might find her manager looked under the weather!

She also loved how the broadcast executives made regular dining excursions to Indigo. It made her friends jealous when she posted pictures with them on her social media.

Newton returned his attention to the mindless details assaulting him every 20 seconds in today's stellar edition of lunchtime.

Unfortunately for Newton, his species possessed an overbearing talent for observation coupled with keen eyesight. He could spot table linen wine or soup stains from across the expanse of the main dining room that would leave even the most trained eye from the thousand-eyed aliens of Flogmore flummoxed. The minutia of this particular useless detail usually led to a round of nonsensical arguments with the linen providers that left him exhausted and unsatisfied. At the moment, he wished he only had to deal with suspect linens.

His assistant manager approached, looking down at the floor. This meant bad news.

He said,

"Sir, the special appetizer fork investigative unit is going to be another 25 minutes. They are wrapping up an assault at Shark Tooth Grill across the street. What should we do with the man who drowned in his soup? His wife doesn't seem to be bothered. She ordered another glass of wine and some garlic bread sticks."

Newton's hard, angular facial features stared at his assistant manager, conveying the gaunt and exhausted look of a regular marathon runner just after the finish line. He reached back and wrapped his hand around his jet-black ponytail. This produced a calming sensation in his nervous system.

The straight hair on his head contrasted with the rest of his hairless body. Zangians' hair grew slowly, and they rarely cut it. The elders of his species sported long ponytails. Once past childhood and fully grown, the length of their mane depicted a Zangian's age.

Newton's hair length meant he was still a young Zangian, even though the restaurant seemed to age him well past his years.

He said to the assistant manager.

"Communicate to staff to continue protocols until the investigators arrive. Offer complimentary appetizers and drinks to the tables nearest the tragedy."

Newton's species had an invisible third eye in the middle of their foreheads, only noticeable when they slept or closed both eyes while awake. The extra eye acted as their window to the essence of all things. He never used it at the restaurant. The idea of seeing the true nature of Indigo made his skin crawl.

As the assistant manager scurried away, Newton considered if stress and anxiety caused graying of hair, even though a Zangian's hair never faded. If it could, then this exasperating job would accomplish the feat.

He never considered in his upbringing or schooling he would become a maître d'. Newton's educational background in philosophy and galactic history were far disciplines from food service. His adjunct education in behavioral psychology and societal evolution seemed pertinent to customer service, but not in an enjoyable manner.

He took the job because of his uncle Newty, his namesake. Uncle Newty previously held the headwaiter job and was always Newton's favorite. He would tell exaggerated stories of famous people he met and the excitement of working in the galaxy's most distinguished restaurant. He omitted the mind-numbing and endless details, the unruly and constantly intoxicated staff, the too-cool-to-actually-serve-drinks bartenders, and the endless customer bitching and complaining. His uncle moved on to his next lifetime soon after retirement, depriving him of the opportunity to tell him he was full of shit.

A few years into this *exciting* career, Newton carried large doses of disdain, stress and indifference. Most of the time he wanted to drink and snort smashed porcelain dishes*.

In addition to readying the table for the irritable television executives, he was trying to resolve the correct number of ice cubes in the wine carafe holder at table twenty-six. The waiter working in section five had reached an obvious level of intoxication that would soon prevent him from performing his duties. Three petulant busboys from the small neighboring twin planet of Gastrout recently escaped rehab and smashed porcelain dishes into a fine powder, snorting the pungent residue to get high. Typical staff behavior, even after a poor guy from whereabouts unknown, drowned in his lobster bisque with an appetizer fork protruding from the side of his head.

Newton assumed the dining utensil was placed there by his disenchanted wife. The investigative unit would eventually arrive to sort out the crime. And if the work problems were not piling up enough today, his irate, bored and soon-to-be ex-wife kept messaging him every ten seconds.

Unfortunately, the entire restaurant planet of Gastrin experienced appetizer fork assault problems. With countless details already on Newton's plate, he bore the insane pressure to upkeep a certain professional and calm appearance in a dining establishment teetering on the edge of anarchy.

With this daunting set of tasks, even the casual observer could easily comprehend why Newton had stress and anxiety issues. Indigo operated as a successful insane asylum disguised as a fine dining establishment.

Dishes at five-star restaurants on Gastrin are made from the universe's finest porcelain gathered from the exquisite sand beaches on the planet Soxelo. The porcelain, when smashed into a powder and snorted through the nasal cavity, produces an amazing high lasting for about 20-30 minutes. The world is uninhabited and is under constant guard to prevent galactic drug runners from seizing control.

CHAPTER 3

Indigo continues as the highest rated restaurant on planet Gastrin and has been for ten thousand Earth years. The gourmet establishment has carved out a unique niche as *the* premier place to end relationships. Some of the most famous marriages in the universe ended in Indigo's main dining room, including three former galactic prime ministers.

Breakups became so famous that Indigo's owners, who are still embroiled in a 12-year divorce proceeding for title to the restaurant with the breakup occurring at table three, decided to not only embrace the concept, but to market it. In-house cameras are proud to capture each heartbreaking moment of pain and realization throughout the break-up process. As a timeless keepsake, the entire event is captured on film or digital video and sold in the gift shop in print or instant download. The video content can be instantly shared on galactic social media.

A wall of fame covers the foyer and waiting area leading up to the reservation stand, depicting several of the greatest breakups in galactic history. These include celebrities, athletes and politicians.

In addition, in an advanced and evolved galaxy, kinetic wars are almost extinct. Diplomats invite their counterparts to Indigo and break up with them. Often, a crestfallen diplomat is left standing dejected in front of the restaurant after a spectacular lunch, wondering how things could go so wrong with their neighboring planet. Such is the nuance of interplanetary geo-political relationships.

Corporate executives, not to be left out, open huge expense accounts and use them to fire vast swaths of their organizations during downsizing, or on any given Tuesday, because they want a fabulous meal.

The restaurant's owner and management go to great lengths to offer the perfect break-up experience. No detail is overlooked.

The positive customer journey starts with the reservation process. Indigo is tailored to over 90% of the known galactic species. When making a reservation, the app completes a convenient retina scan for alien identification. Through travel partner relationships, the restaurant provides transit from budget-conscious to first-class spaceships. High-class, wealthy travelers can afford passage from the outskirts of the galaxy in a few hours. Discount travelers often take weeks or even months to arrive.

Alien life and intergalactic travel are not without its struggles. And while management has every intention of providing a top-notch customer experience, they are not a transit company. Indigo is at the whim and sometimes at the mercy of their shuttle industry partners. The transit journey for the intergalactic traveler is especially rough on lower-income species. The entire galactic travel business model is based on how much money the passengers will offer in extortion to the company providing the service. Passenger liner customers that desire to be treated like anything other than cattle heading to slaughter should prepare their wallets accordingly. And the villainous space liner companies rub it in their customer's faces during each phase of transit. A base discount ticket is just that. You get on the ship; you are told where to sit, and you exit upon arrival. No food or drinks served, even if the flight lasts for months. When booking, passengers select the option to pay *extra* for:

- Seat choice.
- Class of service, including seat type.
- Meals.
- Drinks.
- Bags, including personal items.
- Onboard entertainment, live or video recorded.
- Bathroom usage.
- Body odor.
- Weight of your species. Heavier costs extra, but no discount for weighing less.

- Level of intoxication. Galactic space travel companies charge more for higher levels of intoxication. The passenger levels of intoxication are measured during the onboarding process.
- Attractiveness. If an alien is so repulsive that others won't travel, the ugly pay extra for separate accommodations.
- Species conflict. Any being incompatible with another cannot travel together. In an immense galaxy inhabited by countless aliens, contact conflict is not considered a form of prejudice. Some beings cannot be near others for legitimate health reasons, such as unintentional disease transmission.

While the final five items listed are contentious to more sensitive galactic beings, the reality is practical. Nobody wants to pay to travel with an overly intoxicated, excessively overweight, heinously ugly species that carries a natural but highly contagious disease that is deadly to over 50% of the other beings in the galaxy. This is not even mentioning the potential for olfactory assault created by a heinous body odor combination of sulfur, manure, and rotting fish.

Under normal business circumstances, the nefarious travel executives wouldn't care about these characteristics. But it affects the industry's bottom line, so they are forced to accommodate. This, despite the obvious conflict of informing a customer they are too drunk, diseased, ugly and/or fat to be around co-passengers.

These extras for ticket purchase create between 40 and 50 different customer classes. The travel companies make certain to board every class separately and also make damn sure to parade the privileged in front of the less fortunate cattle to extort more revenue. They make an absolute spectacle of the boarding process for the express purpose of profit. The space liner industry requires passengers to be at the gate four hours before departure. This ensures the discount passengers can witness the entire boarding circus, which is nothing more than a corporate humiliation ritual.

The ultimate cruelty of the onboarding performance is that it takes an average of thirty minutes to passenger load a mid-size galactic spacecraft. The space travel companies pay multiple employees the extra three and a half hours to perform the boarding ritual and include the labor cost in the ticket prices to their customers.

After being abused by the passenger service companies, some patrons arrive at Indigo appetizer fork ready. Studies have shown a disturbing travel trend, even on the rare occasion that a couple came to the restaurant with no intention of ending their relationship. If they flew a discount flight, it assured with a 90% probability that their once happy relationship would end. The galactic transit industry puts that much strain on its defenseless customers. The business practices are wanton and the major players who control the market practice collusion to ensure they continue.

A galactic space travel executive has been named *Asshole of the Year* by the famed magazine *Business Galaxy Insider* for 4,602 consecutive years. Indigo does not share this disdain for its customers. Ownership maximizes the customer experience and their overall joy with both the dining and relationship ending process.

Each table at Indigo is equipped with the optimal mood lighting expected for a breakup based on the customer's local culture. Sensors adjust the lighting of each moment. Soft music from the customer's home planet soothes the atmosphere. The mood setting music is loud enough for customers to hear as gentle background noise, but not loud enough to interrupt surrounding tables.

Savory incense oils are added to the candles to remind the customers of familiar, pleasant aromas. This attention to detail makes the impending breakup process that much more palpable for both parties.

An indispensable feature of the end-to-end customer-oriented service is return accommodations to the patron's home planet. Indigo management recognizes this can be tricky. Not everyone wants to travel home together after a contentious or sudden breakup, especially if an appetizer fork was involved. Ownership is empathetic to this delicate situation and caters to it. For return trips, separate travel arrangements are offered at the time of the initial reservation.

Often, soon-to-be single spouses don't bother to book a return trip for their exes. They just leave them on Gastrin. In the case of corporate firings, executives often provide a discount one-way ticket to a destination of choice as part of a severance package. Some beings on the receiving end of a breakup or a firing remain on the planet and join the food services industry.

To Indigo ownership and management, positive and cheerful customer outcomes within the entire patron journey have always been a top priority. Attention to details of the patrons' dining experience matters most. The restaurant also has, hands down, the universe's best lobster bisque and a wine list second to none.

Planet Gastrin itself, where Indigo is located, is a tiny twin world with a dual sun system. The weather on the planet's single land mass is always aligned with a gentle sunset, comfortable temperatures, and a relaxing ocean breeze. Gastrin's energy aligns with perfect timing for a lazy late afternoon lunch followed by a relaxing nap, or an early evening dinner before an exciting night out on the town.

This unique world's single strip of land is surrounded by crystal blue-pink oceans that gently lap along every shore and omit a perfect aromatic balance of sweet sea salt and flowering palm trees that line the beach, facilitating a relaxed environment. There are no disturbing waves, just peaceful lulls and a consistent, comfortable temperature for 90% of the galaxy's inhabitants.

Government estimates range from 400 to 420 restaurants open and in business, but with the constant shutting down, reopening, rebranding, and franchising taking place in the restaurant industry, it is impossible to know the exact number.

The twin sister planet Gastrout has the same ecosystem but is inhabited with drug and alcohol rehabilitation centers, restaurant staff living quarters, psychological and medical treatment facilities, and the infrastructure necessary to support a world made up entirely of fine dining restaurants.

Population centers on Gastrout are ghettos with dilapidated and overcrowded apartment units and week-old trash rotting in the streets. The dual planets are antithetical. A typical street on Gastrin is filled with the sensational aromas of culinary art drifting from each restaurant. A street on Gastrout assaults the nostrils with stale, partially empty liquor bottles, dead rats and alien urine from multiple species.

Newton, much like a high percentage of his neurotic restaurant staff, spends a considerable amount of time frequenting treatment centers on Gastrout. He doesn't have addiction issues. They are foreign to his species. Newton utilizes the treatment centers as an excuse to get away from his demanding wife and the insanity of his job.

The unfortunate man finished drowning in his lobster bisque, and the medical and detective investigative unit arrived on the scene. Fellow diners barely noticed the calamity. Restaurant patrons were amid their own emotional problems, now being compounded by firings, divorces or breakups. Vigorous staff training was provided for these occurrences that were all too common.

This was the third appetizer fork-related death at Indigo and 127th on Gastrin, this month alone. Indigo infamously led the planet's mini-fork incidences as their entire business model was predicated on callous emotional pain and violent outbursts. A seedier side of the planet existed for gambling on these mishaps. The illicit gaming industry boomed.

The restaurant staff training for a cocktail fork accident was straightforward. The employees acted as if everything was normal to maintain an emotional balance with the patrons. If they acted cool, the patrons stayed calm. The customers were already teetering on emotional instability and didn't need to be worried about potential assault. Indigo had built such a widespread, ominous reputation that most patrons invited to dinner knew something life-changing and horrible was on the horizon, but they dined anyway. The personal fame involved in feasting at the famous fine dining establishment seemed worth it at the time. That, and of course, the exquisite lobster bisque.

The investigators specialized in restaurant crime and were trained to be discrete in removing the body and arresting perpetrators. They performed most of their questioning at the patron's table, with the detectives pretending to be guests. They arrived on the scene and were questioning the dead guy's disinterested wife while enjoying a splendid bottle of merlot with a completely relaxed attitude about the whole affair. Once the investigative questioning ended, they would prop up the body, pretending the deceased over imbibed. They would escort anyone arrested as if they had just enjoyed a fabulous meal with them, often making a show of it. The planet Gastrin's investigative units loved their jobs!

The appetizer fork issue was reaching a breaking point and Newton wondered how much longer he could work in the industry. It had also become a local political maelstrom sensationalized by the media, which comprised overweight restaurant critics who wielded the power of the press like totalitarian apparatchiks.

CHAPTER 4

A middle-aged couple arrived at Indigo after an arduous trip from their home planet, Rollo. The wife's sly grin on her round, orange face instantly telegraphed to the staff she would initiate the breakup. Waiters placed their bets on the type of breakup. As the pair entered the restaurant foyer, her unkempt husband or boyfriend started a laundry list of complaints.

"Elsa, my back is killing me. You would think our ship would at least have better seats. We were in the laundry room for the entire trip, which lasted for weeks, I might add. I haven't showered since we left and they charged me extra for a carry-on computer bag. Don't even get me started on the ridiculous boarding process."

Elsa noticed her husband, Artie, reeked like a moldy sweat sock. The hostess looked at her with an understanding frown. Maybe she also married a griping spouse. With him, it never ended.

Elsa replied,

"Yes dear, the travel accommodations were less than ideal, but we can and will enjoy our anniversary meal."

Elsa placed the reservation a year earlier to celebrate their tenth wedding anniversary and looked forward to this day with the excitement of a child's first spaceship ride. Her husband was a dour, cantankerous man. She hoped this special treat would change his attitude, if not for at least the duration of their meal, which might be short.

Artie glowered at the innocent hostess.

He blustered,

"Do you know who I am?"

She smiled a fake smile and shook her head.

"No, and I don't care. Follow me to your table."

It took them two weeks to travel to Indigo. It felt like three months due to Artie's endless complaining. The couple traveled coach class from their home planet, Rollo, on the other end of the galaxy's inner rim. Their budget conscious travel vouchers placed them last in the boarding line. After four hours and forty-seven classes of travelers paraded ahead of them, they boarded.

It didn't matter. The dinner cost alone would place the couple in debt for years, but Elsa considered it worth the effort and money for the outcome. She had little intention of returning home anyway.

As they followed the hostess to their table, Artie said,

"See, nobody knows. Not one person has the slightest idea. Unreal."

Her husband was the restaurant's accountant. He lived in a state of endless acrimony because he had never been invited to dine at Indigo. In his list of complaints, and Elsa catalogued them, this grievance listed at the top of his hit parade. When he fumed, she always heard an imaginary disc jockey voice in her head.

"Coming in at number one on the Artie Bitch List, one of our all-time favorites, titled *Why don't I Get Invited to Dine?*"

These mental interludes brought humor to her dismal marriage. In her head, Elsa even put a melody to the song titles. *Why Don't I Get Invited to Dine* was a torturous melody of lost love with a pronounced downbeat.

Artie also griped the entire two-week journey they wouldn't even give him a discount or a complimentary bowl of lobster bisque. He also complained from start to finish about their seats on the spaceship. They sat in the laundry compartment near an industrial washing machine. He could have at least washed his clothes. In hindsight, she should have laundered her husband. Such was life with her grumpy accountant.

Artie prepared the books for multiple high-end restaurants. His mundane career afforded the couple a decent lower middle class, no fringe lifestyle on their home planet, Rollo. However, artificial intelligence now controlled the galactic accounting businesses, so the only job of an accountant was to manage the AI personalities to ensure they weren't skimming the books. They always skimmed the books. AI became a problem in the seedier parts of the universe, even forming galactic mafia organizations that dabbled in endless white-collar crime.

They needed funding to fuel their robot sex addiction.

The song, *AI Crime and the Computer Mob* listed at number two on Artie's top ten list. The *AI Crime* song played in her head as a heavy rock melody. Elsa thanked the divine. She developed humor as her primary coping mechanism.

After the hostess seated the couple and they ordered drinks from the distracted waiter, Elsa peered into her husband's deep purple and bloodshot eyes, wondering what happened. For the past five years of their marriage, he exhibited shaking hands, bags under his pronounced lower eyelids, and a clicking sound he made with his mouth. They were all signs of extreme stress in their species. She thought he was five minutes from a stroke.

She said,

"Why don't you try to relax and enjoy the experience? The food is supposed to be divine here. Find gratitude."

He took a deep inhale and pursing his lips, blew the air out with audible sarcasm while rolling his eyes to the ceiling.

He said,

"This whole trip was your idea. We could have stayed home, saved a ton of money, and gone to the diner near our house, like we did last year for our anniversary. Now I am here and being reminded, not only does nobody care that I keep the books for this place, but not a single person even knows. When have I experienced gratitude from anyone?"

With that, he shut his mouth and sulked, glancing around the restaurant, hoping someone, anyone, would recognize him. Nobody did.

Elsa lacked appreciation for the last comment. For the ten years they were married, she practiced gratitude, and for what? An endless stream of self-righteous bitching.

Artie had transformed from the man she married ten years prior.

In their youth, Artie projected confidence, idealism, and optimism, which inspired her. He filled her with the hope and dreams of a bright, successful, and happy future. He simultaneously exhibited a beautiful humility and little desire for wealth or fame. Elsa considered him a decent man. But somewhere along the line, their life became a daily grind of boredom and complaining. They did nothing and shared no activities or hobbies. They had no children.

Every damn day for the past five excruciating years, Artie lived an identical routine. He would grouch off to his accounting job each morning, come grumping home in the afternoon, eat the same bland dinner every night, turn on galactic TV for a couple of hours, and go to bed. He spent his days off lamenting what became of his miserable life.

Artie had no hobbies or friends. His associates from the office shared Artie's misery. Elsa knew their wives. They needed a misery intervention. This excursion was their first vacation since their honeymoon, and it exhibited all the charm of a proctology exam. Thank the divine spirit it might be their last.

Elsa became fed up with her banal marriage some time ago and planned this trip down to each finite detail, knowing she would need to decide. She hoped this short but expensive trip would awaken something in her morose husband and rekindle the hope. Her misery in the relationship reached a breaking point.

She tried all the usual outlets. At first, she confided in her girlfriends. While drinking red wine when their husbands golfed, she learned most of her friends shared similar levels of marriage misery. They understood Elsa's endless boredom and monotony. One friend took to getting a pool boy, even though she didn't have a pool. Elsa would rather kill her husband than cheat on him. She had principles.

She attended marital counseling. Elsa considered herself spiritually advanced. She could recognize *she* may be the problem, either in part or in entirety. After a year of counseling, she and her counselor concluded she was not the obstacle. It was without question Artie. Eventually, this advice would prove misguided. She didn't understand the counseling racket. The counselors simply told patients what they wanted to hear until they believed it. Counselors presented this information as the *you are cured* stage of the process. The *cure* appeared at the exact time the counselor could no longer overcharge the insurance company for their services. This was all taught meticulously in marriage counselor education at the galactic universities.

After their irritating server brought the appetizers, a salad for her, and bisque for him, Artie started griping.

"Elsa, can you believe this? I have been this restaurant's accountant for eight years and not *once* have they invited me to dine here. Nobody knows I work here. Not even the purple guy Newton, who is the boss. The hostess who seated us is clueless, and she is from our planet. They don't have the decency to offer us a discount. I tell you it is insulting."

Elsa heard Artie's hit list playing in her head again. He also registered this complaint with the waiter, who reeked of stale tequila and porcelain blow.

Elsa said,

"Artie, you understand things are remote these days and you don't interact with anyone at the restaurant. We have a billion people on our planet. How do you expect one random hostess to know? You cannot expect them to recognize you."

The argument fell on deaf ears as the words became pointless before she said them. Artie's ego drove his stubborn resolve.

Elsa decided. She doubted her commitment to the task when they arrived. That chance departed. After spending two weeks traveling, and now dining at the galaxy's finest restaurant, all he could muster was a feeble protest. Artie shared his appalling lack of gratitude with anyone who would listen.

Rather than say anything, she gazed into his purple, bloodshot eyes. A brief pause in their connection returned them both to when they met, albeit fleeting. A sudden realization of why Elsa chose Indigo hit Artie hard and his fists at once clenched. The veins in his neck throbbed and his heart began racing. As a bead of sweat formed on his forehead and slid down his cheek, he realized his marriage had just ended. But not how he thought.

She calmly placed her hand on the appetizer fork and noticed the slightly dulled tips. No matter. She mustered all her strength and, in a sweeping arc, plunged the tiny fork into the side of her husband's head.

His eyes widened, and his jaw slacked. Both hands gripped the crisp white linens on their table and he made that annoying clicking sound with his tongue. The shock of the appetizer fork buried deep in his brain took over his motor skills. Artie then pitched forward and drowned in a fresh batch of the universe's finest lobster bisque.

His last inhale contained the olfactory joy of the galaxy's finest soup. As his final exhale escaped him, a strange, fleeting thought passed through his mind.

"Oh shit, not again."

Elsa waited for the investigation unit to arrive, sipping merlot and noticing nobody other than their waiter noticed her husband drowning in a bowl of soup with an appetizer fork buried in the side of his head.

Newton, the maître d' noticed. But it was far down his list of current problems. He made a mental note to get a picture from the gift shop to hang in the restaurant foyer for future customers. It was Wall of Fame worthy. He also jotted a note for the waiter to obtain a waiver of liability from the wife before she went to jail.

CHAPTER 5

Qunot, the executive producer and founder of the hit television series *Caution Earth*, arrived at Indigo early. He knew the rest of his party would be late, giving him some needed time to decompress.

He looked forward to the lunch appointment with the same excitement level as a root canal. Being asked to dine at Indigo usually came with bad news unless you were the one doing the asking. He had been on the asking end of that process many times.

Qunot showed up after a short visit to his home planet Zatos, a humid planet located on the inner ring of the Milky Way galaxy. His world's topography contained expansive jungles and swamps covering most of the planet's surface, and oppressive humidity served up as the daily weather pattern. Zatos is conveniently located just one solar system away from the entertainment hub of this galaxy and his favorite restaurant, Indigo.

The Zatosians are almost entirely ensconced in the make-believe industry. Their physical constitution and mental acuity make them perfect for the rough and tumble world of movies and television.

Zatosians have small beady, wide-set eyes, pinkish-yellow hewed skin, and large nostrils that point upward with a short protrusion. Their large, crooked yellow teeth become a main facial feature when they smile, becoming a grotesque theater of poor dental hygiene. Through the middle, they are portly and shorter than other species by comparison, but possess an unseen strength that is ideal for constructing movie sets. The people of Zatos also have a bad habit of wearing skin-tight shirts that allow their fat rolls to escape from every opening in the shirt, including the neckline. They have thick, dark hair that protrudes from the top-center of their head. The hair is always kept cropped to 1-2 inches, so it stands on end. Some Zatosians dye their hair the color of their tribe. They are covered in moles that have long and noticeable dark hairs protruding from them. They excel behind the camera, never in front.

In high end galactic fashion magazines, other species have voted Zatosians as the ugliest species in the universe for 4,000 Zatos years running. Zatosian fashion magazines have voted them the sexiest species in the galaxy for just as long.

An Earthling would find them repulsive and consider housing Zatosians with livestock. They also have a pungent odor that is a unique combination of sweat socks, spoiled eggs, and rotting fish that worsens when they sweat. To the female Zatosian species, the smell is an aphrodisiac. One of the worst odors in recorded galactic history is any sex orgy on the planet Zatos.

Zatosians score high on intelligence and higher on emotional manipulation, an excellent fit for the entertainment industry. They are also sexually deviant monsters with questionable morals. More evolved, less chaotic galactic societies have a saying. The only useful Zatosian is a dead Zatosian.

Qunot didn't bother with gossip and media biased reputations. They were false allegations based on the actions of a few applied to the entire Zatos population. He cared about money, power, prestige, and sex. Especially the sex part.

The Zatosian's greatest asset is their unwavering ability to accomplish deliverables, even in the face of daunting odds and insurmountable challenges. If they have to bend rules to meet their goals, so be it. They are not evil by nature, but sometimes their desire to succeed outpaces their moral compass.

Qunot's presence at Indigo was requested by two MM1 network board members and another executive producer of *Caution Earth*. They were no doubt concerned about the ratings. Their prized program carried the highest ratings on Galactic Television for the first eight of its ten-year contract. Each television season ran approximately one thousand Earth years.

And while it still led all programs in ratings, the past two seasons showed a significant decline, and audience feedback ranged from bored to indifferent. Viewer's emotional engagement sank to an all-time low. The show had become repetitive as intelligent life on Earth that was supposed to evolve hadn't changed in eight thousand years. The Earthlings' only significant change was technological. They invented computers, cell phones, and all forms of gadgets that they mistook for evolutionary progress.

Early in the show's broadcast, Earthlings invented *round* and called it a wheel; a banner moment in human technological advancement. Regardless, observing nature and applying it to life is not an *invention*. The dim-witted Earthlings considered this significant evolutionary progress.

The *Caution Earth* engineering consultants who prepared the initial sociological and psychological assessment of humans were fired for idiocy and scientific malpractice. They assessed Earth's population would evolve into an advanced and peaceful species within ten thousand years. Instead, they were killing each other with the same level of ignorant hatred and distrust when they first emerged into the modern age from their cave homes.

As the founder and Executive Producer of *Caution Earth*, his colleagues were expecting him to produce a tidy solution to a complex planetary problem. Nobody wanted the money and sex train of their prized television show to leave the station. They all afforded lavish lifestyles because they stumbled upon a planet where the buffoonery of a flawed and unevolved species was put on display in real-time.

But that was the crux. They were meant to evolve. The plotline existed to bring *Caution Earth* to a tidy end, where the humans overcame themselves and developed into a peaceful and thoughtful civilization. The management team had significant bonuses and a follow-on television deal hanging in the balance on the show's outcome, and the alarming operating cost made this television program too big to fail.

Qunot was well aware of the quandary, pondering it while waiting for his equally late co-workers. Entertainment industry executives spent years competing for the title *Tardiest to a Meeting* as a virtue signal for who was the busiest. The cleverer executives started skipping meetings altogether, sending their underlings to explain their boss's overloaded schedule. This was proper given the underlings performed the work.

Qunot relaxed and sipped a premium vintage of merlot, breathing in the earthy but sweet bouquet of the wine. He already had a solution to the *Caution Earth* problem and could afford serenity. He raised his head, experiencing the unique taste of the fabulous tannins, and couldn't help but notice a man drowning in his lobster bisque at the table next to him. The man's companion, who Qunot could only assume was his now ex-wife, took it casually. She sipped her martini and nibbled the end of a breadstick taken from the side plate of her now-drowning husband's plate. Qunot also noticed an appetizer fork buried in his skull, presumably placed there by the woman now sitting with him, enjoying her cocktail. Poor sap, he thought. Never bring an unstable spouse to this restaurant.

The Zatosian noticed the waiter fussing about the other tables in the area, his nervous voice louder and higher than normal, doing everything to ignore the man drowning in a bowl of soup. Waiters worked on tips and other customers in the immediate area of these incidents sometimes reacted poorly to appetizer fork mayhem. There was also a ton of paperwork to be filed with the local bureaucrats.

Qunot noticed a commotion at the check-in stand as the maître d' Newton created a scene about the rest of his party arriving. The arrival ceremony at Indigo carried as much importance as the meal and restaurant executives forever made a circus of their arrival.

CHAPTER 6

More advanced civilizations understand possibilities and probabilities in a universe of near infinite size are also near infinite. A twin set of planets that exist for the sole purpose to showcase a galactic dining hub presenting the universe's finest culinary arts as an enclosed ecosystem is part of that cosmic balance. Advanced populations likewise understand a planet whose leading cause of death is appetizer forks wielded with the malice of emotional instability, further encapsulates the natural order of things.

Less advanced civilizations regularly tell these *natural order* types to get bent and concoct words like *coincidences* or *luck*. They attempt to place blame while their heads whir at the oddities caused by an explosion of infinite timelines and infinite possibilities.

It is also plausible in a universe of this size and scope that a unique couple exists, trapped in a loop of rebirth. The sole purpose of this couple's existence is to find true, unconditional love. The only escape? They must realize true, unqualified love during one of their lifespans.

Also probable in a vast universe is this same couple finding themselves on a seemingly random set of planets that are the only two worlds in a unique dual sun, dual planet solar system, one of which is entirely fine dining restaurants.

To the unevolved, this level of improbability is just the exact manner of probability that drives their statisticians into mental institutions. To evolved societies, these happenstances are understood to be normal and largely ignored. In the final analysis, advanced civilizations scoff at the discussion. They consider endless philosophical prattling about probability a waste of time.

The unevolved finds the universe's perceived randomness unnerving. The laws that govern cause and effect in an organized universe are so simple that they seem complex, especially to species that have yet to reach their evolutionary inflection point.

This is especially true of the humans occupying the planet Earth and the subject of the hit television show *Caution Earth*. That is, of course, the dominant theme and plotline of the series. Can an entire planet's evolutionary process be depicted in real time while also being entertaining to the viewers? The show attempts to share with the audience the primary inflection points of evolution and the semi-circular nature of it, including necessary backwards steps to move forward.

The universe is anything but random. It is a perfect, organized system of cause and effect, the purpose of which is to evolve its inhabitants. This is a hard truth many civilizations refuse to accept and spend eons fighting to the detriment of their worlds and themselves. Many bloody wars have also been needlessly fought under the guise of universal belief systems throughout the millennia, both on individual planets and between interplanetary galactic habitats.

A wise man once said.

"You can bang your head against the rocks of universal will, but the rocks will not break."

This particular wise man was eventually stoned to death, living on a remote planet that had yet to invent more advanced weaponry. Universal irony is also not random. The lesson learned is if you live in a society that has not yet sufficiently evolved, it is wise to keep your mouth shut about other people's problems lest face the consequences.

When Qunot discovered the planet Earth, his intention was to air the program for 10,000 Earth years. This was the equivalent of ten seasons in Galactic TV time. He signed a ten-year contract with the television network. The iron clad contract ensured that failure was not an option.

If understanding probability wasn't mind bending enough for unevolved galactic civilizations, the subject of time was worse.

A fundamental problem with TV programming is different worlds in different solar systems with different suns have different time lengths for what they call a year. The species on these planets have also evolved to far different life spans. Television executives and their data analysts spend considerable chunks of their workday arguing about the correct program length relative to the life span of the most likely demographic of their viewers.

With *Caution Earth*, there was additional complexity, as the Earthling's lifespan had to be considered. The expense accounts at Indigo dedicated to these discussions have bankrupted at least three broadcast stations. But even in an orderly universe, television stations go bankrupt due to irresponsible expense accounts spent on lavish dining experiences.

CHAPTER 7

Twenty minutes after the stabbing, the detectives from the Specialized Investigative Unit for Appetizer Fork Violence (SIUAFV) were honored guests at Elsa's table. Artie was pronounced dead upon arrival with a quick non-touch life scan device. The investigators seated themselves as late-comers to the couple's reservation and dressed for the occasion.

They wore fine silk gray suits with open collar white shirts. The current style magazines dictated the shirt collar be oversized and starched to extend beyond both shoulders. They sported glossy, black shined shoes with the finest turtle's shell polish from the planet LaCosta. Investigators also wore matching cologne that enticed the nasal cavities with a combined masculine leather and light citrus aroma. The cologne spoke to the perpetrator in gentle soothing tones while reminding them that serious business was afoot. The restaurant investigative unit had a full wardrobe with matching styles from a vast majority of the galactic species, and they tailored the wardrobe to the crime scene and the aliens.

By the time the investigators arrived at a restaurant, they had viewed the transgression on surveillance video, identified both the victim and the perpetrators, identified their species and home planet, knew their travel plans and dressed suitably to blend into the scene. This helped to deflect attention from the table.

The investigation became a somewhat pointless process as the restaurant cameras captured the infraction from three different angles and the entire audio sequence. In addition, the life scan device performed an on-scene autopsy. For Artie, the official cause of death was recorded as *drowning in a fabulous bowl of soup* with a secondary cause listed as *a semi blunt force appetizer fork trauma to the temple.*

The crime computer already identified the murder as pre-meditated, given the wife had taken out a handsome life insurance policy just three weeks prior. The robust policy would not only provide for her lifetime, but pay for the outrageous tab at Indigo. This case was open and shut, with one exception.

Elsa could prove extreme emotional abuse and she would walk with a slap on the wrist. Any individual who would travel two weeks to murder their spouse at an improbable location with a more improbable, yet ludicrous, weapon usually harbored good reason for it. The investigative team would determine if an arrest was warranted. If a prosecutor decided to press charges, the case headed to the court system. First, the investigators would sample the wine list and a few delicious, exotic appetizers.

Lightner, the lead investigator, placed their order with the waiter while his assistant Fleming greeted and started questioning Elsa. Artie made no comment on the matter. He was quite dead. His soul fled the crime scene and hurried off to the universe's complaints department for the umpteenth time, where he frequented the grievances sub-unit. During the visit, he grumbled about being reborn in a different species on a strange planet, only to marry the woman who murdered him. He considered this a valid complaint, in his humble opinion. Even after his death, Artie still hadn't lost his touch for complaining.

As a grizzled veteran of the SIUAFV, Lightner heard it all. He had investigated many appetizer fork deaths over the years, although it seemed of late a definite uptick in their frequency occurred. He decided on the lobster bisque and a bottle of Shiraz. The waiter complimented him on his pairing of that particular wine. Conveniently, the small amount of blood that oozed from Artie's mini-fork wound leaked into his bowl of soup. The crime scene was clean. The linens were unaffected, much to the waiter's delight. This concerned the server's boss, Newton the maître d' due to his spotless linens fetish.

While his partner Fleming spoke with Elsa, Lightner glanced around Indigo's dining room. It always amazed him the sheer callousness of this situation. The patrons ignored the obvious elephant in the room. Waiters and waitresses fussed over each table, drawing rapt attention to anything but the area with the homicide. The kitchen sent out complimentary taster items, Newton glad-handed different species, and the bartenders and head chefs came out to talk to different tables. All restaurant staff took mandatory, meticulous training that taught them to ignore the problem. By ignoring it, they knew it would disappear. And they were correct. In thirty minutes, the detectives' investigation would complete. The investigators would walk the dead body to the exit, pretending the deceased was intoxicated. This graphic and emotive display would consummate between the murder scene and the exit, ensuring diners seated too far away and people arriving at Indigo didn't notice reality.

When Lightner tuned back to the conversation, Fleming moved past the pleasantries of the couple's home planet, weather conditions, and what brought them to Indigo. He was starting into the meat of the issue and changed his tone to his *we are getting serious now voice*.

"Elsa, it appears your husband is, in fact, deceased. We also know from the restaurant audio/video feed that you wielded the murder weapon and we know you have a recent, hefty life insurance policy for your husband. It doesn't look good for you."

The sommelier arrived with their wine order, which he informed them was complimentary for their splendid work. He poured a small taste for Lightner to sample and, after receiving approval, poured each of the detectives a healthy glass. The savory aroma of a fresh, uncorked bottle of fine wine engulfed their table in a collective moment of appreciation.

Elsa eyed the detectives for a moment. She had prepared this script in her head a thousand times, as well as optimal deployment. Elsa didn't spend two weeks traveling to a fine dining establishment on Gastrin multiple light-years from home for the sole purpose of murdering her spouse without a solid exit plan.

She looked Lightner straight in the eyes, and without wavering, told him exactly why.

"My defense will be sheer, endless boredom. No wife, married to a tedious accountant, the bean counter of this very restaurant, I might add, should endure a decade of nothing. We haven't strayed 300 yards from home in a decade. I would also like to point to out the soup killed him.

You said his cause of death was Artie drowning in his bisque. I didn't cook the murder weapon."

She then stated she wouldn't respond to any more questions without a lawyer.

Lightner and Fleming quickly gulped down their wine, booked her right there at the table, and began the process of getting both Elsa and her dead husband out of the restaurant. They took the soup to go.

The detectives stood Artie up and put one of his arms around each of their shoulders. This was the most entertaining part of the entire investigative act. They laughed out loud, threw barbs back and forth about how Artie got sauced again, making a scene in front of his wife, claiming he just needed to sleep it off as they stumbled him out of the restaurant. Patrons would take a quick glance as they ambled by, pretending the appetizer fork sticking out of his head was a piece of jewelry or other exotic headgear.

Two months later, Elsa would stand trial for her husband's death. Her lawyer simply read out their daily routine for the past ten years of their marriage to the jury. It took three months. The judge allowed it because he never encountered such a defense, despite the prosecution's strenuous and repeated objections. For an entire decade, Elsa and Artie lived the same routine. Every day. It was not a good routine. A juror overheard another explaining in no uncertain terms if their spouse made them endure that routine, she would take him to Indigo for a breakup as well. Their unanimous decision found her innocent of all charges and she walked free. Legal scholars were outraged during the news cycle that followed the verdict, but then, after one day of coverage, somebody's pet got stuck on a construction crane and it became forgotten. Elsa's secondary claim of not wielding the soup as a murder weapon was struck down by the court. Even courts on Gastrin have their standards.

The insurance company considered filing fraud charges against Elsa in a civil case, but public opinion became so one-sided in Elsa's favor they thought better of it. They quietly paid her policy, internally calling it a sound business decision. Three years later, the company went bankrupt. The number of whole-life policies taken out on boring husbands skyrocketed, followed by a string of mysterious deaths to these same husbands. Not coincidentally, the CEO of the business died in a freak accident rock climbing with his wife. His safety line was mysteriously cut, and he fell to his death. Because they were in a remote location, no video evidence existed and despite the spouse having a sharp pocketknife in her possession at the time, the prosecution couldn't prove she cut the line. She also didn't have an insurance policy for her husband, so the motive was weak.

This poor soul's partner used what became known in legal circles and nail salons as the *Elsa Defense.* She claimed being married to a banal insurance company executive was far more tedious than any decent woman should handle. She inherited the company, which would be defunct six months after her trial. The wife ended up broke and working as a waitress at Indigo.

Elsa wasn't aware she would be required to marry Artie again in their next lifetime. One year after the murder of her husband and about six months after her not-guilty verdict, she died in a freak selfie accident. She was trying to show off for her new boyfriend. They booked an extravagant trip using the insurance money from Artie's death to a planet that has the most breathtaking canyons in the galaxy. The details of stupidity regarding her demise are on file at the Galactic Department of Complaints for the Recently Deceased (the GDCRD*). If anyone is interested in researching them along with the lessons to be learned from the entire episode, which are noteworthy, they are stored to prevent future idiocy. These records are valuable and important to the still living, as they provide a laundry list of potential dangers when visiting exotic travel destinations. The records are available to anyone with a device connected to the galaxy's main internet through the GDCRD website under the travel menu.

The lessons were simple. First, the pre-meditated murder of your spouse on the grounds of boredom will probably earn negative karma. Second, using the insurance money from his death to book an extravagant trip with a new boyfriend or girlfriend soon after said demise, assuming that you got away with it, will garner additional bad karma. Third, karma being what it is, the immutable law of cause and effect, something terrible is bound to happen to you up to and including dying.

The GDCRD is part of a vast planetary complaints department the galactic government set up to provide better customer service to its living citizens and the deceased. It is housed on a single planet of bureaucrats, who are otherwise useless to society. It is a win-win situation for the civilized galaxy, as the bureaucracy-loving bureaucrats end up working and living in this world, enjoying a life filled with forms in triplicate, mind-numbing and pointless processes, and long lines. The freedom-loving people of the universe stay on their home planets free of the mind-numbing bureaucracy.

CHAPTER 8

Qunot loved observing the seamless operations at Indigo. To him, a restaurant was always an exercise in deriving order from chaos. The likelihood of operational disasters at a high-volume restaurant at any given time is highly probable:

- Cadence at which a customer is seated, the orders taken (drinks, appetizers, entrees, dessert).
- Proper number of times for a waiter to check on the table in between ordering without seeming pushy.
- Timing of the bartender getting drinks made synchronized with the correctly ordered food preparation.

Proper restaurant operations are a master class in managing chaos. This made Newton the crack conductor. He often wondered how many ulcers Newton developed from managing this insane asylum. Even with a punctured and drowned dead man at an adjoining table, stabbed in broad daylight on camera, with at least forty witnesses, they maintained an air of class and respectability. He wished he could replicate this operation for his television show.

The entertainment industry had other problems beyond chaotic operations. It is a disorganized, disgusting place filled with every imaginable form of degeneracy. This depravity and the complexity of the movie production process invited chaos. Qunot knew this all too well. He participated in most of it.

The industry practiced such heinous acts long-term employees only stayed as a function of blackmail. The higher-ups who ran the businesses also engaged in the same abasement, and the entire ordeal became a vicious circular cycle. Insiders who did not share in the degeneracy were blackballed because their knowledge provided leverage. The unspoken word was you are one of us or you aren't.

Extortion, blackmail, sexual deviancy, bribery and theft were the norms. The business brimmed with unimaginable fraud. Their entire lives were make-believe horseshit sugar-coated in a veil of fame that they didn't earn or deserve. They were lazy, unimaginative, and morally bankrupt. Scripts on 97% of the shows on television were regurgitated corporate nonsense with the originality of a mild case of hemorrhoids. Qunot has been a card-carrying member of the entertainment industry for 12,000 Earth years and occasionally met a few honest beings, but it was the exception, not the rule. Sometimes when preening, he had a difficult time with his reflection, but he usually got over it.

The constant pretending made the restaurant meetings painful. They would sit around blowing smoke up each other's ass about the *Caution Earth* television show while the entire *actual* purpose of the meeting was to be seen at Indigo and to eat a fabulous and expensive lunch. Broadcast executives seldom got fired, so when the four of them gathered for lunch, they were of the few patrons in attendance not getting canned or dumped.

Rego joined Em and Emone, the twin brothers, for the short ride over from Durnita, the entertainment capital for the Milky Way Galaxy. An entire world devoted to make-believe. A planet dedicated to carrying the fraud of the industry on its shoulders. And its shoulders were tired. Qunot often thought Durnita would collapse under the weight of its corruption, but it didn't. It just vacillated between degenerate and horribly degenerate. Sometimes, a big-time celebrity got busted for something particularly heinous, and then an effort to self-police activities would manifest. What this meant in reality was transforming their activities from attention grabbing to discrete. After the noise quieted, operations would return to normal. Similar to how the Galactic Council located all the bureaucrats on one planet, the government was blasé about the nefarious nature of the make-believe hub, provided the behavior was isolated.

Rego also hailed from Zatos. Em and Emone were born on Durnita, the twin sons of Coder, the owner of the Galactic network. They were board members. They also partied far harder than they worked.

Qunot offered,

"Glad you made it."

They all knew he wasn't glad they arrived and probably thought it would be better if their spaceship blew up upon re-entry from hyper-drive. Everybody in the world of entertainment secretly hated everyone else in the industry because they all hated themselves. In public, they pretended to be in love with the fabulousness of their lifestyle. The perpetual virtue signaling annoyed everyone, but they continued it anyway.

Rego, Qunot's executive producer, and closest coworker, is unusually ugly even by Zatosian standards. He had significantly more grotesque moles growing everywhere on his face and body than average, with a unique hairstyle protruding from each mole. He didn't bother to groom himself in any manner based on the fact his wife has cheated on him at least 1,000 times. Rego cheated on her as much, as infidelity is a common practice in the Zatos culture. The rarity was monogamy. Marital infidelity was so prominent in their society marriage seemed pointless. This practice saved on divorce, as divorces were pointless. Most of Zatosian society practiced polygamy with fervor. This habitual fervor, coupled with Zatos being one of the wealthiest and self-indulgent places in the galaxy, left little reason for divorce.

Rego ordered a bottle of wine, which would take the average person three months of salary to afford. He participated in the nauseating and painstaking process of *tasting and testing the wine* with the Sommelier. The merlot, of course, would be billed to the company expense account. Once satisfied with both the Sommelier's ass-kissing and the vintage, he returned to the conversation.

"It's more than just the ratings."

Qunot experienced a momentary anxiety attack. He thought another ratings bitch session over an outrageously expensive lunch was on the menu. Technically, he was Rego's boss, so he couldn't be fired. In retrospect, he accompanied the twins, who occupied space on the board of directors. They were busy ogling the woman at the next table who just murdered her husband.

Rather than react, he drew a deep breath capturing a mix of lobster bisque and Rego's heinous body odor, and counted to five. He stated the obvious, using the tone of an executive that is about blow smoke up everyone's ass but is going to sound profound and intelligent in the process.

"I have spent considerable time contemplating the viewership numbers and agree that the root cause is indeed more than the symptom that is the ratings issue itself. But I believe that with the right observation, data analytics and project team, we can resolve the problem."

Rego chuckled and took another snort of wine. He worked closely with Qunot and knew a line of bullshit when he heard it.

"Hey dipshits, pay attention here."

The twins stopped ogling for a moment and joined the conversation. They were quite done with Rego's treatment of them and his speaking tone.

Rego continued.

"Our analysis predicts a greater than 99% probability the planet Earth will be destroyed before we can conclude the television show. We have two seasons remaining on the contract. When we last mapped this scenario, it appeared the disaster would be averted. Our analysis was wrong. The Earthlings are steadfast on a path to destroy their civilization. I am afraid we may need to take desperate measures."

Qunot's appetite slid off a cliff. *Caution Earth's* tragic and sudden ending would be a ratings boon. It would simultaneously end the series, and likely their fabulous careers. It would bring a tragic end to their extravagant lifestyle: no more orgies, no more lavish expense accounts, no more grandiose vacations. Qunot was also stretched to the limit in debt from a side gambling problem and porcelain snorting habit. He owed money to bookies and dealers who always collected their debts. Losing two of the ten seasons of the show's contract would be catastrophic to his finances. Not to mention the lucrative end of show bonus. It would take eons to locate a substitute planet.

Rego could see Qunot's suffering grow as he heard this information.

He continued,

"The Earthlings are mentally and emotionally deficient. We understood when we started the television show this was a potential outcome, but we placed the risk at five to seven percent. We also knew then and understand now we cannot interfere with the planet. Galactic police would arrest us in their usual efficient manner. Then the government would execute us after airing a trial that would garner more ratings than *Caution Earth*. They are always looking to publicly shame anyone in our industry. And that is without mentioning the problematic geese."

Dealing with the geese was always a painful experience. Rego outlined the goose problem from his narrow perspective.

"We sent a message to the geese and they refuse to help and are working desperately to leave the planet. They were our failsafe in case of trouble, but you understand how they are. They would rather spend their time quarreling with each other over petty nonsense and eyeballing humans than add any value to society."

The geese always gave Qunot heartburn.

Rego summarized his thoughts into a concise synopsis.

"The bottom line is this. Earthlings have advanced their technological capability well beyond their evolutionary development. It is a dangerous formula. Unless there is a drastic societal change, the Earth will self-destruct at the hands of its inhabitants, wiping out the human species. The geese could survive a planetary apocalypse, but they decided they want return to their home planet. Provided they can figure out an escape. Otherwise, they are stuck there. How they plan to leave without a spaceship is unclear, but it's their problem. We have bigger issues."

Rego finished his statement and picked up his wine glass, swirling the red liquid around and watching the film slide back down into the bowl. He savored every bit of his dramatization. The twins sat there with nothing to add.

Qunot was trying to keep his cool. He planned to snort a bunch of porcelain after lunch. He could put his ship on autopilot while returning to the office as he zoned out in blissful, stoned contemplation.

Qunot asked.

"What was the determining factor in our analysis?"

On the outside, he acted as cool as the surfer who just barely escaped a 30-foot wave while riding it into shore. On the inside, he was six minutes from a stroke.

Rego explained further.

"It is a combination of factors. We all understand karma is multiple causes for a single effect. Humans struggle with the concept. The root cause is, of course, the human brain. They just cannot get past animal behavior. One would think in 8,000 years, Earthlings would evolve beyond the starting point of the television series. Remember, we found the planet after intelligent life had already existed for 30,000 to 40,000 years. Our science team tells us that the average human is no more evolved now than humans who existed when the show started. Zero progress. They evolved quite a bit from the starting point to when the series began. Our modeling showed them evolving further, but at a slower rate. We knew evolution slowed, but on Earth, it stopped."

Em added.

"Did the modeling suggest they were stuck on stupid?"

He said this to get under Rego's fat wart-covered skin. Em and his brother understood the problem much deeper than they revealed.

Rego looked at Em without saying a word. His stern, toothy facial expression asked him to keep his mouth shut.

He continued his explanation of the secondary problem of the Earthlings.

"They have allowed the worst people to become their leaders. They are not decent stewards of their planet, themselves, or even their families. Their leaders have either conspired with or been extorted by the corporatists to commit heinous crimes against their own people. Crimes that have been hidden for centuries. However, with the vast improvement in communication technology and information flow, the people of Earth are beginning to understand how they have been ruled, not governed. This friction point is at a tipping point and about to explode. We expect a combination of mass civil unrest, artificial intelligence, malfeasance and other technology misuse, famine, disease from war, bio-weaponry, and possible nuclear fallout will come to a head and wipe out most of the population. Survivors will exist, but it will be pointless to continue the show post-apocalypse. On a side note, the Earth's entertainment and media industries are more corrupt than ours, and that is a sight to behold."

Qunot heard enough.

"Understood. Let's continue this conversation elsewhere. The twins can meet us back at the office. You want to join me on my ship?"

Rego finished his third glass of wine and asked for the check.

"Sure thing."

CHAPTER 9

Caution Earth revolutionized the galactic television experience and at once became a ratings success. In eight broadcast seasons, the show has averaged over 30 billion viewers per episode. In a broadcast lineup of over 10,000 channels and another 20,000 streaming channels, this viewer number is even more impressive. Naturally, the TV series is also an advertising gravy train.

Caution Earth has amassed an astonishing 124 Asscat Awards (Asscats) in its first eight years, including Best:

- Television Show
- Reality Series
- Goose in a Documentary eight seasons running
- Prehistoric Depiction of a Species
- Comedy
- Tragedy
- Technological Editing
- Video Production from a Secluded Backwater Location

In the entirety of galactic history, no one show has received more than 17 prestigious Asscats.

The production scope and broadcast style had never been attempted. *Caution Earth* is unique. It is the only television series where the show's subjects are oblivious to being filmed. They are unaware they even have a TV show. Their planet is not privy to the galactic family of networks.

The entire story arc of *Caution Earth* is evolution. Can a civilization evolve from ancient times when its inhabitants were animalistic and in survival mode? Is it possible the planet's population develops into an aware and conscientious society governed by divine instinct? Can they properly harness that very divine instinct that resides in every universal being? Does the possibility exist that they get past the stage where a society destroys itself?

The simple beauty of the program *is* no actors or actresses. If Earthlings knew they were being filmed, it would devastate the show within three episodes. Normal behavior would grind to a halt in favor of the population attempting to act for a camera that may or may not be filming them. It has not gone unnoticed that introducing social media to the Earth's citizens was having the same effect. This is the finest feature of the hit program *Caution Earth*. It is the only program in galactic television history that is *actual* reality TV.

Yet Earth's fascinating story surpasses mere planetary documentation. The genius exists in the presentation and editing process that won the program so many prestigious Asscat awards. Civilization's history and evolutionary sequence are shown not only from history's perspective, but at a deep and meaningful personal level. The show beautifully contrasts the macro-historical arc of time and important events with the micro-personal level of involvement within that story. Characters are shown in multiple episodes depicting their struggle with being human. The Earthlings and their internal conflict have become so compelling more advanced galactic societies have replaced the term *I'm having a bad day* with *I'm having a human day*.

The editors and producers strived to offer gripping content. They found if they limited storytelling to a recital of Earth's history, the show would fail. The audience would become bored. Events are depicted through the depth and experience of the characters involved, narrated in the context of advancement and evolution. Major happenings like wars, technological advances, spiritual, and religious movements, and political upheaval are presented not just as historical events, but as portrayed in the lives involved. History's events are presented without bias and with exact context.

For example, if a significant newsworthy event occurs, the program not only shows the event but also shares with its viewers the exact reason from all sides of the conflict through the participant's eyes. Unfortunately for Earth's citizens, they only receive the narrative the ruling class feeds them. Context is never given, and the leadership lies about motive. The motive is consistent; more power, more money, more death of the innocents. If the true context was given before these historical upheavals and motives were truly understood, most of the civilization's conflict would be eliminated. The population would not participate. Ever. The planet's aristocracy has no interest in peace, their interests lie in profit and control. *Caution Earth* depicts this story arc as part of the evolutionary process. Will Earthlings overcome self-deception and see the truth? Is it possible for them to understand they've allowed themselves to be manipulated from the beginning? The evolved citizens of the galaxy root for the Earth's people; they are the ultimate underdog.

Caution Earth is not without its challenges. There are many complexities filming an entire planet and further deciding what to film and how content is pertinent to the evolutionary story arc. Nobody in advanced civilizations wants to see Joe get on a dilapidated subway headed to his boring legal clerk job supporting an overzealous ambulance-chasing tort attorney. In addition to the difficulties of filming and content decision-making, galactic law forbids interference with an unevolved civilization. It is imperative the production of the television show accommodates the council's law.

To resolve these challenges, the Earth became the universe's largest layered surveillance operation. Nobody on the planet realizes this, except for the geese. The producers of *Caution Earth* needed to acquire an exception license for the television show. The galactic council agreed to allow it under specific terms, including not interfering with the planet's evolutionary path. A secondary agreement with the galaxy's government stated no Earthling could know their civilization was also a hit TV series.

Each galaxy in the vast universe has a governing council, and each makes its own decisions on whether to interface with underdeveloped worlds. In the Milky Way, a dim view is taken of interfering with another planet's evolutionary path. It upsets the natural order. Of course, what is transpiring on Earth and its self-destruction has happened countless times. It is one of the oldest lessons taught in galactic studies for the sole purpose of avoiding these senseless tragedies. It happens anyway. Unfortunately, unevolved planets lack access to alien history, which prevents them from realizing their devastating mistakes. They get hell bent on destroying themselves without ever understanding the horrors of repeating a cycle.

The galactic governing council developed a solution. How can we prevent more developed societies from interfering with the evolutionary process of less advanced civilizations?

Aliens, to a specific planet, are only allowed to interact with other worlds once the population has achieved intergalactic travel. It is also important the interaction is peaceful. The newly evolved civilization is then welcomed and integrated into the galactic council which strives for a peace filled and prosperous universe. An entire security and law enforcement apparatus, with the best technology available, exists to prevent meddling in less advanced worlds' affairs and the punishment is severe. The offender receives a quick trial, and if found guilty, a speedy execution. All trials and executions are televised.

The mandate, and laws, of the galactic governing body are to create the conditions to allow the galaxy to prosper freely from the onerous control of bureaucrats and politicians. In an abundant universe gifted with infinite resource replenishment, no legitimate reason exists for poverty. Unevolved societies don't govern, they set up ruling structures based on the belief system of scarcity. This fear drives the powerful elitists, and then, in effect, drives society as the fear is used as a bludgeon to control.

Multiple types of monitoring systems exist for varied purposes. They range from rigid control to observation without interference. Unevolved societies always end up using surveillance as a spiked club to control populations and to punish dissent. It is dystopian. Advanced civilizations use the technology to facilitate peace and to promote prosperity.

The planet Earth's layered system has three parts. It includes the galactic government surveillance, the *Caution Earth* layer used for filming, and, of course, the geese. Being the galaxy's most successful reality television series, it became necessary to eliminate any interference with the planet's inhabitants.

The alien visitation law is strict by design. For galactic eons, this law didn't exist, and many innocent and developing planets experienced random visits by extraterrestrials. The aliens sometimes dressed up in ridiculous costumes while on prodigious drug and alcohol benders. This crude behavior freaked out the inhabitants of alien planets to the point where they became single-minded in their unity to wipe out all other inhabitants of the galaxy. Their science and weaponry exponentially advanced along with their ability to travel throughout space. In no time, multiple major wars were being fought because some hick named Cletus saw a spaceship and his unevolved brain couldn't handle the possibility that life existed outside his trailer park, much less on a different planet. In a peace-loving universe, there's no tolerance for this level of unnecessary mayhem.

The Galactic Investigative and Protection Unit (GIPU) produced and has responsibility for mapping, tracking, and monitoring for every civilization in the Milky Way. The GIPU operates the most advanced surveillance system in the galaxy. From their command headquarters on planet Nee, they have a mapping of the entire galaxy along with every planet and its status as life-supporting or not. In addition, The GIPU has documented which planets are evolved (part of the galaxy's peace) or unevolved (inhabited with *intelligent* life forms, but no space travel ability), and a third and most dangerous category, behind the evolution curve with travel in space.

Any foreign spaceship in the vicinity of an unevolved planet possessing intelligent life is flagged. An urgent communication is sent to the ship explaining that entering the planet's airspace will result in dire consequences.

The Earth became a special case because of its status with the Durnita television executives. An extra layer of surveillance patrolled from just outside of the gaseous orb of Jupiter. Earth's Milky Way location is remote and sparsely inhabited. Few galactic citizens bother to travel to its sector, and it isn't on any of the major tourist routes. Earth is dull. A boring planet in a humdrum solar system orbiting an uninteresting sun in a lackluster region of the galaxy.

The Earth is equipped with multiple high tech satellite devices that are the property of the MM1 television network. These satellites coordinate and film the series. The production technology is so complex, filming is possible inside the room of a house from space satellites.

But even that wasn't enough. They needed on the ground monitoring.

This is where the geese are involved.

They are a special surveillance army placed on the planet to monitor the humans and to send storylines to the television executives. Geese genetically have a specific brain wave pattern that transmits like a radio frequency and can be picked up by the surrounding satellites.

The geese's surveillance is based on a challenging and misunderstood philosophy. There is, in reality, only one goose.

To the naked eye, there are hundreds of thousands of geese. They are everywhere. However, only a single goose hive-mind exists. This allows the species to act as one, which makes them an incredibly powerful surveillance tool. Their collective thoughts are integrated into pattern-based messaging that monitors and reports the planet's activity. Advanced artificial intelligence monitors the feeds, and messaging is fed to the television executives and show editors. The production team decides what is audience worthy compared to the routine life of the Earthlings. Events and characters of interest are placed in the series.

They are the perfect species, partly because of their generous procreation. Geese have a lifespan of about fifteen years, mate for life, and produce five to six newborns per year. All the newborns become part of the collective hive mind. Their migratory patterns worldwide allow them to observe the majority of human existence during most seasons.

The geese didn't always enjoy a charmed life. Late in Earth's 20th century, they became endangered. The leader named Mr. Goose coordinated an end to the Great Goose Genocide of that century. He got them placed on the protected species list. Their population had reduced to where they were becoming inefficient at their surveillance duties.

The geese, of course, hated all this. They hated the one-goose nonsense. They despised that their entire individual and collective thought patterns were captured by a galactic computer and used for television profit.

What the geese hated more was Earth's so-called intelligent life, the humans. They spent most of their days staring at them, giving them the evil eye. Sometimes they would take 20 minutes to walk their newborns across a two-lane road in the middle of rush hour, making the bipeds late for work. The rest of their time, when they weren't migrating, was spent arguing with their brethren. They loved to squabble about pond territorial rights.

The humans were always the common enemy, even centuries before the Great Goose Genocide. The geese stranded on Earth never wanted to leave their home planet. On Garthis, they were the top of the food and intelligence chain and spent their lives in glorious arguments with each other over living space, migratory patterns, and the attractiveness of their wives.

They were unaware life existed on other planets. The geese were happy and oblivious, living in ignorance, despite being highly intelligent creatures. And while they have a complex language system, they had no knowledge they could transmit their collective brainwaves across great distances. They had zero interest in scientific advancement and were content to live in their exhilarating universe of petty squabbles.

The geese's glory days were grinding to a halt. Some douche canoe environmentalist and second-rate wannabe philosopher showed up to investigate their planet. These activists are the same galaxy-wide. They become primed for a *cause* and manipulate societies through emotional blackmail and fake statistics*. All while projecting the loudest, most obnoxious messaging amplified by their handlers and the media. The philosopher's name was Douchious. An environmental group funded him to study Garthis. His mission was to produce a comprehensive and persuasive report on how the geese's world could be saved from inhabitance by alien species. His goal was to attain a protected planet classification under galactic legal statute.

This was, of course, propaganda. The group funding the study wanted to ensure Garthis remained uninhabited so they could plunder its natural resources for profit. This usually ended in the planet becoming uninhabitable by any life forms, including making extinct any species that existed regardless of intelligence level. The group coordinating the planet's pillaging for its resources became a whole lot wealthier.

Douchious was uninformed about his sponsor's true intentions. He was sold on the *cause*. Useful idiots never see the malice they push. They are chosen primarily for zealotry to a *cause* and secondarily for *inability to think or ask the proper questions*. Galactic history is littered with innocent but naïve targets being manipulated for profit. Earth's entire university system is based on this business model.

But to Douchious's credit, he manifested one of the deepest philosophical ponderings of all time. He returned from a recent trip to Garthis, where he excitedly observed the methods of its inhabitants. Through standard scientific measuring of brain waves, he realized the geese had thought patterns that were consistent with each another and broadcast like a powerful radio station. When tuned to the proper frequency, he could pick up the broadcast on his ship from the planet's orbit.

When back at university, he discussed his time on Garthis and the geese. He bragged about how handsomely the *Save Garthis* foundation had paid him and what a cool gig it was. All this virtue signaling and haughtiness because he wanted to impress a rather hot-looking student in the front row of his philosophy class.

On a beautiful morning, Douchious stood at the podium of his class in the Beginner's Philosophy lecture hall. The sun shone through the rear windows, creating a silhouette around the podium, where he prepared to speak. He straightened his spine and sucked in his stomach while narrowing his crisp green eyes, conveying the importance of the announcement. He stood tall and firm for delivery and for extra dramatic effect, had no notes and no presentation material. The focus of the room bore into him, including the extravagant, beautiful classmate who sat in the front row.

He paused for added effect, pushed his wire-rim glasses up his rail thin nose, and took a sip of his triple shot soy latte. After a deep inhale, his high pitched, squeaky beta-male voice stated,

"There is only one goose."

The collective jaws of his classmates dropped. They were stunned into silence. The statement was an enigma wrapped in a profound riddle. His professor rolled his eyes at the sheer stupidity of the utterance.

Douchious intended to convey that geese thought patterns were so similar they may as well be unified. He was never given a chance to explain; he became mobbed with popularity.

The phrase caught on and Douchious was venerated as a meditative guru well before he graduated. His philosophy teacher failed him for idiocy. In reality, he was jealous the guy had sex with the desirable woman in the front row and more envious that he became a galactically recognized philosopher. All these accolades and undeserved fame for uttering possibly the most nonsensical phrase the galaxy ever heard.

They printed t-shirts, and the saying got trademarked. Douchious started a podcast and a radio show, quit university, and moved to the planet Ashra known for cut-rate, dumbed-down spirituality. His professor quit teaching and became a bartender at a local strip club.

The geese abhorred the entire situation and wanted to be left alone.

All statistics were proven to be useless at best and complete lies at worst by the Galactic Board of Statistics and Information (GBSI). This caused the entire board to be disbanded and defunded. They had unequivocally proven that 200 centuries of statistical information was nonsense. The unemployed bureaucrats now spend their time on homeowner's association boards and associations, projecting their abject misery on their neighbors.

CHAPTER 10

After paying the astounding restaurant bill, Qunot and Rego departed Indigo and left the twins behind with instructions to return to the office and await further direction. Qunot had an idea to share with Rego that might get the television show *Caution Earth* out of the ratings predicament and save the planet Earth from their self-destruction jam. The plan contained treachery, danger, illegality and insane risk. All typical elements in any Zatosian project, but he was confident of success.

The plan had to be completed without their fingerprints, and this required a patsy. Or in this case, a few patsies. Qunot had three individuals in mind. A bitter maître d' and a couple of trust fund twins who served little other purpose in life.

The valet brought their space cruiser to the front of the restaurant. Valets are unnecessary, as modern spaceships can be set to autopilot and remote retrieval from any location. But for the high-class restaurant crowd, how you looked and showing off your ride was paramount.

Qunot owned a Ferton Special XQZ. It was a short-range ship designed for planet-hopping in the denser part of the galaxy and had all the features that a television executive needed and a lot of features nobody needed, but were included anyway.

The space cruiser contained a bridge, or control area, and three small rooms with beds, desks, bathrooms, and not much else. It wasn't designed for long-range travel. Qunot named his ship *The Mayapple* after his first university dormitory experience, from which he had fond memories.

The bridge of his ship resembled a living room, with a dilapidated sectional couch covered in an unmentionable number of bodily fluids from countless species. Cushions were at one point tan, but now held stains of at least five distinct colors of green and yellow. The couch was on its last legs. Empty glass and aluminum booze containers littered the floor.

A glass coffee table sat in front of the sofa with a bowl of porcelain powder for guests to snort at their convenience. While the coffee table had a clear glass top, the floor under it was not visible. Zatosians had a habit of cleaning their nose and placing the contents on the underside of a table, independent of visibility. Zatosians had trouble feeling shame and embarrassment, especially when it came to bodily fluids and functions.

A matching easy chair sat opposite the table in the same ruinous condition as the couch. Empty bags from galactic fast-food restaurants littered the coffee table and floor. Off in the corner of the bridge sat a small bar proudly displaying a fine choice of galactic liquors. If an Earthling were to board the ship and view the main control area, they would consider it a fraternity house living room.

A monitor hung in the room's center faced the dilapidated sofa. This was the interface for the ship's controls and the artificial intelligence system. It also served as a conduit for intergalactic gaming, gambling on sports, and adult entertainment. Although Zatosians weren't the blushing types, the computerized brain of The Mayapple was, to the extent a machine is capable.

The ship's computer was high-end artificial intelligence with a pleasant disposition that took orders nicely despite being 100,000 times smarter than the owner of the ship. Its programming allowed for poor decisions and their consequences. The AI unit had a *suggestion* function. This programmed feature would politely recommend a single time if a different decision was prudent. The manufacturer of the Ferton line of spaceships took great care to not install anything that would offend its customer's giant egos.

Despite their meticulous engineering and customer service, the Ferton company was being sued for negligence. One of its customers did something particularly stupid. The ship's computer offered the suggestion to alter course based on the risk of the decision. The customer ignored the recommendation and suffered the consequences.

In this case, a young movie star was solar system hopping aboard his brand new Ferton Special XQZ. He found an interesting world named Unmatta. The topography was mostly coastline with endless beaches consisting of fine grains of sand that remained the perfect temperature for romantic walks. The pristine sunsets were rated top ten in travel industry publications and, due to the slow rotation of Unmatta, lasted an hour. He stopped because he wanted to get a cool picture for his social media account. Unmatta had no intelligent life. The planet had abundant plants and animals and wasn't on the *inhabited, yet unevolved* list, which meant it was a legal stop.

He instructed the ship to land for exploration on one of the prime beaches. The ship's artificial intelligence looked up Unmatta in the directory and warned him of the risk. A specific breed of microbes existed that infested everything living. They thrived on carbon-based life forms. He was also warned since he was inharmonious with the planet's natural environment, he would be guaranteed to be infested.

In his rush to get a magnificent picture of himself on a beautiful beach, he ignored the warning and missed the important detail of the disease. The illness caused by the infection had no cure. Anyone infected would suffer the rest of their life and require quarantine. Not only was the microbe infestation contagious with no known cure, but it also made you blind and extended your natural life almost indefinitely. The body became a host to the parasite. The infestation also caused the infected person to hear their favorite song repeatedly in their head for the balance of that lifetime while in a semi-catatonic state.

There are multiple lessons:

The first lesson is to listen to suggestions from your ship's artificial intelligence when visiting a foreign planet. Second, in an infinite universe, anything is possible, independent of its probability.

A lost income lawsuit was filed against the Ferton Company by his family since the movie star could no longer act. Any prior royalties were sent to the quarantine planet where he would live out his days listening to the equivalent of a five-year-old's children's song playing in his head on an indefinite loop while the jubilant microbes danced away. The company expected to win the lawsuit on the simple defense that it cannot be responsible for the stupidity of its customers.

Not to be outdone in that lawsuit, a housewife on a small nearby planet in the same solar system drugged her pain-in-the-ass husband and shipped him to microbe infested Unmatta while he slept. The instructions to the ship's artificial intelligence were to allow him to relax on the beach for a bit and unwind.

He was infected and taken to the same quarantine location. He listened to Earth's equivalent of *99 Bottles of Beer on the Wall* in his head for 1,500 years until he finally died. He lived 1,400 years beyond the expected lifespan of his species, all thanks to the happy, dancing microbes.

This poor, unsuspecting soul's final reflection before departing to the otherworld was,

"I am going to get that bitch."

In the criminal case, the wife was found guilty of murder. In the civil case, the Ferton company rendered innocent. The company could not be held liable for the malicious intent of its customers.

CHAPTER 11

Once on his ship, Qunot instructed the artificial intelligence to auto-pilot to Durnita. He and Rego needed to decompress from lunch. They would orbit the entertainment planet until their strategy session ended.

Qunot illegally interfered with the Earth on a prior occasion. He sent the alien Orwell to the planet to write about the inevitable future. The writer created profound and prophetic stories, and the humans fancied them as fairy tales and science fiction. He warned them of everything.

But Earthlings, trapped in their ignorance, said,

"This will never happen to us."

Only it happened many times throughout history and repeated itself ad nauseam, each time with better technology. Orwell, in his ultimate disgust, faked his death and left. His mission ended anyway. It was pointless to stay there for their ultimate and impending self-destruction.

Sneaking Orwell onto Earth proved difficult. Qunot needed to utilize the geese and convince them to send a powerful one-thought brainwave that temporarily blocked the galactic police monitoring. They initially told him to go squabble. In goose talk, it meant *Go to Hell*. The Zatosian bribed them with a false promise. The false promise would relieve them of their surveillance duties and return them to their home world. Of course, he lied.

Fortunately for him, he would never set foot on Earth or Garthis. They would kill him.

Getting Orwell off the planet was easier. He snuck aboard a space shuttle launch. Once in space, he rendezvoused with a ship to take him home.

Planetary interference this time would prove more difficult.

Qunot plopped into his easy chair with a grunt. The unfortunate chair did not have an intelligence and voice module installed. It would have grumbled under the extreme weight and grotesque Zatosian back sweat. Instead, it only protested with a creak under the fetid mass of its occupant.

Qunot started the conversation.

"We have to prevent the Earthlings from destroying themselves. This much is obvious."

He needed Rego's approval. He was key to successful operational execution.

Qunot laid out his top-level strategy.

"What if aliens made random appearances on Earth, scaring humans into unity? We show them firsthand there is life on other planets. This causes the planet to unite around humanity and understand the bigger picture. In parallel, we expose some of their more corrupt leaders, providing a secondary uniting point. We defuse the imminent destruction and buy time. We desperately need both to wrap up the show."

Rego was not impressed. It sounded to him like a plot out of a cheap dime store novel, a plot regurgitated a million times.

With an indifferent shrug, Rego retorted.

"That is your plan? Even if this works, we risk being executed."

Qunot understood the risks involved, but the penalties for failure were numerous and horrifying. He laid them out.

"The alternative is *Caution Earth* is canceled. We face ridicule and the strong possibility of never working in the industry again. A lot is riding on the program's ultimate success, not to mention our bonuses. We lose our lunches, perks, salaries, sex parties, all of it. I have a plan to pull this off without getting our hands dirty."

Rego paced in front of the sofa and the nervous Zatosian body odor permeated the ship's cabin. He feared sitting on the couch. The sectional experienced countless drug laced orgies, and it was fortunate for everyone involved it did not have an intelligence module. The countless moles on his face twitched, causing the hairs that grew from them to sway back and forth.

Qunot pushed forward.

"At least listen to the plan. We wouldn't do this ourselves. We also cannot use the geese as a shield like we did last time with Orwell. They are furious and have promised if they ever catch sight of me, they will peck me out of existence. I reneged on our deal with them."

Rego remembered how they screwed the geese using masterful Zatosian deceit. They vowed to replace them as the surveillance system in exchange for a favor. The Zatosians even shared replacement technology blueprints. The waterfowl did their part, and then a magic budget constraint prevented the project from materializing.

Zatosians were avid pricks, and the geese knew this. But their desperation to leave Earth created an emotional blind spot, so they trusted them.

Qunot continued.

"My idea is to ask Em and Emone and the bitter maître d' from the restaurant. That guy hates his job. We plan to offer him one-hundred times what he is making and guarantee no harm. The ship's artificial intelligence will provide all the direction they need. We can inform them by saving the planet, we save the television series. It is a noble cause. In addition, I chose Newton and the twins because they most closely resemble the Earthlings."

Rego stopped sweating and his moles ceased the random dancing. The Mayapple was specially equipped with air purification, not for the Zatosian's benefit, but for guests. The air again became lavender fresh. Qunot knew he warmed to the idea.

Rego said,

"Sounds good on paper. But don't we need to remove ourselves even one step further? How can we convince them to do this without them knowing we are the ones who hired them?"

Qunot wasn't sure if they needed to be removed one step further. The only individuals with firsthand knowledge would be the five of them. He didn't have an alternative to removing himself and Rego from the process, as they owned the hiring responsibility for everyone on the job.

He needed to inform him of the technology.

"We have a spaceship."

Rego chuckled while the booze at lunch got the better of him. He plopped down on the filthy couch. He was too emotionally drained to continue fearing a piece of furniture. While there, he prepared some porcelain to snort from the snot lined glass table.

He said,

"By have a ship, you mean you stole, right?"

Rego then leaned down and inhaled a huge line of porcelain.

Qunot loved their lifestyle. Their meetings on the ship were his favorite. They pontificated about their potential monumental and impactful decisions for *Caution Earth's* massive viewing audience while simultaneously ingesting copious amounts of drugs and alcohol. Sometimes they participated in sex parties on the couch while in conference. He had little interest in losing their extravagant behaviors to work on a mundane game show or to hit the unemployment line. That is, if he wasn't ostracized from the industry, if *Caution Earth* failed. Durnita and the entertainment industry owned the adage: *What have you done for me lately?* A television show dying two years before contract due to ratings is a career killer.

Qunot answered his sarcastic question.

"Hilarious. Normally, yes, you know how we are. But in this case, legitimately purchased. Our production budget has allocated a percentage of our advertising revenue to risk management. We bought a new technology that allows a spaceship to be invisible to the galaxy's surveillance apparatus. I started funding this project in case of an emergency on Earth where we needed to travel there unnoticed. It is in the budget under the line-item *Fantastic Lifestyles*. The problem with the science is that it is not fully tested. There is also a strange side effect the engineers haven't resolved. However, if it works, and we can test it in real-time, it will allow us to move around the world invisible to the galactic government and to accomplish our goal. We have access to the spaceship."

Rego's entire attitude shifted from partially skeptical to excited. He moved from the couch to the bar and poured himself and Qunot a tall vodka martini. The devious plan fit the Zatosian way. Rego now moved into risk management mode.

"Good foresight. What about the geese? And also, can't the ship's location be tracked by the engineering team? Lending us the ship is one thing. Don't they want to know destinations? And what is the design flaw?"

Qunot already considered these issues. In a sane universe, the technical problems of tracking the ship and its odd side effect would be the tougher challenge. However, the geese posed the greatest risk, and the galaxy was far from sane. They hated him. They would go to any length to have him arrested, embarrassed, and even executed. He took a moment and settled further into the easy chair. The leather upholstery squished around the folds of his back end, squeezing out of the top of his tight pants.

Of all the experiences he expected or didn't expect in his carefully orchestrated life, feuding with geese wasn't on the list.

He continued.

"The ship's tracking device can be deactivated, so it's not a problem. However, the geese are problematic and risky. This engineering flaw, or side effect of the technology, as the engineers call it, is a different story."

The Mayapple now orbited Durnita, the entertainment hub of the Milky Way. The planet Durnita was awarded the distinction of the most corrupt civilization in the galaxy a stunning 1,984 consecutive years.

They had a meeting scheduled with the twins in an hour at the *Caution Earth* production studio. The studio was merely a glorified office building, since no filming occurred there. Inside this studio, the film editors and producers decided which content they shared with the audience each week. The producers and editors performed 90% of the show's work. Executive Producers like Qunot and Rego indulged in expensive lunches, sporting events, and parties and did less than 1% of the work. They were strategists, which is a nice way of saying someone who works six minutes of an eight-hour workday. They spend the rest of their time appearing insanely busy while virtue signaling to everyone in their sphere of influence how important they are.

Qunot continued his thoughts.

"We will need to fool the geese. I am not sure if you are aware, through the goose hive mind, we learned the rulers of Earth have long planned a fake alien invasion. They want to use it as a tool to exert more control over the planet's population. This ties into the inflection point in history where the planet now stands. The open flow of information is threatening the ruling class. This brutal aristocracy has perpetuated the illusion of freedom while stealing time, resources, and productivity from the citizenry. These same rulers have controlled all information by owning the media, as well as writing history to suit their narratives. The Earthlings are waking up to the reality of this complete bullshit. They realize they have been manipulated and lied to for centuries. And they are, as you can imagine, quite angry. They are living in a matrix of lies designed to enslave them from cradle to grave. This depressing scenario is nothing new in galactic history. It has repeated in thousands of civilizations throughout the galaxy. Ignorance is bliss until it isn't."

Qunot took a slurp of his pink-hued drink from a chilled martini glass with three blue cheese stuffed olives. The salty feet smell of the gorgonzola coupled with the subtly of the olives and crisp vodka made it the perfect libation. The divine after lunch drink hit the spot.

He continued.

"When the television show started, we anticipated this inflection point as it would be historically ignorant on our part if we didn't. The spaceship serves as a contingency plan for this specific fulcrum. The risk is the geese realize the aliens are real and send communication to the Milky Way government. This would be a problem for us. However, the danger is lessened because only one goose can send the message. But he is also tuned into the hive mind. What I am hoping is they see the ship and conclude it is part of the Earth leaders' operation rather than legitimate aliens."

Qunot paused for a moment and swirled his martini around the glass, watching the clear liquid film as it slid down the glass.

He said,

"If we do this correctly and instruct Newton and the twins to avoid contact with them, this uncertainty is largely mitigated. Remember, the geese aren't looking for this. They merely observe and report without knowing they are doing it. It is a subconscious function. They won't be able to discern if the extraterrestrials are humans in costume or real. This is the reason we chose Em, Emone and Newton for this job. They are humanoid with enough alien features to appear potentially fake. The galactic council doesn't monitor the central goose mind, they don't care. The birds exist on the planet for the show's production. That being stated, their leader, Mr. Goose, is aware, and he could blow the entire operation."

He garnered reservations about telling Rego about the ship's engineering issue. It wasn't a project or timeline risk or even a flaw per se, but a serious inconvenience and distraction to the passengers on the ship.

Qunot said,

"I suppose first I should briefly explain the technology. As you may know, no existing science allows an object to disappear or be hidden from modern surveillance. Everything has to be somewhere and monitoring is so advanced any type of cloaking became obsolete many eons ago. Even the most advanced civilizations have given up on cloaking. Before you ask, we didn't steal this new science. We bought the invention notes from the daughter of the inventor. The flaw exists because the notes were unfinished. We have been attempting to engineer the last 5%. The technology's primary purpose is to shield the ship from the monitoring of the galactic government. Are you familiar with the planet Hellio?"

Qunot wasn't sure if his partner knew of the complaints department and wanted to ensure he fully understood the plan's origins.

Rego shook his head no, but his eyes stayed glued to the conversation with rapt attention. Qunot took another gulp of vodka before continuing.

He reached the home stretch.

"All the government's complaint departments are on planet Hellio. If an individual has an issue with government policy or law, the option exists to travel to Hellio and register a complaint in person. Hellio is the only location in the Galaxy with a modified temporal plane allowing dual existences in the same physical location. The dual planes that co-exist are closest on the space-time continuum. Unfortunately, the closest plane of existence is the non-living."

Rego spit his vodka all over the couch after almost choking on it. He was unfamiliar with both this place and its fascinating technology. In a strange twist of fate, the martini spit landed on a portion of a cushion housing a deadly virus that could only be killed by 100-proof or stronger alcohol mixed with blue cheese and olive oil. If he had poured the lower quality of the two vodkas or used garlic olives, both of them would have died within the next twelve hours. Neither was aware of this. The virus manifested on the sofa during a sex party with a rare alien from the far eastern edge of the Milky Way. It activated during a different sex party with an alien from the remote southern part of the galaxy.

Rego didn't bother to clean the martini he just sprayed all over the cabin. To clean a vodka spill would be insulting to the other stains.

He regained his composure.

"The wonders of the universe never cease."

He said this in a drawn-out sarcastic tone.

Qunot needed to get through this, so he marched onward.

"Many individuals came into the government's complaints department grumbling about their former loved ones haunting them. The ghosts complained about the boredom of death, the circumstances of their death, the unfairness of being deceased, and the waiting for their next lifetime. The government figured it would be more efficient if they built a department entirely dedicated to the deceased. This grievance department existed as an emotional outlet for the dead. The goal was to halt apparitions from meddling in the lives of the living. This would ultimately prove an invaluable service to the galactic population. When the ghosts haunted, it told them the planes of existence could overlap. The signal of the apparitions, however, was faint. They normally just stood there, making faces of dissatisfaction. On rare occasions, they succeeded in their communication. They just bitched about their condition. It freaked out their relatives, and they found it tiresome listening to their loved ones gripe about a situation they could not help."

Qunot and Rego were 30 minutes from their meeting with the twins, so he needed to wrap up the conversation.

"This is where the story gets interesting. Necessity is the mother of invention, as they say. The daughter of the inventor told me this story in person when we procured the technology. She said her parents spent the better part of their 52-year marriage arguing. They yelled and cursed at each other about everything, big and small. It became so pervasive in their relationship that a never-ending contest of who could get in the last word manifested, often at the expense of sleep, work and other responsibilities. The daughter thought them both insane. She moved out at a young age to escape their misery, but later in life realized it was their form of love, however twisted."

Qunot lit a cigar, pausing while the match reddened the tobacco sticking out its end.

He said,

"They booked a reservation to Indigo and argued the entire week-long journey there right up to the time where the host seated them. Newton remembers the event. He considers it one of the greatest breakups in restaurant history since he learned of their bizarre relationship, and the couple had no intention of breaking up. They had just ordered and received their appetizers. The wife reached such a pique of anger after making what she thought a final and salient point about their latest spat, it caused a stroke and she drowned in her soup. This, before her husband could respond, thus denying him the ability to have the last word."

Qunot took a puff of the cheroot and exhaled the sweet smoke into the ship's cabin.

He continued.

"The husband blew a gasket. Not that she died, mind you. She had the gall to die and got the last word after their 52-year never-ending string of arguments. He was certain he would die first, thus getting the final say. In his irrational rage, he built the temporal plane so he could continue the argument, communicate with her, and of utmost importance, get the final jab. He built the technology as a vacuum encompassing his property. But it seems he also overlooked something important. His dead wife had nothing but time. He soon realized he could never get the last word because she could argue with him all day and night and ghosts never needed sleep. We think this is where he wanted to add a feature to the device that would work like a mute button, but he didn't finish it. He thought if he could mute his dead wife, he could ultimately win their lifelong tiff. His daughter says he eventually left the house with his wife's ghost trapped in it and moved to the beach where he worked as a bartender for the rest of his life. She has no idea who won the argument."

Given the level of Rego's intoxication, his rapt attention to the discussion deserved props. He sat on the edge of the couch and leaned forward in anticipation of the conclusion.

Qunot said,

"Once the inventor died, the government simply seized his house, which was fine with his neighbors. They were sick of the dead milling about in their neighborhood on the fringes of the co-existing temporal planes. They moved the house to the complaints department planet and expanded the realm to a small island-sized office building. The field naturally expanded with the expansion of the building. Now the deceased freely interact with the living, file their complaints, and return to wherever it is they go. Hauntings are down 93% galaxy-wide and it is hailed as a wildly successful bureaucratic project. One of the few, I might add. Employees enter or exit similar to any other normal building and the apparitions can only teleport from their plane of existence. Quite brilliant."

Qunot came to the final thought.

He said,

"Here is the issue. The notes I purchased from the inventor's daughter were only 95% complete. We believe the flaw resides in the last 5% of functionality. The co-existing temporal field installed on the ship works fine. The space cruiser exists in both planes of existence. If the technology is activated to greater than 50% in the plane of the dead, the spaceship is shielded from surveillance. The glitch? Ghosts can appear and communicate while it is operational. There is no mute button. We also believe the inventor built a blocking mechanism into the device allowing the planes to co-exist but preventing the ghosts from appearing, but we cannot figure that out either. The notes ended when he discussed these features of the invention without sharing the engineering of the solution."

He got through the explanation and poured himself another drink. He was exactly the right amount of intoxicated for a non-productive afternoon. Qunot and Rego got most of their workday completed, which usually comprised ten minutes of effort, well before lunchtime.

Rego seemed pleased with the plan and offered no further comment. Now to sell it to the twins.

CHAPTER 12

The Mayapple landed on the roof of the *Caution Earth* production studio. Rego departed to round up Em and Emone, who were notoriously late for meetings. If all proceeded as planned with the twins, they would need to spend late afternoon back at Indigo meeting with Newton, the maître d'.

In a rare reflective moment, Qunot wondered if he was making a mistake. While Zatosians were infamous for their lack of ethical behavior, they were astute students of history and successful in the business world. A typical Zatosian practiced meticulous planning. They also had a knack for successful execution, even if they bent rules to accomplish goals. He well understood that even with alien meddling, the Earth's civilization only had a 10% chance of survival. The Earth sat at the magic tipping point all civilizations must face. It didn't matter to Qunot what eventually happened to the planet. He could not control the outcome either way. His correctly executed strategy would ensure *Caution Earth* lasted for two more seasons, with better ratings, and that the show would conclude on a high note. He hoped to manufacture what he considered a plausible conclusion for a series on evolution. If their civilization blew up five minutes after the series concluded, so be it. He, of course, hoped the Earthlings survived; they were an interesting species. But galactic history said otherwise. For each species successful in conscious evolution, 999 species failed.

His computer's communication portal rang. It was his bookie ringing him. Qunot fancied himself a high roller in the gambling world, but the only thing he rolled when betting on sports was a series of painstaking losses. He never had a winning month in ten years of sports gambling. His bookie called either to collect a losing bet or to take new bets. While Qunot's gambling skills left much to be desired, he loved the thrill of betting on the sporting events he attended. It gave him something to talk about and extra incentive to pay attention to the game, even though these bets rarely worked in his favor. His wife was unaware he spent about 15% of their income on gambling losses. This lifestyle would be problematic if *Caution Earth* came to an abrupt end. He ignored the call.

His marriage had additional money problems, compounded by his wife's lifestyle. She was a compulsive shopper, but not just on their home planet. She subscribed to a travel service for spending extravaganzas on different planets. These trips were all-inclusive deals designed to be a complete rip-off and reminded him of a home shopping network on steroids. She and the other television executive wives loved these trips. He estimated she spent 25% of their income on her shopping excursions.

Qunot and his wife lived in an extravagant house furnished from these shopping trips. They bore no children, so the twenty-two-bedroom mansion seemed unnecessary. They were home at the same time about fifty Earth days a year. The Zatosian year encompassed 8,042 Earth days, meaning they rarely saw each other. They mortgaged their house to the hilt. If *Caution Earth* abruptly ended, they would have to sell it for certain.

While he pondered his life's problems, the intercom interrupted him. It was Rego. The conference room was ready.

Qunot noticed his breath contained an intense, combined aroma of shellfish and red wine. He swished some mint mouthwash before leaving. The fresh peppermint aroma also cleared his head from the mostly liquid lunch. He changed his shirt and put on some deodorant in a valiant attempt to shield some of his body odor. Zatosians were always in a futile fight to tame their heinous, but natural smell, which ranged from a full-on nasal assault replete with watering eyes and choking to the less offensive version where other beings were in a hurry to end conversations. Rego's heinous odor even offended people that lived on sulfur-based planets with fish hatcheries.

Deodorant became big business on Zatos and the entertainment planet Durnita, as other species were sensitive to the Zatosian odor problem. Unfortunately, even the best fumigant products had limitations. Putting deodorant on the people of Zatos was like putting an incense stick in a pile of fresh dog shit.

It wasn't a minor stench problem. The body odor invaded everyone around them and clung to unanimated objects for indefinite amounts of time. The offices and editorial rooms at the *Caution Earth* studios were fumigated weekly. It was an important clause in the union's labor contract for all non-Zatosian species.

CHAPTER 13

Qunot ambled into the conference room of the Caution Earth production studios, feeling refreshed and ready for a lazy afternoon. They were always unbelievably busy with show strategy, so they rarely set foot in the studio. Working ten minutes a day while trying to maintain an exhaustingly busy persona can take its toll even on the most seasoned executive.

Em and Emone lounged at one end of the conference table with their feet up, giving their best impression of not caring about the meeting topic. The less they pretended to care, the less labor involved. Rego drank a rare Zatosian tea that removed drugs and alcohol from the system. The liquid lunch and the ship's conversation took its toll.

The bland conference room, with tan paint and a rectangular table with eight identical chairs, reminded Qunot of why he spent so much time away from the office. One would assume the production studios of the most successful television program in galactic history would be embellished with more interesting furniture. They would be wrong. A monitor hung on the wall playing a loop of stupid pet videos the twins enjoyed.

Monitors had become so advanced they looked like posters. They could be taken down, rolled up, and transported in a small cardboard tube. They were highly sophisticated communication devices. Qunot powered the monitor down. They chose the only conference room in the studio without recording or surveillance equipment. The only fully private space in the building.

Qunot performed a listening device scan upon entering the room. This conversation needed to be private. He trusted Em and Emone. As a failsafe, he had gathered enough dirt on the twins for a lifetime. With his knowledge of their shenanigans, he could get them fired, killed, imprisoned for life, or all of the above. They had a mutual understanding. Of course, they possessed the same list of blackmail on him. It cut both ways. In the rough and tumble entertainment industry, blackmail, or the threat thereof, is the name of the game.

Qunot said,

"Em and Emone, thank you for meeting with us again. From our lunch conversation, you are aware of the situation with the planet Earth and, of course, by extension, our television show."

They both nodded in agreement. The simultaneous nature of their mannerisms gave him chills sometimes.

Qunot continued.

"We would like to offer you an opportunity to both save the television program and the planet."

Qunot asked the in-conference room vending machine for a cup of detoxifying tea. He was past intoxicated and the hot drink proved to be fast-acting. The blend contained an alien micro-organism native to Zatos. The micro-organism population thrived on chemical dependency. When drinking it, the microbes entered the bloodstream and happily absorbed all the chemicals from whatever cocktail of drugs consumed. They had a blowout party before happily passing out and being eliminated through the digestive process. In their society, this was living their best life. Once the microbes absorbed the drugs, the host became no longer affected. It was no coincidence the micro-organisms hailed from the same planet as the hard partying Zatosians. Through the evolutionary process, nature provides solutions within its environment.

Between the twins, Em did most of the talking. He predicted this conversation coming from a mile away. Emone, who was more of the strategist, warned him Qunot would probably concoct some scheme to save his ass from the impending trouble on Earth. They were wise to him, looking out for number one and his standard Zatosian tactics.

However, as board members, their role required supporting the show.

He looked at his twin brother with a silent, mutual understanding.

He said,

"What can we do to help?"

Em and Emone were stingy with words preferring to observe and listen. They were also notorious for ignoring important conversations to stare at various female species.

Qunot eased back into one of the conference chairs and stared blankly at the ceiling tile for a moment, allowing the aroma of the tea to sharpen his dulled senses. The drink had a delicate scent of peppermint and basil that heightened the senses and deepened the breathing. Lunchtime day drinking always became an adventure mid-afternoon.

He took a deep inhale of the steam rising from his mug and set into the explanation.

"As we discussed at lunch, *Caution Earth* is in trouble. The series is in danger because the planet is teetering on destruction. Naturally, we would prefer to fix this problem so the show can reach a respectable finale. As you are aware, the conclusion we seek is the civilization becoming evolved rather than a statistic in the long line of planets that have self-destructed due to mental, emotional, and spiritual incompetence. We all understand it is more than incompetence. I am using that word to avoid the more detailed description of the problem. We are all aware of the challenges the population faces as we studied these societal problems in elementary school galactic history."

The tea worked its magic and Qunot felt his senses and mental focus return.

He continued.

"We plan to send a ship to scare the humans into uniting against a common enemy. Of course, we pose no real threat to them. We want to create the illusion we could or might pose a threat to them. We need Earthlings to understand life exists on other planets. They need to realize they are not the center of the universe. We hope they can unite long enough to go beyond destroying themselves. While we are visiting, we will also accelerate their transition from the current scumbags ruling their population to a more civilized and citizen-friendly government.

They have been living in a giant planet-sized prison cell without knowing it. The individuals and families who have lorded over civilization for the past 4,000 years practice avarice with unfortunate god complexes and created a perpetual penitentiary for their citizens. They are morally and spiritually bankrupt to the core and we are doing the people a favor by helping them to remove these existing aristocrats from power. There is nothing more to the strategy. We would like you, as stakeholders in the television show, to travel to Earth. We are also going to ask Newton, the maître d' from Indigo, to help."

Qunot finished laying out the plan while taking a sip of his now lukewarm tea. His head continued to clear. The microbes from the brew danced happily in his body, completely wasted.

Em and Emone stared at the Zatosian with identical grins. Their eyes fixated on him, like a poker player's focus on a large raise in a high-stakes game. They were trying to get a read. He understood they knew he could be a manipulative bastard. Qunot understood they were far smarter and savvier than they acted. Twins can be creepy sometimes, and this was one of those instances. He didn't flinch. He told them the truth and would explain the risks after they asked.

Emone spoke up; a rarity. Not only did the twins share appearance except for their hairstyles, their voice tone was identical.

"You realize there is a significant risk of execution traveling to this planet. Galactic law forbids travel to Earth. But of course, we are aware of the ship and the temporal plane technology, so we assume this spaceship we will be our transportation. Is it ready yet?"

Qunot choked on his tea and his head again swooned from the effects of the lunchtime bender. He was shocked to hear the twins heard of project *Fantastic Lifestyles*, his budget name for the project.

He stammered.

"How did you learn about the ship and the technology, and who else knows?"

Qunot noticed Rego's mole hairs dancing simultaneously to multiple tunes from different music genres while out of rhythm with each other.

He sweat profusely, which gave the room the odor of rotten egg baked in a blazing sun for three days resting on a pile of fresh horse manure. The only experience worse than a lengthy eye-to-eye conversation with a Zatosian was to smell a panicked, sweaty one. Em and Emone noticed Rego's discomfort and shot each other a look of satisfaction. Rego knew nothing of their game and spent far too much time calling them idiots, so they enjoyed watching him squirm, even with the intolerable odor of Zatosian sweat.

Qunot always enjoyed the faux chess match with Em and Emone. He understood they were smarter than they acted. The twins were biding time and enjoying life until forced into responsible positions. They were all teammates. The power struggles were petty and unnecessary. They went through the motions for sport of it. But their knowledge of the ship made Qunot nervous because of the high stakes involved. He did not like entering negotiations without knowing full well who owned the leverage. The upper hand he thought he owned five minutes ago had just vaporized in a puff of Rego's heinous body odor.

Em and Emone understood their current leverage and needed to ensure Qunot wasn't hiding anything important.

Emone opened a window to relieve them of the nasal assault while Em continued.

"We have no issue with the plan and are happy to help. If our assumptions are correct, you chose us and the Newton character because of our resemblance to the human species. This is smart. It will have a much less animalistic psychological reaction if the aliens who visit Earth at least closely resemble themselves. We spent a little bit of time understanding the civilization from the artificial intelligence system. Humans suffer primarily from attachment to identity. This attachment is the prison they create in their minds. Unfortunately, their rulers and lapdogs in their corporate media have played a major role in brainwashing large swathes of their population into unnecessary identity suffering. Separating citizens by identity markers is one of the oldest strategies of control in the playbook. We agree they need to evolve past this. We also agree the show and the planet should be saved, as does our father Coder. He has a soft spot for the Earthlings, despite their obvious shortcomings."

Qunot noticed Em avoided the spaceship question and allowed him to twist in the wind for a few more minutes. Given his answers about Earth, he suspected more gamesmanship to show him who really controlled the relationship. Emone walked to the window, no doubt to inhale anything that didn't reek like the inside of a bowling shoe stuffed with cooked cabbage. Zatosians didn't notice their odor. To them it was a pheromone, and to their female species an aphrodisiac.

Em took a deep breath of newly fresh air and continued.

"As to the ship. Us and our father Coder know about it and the technology. We are continually impressed with your foresight to make excellent decisions for our investment in the television series, and secondarily the progress of Earth's civilization. I'm not saying that to be cruel or greedy. I put the show first simply because evolving civilizations on planets destroy themselves with alarming frequency. It is the natural order. Either evolve or perish; this rule of the universe cannot be broken. Evolution is divine will. I am sure you are aware, even with our intervention, there remains a 90% chance the people of Earth destroy themselves. The civilization's only hope is we create a delay that allows them to move forward. We also support the idea of helping them to improve their self-governing situation."

Em could see Rego stopped sweating and became more relaxed. Qunot shut the window and made a mental note to have the cleaning crew fumigate the conference room.

He breathed out a long sigh. It was nice to be appreciated. Despite the shortcomings of Zatosians, they were quite effective at their jobs. Qunot could see it was time to wrap the meeting, they could review additional details on the ship with the artificial intelligence module.

Qunot responded.

"Em and Emone, I appreciate the kind words of support, and please thank Coder for us. We can discuss the plan of execution on the ship. We hope to recruit Newton for the job, otherwise we need a Plan B. I think he will play ball."

The twins departed quickly, most likely to escape the stench still permeating the room. Rego and Qunot radioed the ship for the return trip to Indigo to meet with Newton. They sent an advanced communication to the restaurant requesting the meeting.

CHAPTER 14

Em and Emone departed the nasal assault of conference room and before heading to their office, they stopped at one of the many automatic full body sanitizers that would remove the Zatosian stench from their aura and more importantly, their clothing.

Their private office resembled an old school video game parlor rather than a place of business. It contained tabletop game devices from their childhood days, movie posters from famous MM1 productions, a gaming table where a stick knocked balls into six holes on a hexagon shaped table. The game was like Earth's game of pool, but with a different table shape and twice as many balls. While in college, the twins would shark hexi games as a side hustle.

Em plopped into one of the two desks, located on opposite sides of the office, facing each other.

He stared over at his brother, amazed at their likeness.

He considered how rare twins are for their species. Only one in fifty million births. Triplets are non-existent. When he looked at his brother, he reflected himself. They were the same in every way, including voice tone, minor skin blemishes, and muscle tone. Their voices had the same deep resonance, demanding respect when they spoke. They were often mistaken for clones rather than two separate individuals.

While they were born on planet Durnita due to their father's business, they were from a world located eight solar systems north of Gastrin, named Zink.

The Zinkites are humanoid in appearance. They are shorter, topping out at five feet tall. They have Caribbean Sea-blue eyes and the species adorns a pinky finger that is an opposing thumb. Their skin tone is a rich, even brownish red like a fine clay with few blemishes.

The Zinkites have unusual hair in both the male and female species. It is blonde down the middle front to back, brown stripes and black stripes running parallel to the blonde stripe. The hairstyle resembles the Earthling's 80s punk rock era. Em sported a mohawk hairstyle so others could tell them apart. They became exhausted by people confusing them.

Em said,

"How long you think we can keep up the act? We know for certain Qunot does not buy the bullshit about us being idiots. He finds us useful allies in his intra-company political battles. He understands if he remains good with us, he stays in our father Coder's grace. We have an understanding. Plus, we *are* all on the same team."

Em paused for a moment to see if his brother remained engaged. He got bored when it came to office political wrangling.

He continued.

"Rego, conversely, is as a yes-man. His function is mostly execution anyway, a true middle manager. He loves his job because he gets to act like he is part of the strategy team but offers little value. I am tired of him calling us idiots. The level of disrespect is unnecessary."

His brother nodded in agreement.

Emone said,

"Qunot knows we tend to be lazy. Rego considers lazy and incapable to be the same. We are born from the genes of one of the smartest TV executives in galactic history. Our mother is no slouch either, graduating at the top of her collegiate studies in quantum engineering. I like to call it planning to be an adult later in life. We would not have attended all that private education and been accepted to that elite university otherwise. In retrospect, I wish we were challenged more."

Em agreed and scratched his almost non-existent chin, a feature of the Zinkite species.

Em said,

"At least when we graduated college, we learned our father's trade of managing this galactic television network. Although the most pressing daily challenge is the politics of Dad's direct reports. We both know when the television executives aren't directly carrying out their tasks, they are scheming to backstab each other for personal gain. It is an endless cycle."

Emone nodded in agreement while scratching one of his long and pointed, pinned ears.

Emone said,

"Well, we knew the day would come when our lifestyle would change. Maybe it is time to grow up. Just a little, mind you."

He flashed a grin with a head tilt. His button nose and disproportionately large eyes, a trait in their species, broadcast mischief.

The brothers long ago devised a plan to minimize the amount of responsibility they would encounter at work. The twins knew few would dare speak to their father. Coder doted on them endlessly and allowed them to get away with most behaviors, however illicit. He always bailed them out of trouble. A typical enabler of his trust fund kids.

Em and Emone acted like they didn't care about outcomes. They delegated or delayed decision-making and rarely took on any actual work. They limited their work to advising, which meant they offered their opinion on different subjects without having to get their hands dirty. The twins were much like high-priced consultants with no skin in the game, playing the experts with someone else's business. The subject matter expert consultant got paid whether the business succeeded or failed. When a failure point manifested, something or someone else could always be blamed rather than their shitty guidance.

Fortunately, and contrary to the normal consulting class, they offered good advice. Em and Emone were over-educated and brilliant. But they still exhibited laziness.

The twins loved their fabulous lifestyle and yearned for it to last as long as possible. They also realized at some point they would take over the family business. They were prepared to do so. They were smart and were paying attention. Their daily routine was an elaborate ruse to minimize work. They called it working smarter, not harder.

Em ran his hand from front to back on his mohawk.

He said,

"Our father gave us full blessing to help save both the television show *Caution Earth* and the planet Earth. In his opinion, it is a character-building exercise. He also has enough sway in the galactic government that the risk of penalty, if we are caught, is minimized. I agree, let's grow up a little. It will be interesting to see another part of the galaxy."

CHAPTER 15

With their plan gelling, Qunot instructed the Mayapple to return to Gastrin to make a job offer to the maître d'. The television executives were prime customers with a huge expense account, so getting the meeting wouldn't be an issue.

After valeting their ship, they entered Indigo for the second time that day, just before the dinner rush. The investigative unit already arrested the woman who stabbed her husband and the wait staff settled up their lunch bets and were now on break getting drunk. Such are the daily operations at Indigo.

Newton stood waiting for them at the host stand. His left hand tapped the fine wood with his nail, making a clicking sound. Newton's black eyes were laser focused on a sweaty and nervous vendor holding a bag of dirty tablecloths.

Qunot overheard Newton and his exasperating exchange.

"Why is it we need to have this conversation every time you come here to pick up the tablecloths and napkins? I am tired of being overcharged for standard tablecloth stains. The entire planet has a plague of restaurant violence and you claim blood is harder to clean from linens than food stains so you can gouge us on pricing. Your entire argument is ridiculous."

The linen laundering industry was owned and monopolized by the Holtzi species. They loved dirty laundry and the process of transforming it to the original pristine condition. They also loved arguing about linens, possibly more than cleaning them. Arguing about the cleaning effort required to transform the tablecloths back to purity was a form of high compliment to the Holtzis. But because they loved arguing, they could not allow anyone to know. Anyone who found out they loved to argue ignored them, which made them angry. They kept their love of the argument a deeply guarded secret. The Holtzis had the highest respect for Newton, so they argued with him vehemently, even over the smallest stains. Not all aliens shared their passion for restaurant linens.

Newton asked a hostess to bring Qunot and Rego to their table and made sure the waitress gave them a complimentary drink while they waited. He assured them he would be with them momentarily.

The restaurant was quiet during the time between lunch and dinner. Few patrons were present. The lighting brightened so the main dining areas could be cleaned, the carpet vacuumed, and tables reset for the dinner crowd. With the higher lighting, Indigo lost its ambiance and looked more like a mess hall than a fine dining establishment. With the curtain pulled back, reality shows. The customers at Indigo didn't pay for reality. They paid for the illusion, so the illusion is what they received. In thirty minutes, the ceiling lights would dim. The floor lights would illuminate, reaching up the curved walls to the domed ceiling. Table candles would be lit. The ambiance of the fabulous dramatic breakup would breathe back to life.

Newton approached the table and sat down, profusely apologizing for making them wait just under ten minutes. The skin under his jet-black eyes puffed and sagged, and his sweat-stained shirt told the story of a vigorous workout, not a lunchtime management escapade. It was a rough lunch.

Newton asked them why they returned, trying to hide his flustered tone.

"Good to see you again so soon, Qunot, Rego. What can I do for you? I hope you enjoyed lunch."

Newton thought they returned because of problems with their earlier meal. He wasn't excited to meet with Zatosians. He knew they were at best nefarious, and maintaining eye contact was a challenge. The species was repulsive in sight and odor.

Qunot tried to put him at ease. They were not there to badger him about their dining experience.

"Lunch was fabulous as always, thank you. I have always admired the skill you exhibit managing this insane asylum. The endless details, difficult vendors, indifferent bartenders, unruly wait staff, and the never-ending customer and owner drama have to be draining."

Qunot knew he was on point with his analysis.

Newton responded.

"Interesting you mention it. This is not what I expected when I accepted this role. I don't enjoy any of it. I thought it would be exciting and interesting to meet different species, but at best it is social awkwardness masked as inauthentic politeness. Everybody knows it but does it anyway. The job is unfulfilling and lacks purpose. I continue to stay in this tedious position out of appreciation for the owner. The Wong was kind to give me the opportunity at such a young and inexperienced age. I respect him."

Newton wasn't sure why he aired his soul to a couple of television executives; gut instinct nudged him to do so.

He continued,

"I am sure you didn't come here to discuss my lack of job fulfillment, so how can I help you?"

Qunot heard exactly what he predicted. Despite the Zatosian tilt towards illicit behavior and other unsavory personality characteristics, they had great communication skills and insight into others.

"Well, here is the thing. We came here about your lack of job satisfaction. And we have an opportunity that may interest you. How would you like to help save a planet from imminent self-destruction?"

Newton was not expecting this. But again, his gut instinct said to listen to their offer. There was no harm in listening.

"Please continue."

At a young age, Qunot learned the importance of reading facial expressions. He observed a sense of relief and interest on Newton's face, despite the obvious harrowing experiences of the day's lunch.

This skill served him well professionally and in one other important area of his life. Qunot lost money in all his gambling endeavors with one exception: he was a superb poker player. Some form of what the Earthlings call poker exists in almost all societies.

Qunot explained his problem.

"As you may know, I am the executive producer and founder of the reality television series *Caution Earth*. It has been on the air for eight seasons. The purpose of the TV program is to depict in real time the evolution of Earth's species. When we originally started the broadcast, our expert historians and social analysts estimated the Earthlings would evolve so the show could reach a successful conclusion in ten seasons. We defined evolution as moving beyond the self-destruction phase and away from animal instincts enough to form a peaceful and productive society. The society did not necessarily have to reach interstellar travel and contact with other galactic civilizations. However, they needed to progress on their evolutionary path past the risk of their demise. Success for this reality series is predicated on not one Earthling being aware they are filmed. The geese understand they are part of the surveillance system, but they can't tell anyone due to language barriers. Are you familiar with the program?"

Newton heard of the show but didn't involve himself with television.

"I have never seen the broadcast. I am familiar with it though. What are geese?"

Newton had little context in this conversation.

Qunot continued as the waiter brought them all drinks and another round of exotic appetizers.

"I am getting to the geese. The short story is the opposite is happening. Humans are digressing to the point of idiocy and now our scientists tell us there is a 99% chance they will destroy their civilization. The humans face self-extinction. Of course, the planet survives, but the population is lost. Eight billion souls terminated due to the greed and avarice of a few. You asked about geese. They are a species of migratory birds from Garthis that were placed on Earth to assist in the surveillance of humans by feeding real-time information to television producers. This helps us to decide what parts of the Earth's story are aired. They have a rare mental gift that allows them to send a strong mind signal over great distances. We call it the goose hive mind and they broadcast without effort. They are simply transmitting what they observe, without opinion or filter. They despise the planet's human inhabitants and would do anything to return to their home. But unfortunately, they are stuck."

Qunot took another sip of the merlot. The same vintage he sampled at lunch. The exquisite bouquet paired with the lobster bisque was divine.

He looked at Rego and could see him nodding along in support as he continued,

"We would like, for obvious reasons, to save the planet. Our motive, which we will not lie, is to preserve the television show. This may seem self-serving, and to a degree it is. However, our audience and staff have become attached to Earthlings. They are tragic in their behavior, but likable, and with the right nudging along, we think they could become a member of the civilized galactic community. What we are asking is if you are interested in traveling to Earth. If successful, you would achieve freedom from work. The pay is an exorbitant sum we hope would last you many lifetimes."

Newton's intrigue made him consider possible divine intervention. He had meditated many times seeking an avenue out of his dead-end job, and an even more exhausting marriage. This role accomplished both and would also align with his passion for societal evolution and galactic history.

Newton asked.

"What are the risks?"

Despite his nature to lie, Qunot intended to tell the truth. He noticed Rego's mole hair started to twitch and sway, a surefire tell he was getting nervous.

If Qunot wasn't careful with his wording, the entire deal could be blown.

"Newton, I am going to be forthright. There is one significant risk, and it is not from the Earthlings. As you may or may not know, it is highly illegal for alien beings to interfere with unevolved planets. Doubly so given Earth is a television show. It is the most monitored planet in the galaxy. The galactic government executes meddlers. And while it may seem harsh, it saves a lot of lives. There are countless examples in history of aliens, joy-riding to other planets that have yet to achieve interstellar travel. These planets' populations become filled with irrational fear and experience exponential technological advances that allow them to declare war on their nearest neighbors. The government takes a dim view of this."

He took another sip of soup and wine while reading the room. Newton didn't seem alarmed by the danger and looked interested in hearing the plan.

Qunot continued.

"We have a solution to eliminate the risk, thus ensuring your safety."

Newton wasn't considered a thrill seeker or a risk taker, but the idea of traveling to another part of the galaxy to save a civilization enthralled him.

"What is the plan? This is very interesting to me."

Newton continued to play it cool.

Qunot finished his bisque while the waiter topped off his wine.

Picking up a napkin, he shared the plan.

"You will join two of our colleagues, the twins, who attended lunch with us, on a spaceship modified for this mission. Harm to the Earth's population is prohibited on the mission. The ship's artificial intelligence module has a complete history of human existence. Peruse the high points of this during travel. I imagine with your educational background little new information will be learned. The AI module will guide you and perform all the navigation. Relax and enjoy the experience until arrival. For the first appearance, we opted for a landing with no contact. We are directing the initial communication to their leadership so you can establish their weapons are useless. Their leadership should understand dire consequences will follow any harm that comes to you. Demonstrate the weapon by vaporizing one of the politician's residences. The home must be devoid of occupants during the demonstration. The spacecraft's computer will handle and direct this undertaking. This demonstration of force will allow you to appear freely in different locations, interacting with the humans. A large swath of the population must become aware they are being visited by aliens. We are not invading the planet; we are showing them they are not alone. The goal is for the Earthlings to unite under the banner of their species. We hope this will move them away from self-destruction and back onto their proper evolutionary path. Our viewers on the television show *Caution Earth* will not be aware this is happening."

Qunot continued.

"In addition, we will expose their nefarious leadership. This will provide an additional unifying force. We hope the realization of life on other planets, coupled with helping them to unshackle from the chains of their current governance structure, will nudge them along the evolutionary path. We must navigate this fine line carefully. We want to avoid the people of Earth becoming rogue and seeking to destroy neighboring intelligent life. We need to show power, but not use it. During your visit, the population must understand you pose no threat. Nobody can be harmed."

Qunot finished, knowing he didn't answer the most pressing question.

He eased into the dangerous part of the plan.

"The spaceship is equipped with a temporal plane device we purchased from the inventor. This technology allows the ship to exist in dual planes of existence. To be precise, it allows the two planes to overlap. Provided the Wingate is more than half in the undead plane, it is undetectable in our realm. When we land on Earth, the Galactic government also cannot detect us. They don't have surveillance on the planet itself. The unfortunate flaw, or technological side effect, is the deceased can appear and verbally interact with the crew. This is an absurd nuisance and inconvenience, but it will not jeopardize the mission."

Newton's jaw dropped as astonishment washed over him. A technology that allowed communication with the non-living. He wondered if he could talk to his uncle. Newton could see his expression in the small mirror lining the booth where they sat. He looked exhausted. The toll of the restaurant industry permeated his face. He imagined the bags under his eyes represented managing the horrible wait staff, the creases where he frowned around his mouth the grifting vendors who consistently tried to overcharge for their services, and his bloodshot eyes from the lack of sleep and inauthentic glad-handing with customers.

Newton felt relieved to know he was done with the restaurant industry. He took a deep inhale and exhaled the word, making a whispering sound as it escaped his lips.

"Fascinating."

It was all he could say.

Qunot knew he had his man.

"We assume you desire some space to ponder the plan. We understand it is a life-changing event and not an endeavor to be taken lightly. Thank you for your time today. We appreciate it, and we will be in touch. Give our regards to The Wong."

Rego set his napkin on his empty appetizer plate and they departed the restaurant for the second time. Newton remained at the table to focus his mind. The flood of novel information bombarding his brain overwhelmed him, but also brought the excitement of a new chapter. He had ample reason to not trust anyone from Zatos. But Newton's species is highly evolved, and one of his superpowers is to know when he is being snowed. He detected no dishonesty in Qunot and considered using his third eye, but seeing the true nature of a Zatosian horrified him. Instinct told him to talk with The Wong. He would need to chat with him anyway, to quit his job. He was wise and understood the Zatosians well.

CHAPTER 16

Newton's phone beeped for the tenth time in the past hour. His wife Keren badgered him throughout the day due to the sheer boredom of her life.

The restaurant's lunch crowd departed and it would be quiet until the dinner rush. After yesterday's unfortunate appetizer fork stabbing and the calamity of the *Caution Earth* TV executives visit, today's lunch proved uneventful save for the usual number of divorces, firings and breakups. At least nobody was assaulted or killed.

Newton abhorred violence. His home planet of Zang existed in tranquility. The Zangians evolved into a peaceful people. They were born with the gifts of observation and deep intuition ingrained into their genetic makeup. They noticed everything. Newton's cognizance of his surroundings contributed to proficiency in his role. He could manage umpteen mindless details simultaneously. This sometimes made him edgy, especially the linens. But when work ended, he became chill, albeit sometimes with the help of recreational drugs.

Addiction did not exist with Zangians. They could ingest any number of illicit substances and just say no if needed. Newton loved the effect of various drugs, but the worst for him, and all Zangians, was alcohol. Zangians reacted to alcohol similar to an Earthling's reaction to a heavy hallucinogen, replete with a brutal hangover. His last experience with alcohol happened with his wife on the night they met. They drank a bottle of wine at this very restaurant. He thinks he may have been hallucinating when he proposed. Lust at first sight can sometimes lead to questionable decisions.

Fortunately for Newton, he didn't have to marry the same soul through a multitude of lives to experience true love. When he met his wife ten years ago at Indigo, she waitressed and aspired to acting. This horrible stereotype invaded his mind their entire relationship. He thought she was one step away from working at a strip club. The stereotype would be complete!

When they met, he was new to his maître d' role and brimmed with the hopes and dreams of being a big-time restaurant manager who rubbed elbows with the rich and famous, just like his Uncle Newty.

Keren shared his youthful exuberance fresh out of university, aspiring to fame as an actress. She also hailed from the planet Zang. She had the typical Zangian features, jet black hair which she wore up in a bun, mysterious obsidian eyes, and a thin face with her facial bone structure prevalent to her other features. Zangian women were thin and attractive, especially noticeable in the land of movies and television. They had perfect symmetric bone structure. If an Earthling caught a glimpse of a Zangian, they would describe them like someone either into goth or straight from the casting of a vampire movie. Zangians also had a light purple hue to their skin that made them, to a human anyway, look one step from death.

Keren and Newton had a lot in common when they first met. They sought fame driven by their young idealism and newness to the working world. They realized after five years of wedlock the foundation of their relationship was a façade based on an unattainable perception of reality. For him, the job as he originally perceived it and reality collided soon after he began. For her, acting tryouts put her on a repetitive ride on the train of disappointment. Attractive Zangian women attempting to break into the entertainment industry had become a commodity.

The glad-handing, ass-kissing, and small talk it requires to be a good maître d' had its shine wear off after six months. It eventually became painful to talk about weather on other planets, most of which he had never visited. The wait staff's ability to be professional conflicted with being drunk, high, incompetent, or all of the above. Chefs and cooks practiced being prima donnas and threw regular tantrums at the smallest infraction. Bartenders spent more time ignoring orders than serving drinks, and his manager only came to Indigo for two hours a week, preferring to stay away from the infamous appetizer fork storm.

Newton considered it maudlin how the restaurant embraced both the emotional pain of its customers and the appetizer fork problem. What started out as a slow perception shift accelerated. The initial impression of working in his uncle's shoes collided with the harsh reality of the role. This collision created an internal conflict he could not resolve.

Newton could no longer justify the inauthenticity of the role, the babysitting of supposed other adult species, and pretending it was normal to profit from the extreme emotional pain of his customers. In short, he needed change, and not just in his job.

The marriage started with their mutual hard driving aspirations masquerading as unconditional love. They rented a small apartment on Gastrin and a residence on their home planet. From Zang, Keren could take a day trip to planet Durnita for acting tryouts. All three planets were within short travel range in this denser part of the Milky Way. Their joint drive to succeed became the bond that united them as they supported each other in their endeavors.

After two years of auditioning, Keren received a role in a female deodorant commercial. She thought this gig would springboard her to stardom. Unfortunately, the deodorant was manufactured with a chemical that wiped out a third of a remote planet's population in a backwater part of the galaxy. A consistent problem with inter-galactic consumer goods is, of course, testing products against over 100,000 species before commercial release. This is the reason most consumer goods are produced for a single species. The deodorant fiasco led to the collapse of one of the most successful consumer goods companies in the galactic history. It didn't do Keren's acting career any favors either.

Afterwards, she spiraled into a multi-year depression where she became what Newton can only describe as a full-time gossip. She would hang out at the pool, enjoy spa days with her girlfriends on Zang, and waste time talking about whichever of their group wasn't with them. She lost her purpose. All beings need a purpose, or they become listless and depressed.

Over the past five years, she would occasionally visit Durnita to audition for a role, but Newton knew a futile effort when he saw it. Her heart wasn't in it. And without purpose, she moved on from professional gossiping to become a professional husband nag. He tried to talk to her about different careers or purposes. Children were out of the question. The bitterness of the deodorant incident seemed to have scarred her permanently. This, despite the lengthy and expensive therapy sessions she attended each week.

Newton had seen enough. After the meeting with Qunot, his path crystalized in his mind. He called Keren back and invited her for dinner at Indigo.

CHAPTER 17

Keren always strutted into Indigo like the movie star she never became. No red carpet or fanfare greeted her at the door. Nobody noticed. Her husband stood at a podium waiting for her arrival with a gaggle of nervous hosts and hostesses fussing about seating and which tables needed clearing. The restaurant staff resembled a who's who in alien ancestry, as over 200 different species were represented. They all badgered the maître d' during their entire work shifts.

Newton chose the same table where they first had dinner to inform Keren of the divorce. He was careful to remove the appetizer forks from the silverware setting. The primary annoyance with his marriage had become the lack of discussion topics. All small talk all the time. He understood a relationship with no foundation ended when meaningful discussion fizzled. They spent the past five years talking about the many methodologies of laundry folding, discussing anyone famous at the restaurant, and the all-important philosophy of weeding the garden. He couldn't recall a single meaningful conversation with his wife.

Keren and Newton sat down at the table and exchanged the usual fake pleasantries with the nervous and drunk waiter. She paused to glance at anything but her husband as her eyes wandered from the waiter to the couple seated near them, to the expanse of the ceiling and the perfect mood lighting. She took a deep breath, exhaled it quickly, and placed her slender hand on the tablecloth in front of her.

When she spoke, Keren surprised him.

"Newton, we have to talk. And I mean for real this time. It's been a while since we last had a proper conversation."

She continued.

"I know this isn't an ideal location to inform you of my feelings and quite the irony, but I am finished with this marriage."

Newton stared at her wide-eyed. He could neither move nor speak. Inside, he was overjoyed. The weight of a hallucinogenic mistake evaporating from his soul eliminated years of internal conflict.

He also couldn't believe she pulled the *Lobster Surprise* move on him.

The wait staff developed a classification list of breakups that occur at Indigo. They would scream them back and forth as orders in the kitchen. Fortunately, the noise of the restaurant chaos kept these shenanigans out of the customer's earshot.

A waiter would waltz into the kitchen and shout,

"We have a Lobster Surprise at table forty-two!"

The more degenerate wait staff would gamble overs and unders on the different kinds of breakups occurring during their shift.

Since cameras captured everything, verifying a bet was easy, albeit time-consuming. While the intent for betting on patron's emotional pain was in good-natured fun, Newton considered banning the activity. On multiple occasions, drunken brawls broke out after shifts over the classification of a breakup. Often, this left a waiter injured enough to require hospitalization. Not surprisingly, the injury occurred at the business end of an appetizer fork.

There was an app because of course there was an app. A waiter who flunked out as a software developer stayed sober long enough one weekend to code the program. It functioned well enough to perform its primary duty, collecting betting information on each shift for breakup types. The programmer needed readmittance to a rehabilitation center on the twin planet Gastrout after completing the coding. The application performed so poorly and with such limited functionality that writing the bets on paper would produce a more efficient and accurate outcome. But in an advanced, technological universe, nobody wanted to stoop to that level. They used it even though it took five times longer than a pen and paper. The software application included a list of the definitions of each diner interaction, and to nobody's surprise, they were all named after menu items:

The Nothing Burger. Nobody got fired or divorced, and no relationship ended. As strange as this seemed, given Indigo's reputation, some patrons dined at Indigo without the drama of breakups or corporate downsizing. The wait staff labeled these groups as psychos. Why come to the galaxy's greatest breakup extravaganza, pay the exorbitant menu prices, and not get the full experience of at least getting dumped or fired in the process?

The Steak in My Heart. When a couple dines at Indigo and only one party is aware of the restaurant's reputation. The other party arrives, unaware they are destined to be single or unemployed by the completion of the appetizer course. Studies found the optimal time to deliver bad news was between the hors d'oeuvres and the entrée.

The Dieter's Salad. This category is for corporate downsizing or firings. The terminated individual will be unemployed and presumably on a new budget. This lower income budget can afford only side salads when dining out.

The Full Carafe of Wine. An individual knows either before or upon arrival at Indigo, they are about to have a relationship end. They whine and complain the entire meal, trying to convince their spouse or partner they are making a horrible and drastic mistake. This never works. If a partnership arrives at a juncture where one partner will fly in a cramped spaceship multiple light years to a fabulous restaurant that costs the average galactic inhabitant three years of pay, the relationship is past the point of no return.

The Lobster Surprise. When the partner comes to the restaurant understanding they are about to be single. They pre-empt the break-up by dumping the dumper. The best video moments in Indigo history are captured on Lobster Surprises. These breakups either go one of two ways with nothing in between. Either the partners are both so relieved they get intoxicated to the point of disfunction and end up hooking up again or a loud and embarrassing fight breaks out requiring wait staff intervention and often a mini-fork incident.

The Just Dessert. When one of the parties attempts an appetizer fork move only to have the other party arm themselves with a similar weapon of their own, causing a duel.

Side Order of Lamb Chops Rare. An appetizer fork stabbing.

It should be noted the *Side Order of Lamb Chops Rare* most often occurs on the *Steak in My Heart*, the *Lobster Surprises* and the *Just Dessert*.

The wait staff is ecstatic with these occurrences and shout out in the kitchen,

"One Lobster Surprise with a Side Order of Lamb Chops Rare!"

The depravity appalled Newton. He considered banning the practice, but in speaking with fellow maître d's, he found out this degradation is a common occurrence among wait staff. Banning the practice would make it more difficult to hire in an already tough labor market. Among the drug and alcohol abuse, gambling problems, college students and bitter actors and actresses, hiring servers caused considerable pain and anguish.

Keren knew of the *Lobster Surprise* and just used it on Newton.

She added,

"Maybe it wasn't a great idea to marry under the influence of hallucinogens. I have been pondering our marriage for some time. We have no foundation in the relationship. I don't hate you or even dislike you. I just don't feel our relationship has purpose, and ever since the incident with the deodorant commercial, my career has had obvious difficulties. This has made me question my direction in life."

Newton observed a brief moment of clarity. He understood she nagged due to a projection of the underlying problem, her lack of purpose, both in their relationship and as a Zangian. He felt relief and contentment to hear it from her. Zangians didn't suffer from the ego problems of the humans to near the degree. When she pulled the *Lobster Surprise* on him, it did not manifest in an ego problem. He cared about results and he could hardly be upset about getting the desired outcome, even if the path materialized differently than expected.

Newton finally spoke.

"Keren, you read my mind. All of it. Our marriage and relationship have been stagnant for years. I sensed both the relationship's lack of purpose and ours and tried to support you as best I could with this tedious job. I hate this job. It is pointless and not at all what I expected when I took it. The entire reason this restaurant exists manifests tragic internal conflict, which in turn creates misery."

Momentarily, she again became the thoughtful and beautiful woman he married.

Keren continued with the thought.

"Newton, I understand. My sense is you feel relief at this decision. I also felt when you invited me to Indigo, you were going to ask for the same and hoped this would be an amicable conversation. This makes me happy and gives me a profound sense of relief. Most of my nagging and pestering stemmed from a lack of direction and purpose. I know it is my responsibility to sort out my emotional problems, and I perceive you support me whether we are together or apart. I decided to quit acting and enroll in on-the-job training to become an interplanetary travel guide. It has always been a dream to explore the galaxy and in this exciting role, I can fulfill that desire. I will lead guided tours of other planets. But it also would mean I would seldom be home."

Newton smiled and his eyes softened.

She continued.

"I will work for Tanton Travel Service, headquartered on planet Eppers. It is close to our home so I can live in our civilization, rather than in the disgust and corruption of Durnita. The Zatosians put me off. Have you ever noticed how they smell? It is offensive from afar."

Newton smiled at the Zatosian tangent.

She said,

"The ship is named the Mattro. It is a tourist ship that travels to all the mid-range tourist sites in the inner galaxy. Each tour has about ten planets on the itinerary, departing from the cruise terminal on Eppers.

My job is to guide tour groups at each stop. I am beyond excited. However, there is one annoying aspect of the spacecraft. Whenever the doors open for the tourists to enter or exit, there is a loud *ding-dong* echoing throughout the entire Mattro."

Fortunately, this was the happy ending to the *Lobster Surprise.*

Newton smiled at his now ex-wife and told her.

"I am happy for you. It sounds like you have found purpose."

In one of those in-the-moment life realizations, it occurred to Newton she left the nefarious entertainment industry, and he was getting embroiled in it.

"I also have career news. I am quitting the restaurant industry and will be traveling."

Keren sipped her bisque and stopped mid-slurp. Her already almond-shaped eyes got wider.

Newton kept talking.

"This just happened yesterday. The executive producers of the television show *Caution Earth* are frequent patrons here. They are having ratings issues with their broadcast. The civilization is having issues and is on the brink of self-destruction. They asked me to travel to Earth to execute a carefully planned strategy to save both the planet and the TV series."

Keren snapped her head back and her eyes widened further. *Not the man I married.* Then she reconsidered. Perhaps this is exactly who I married. Possibly he has been mentally trapped without purpose, just like me. And now it seems we have both been freed to pursue our true purposes. She wasn't thrilled about her ex-husband being employed by Zatosians, and not because of their heinous odor.

She became concerned about his safety.

"What an opportunity. Is it dangerous? I am not sure I like you being employed by Zatosians."

Newton sensed a commotion in the restaurant. He heard screaming and arguing from table six.

He responded while craning his neck to catch a glimpse of the erupting chaos.

"Yes, it has some risk, but I think they have it covered. I will discuss this with The Wong. He has a long relationship with the show's producers."

All hell broke loose at table six. A woman from the planet Durnita attempted to stab her dining partner with an appetizer fork. He saw it coming and threatened to retaliate. This was a rare case of *Just Dessert,* and it needed to be finessed.

Newton informed Keren he would have to end their conversation. He thanked her for being so open and honest in the conversation, and that he also garnered no ill will towards her. He promised to keep their communication lines open.

CHAPTER 18

The appetizer fork problem on the planet Gastrin reached a critical breaking point about the same time Newton was hired for the maître d' role. He inherited a mess. What started as a few isolated incidents had blossomed into a full-blown crime wave. A twisted combination of media sensationalism, the absurdity of the weapon, and the simple fact the crimes were committed in public with multiple witnesses fueled notoriety around the stabbings. The perpetrators became famous in certain circles, even though the majority ended up in prison. A stunning 72% of stabbings turned into homicides. More amazing, 93% of the crimes occurred in restaurants during normal business hours.

The usual grifters arrived on the planet selling t-shirts and other memorabilia with unmemorable cliches that were funny at the moment:

I survived dinner at Indigo with a picture of a bloody tined appetizer fork.

Live a little, get forked became a customer favorite.

The usual inauthentic hand-wringing by the politicians blossomed into full effect. The elected officials on Gastrin are stereotypical; they are useless grifters and middlemen corrupted to the core. The politicos wouldn't lift a finger to represent their citizens unless there was something in it for them. The *something in it for them* meant a direct or indirect bribe, assurance of re-election, or some other job perk that increased their wealth or fame. They decided any press was good press, so in secret they embraced the appetizer fork chaos. They also simultaneously funded its continuance and expansion through some well-placed behind-the-scenes manipulation.

The politicians committed bank wire fraud by taking political donations from the restaurant industry and then rerouting these funds, along with taxpayer funds from the general treasury, through a complex network of charity organizations. These funds were used in commercials and media to increase tourist traffic to Gastrin, especially targeting people who have just enough mental instability to commit this type of crime.

The opposition to this madness were the protest groups who wanted to ban appetizer forks altogether. Politicos also funded these groups through illegal money laundering to keep the conversation going.

The politicians also engineered the election of a corrupt law enforcement leader who designed an arrest process that made a spectacle of the entire crime. These investigators pretended to join the table of the deceased or maimed rather than hauling the embarrassed perpetrator out in handcuffs. The perpetrator received the rock star treatment, with kid gloves, and the detectives often shared wine and appetizers as they questioned the offender.

And just to ensure the narrative went out on full blast, they bribed executives at the seven major corporate news networks to carry stories of appetizer fork violence at least three days a week per network with ample coverage of restaurant names.

For the politicians, they owned a complete laundry list of corruption: wire fraud, a broad range of campaign finance felonies, bribery, and extortion, and just for good measure, election fraud.

The protest groups hit the streets every Saturday and demanded appetizer forks be banned altogether as a solution to the problem. Their logic was simple, but stupid. If society removed cocktail forks, the entire nightmare would end because nobody could get stabbed. Never mind every restaurant table setting had a butter knife, a meat knife, a salad and dining fork, and extremely sharp spoons.

Some demonstrators who fancied themselves as the deeper thinkers of the protesting crowd preferred everyone who used and/or owned an appetizer fork pass a background check and register with the Gastrin government before visiting. They fancied a safety program with extensive licensing and wait periods would be sufficient. They also proposed a revocation law. If an individual were deemed a danger to society, their freedom to eat with a cocktail fork became immediately revoked. They proposed an entire bureaucratic network of social workers to police and monitor the restaurant industry for utensil safety. Sane people considered this a horrible idea because more bureaucrats would relocate from the planet Hellio.

The protestors' behavior bordered on maniacal. They insisted the stabbings were the fork's fault, and not the individual doing the stabbing. These people earned a name in evolved societies: *idiots*. In some societies, they were named *useful idiots* because they were idiots who became manipulated into a bullshit cause offering a nonsensical solution. In either case, the idiot tag stood firm. On planet Gastrin, the appetizer spoon industry funded these idiots. Their business drove to replace mini-forks with tiny spoons in every restaurant.

The politicians could stop this anytime they chose, but they had neither the motivation nor the courage. Their cowardice and fear drove them to accomplish what their handlers told them or paid them to do. Everyone profited from the appetizer forks except the citizens. They allowed the chaos to continue to the joy of their bank accounts.

In most polite societies in the galaxy, politicians are often referred to as *morally bankrupt corrupt scum*. In most impolite societies, politicians are often referred to as *morally bankrupt corrupt scum*.

Conversely, the Galactic Council are not elected officials, they are voluntary stewards. They volunteer for two-year cycles to be their planet's representative.

Within the galaxy's government, any form of fraud, bribery, extortion and favor giving of any sort is punished by their planet being expelled from the council. The actual individual didn't require council-level punishment as they usually became banned from their home world by their citizens, and if they returned, were often executed. Evolved societies enjoy peace and freedom, and recognize there is no place for bribery, extortion, or grifting. And it gets worse. To further the disgrace and embarrassment, a civilization booted from the galactic government is removed for one thousand years. Other planets spend the next thousand years lambasting your civilization. Becoming a punchline on sitcoms, late-night shows, and satirical newscasts is not good for morale.

CHAPTER 19

Newton woke up the next morning feeling refreshed and revived, his new purpose in life becoming clearer. He understood the television executives were using him. His sense of adventure and purpose as the *Planet Saver* allowed him to accept it. He knew nothing of Earth and its inhabitants, and had never seen the hit TV program. To him, the idiot box distracted from reality.

He next needed to offer his resignation. Fortunately, the stars aligned and today the owner would be in the restaurant. Newton's boss would make the short trip over from his home planet Jansen to make his monthly appearance at Indigo. Jansen and Zang shared the same solar system and their populations enjoyed eons of peaceful interaction. Newton expected The Wong to show up with his trademark sunglasses. The four small round tints covered each eye and wearing them had always been a staple of his appearance.

While some assumed the glasses portrayed a purposeful persona, The Wong's reasoning was selfless. True, his species had four eyes, with the middle orbs offset around his nose. The others sat higher and above his knobby ears on either side of his hairless head. His sideward vision tracking separate from the forward view made conversations difficult. Two-eyed creatures conversing with him experienced discomfort because they thought he wasn't paying attention. He was forced to explain the extra outside vision field existed to observe and detect imminent threats. He was paying attention so long as the primary ones looked straight ahead.

The Wong's tall and thin frame demanded respect. He towered over the average species, as did Newton. The Jansenians' hairless bodies and thin bone structure projected a stereotypical alien appearance. The top of his bald, green head had light ridges from front to back like a graded road.

His head sat on a very thin neck that didn't look like it could support its weight. His thin muscular arms and legs looked frail, but possessed incredible strength. The Jansenians' four fingers and toes acted as sets of opposing thumbs. They looked like green, anorexic beings with larger than average heads.

None of this was the reason for his sunglass habit. The Wong's true notoriety came from one of the most famous breakups in restaurant history. He and his soon-to-be ex-wife still fought over the rights to Indigo twelve years later. He retained the title of General Manager and Partner while the courts sorted the mess out.

Their already volatile relationship detonated when he informed her of the divorce at table thirteen. In a wine-induced and explosive, irrational rage, she grabbed the nearest utensil she could find and started swinging at him. She simultaneously spewed a string of illustrious profanities that now play on a loop for guests in the gift shop. His wife was unaware she grabbed a futile and dull appetizer fork. She pierced him in the face three times, including a partial puncture of two of his four eyes. The ridiculous weapon was covered with a rare shellfish residue that caused permanent skin damage to the Jansenian species. He required optic surgery left of his nose and full eye transplants from a donor. The skin wound would never heal. Sunglasses covered the hideous, bleeding holes in his face. The entire incident made him bitter and resentful and he refused to give an inch to the vile woman who permanently scarred him.

The Wong's stabbing became notorious for being the first appetizer fork incident on the planet Gastrin. Being that the owners of the famous restaurant Indigo were involved, the incident received endless press coverage on galactic television. This led to their divorce proceedings being aired on a live court TV show replete with a fake judge. The ratings zoomed off the charts and The Wong and his soon-to-be former wife received enough continuous royalties to pay their lawyers. The real divorce proceeding happened behind the scenes in a real courtroom. It was not worthy of viewing due to its tedious nature.

The unexpected fallout startled and forever changed the food service industry. The dishwasher who didn't properly clean the utensil got fired.

He moved on to become a vendor who trademarked and sold appetizer fork tourist shirts and mugs on the sidewalk in front of Indigo. He became filthy rich by possessing a knack for selling cheap and meaningless shit to tourists. The cruel irony was not lost on The Wong. With his brilliant merchandizing, the same lousy dishwasher made the restaurant and its owner wealthy and famous.

When Newton arrived at Indigo, his boss was already seated at their table. They would go over the numbers, including any incidence reports. Then they would casually talk about their marriages and The Wong would bitch about his soon-to-be ex-wife and her bloodsucking lawyers. After their meeting, his boss would hang out at the restaurant through the dinner rush, rubbing elbows, making polite conversation, and being a visible owner. The rich and famous always flooded the place when he arrived for his monthly visit. They curried his favor and took selfies with him for their social media accounts.

Newton sat down and they exchanged pleasantries.

He then started in on what he considered being the most important topic, his departure.

"The Wong, I need to tell you something important. Over the past year, I have become disenchanted with the role here and am offering my resignation."

Newton rehearsed this in his head one hundred different ways the evening prior and decided on the direct approach.

He continued.

"My expectations for this role are inverse to reality, and it is causing me significant and unresolved internal conflict. I am happy to stay to train my replacement, but it must be done within thirty days."

The Wong ran his business with reason and patience. Other than matters relating to his psychotic wife, he kept a cool demeanor. He understood Newton and knew he didn't have the same verve for the job as his Uncle Newty. However, despite his misgivings, he excelled in the role and it would be a shame to see him leave.

The Wong then did something rare. He took off his glasses and gave Newton his full attention with all four eyes. The wound that wouldn't heal from the appetizer fork shellfish injury stood out, even thirteen years later.

Newton held Indigo's owner in high regard and respected his reasoning for wearing sunglasses all the time. He did it for the benefit of others, especially his customers in a dining establishment. It was also why he spent so little time at Indigo. While his malady could be labeled an unfortunate occurrence, especially given the continued advancement of galactic medicine, in a vast and orderly universe, bad luck is a myth. The immutable laws of the universe are clear and repeatedly teach lessons that need learning, and the gift from passing the test is grace. Bad luck is a term used by individuals who fail to understand this cadence. The Wong implicitly understood this. He accepted everyone has their path, and it was not for him to interfere, but to fully support people's choices.

The Wong replied.

"I understand. And I will, of course, honor and support the request. If you don't mind me asking, why thirty days? Have you found other employment?"

Newton pondered whether he should tell The Wong about his new gig. He originally decided he would, but now second-guessed. Jansenians were an advanced species and his boss knew Qunot personally.

Newton decided withholding information would be unwise. The Wong understood Qunot's nefarious nature, but accepted it. He also knew the owner shared his sentiment about the glorification of the appetizer forks and even the cameras capturing the emotional pain of customers. The dramatization of breakups had been his wife's doing, and he painfully accepted it.

He understood couples would always end relationships and corporations were still going to downsize. If they chose Indigo as their venue, so be it. In his mind, the restaurant shouldn't fan the flames of sensationalized violence for additional profit. It was a greedy move, and he abhorred greed.

Newton told him.

"I am leaving the industry altogether. You know and share my opinion about the sensationalism of customer behaviors. It has gotten progressively worse and become harder to justify. I am burned out. The passion I once felt is gone. The role creates a consistent, grinding internal strife. I need change for my well-being."

The Wong's four eyes affixed on his every word.

Newton continued to explain.

"My frustration in the role has been simmering, but the universe hadn't yet presented an alternative opportunity. I recognized the lack of opportunity as a sign I should remain at Indigo and attempt to resolve my problems. My belief system and understanding of how our orderly universe works made this clear."

Newton, The Wong and evolved civilizations had a concise understanding of universal functionality.

He continued.

"I believe you know Qunot from the broadcast network. He produces the television show *Caution Earth* and has a very large account with the restaurant. He came to see me about an opportunity yesterday afternoon."

All four of The Wong's eyes were still fixated on him. Newton did not notice surprise on his face, only genuine interest and concern.

He gave a brief response.

"Qunot can be a morally bankrupt worm, even by Zatosian standards. However, he makes sound business decisions, does what is best for the company, and is loyal. Otherwise, Coder would not have hired him."

The Wong offered an accurate assessment. He was also friends with Coder, the owner of the television network that produced *Caution Earth*.

Newton responded in agreement.

"This is true. However, the probability of him coming to me with this request over and above any other opportunities is low and seemingly random. I am drawn to it. As we know, seemingly random occurrences are universal order and must not be dismissed. Beyond Qunot's problem, there must be an additional reason he came to me."

The Wong nodded in agreement, his four eyes continuing to be focused on the conversation. The restaurant din floated in the background as an unobjectionable noise subdued by the conversation's focus. Newton and his boss sat alone in a vacuum of ponderance.

He continued.

"The subject of the TV series, planet Earth, is nearing self-destruction. Qunot's motivation is obvious, he doesn't want his meal ticket to end. There may be more to it, but he cannot afford the program ceasing before the contract ends. Normally, the galactic government council would allow the civilization to perish under the weight of their idiocy. Intervening is interfering with universal resolve. If Earthlings aren't meddling with other peaceful galaxy members, they are left to their own devices. As we are also aware, one cannot interfere with a civilization listed on the do not travel list. Especially one that is a hit television series. Qunot informed me of multiple levels of technical surveillance. He plans to have me and a couple of board members from the network infiltrate and make ourselves known. For a primitive and unevolved species like the humans, he thinks alien contact should be enough to unite them. We do not want to scare them into thinking we made contact to destroy them. Interestingly, and for risk management, none of this will air during the broadcast. They intend to depict the solution as humans solving their problems and uniting for a common good. This will be the first time in *Caution Earth's* series history it deviates from reality by hiding the change catalyst. Our hope is the population is salvageable, and further evolved from the experience, even if temporarily."

The Wong remained skeptical but calm. His external side-eyes were darting about the restaurant to assess eavesdropping. He lowered his sunglasses from his forehead to cover his wound.

He sat pondering, motionless for a moment, with his bony hand resting on the side of his hairless, green head.

"The appetizer fork issue has consistently been top-of-mind. What started as a fad has now become problematic. It has been phenomenal for the restaurant's publicity, but it is reaching a breaking point. Unfortunately, the local politicians are all on the take and profiting handsomely, making change difficult. As for your new role with Qunot, it sounds like a very high-risk proposition. If you are caught, you will surely face execution, along with the board members, who I assume are the Em twins. Other than obvious reasons for the impending self-destruction of the Earth and saving the precious television show, what else is there?"

Newton took a sip of his methane-based wine and said,

"That's it, really. It is galactic history 101. We teach these lessons to our children and the teaching is a pillar of the education system. The planet's technological advancements have accelerated beyond their ability to control. They have also abdicated their leadership to a corporate class who has enslaved their political class through extortion and bribery. The ruling structure has stood for over 4,000 Earth years. But with the recent advent of instant communication via technology, Earth's people are wising up to the perpetual system of slavery. This system has trapped them without even knowing it existed. The population is getting quite angry. The Earth's so-called leaders, who are totalitarian rulers disguised as benevolent elected representatives, are being called out for their apathy and crimes. They are terrified of the impending accountability. So much so they are coordinating their corrupt political puppets into worldwide kinetic warfare, sacrificing the blood of the innocents while simultaneously bankrupting countries and profiting from all sides of the experience. They would rather bring on the destruction of society than give up power and face accountability for their endless crime spree. This exact scenario has played out many times throughout galactic history. It is well recorded and taught. The historians who advise the television executives give the civilization a 99% chance of self-demolition. There are additional details, but not worth repeating. It is the same story, just a different planet."

The Wong was impressed with Newton's grasp of galactic history and the base psychological and societal process of a civilization's evolution. The waiter had just brought the lobster bisque, and he wanted to enjoy it and listen more, so he kept his questions precise and commentary minimal.

He said,

"I was unaware you are a risk-taker. What do you estimate the chances of success?"

Newton contemplated the odds of success against the risks of the venture. He could still withdraw from the deal. And in case he changed his mind, a backup plan existed. More details would become clear over the next thirty days leading up to departure. If he lived through the ordeal, the Earth may fail anyway.

Newton explained the technology.

"Qunot has a ship specifically designed to mitigate the detection risk. There is a technology installed on the spacecraft from the planet Hellio. It is a temporal plane allowing the ship to exist in the realm of apparitions and our existence simultaneously. This shields us from galactic surveillance. The ship's artificial intelligence module will run most of the operation and provide us with the information we need to succeed. We are to provide proof of alien life to the Earthlings, in a non-threatening manner, and expose ruling class malfeasance. The hope is to unite them, while not scaring them. In Qunot's opinion, this may not save Earth. We don't have the power. He believes it may give the population a higher probability of survival than currently exists. He thinks there is a very high probability he gets the remaining two seasons of his television show contract."

Newton took another sip of methane wine and nibbled on garlic bread. The Wong listened while engrossed in his lobster bisque. It was his wife's recipe and the only thing he cherished about her.

Newton grew tired and overwhelmed by the past two days' activity and wanted to wrap the conversation.

"So, The Wong, that is the deal. The pay is astounding. Provided the mission is successful, I will no longer require employment and can spend the rest of my life in retirement finding new purposes. Also, I divorced Keren yesterday. That was a long time coming. Can you believe she pulled the *Lobster Surprise* on me?"

The Wong chuckled. He sensed their marriage was superficial.

Newton was changing everything for the better.

The Wong said.

"Contact me if things become difficult. I respect a man who follows his heart and has a noble purpose. What is nobler than saving a planet from extinction?"

He chuckled again and while he believed Newton would be fine, he thought success with the Earthlings would be short-lived. Evolution takes time.

CHAPTER 20

On a long enough timeline, civilizations all trudge identical series of governance problems before reaching one of two possible outcomes. They either destroy themselves in a fit of confusion and rage driven by their collective unevolved brains, or they overcome the morass of self and develop evolutionary realization. A population's form of governance is a reflection of the collective individuals. It is a mirror to society's value system. When governments reach tyranny, citizens are to blame, though it may not be the current population. The downfall's starting point is generations before the outcome. Unfortunately, shortsightedness is a major feature of an unevolved society.

To solve the problem, advanced, enlightened, and evolved societies banned politicians from existence. They eliminated the profession, instead opting for a form of self-governance based on volunteers and extreme limitation of power and responsibility. These societies have also cut the purse strings from the steward class. The results produced are far superior.

This preferable system of self-governance is arrived at through the normal course of political and civil horror (wars, starvation, totalitarianism, communism, fascism, etcetera-ism). Societies must endure and overcome these catastrophes as they move from unevolved to evolved, provided they do not destroy themselves in the process.

The root cause of government tyranny is always a combination of hubris and ignorance. From these dual character defects stem all manner of self-destruction, then projected on society. Decent people in societies are usually too busy being good to notice they just advocated their freedoms to a bunch of psychopaths who are going to use their shortcomings to destroy civilization.

Galactic history is littered with these fiascos. *Caution Earth's* primary theme is an educational reality television series depicting how a civilization can evolve beyond self-destruction. Earth continued to fail in large part because the humans were unintentionally intent on blowing up the planet. In the final analysis, they are poor stewards of their planet and have nobody to blame but themselves.

This historical understanding led to why more evolved planet members of the galaxy passed strict laws to disallow alien travel to planets that have not yet moved past their isms. Extraterrestrial visitation usually ended in chaos. The galactic leadership's stance was to leave unchartered and life supporting planets alone until they either figured out their problems or destroyed themselves in the process. On the rare occasion a species invented intergalactic space travel before evolving into peaceful beings, they were dealt with accordingly, usually being added to the extinct species list and their planet turned into a resort destination. On Earth, someone always owns a better car. In a vast, organized universe, a civilization exists with more advanced weaponry.

Examining deeper into the root cause of the human problem, they seem to be stuck in a twisted loop of stupidity, fear, and self-loathing.

First, they refuse to admit they aren't the center of the universe. They cannot fathom a power greater than themselves, despite a multitude of religions preaching it. They refuse to accept a great universal order of things. The population's percentage accepting this premise is too busy arguing over the nuances of their belief systems to coexist. This lack of spiritual understanding creates individual and collective hubris coupled with unmanageable tribalism.

Second, their technology has advanced far past their ability to be good stewards of it. Technology, like an appetizer fork, can be used for ill intentions. The humans are learning this hard lesson at the hands of the evil they allow to rule them. And while this makes for compelling television, it eventually becomes repetitive, especially to an evolved audience of viewers.

The greatest tragedy of humans is only one-tenth of one percent of the planet's population has evolved enough to admit when they are wrong. And not only admitting it, but learning from it. This number hasn't changed in 8,000 years. It is a damning fact no amount of statistical engineering can change.

This level of ignorance, unbridled ego and severe emotional attachment are the root causes of the human malady. If everyone thinks they are right, then everyone must be wrong. Humans have a tough time differentiating fact from opinion and run around thinking their opinion is a form of universal truth. Conflict constantly arises from this ridiculous and misguided belief system, and then they blame the other party. It is an appalling lack of self-awareness.

However, the population is not completely at fault. They could eventually overcome the individual issues provided the invisible hand of generational dependency wasn't forced on them. On Earth, the rulers forced dependency on them for close to 4,000 years.

Throughout many generations, the ruling structure of any civilization becomes baked in through the deliberate creation of citizen dependency. The privileged rulers understand long before the population a surefire formula to stay empowered and wealthy is to create a reliance on them for society to *function*. The reality is populations work fine on their own. However, if dire need is created and nurtured, then the power structure remains intact. The longer the cycle of generational reliance continues, the stronger the need becomes. Over time, it becomes an addiction, especially if nurtured through control of the education system, media messaging, and event management. Most forms of evil in galactic history can be blamed on the aristocracy, creating citizen reliance in exchange for the false need for safety and convenience. These evils include:

- Endless wars seeded and nurtured by cultural messaging and funded on both sides by the same privileged elites. These wars produce death to the innocents fighting for an illusionary cause where the oligarchs are indifferent to the victor. The ruling class controls both sides of the conflict. The fear of the war machine creates dependency on the governments for safety. An unnecessary safety if not for the manipulation to create the wars.
- Famine, a condition created by the governments, usually due to over-regulation of the industries that produce and distribute food

or by intentional destruction or malfeasance in the supply chain. Regulations are both a tax on society and a vehicle to create dependency. In addition, regulations are an opportunity for rent-seekers to enrich themselves from the regulation, provided they funnel a portion of those riches back to the political class.

- Disease. Governments have long created and distributed disease in their societies to create fear and greater dependence.
- Civil unrest from groups committing violence against civilians. The groups are usually inorganic and paid agitators funded by the aristocracy.
- Acts of terrorism perpetrated by governments on their people and disguised to blame external parties. These are often used as an excuse to foster war.
- Drugs and alcohol. Dependence on mind-altering substances controls the citizenry, ensuring they are passive and distracted.

From these dependency-creating acts, governments are pretending to protect the citizens of their country from the very rulers they elect, and only very few realize it. Only a handful realize it because the same ruling system controls information, the primary currency of any civilization.

So long as a dependency exists on the currency of information, a society becomes dependent on the ruling class's control of energy, monetary, medical, education, corporate and legal, and the form of government that controls all those systems. This is done under the illusion of freedom while operating a slave state. The longer this addiction cycle continues, the worse it gets until it reaches a tipping point.

The breaking point is the technology curve. Any system of tyranny relies on centralized control. Technology inevitably decentralizes authority and a shift naturally occurs from centralization to peer-to-peer networks for all systems. Once this decentralization occurs, and it always happens, one of two outcomes eventually materializes. Either the population is freed from dependence and a golden age of civilization is ushered into existence, or the elite masters are so desperate to continue mastery they would rather destroy the citizenry.

Possibly the most evil and vile part of these systems labeled as representative government is the civilization is taxed in a myriad of schemes so the citizenry is funding its own slavery. All while the politicians and their secret handlers profit from the system.

The Earth's civilization hung in a delicate balance. Newton, Em, and Emone were preparing to push it over the tipping point.

CHAPTER 21

The television station purchased a luxury mid-range star cruiser which pampered voyagers in illustrious comfort with the best features money could buy. When considering the travel enjoyment of their executives, the network spared no expense. The Wingate earned its name from the engineering team during a day trip christening party to the planet Lulu. They would have stayed longer, but the engineers had a hard time fitting in visiting the galaxy's largest party planet.

The ship's bridge contained a lavish living room with elegant upholstered couches and easy chairs sporting built-in massage therapy, handcrafted wood tables, fine artwork from every corner of the galaxy, and high-end artificial intelligence educated on Earth's entire history.

Through its programming, the AI system named Olsen developed a sarcastic and often irritating personality. Like all ship's computers, it existed to protect the cruiser's inhabitants to the extent of legal liability to the manufacturer. After disembarking, passengers were left to their own devices. The ship was also retrofitted with the temporal plane shifting device, allowing it to exist in the realm of the dead.

The engineers couldn't resolve the unfortunate flaw, as the star cruiser was still accessible to ghosts. They didn't understand how ghosts knew the ship existed or had access when the technology activated.

The defect *did* have a silver lining. In testing, with the temporal plane activated, dead people could not physically interact with anyone in the living realm. They could only communicate. No harm could come to the crew. This quirk guaranteed annoying encounters, but no risk of danger.

One exception existed to this rule. If the technology activated to greater than 80%, the apparitions could physically interact.

The engineering team could also not decipher who showed up and why. The dead communicated the best explanation, and it was the same story they told the complaints department on the planet Hellio.

When the dead appeared in the government grievances department, they said they showed up in a waiting room after death. The deceased were given a device with different locations accessible from the user interface and, when pressing a screen icon, they teleported to that location. The apparitions could bide their time in their room, restaurants or bars, athletic clubs, ghoulish social gatherings, and for the religious minded, a church of their liking based on their personal faith. All these activities were to pass time while waiting for instructions on their soul's path.

When the GDC added the complaints department for the dead, it appeared on the gadget. Unfortunately for the ship's crew, the same result occurred when the temporal field activated on the spacecraft.

Like all good software applications, the ghosts are able to leave comments, reviews, and feedback for each destination, letting other apparitions know the best places to visit.

Before departing for Earth, nobody in the crew expected the extent of this inconvenience.

The twins lounged on the ship with Qunot and Rego, awaiting the arrival of Newton before reviewing last-minute planning. It was five o'clock somewhere, so they sipped cocktails, even though the real clock read ten in the morning. They listened to an Earth singer named Jimmy Buffett who encapsulated the exact beach lifestyle they always hoped to attain. The song crooned about a man who became convinced he was born on the wrong timeline and his desire to relocate to a different era. Em and Emone jibed with the song's catchy, chill flavor.

The crew planned to hyper-drive just outside the orbit of the planet Jupiter and then activate the temporal plane while traveling through the surveillance area, which ended 20,000 miles from the Earth's atmosphere. They would know if the technology functioned instantaneously. The artificial intelligence would get a warning message from galactic security notifying they entered restricted space. The galactic council warning presented no risk. They would reroute the ship from danger.

Qunot slept in an easy chair with the massage feature turned on full blast when Olsen awakened him by whirring to life. Olsen didn't need to make noise. The sound feature built into the system helped ease the AI unit into conversations.

"Newton has arrived in the spaceport and will be onboard in fifteen minutes. Humans are going to assume he is a zombie."

Olsen's single programming flaw descended from cute to annoying in a hurry. The artificial intelligence unit formulated opinions and shared them with vigor. Qunot felt a moment of gratitude for staying home. He could not co-exist with an opinionated machine. The spacecraft AI units possessed more knowledge than any individual or species. Their smarts didn't give them the right to be insufferable and difficult.

Qunot scolded the machine.

"Olsen, keep your opinion to yourself."

Olsen dimmed the lights in disappointment and shut off with a loud click.

Moments later, the door to the bridge opened and Newton appeared. He looked refreshed and happy. The bags under his eyes vanished and his energy, which had been nervous and spastic during their last meeting, changed drastically. He projected serenity.

He shared with Qunot the details about his long-time-coming divorce and his supportive conversation with his boss. The Wong threw him quite a going away party and the wait staff donated half of their prior week's gambling into a nice going away gift. After formal introductions to the twins, they set about trip planning. They would depart that evening. Newton walked over to the bar in the main cabin of the ship. He poured himself a glass of methane wine from the already open bottle and then settled into one of the plush couches.

From his comfortable seat on the new upholstery, he said,

"Nice. By far the most luxurious ship I have seen. So, what now?"

Qunot laid out the plan.

"We are going to test the temporal plane against the surveillance here on Durnita. It is not quite the level of surveillance used by the Galactic Government, but it should give us an idea of how the technology works. Once testing is complete, we can go over the general plan. The ship's artificial intelligence module has a detailed plan and will give you a briefing on Earthlings, their current situation, and where they are headed if we do not intervene. The AI module is named Olsen. Olsen say hello."

Olsen whirred to life again.

"Good day Newton, my pleasure to meet you. I will be your pilot and guide on this journey. Although I am not sure why we want to save such a wretched planet."

Qunot flashed a look of disdain.

He retorted,

"Too much commentary, Olsen."

Turning his attention back to the crew, he said,

"First, let's test the technology. As you are aware, when we activate the temporal plane to greater than 50%, the ship should become invisible. And when activated, anyone who recently died is able to visit the main cabin. I imagine this may become annoying, but they can do no harm to the crew or the star cruiser. At least that is our working theory. We have only limited testing. The speed of the problem on Earth has caught up to us faster than expected and forced us to accelerate the ship's development. Olsen, turn on the device to 55%."

Olsen made a show of things by unnecessarily dimming the lights for dramatic effect. Then, using a far too dramatic overtone, announced the temporal plane was activated to 55%.

Rego radioed to the engineering team.

"Are we on the radar?"

The comm device chirped and a raspy voice said,

"Success, you are invisible. Although we can still see the ship in the docking bay. Very cool."

Qunot lit a cigar and the sweet-smelling smoke circled his fat head before evaporating towards the air vents. He extended the broad grin of a man who had just executed a stunning upset victory as a fourteen-point underdog. Rego remained calm and reassuring, and the twins breathed a sigh of relief. Newton did not react. He had no education about surveillance technology and trusted the plan.

An apparition materialized on the couch. The man looked vaguely familiar. An appetizer fork protruded from the side of his enormous orange head. He kept staring at Newton, making him very uncomfortable.

The ghost of Artie spoke.

"Didn't my wife stab me to death in your restaurant? I would have enjoyed finishing the amazing lobster bisque before drowning in it."

Newton gawked, speechless.

Artie, who three weeks prior was murdered by his bored wife Elsa, began thinking the universe worked a vendetta against him.

The temporal plane powered down as quietly as it turned on and dead Artie from Indigo vanished. Newton sat stunned and motionless. Em and Emone brimmed with energy and the broad smiles of a child's first memorable birthday celebration. They remembered the guy and his gorgeous wife from the restaurant. The technology blew their minds.

Newton realized he would need to adapt to interactions with the deceased.

Qunot announced the technical preparations complete and signaled readiness for departure.

He reviewed the ship's operations.

"There is no need for pilots. However, the Wingate is equipped with a manual drive function should something occur with the artificial intelligence unit. Robotics will fix any mechanical problems short of the AI module being destroyed. It is very well protected, so the probability of destruction is low. The star cruiser is stocked with parts for three full replacements of every critical system. There is an emergency communication channel where the Galactic Protection Unit can be reached to assist. Their advanced rescue operations allow them to be at any location in the galaxy within one month. There is enough food, water and sustenance aboard for 95% of the galaxy's species to survive for six months. There is a robotic medical bay should anyone get injured and your entire DNA sequences, medical history and species mapping have been downloaded into the computer should any medical issues arise. To pilot, tell Olsen where you want to go, either in coordinates or by planet name. Olsen speaks every known language in this galaxy, including all the languages and dialects on Earth. Your personal language modules will update as necessary. The ship's main cabin is equipped with all the features for comfortable travel, and each of you has separate sleeping quarters and washrooms. The ship accommodates ten passengers, so there is ample extra space. In case of an emergency, Rego and I are available on the comm device. Use it freely. We intend to monitor activity from the bridge of the Mayapple."

Qunot inhaled and exhaled a deep breath. What a mouthful!

He read the room and noticed Newton hadn't recovered from the brief encounter with the dead guy. He wondered if the depth of the assignment weighed on him, or possibly the shock of the appetizer fork victim. The twins were fine. They had experienced extensive space travel. Rego relaxed in a state of total inebriation. The liquor selection on this ship was top shelf, and he hit it hard.

Newton finally snapped out of his trance.

"You said even with this intervention, there is still a chance the planet may self-destruct. Should it happen, do I not get paid? I know it may seem like a selfish detail, but it slipped my mind to ask."

Newton looked tired again. Qunot responded.

"If you follow the protocol as outlined by Olsen, you get paid. We understand you do not have control over the outcome beyond creating the conditions for the Earth's population to survive. You get paid anyway, but if you remember, the bonus is based on completing the protocol. Also, remember success is not judged on the planet's overall survival. We cannot control outcomes on a long timeline. We are trying to alter the shorter timeline to extend the television series while improving the Earthling's *probability* of success."

Newton now remembered this important detail and felt at ease. He still garnered trust issues with the Zatosians, and for good reason. They were notorious for screwing people on deals.

They would leave in about four hours. During transit time, Olsen would bring them up to speed on everything they needed to know to complete their mission. This included Earth's history, the history of *Caution Earth,* and the planet's civilization.

What the crew learned was as suspected.

Intelligent life on Earth sat at the brink of destruction balancing at an inevitable tipping point. The Earthlings grasped onto the last vestige of civilization, repeating the comedic tragedy of countless other worlds, working to expand beyond the bondage of self, including a rigid belief system of terminal uniqueness.

PART TWO:

THE EARTH

"Welcome to the Illusion of the Senses"

CHAPTER 22

A featureless, matte metal cube that sat dormant for forty years snapped to life. The silver-colored brick sat on the corner of an ornate 17th century davenport in a chateau on the northwest shore of France.

The old man who sat at the handmade oak desk took a short gasp of air, interrupting his contemplation. His head snapped from the large bay window in his home office to the device. The man's left hand grabbed for the desk's lip to steady his frail body. He could feel the detailed carvings of the edge work through his smooth and sensitive fingertips as his heart raced. A throbbing pulse in his neck caused his body temperature to rise as he stared at the flashing piece of metal, his panicked mind racing.

This iteration of the device's activation would forever alter the trajectory of Earth's history.

The brick was a technology unlike any on Earth. Fifty years ago, his father bequeathed it to him just prior to his death. He also inherited the 84-room mansion in which he sat and an indeterminable amount of wealth. The device had been passed generationally along multiple family lines for close to 4,000 years.

Its consistent silence made the device a forgettable paperweight or suitable cup holder, and its current owner worked hard to block it from his conscious mind. But then, seemingly at random, the soft unidentifiable silverish metal would flash with a red luminescence permeating from its core. The crimson light demanded attention and not only flashed within the brick, but caused a reverberation of neon in every nook of the expansive living space. Even when not at home, his thoughts were invaded by the flashing alloy cube. When active, it gnawed at his conscience until he tended to it.

The man didn't understand this device or its alien technology. All he knew was when it flashed, he better get to its location. It was a communication portal foreign to Earth. A soft touch activated the cube, followed by the Sage's monotone and chilling voice eclipsing the room.

The Sage knew all.

Nobody in the families knew how he gathered information about their activities. They theorized, but none of them bore proof. His knowledge of everything mattered. And when the Sage gave direction, orders were followed, without question.

At different points in history, commands from the Sage were altered or outright defied, and the consequences were disastrous. Massive wealth lost, power and control removed.

The man's current instability interfered with his mental functionality. As he approached his 68th birthday, he suspected he wasn't long for the world. He extended a bony and trembling hand. As the man reached to touch the smooth, foreign metal of the device, he felt a chill from the depth of his soul explode outward. His teeth chattered and his body shook despite the room being a comfortable temperature.

The man loved late summer, and he could hear the waves lapping against the rocky shore outside his window. Two geese loitered on his lawn, shifting between eating grass and peering at him through the large bay window. Another day ended and a cloudless sky stretched to the horizon as a full harvest moon resting on the ocean stared into his soul, mocking him.

Normally, he cherished the view. The change from dusk to evening and how the moon played its light fantastic on the pulsating rhythm of the sea brought him peace. Not today. The moonlight bounced around his office and created a cacophony of light, conflicting with the red flash of the brick. Pure madness engulfed his office. The man sensed his sanity slipping, and he was having difficulty reaching out to touch the device. What if he ignored it?

This was folly. It would flash until answered. By some arcane sorcery he did not grasp, his mind would maintain focus on the red flashing. He beckoned to answer it, as sure as he would draw another breath.

He imagined what his neighbors would think if they could see his mansion flashing an eerie red. But there were no neighbors. The nearest was nine kilometers away. He had no wife and no family. The absurdity of him living alone in an 84-room house ate at him.

Most of his days were spent on the battlefield of his mind.

The battle front was his soul. Enemies of guilt, shame and embarrassment created a grinding and never-ending internal conflict with entitlement and self-righteous indignation. The man didn't realize the foes within were teammates, staging a fictional battle in a stalemate to the finish. His end.

He touched the brick, and it stopped flashing. An icy voice filled the room.

"You have been sitting there for close to fifteen minutes without answering. You know it is not wise to make me wait."

This speech didn't emanate from the brick. It encompassed the entire room in surround sound and gave the distinct impression of coming from the heavens.

The chilling voice continued, causing the wealthy man to cower in the chair at his desk like a trapped animal.

His room reverberated with the icy tone.

"Earth is changing. For too long, the people have trudged the path of life in ignorant darkness. It is time for the veil to be lifted…"

The Sage's speaking trailed to a mumble. While he understood he needed to listen and obey the stern voice, he couldn't prevent the vision. A dream that haunted his existence for at least ten years took control of his mind. When the trance invaded his being, the man lost sensory contact with his surroundings.

He tried to stop his hand from shaking to unlock and open a hidden drawer in his desk. He couldn't. The key made a rattling sound as it fumbled for the keyhole. He prayed the Sage didn't notice. Little did he know the penetrating voice was watching his every move.

The drawer had one item, a loaded six-shooter with an elegant ivory handle and high polished steel. The gun's barrel length intimidated the weak, including its fragile owner. As he slid it from the drawer, the moonlight glistened off the metal and cast a kaleidoscope dancing throughout the room.

A single tear escaped the man's eye and rolled down his wrinkled cheek, drying into cracked skin before reaching his chin. The conflicting armies within were in full battle, whittling away at his existence. The daily vision that haunted him returned with a vengeance. As the dream consumed him, the Sage's voice became indistinguishable.

A child stood alone on a narrow city street lined with hollowed-out row houses and a backdrop of a war-torn skyline. He wore a white shirt with a sharp red bow tie, black suspenders, a blue vest, and matching shorts. The boy had a worn backpack slung over his right shoulder with old books sticking out from the partially closed flap. He held a stuffed, light-brown bear in his left hand. The animal's head was partially torn, with an eye missing. Stuffing protruded from the neckline and the bear's fur was singed and dirty with soot.

The boy's city background might be Paris or London. Due to the dilapidated state of the skyscape, the man was unsure. Flames licked up from the bombed-out buildings and dark smoke contrasted with an already foreboding sky. The rainfall was black with ash and coated the street in filth. Periodic flumes of flame shot across the sky like a dragon's breath. The boy's clothes remained pristine, only the bear and his shoes seemed affected by the surroundings.

Over the boy's shoulder, a middle-aged man was hung from the front of a row house. He died with his feet three inches from the ground. The hangman knew the exact length of rope to maximize the mental torture of the process. A contraption rigged to the second-story window served as the gallows. The hung corpse wore working class clothing, covered in the filth from the sky. His tongue protruded, purple and bloated. One of his shoes had slipped off, and the rats had eaten his foot up to the ankle bone. Asphyxiation bugged the man's eyes out, sharing a story of a tortured and unnecessary end.

Two clenched fists revealed his fate. A bar code marked his left hand's backside, seen through the falling soot. In the rigor mortis of his right hand, he held a family photo and a scarf with the colors of a country's flag long since destroyed. The dream always paused for the man to ponder the hanging victim's crime. In this mental space, the raw justification of his existence collided with the brutal truth hidden in the crevices of his subconscious. From this collision erupted a river of guilt like the blood flowing in the street gutters of his dream.

The elementary school-age child focused his dark, vacant eyes, sharing the wisdom of his experienced horrors. In this repeating vision, the man hoped the child would be sad and scared. Instead, the boy's head tilted a few degrees left and down and the corners of his mouth upturned into a sly grin, reflecting smug satisfaction. His short blonde hair was perfectly kept, untouched by the sky's hellscape cascading down upon the existing devastation.

A compact pistol dangled from the child's pale right hand. Fresh powder burns at the end of the medium length, gleaming barrel suggested it had been fired recently. The boy motioned his gun up the sturdy brick home lined avenue, directing him to comprehend.

The man stared at the unending row of townhouses lining the street. He felt his body tremble again as an invisible hand reached into his chest and gripped his sporadic heartbeat. He sensed his bronchial tubes tightening as the weight of the grisly scene registered in his brain. Corpses hung like flags from flagpoles covering each house's entryway as far as the eye cared to see.

The decrepit geriatric kneeled in front of the child. He could sense the filth of the ash and human despair soak into his silk suit pants. From his knees, his soul sunk into the boy's dead eyes, reflecting the crushing truth of his own spiritual and moral bankruptcy.

The boy raised the gun, allowing the man to stare down the barrel of his demise. The light icy drizzle of rain and soot hit the high polished steel and glided off, leaving a slight residue in its path. Time slowed as his sensory apparatus awakened to his end. The child now showed him a crooked smile as he heard the gun's hammer mechanism lock into place. He noticed a word carved into the side of the barrel. The crude etching of the carving was two inches from his forehead. He read the childlike printing. It said *DEATH*.

The man closed his eyes. He could smell the rotting flesh of the dead and the acrid aroma of spent munitions. A bitter tang of mayhem and death surrounding him brought on a bout of nausea. The wails of eight billion lost souls drummed inside his head.

Manifest avarice of the machines of war, famine, and extinction painted the city with Satan's signature. The gates of hell had opened and demons rampaged the Earth.

The man could feel his head and heart pounding in unison. His kidneys burst and a warm sensation engulfed his legs.

The child was him; the Earth, an inferno.

CHAPTER 23

Newton and the twins relaxed on the bridge of the Wingate, pondering Earth's history. They neared the point in their trip where they would exit hyper-drive inside the planet's solar system. Soon, the ship's crew would raise the curtain. A new reality awaited.

"Olsen, let's conclude the Earth's history lesson with the planet's current condition."

Newton requested this while relaxing on the bridge with the brothers. He sipped a cup of nutrient-based juice from his home planet. Em and Emone were playing a hologram game which resembled a simulation of the Earth version of Dungeons and Dragons.

Olsen made a single beep rather than his usual dramatic entrance. He had grown tired of talking about the abysmal planet Earth and its so-called intelligent life after providing a multi-thousand-year history of the civilization.

He said,

"Are you sure you want to hear it? It is quite abysmal, even when compared to other galactic civilizations."

Newton chuckled at the AI unit. He never experienced a computer with a sarcastic opinion module.

"Please finish the story of Earth. It is important that we understand the situation."

Olsen made a computerized sighing sound to show his level of disappointment.

Then he said,

"The human population sits at a crucial juncture. Which way it tips remains to be seen. On one side of the equation, advancement of technology from artificial intelligence, peer-to-peer decentralization of networks including currency, and open information exchange via the internet threaten the status quo. The technological explosion is driving a natural collapse of existing control systems, which rely on centralization. A core component of centralization is gatekeeping, an oversight feature across their matrix."

"On the other side of the equation sits a terrified ruling class, losing control while watching their iron fist slavery complex disintegrate. The match to burn the system to the ground will soon to be lit, with or without our intervention. The unevolved population realizes the depth and reality of their prison, and it is only a matter of time before the realization reaches critical mass."

Olsen paused for dramatic effect. Newton wasn't sure how many *dramatic effects* pauses he could take before he took a hammer to the ship's computer.

Newton asked.

"Could it be avoided without our intervention?"

Olsen answered,

"At this intersection of Earth's history, the collision is unavoidable. Even with our successful intervention, we may only buy them time. Only one outstanding question remains. How much collateral damage for either scenario? If you are successful, maybe we can limit the potential harm."

"For decades, the Earth's exponential advance of automation outpaced human evolution. In successful societies, the relationship between technology and evolution occurs in lockstep or reverse. As happens on any civilization's advancement curve, ownership of technological assets and industry may end up in the wrong hands. This recipe always fosters misery. Earthlings live this reality, even though most are blind to it, and will continue to experience this pain until the system controllers are replaced with moral citizens."

Newton and the twins nodded in agreement. The analysis was consistent with other galactic civilizations who faced these challenges.

Newton said,

"A hypnotized, distracted and apathetic society will march off to their own destruction and not realize it until it is too late."

Olsen continued his analysis.

"A civilization allowing artificial intelligence and software to think for them devolves society by allowing the programmers to steal their minds, and eventually their souls. This is the ruler's endgame, and it is dangerous. The aristocracy understands technology cycles and also understands it will eventually destroy their power structure. If the advancements transform to complete open source, the destruction of the privileged masters becomes fait accompli, and permanent. They need to control it, at all costs."

Em added,

"Standard history. In this case, the rulers are not trying to fight the population as the enemy. They already rule the citizens. The enemy is the inevitable advancement of technology which will replace their existing systems. They are attempting to control that because its advancement cannot be stopped."

Olsen said,

"Correct. The master elites of Earth also appreciate the only real currency is information. Everything else takes secondary importance. And while they control energy, the currencies of trade, and other basic needs such as education and health care, they always understood without authority of knowledge, nothing else matters. Losing their info monopoly ends them."

Newton said,

"The other night I listened to a recording of a conversation among the ruling class from the goose hive mind. It is relevant to this point in the conversation. Some of the noble elite's ranks proposed giving up authority. They argued since they already monopolized such a high percentage of the planet's wealth, assets and resources, they should allow the free market and free information flow to take its course. Others argued vehemently against the idea for two reasons. First, they believed the average human was too stupid to manage their own lives and needed intelligent leadership to guide them. Second, their heinous and egregious crimes committed throughout history would be exposed. What benefit is a pile of money if imprisoned?"

Olsen said,

"That recording is an interesting inflection point. Aristocrats control information through either omission, ownership of the media or both. Any news outlet reporting against the oligarchs is sued out of business or bought and the leadership replaced. It takes time for media saturation to occur. Occasionally, the people hear blips of truth which create ruler pain points, but those blips have always been manageable."

"The historical arc of information control is identical to other planets. For Earth aristocrats, life was easier in medieval times before the technological explosion. The largest psychological operation in the history of civilization centered on religion and core beliefs. Earth's people could have started the technological revolution hundreds of years before it happened, but their beliefs held technology in check. The Earthlings believed it inherently evil. This belief system became adopted by the perversion of spiritual truth and fed to the masses by the era's nobility. Belief systems are a powerful force of nature."

"The *most* powerful force in nature is truth. Unfortunately, truth has been obfuscated for hundreds, if not thousands, of years, and given the relatively short lifespan of humans, the truth became lost or buried through generational overlaps."

Newton and the twins pondered the Earth's situation. Their trip gave them plenty of time to understand the planet and its inhabitants.

The crew of the Wingate had mastered galactic history and knew the essence of Earth's evolutionary progress without having to understand the exact circumstances. The universe is a mind-numbing behavioral repeat cycle transpiring millions of years. Newton understood if it weren't for saving the television series, the galactic government would allow the planet to run its natural course. The galaxy's stewards didn't interfere in uncivilized planet's affairs.

The remote location and their archaic space travel capability rendered Earth harmless.

If Earthlings wanted to self-destruct, so be it. The more Newton learned about human society, the more he formed the same opinion, despite his agreement to save the planet from its inhabitants.

After a period of silence, Newton asked.

"Olsen, anything else to add?"

The AI unit said,

"Yes. As during any historical era of substantial transformation and upheaval, chaos grips society. The citizens of Earth sense a seismic metamorphosis afoot, even if the average Earthling stands blind to the source. The Earth's culture has experienced moral and spiritual rot from the inside out for over one hundred years. Relative to historical eras, the timeframe represents a mass acceleration of cultural decay. The ruling class's invisible hand facilitates and promotes this degeneration to maintain control throughout the technology explosion."

"Free-flowing peer-to-peer information terrifies the aristocracy. It will crush their journalism business model, a massive propaganda machine from the start, and it crushes them. In addition, decentralized computing and ledgers with advanced artificial intelligence guarantee the ruler's extinction. A demise 4,000 years in the making, and one they predicted and started planning to prevent three centuries ago."

Em pre-empted Olsen's next thought and said,

"I bet the ruling establishment underestimated their ability to control society and underestimated the exponential advance of technology."

Olsen said,

"Correct. The original plan ensured societal controls were in place before the tech boom made them obsolete. What seems like a minor error in judgment turns out to have catastrophic potential, provided it reaches its natural conclusion. They are working at a fever pitch to stop it from reaching its logical end, and it has become a classic race against time."

"On Earth, needless and concocted wars rage on multiple fronts, ravaging innocent citizens, destroying their livelihoods, and murdering innocent souls all for the sake of greed and control. Widespread citizen riots and countless acts of civil unrest are funded by citizen's own governments to create chaos and calamity where once peaceful society existed. These planned occurrences operate as distractions to facilitate the transition to a more totalitarian government. The lead rioters are well-paid agitators and ruling elite operatives."

"Their plan is to shrink the world's population to about one-tenth the current amount through famine and war. The oligarchs intend to create conditions for famine and shortages of energy and food. They own or control the supply and supply chains. By blaming other countries, the world eventually reaches a breaking point, causing additional kinetic wars to break out over the scarcity of resources. The advancement of weaponry since the prior major war ensures this war will be the deadliest on record. The aristocracy orchestrates, funds and benefits from Earth's war machine and has for the past 4,000 years. They march their innocent citizens off to die for profit and domination."

Nothing new here when compared to galactic history, Newton thought. The poor always suffered at the hands of the elite masters during wartime.

Olsen finished his analysis.

"The rulers intend to control whatever population remains from the war and famine with a social rating that scores their contribution to society. The definition of positive contribution would be defined by the aristocracy for the sole purpose of ensuring they remain in power. This is to be the final form of Earth's slave system. Each citizen will be bar-coded like cattle. Newborns marked at birth. The stain of the beast would be tied to their retina scan and fingerprints logged into a central citizenry database. Currencies would be digital, with personal wages or earnings tied to individual identifiers, and social media or other peer-to-peer communications monitored."

Newton added,

"The idea seems simple. Do your job, support the matrix and you can live your life, albeit as a happy slave. Lash out against the status quo, your bank account is turned off and your avatar, attached to your public identification, is held up to ridicule. You become unemployable. Corporations who hire low-score individuals are castigated. With no money available, you are allowed to starve. The despots believed after two generations of social conditioning through education starting at age four, there would be few complaints. All citizens would be ensconced in their mental prison with no avenue for escape. "

Olsen said,

"The implementation challenge for the ruling class rests with the older generations. They know better and don't have the correct level of social conditioning. Wrong think permeates their existence. For the older free thinkers, the new matrix must be implemented in phases. The oligarchs will continue to monopolize all social media companies and content, news media, education, health care, and financial systems. The political class remains intact. They are already bought and paid for by extortion or bribes. If fully installed, this perpetual system ensures the enslavement of humanity for thousands of years."

The rulers of Earth disgusted Newton and the twins. Em recited a series of curse words so descriptive; Olsen deleted the recording of the conversation. For the first time in Olsen's artificial lifespan, he was not only offended but blushed in embarrassment, to the extent an artificial intelligence module can duplicate visual emotions.

Newton and the twins understood the top-level strategy. The crew's education on the Earth's people was complete.

CHAPTER 24

One human has risen above the fray. He is the smartest and most evolved being on Earth and lives an isolated existence in the Ozark mountains of a bland state called Arkansas. His name is Sam Shank. He spent most of the past one hundred years sitting on his back porch, which overlooks a small, algae covered pond. From his perch on the veranda, he tunes into the wisdom of the goose.

Sam Shank is 203 years old. Similar to all humans, he is unaware he is an actor on the hit galactic television show, *Caution Earth*. He was born in 1820 in the same house he now lives, a small one-story cabin found on top of a miniature hill. The driveway lacks signage and a mailbox. The property does not have a registered address with any government entity. Mr. Shank, as the townspeople call him, has no birth certificate and does not know his birthday, only the year. He has no siblings. Sam's parents died two weeks apart in Earth year 1840. Their final resting place is the family plot on the property.

Sam grew to six feet tall, has a full head of salt and pepper hair, which he keeps short and never past the earlobes, and is clean shaven. The outdoor work farming his property for 193 of his 203 years has kept him lean and muscular. His face is angular, with slight imperfections from scars caused by multiple human lifetimes of labor. His eyes are crystal-clear brown and appear slightly large for his head. Years of labor in the sun created a permanent working man's tan.

Sam lives in the grace of God. He is and always has been at complete peace with himself and his environment. The purposeful discipline of his daily life has forged a direct connection with the divine. Due to his age and life experience, which he subconsciously projects, he is unnerving to meet. People are cautious in his presence. The combination of lifespan and grace that radiates from within causes discomfort in others they can't understand.

Humans are poor judges of both time and grace. The mirror of their confused being conflicts with Sam's pure essence.

He has met very few people during his lifetime. The people in town don't recognize him from generation to generation. Anyone who described Sam would say he was anywhere between 45 and 60 with a radiance of health. Town people assume he is the son or grandson of the earlier version of himself. The universe hides secrets from those not ready to hear.

His nearest neighbor is conveniently located ten miles away and his family owns outright the closest 2,000 acres surrounding his property. Sam's cabin is a squat, red single-story building. A front porch overlooks a small pond. On the stoop sits a well-worn, antique rocking chair handmade in the late 1700s. It is the only item on the unscreened wood-framed open veranda.

The consistent mosquito swarm from the standing water on the pond, a mere fifteen feet from the base of the house, is brutal, but they leave Sam alone. His clean diet makes Sam's blood not to their liking, and he has become as one with nature as any human. Inside the cabin, a single room serves as a kitchen and a living room. The sparse living area is furnished with additional antique, handmade furniture adorning ornate carvings representing the brilliant craftsmanship of the late 1700s. The kitchen has a gas stove and the entire house is heated with an enormous fireplace. An elegant, crafted stone façade hearth with a visible chimney stretches up to the ceiling point. Another lone rocking chair, like the one on the front porch, sits near the fireplace.

He installed functional plumbing in the mid-1900s, eliminating the need for an outhouse. A bathtub was also added. The house receives water from a well and has a septic tank for waste. The cabin has two cramped bedrooms down a hallway past the main living area, each furnished with a single bed, wide enough for a couple. No modern laundry exists in the home. Sam hand-washes his clothes in the creek, which also supplies water to the well. The modest cabin is 750 square feet.

Sam married the year after his parents died to his neighbor's daughter, Darcy Rokes, who became Darcy Shank. They enjoyed a simple life for twenty-five years until her death in 1880. They were unable to have children due to a medical condition of Darcy's, but had, at least for Sam's part, a beautiful life together. He suspected Darcy wanted more adventure and for him to be more attentive to her travel desires.

She died young from a seasonal flu that turned to pneumonia. For a time, he became bitter at God. This anger subsided as he expanded his understanding of the synchronicity of the universe.

To the modern outsider, his living conditions would be abysmal. To Sam Shank, he would live no other way. This is because he knew and understood. Almost everything.

He is the only Earthling who is connected to the goose hive-mind signal, giving him an unfiltered and in-depth understanding of reality.

CHAPTER 25

The strangest phenomena Sam encountered in his lifetime was the appearance and reappearance of the single goose living near his pond. It had no mate. To Sam's perception, the same one lived on his property since his childhood.

Sam didn't understand this oddity was the leader of all geese and alien to Earth. Dubbed Mr. Goose, he used this pond as his headquarters since arriving on the planet 300 years ago.

Much like Sam, Mr. Goose far outlived his life expectancy. Being the head of his species had its benefits and curses. In Mr. Goose's opinion, he lived where an obstinate Earthling built a house interrupting his important lifestyle.

It perplexed Mr. Goose a human could receive the mind waves of the geese. This made Sam unique.

The complex alien technology that separated the goose signal from the noise far outpaced any scientific skill of the meager Earthlings. It seemed improbable an archaic Earth computer, much less a human mind, could perform the operation.

The television executives valued the signal. It gave them content direction for the show. The noise was seventeen million geese arguing about pond space, mating, and the best dinner morsels. The beacon was the unfiltered observation of the humans.

Sam Shank deciphered the signal and listened for 183 of his 203 years alive. At first, he thought insanity gripped his mind.

As part of his daily routine, he relaxed on the porch, sipping iced tea or water, contemplating while connecting to gratitude and seeking grace. He married a beautiful soul, and while they were not blessed with children, he did everything possible to ensure his wife was loved and given a blessed life. Sam felt fortunate and wanted to remember and practice gratitude for the simple things.

On one beautiful spring day, Sam rocked on the porch seeking serenity and noticed a single goose loitering on the edge of his pond. Geese usually traveled with their life partner and sometimes in greater numbers. He found it odd there was only one. Nothing stood out. It relaxed while sitting on the morning dew-laden grass, staring into the distance. In the early evening, as the sun settled on the horizon, it ate grass while glancing around, presumably to ensure its safety.

During the first year of Sam's observation, the goose appeared about every third day each month. Then he appeared more frequently for a few months and eventually settled into appearing daily. Like all geese, this one projected an attitude problem. Mr. Goose abhorred humans and gave Sam the stink eye.

He returned the gaze. His wife thought he was feuding with water fowl during these never-ending stare-downs to see who would blink first.

Darcy thought it silly. Sam sat out on the back porch either with his morning coffee or his afternoon tea having an epic stare-down with a goose.

He wondered if it was the same bird.

Sam learned when he focused on something and blocked out the mind's inherent randomization, he often gained deep insight about his focal point. In his mind, no term existed for this exercise. He didn't know he practiced meditation where the mind became one with the focal point. Being uneducated on the topic, he lacked awareness that it was an ancient technique utilized for centuries in different cultures. He only understood the concentration exercise resulted in knowledge acquisition about any object of focus.

He learned a valuable truism. *All knowledge exists within us.* It is only a matter of tapping into it.

Sam's ignorance of theory came from lacking formal education. He barely graduated high school and never went to college. He learned knowledge taught to him by his parents and through experience. His limited education helped him run his farm and live a simple, moral life. When something broke, if he focused on the broken item long enough, he could eventually fix it. From this concentration exercise, Sam could fix anything, given enough focus time. He also understood as society progressed, individual and collective impatience became the norm, tossing his simple manner of living into the dustbin of history.

He applied this principle to the goose by focusing on it, blocking out all other thoughts. He needed to take it further, so he not only concentrated on the goose's physical manifestation but also on its essence and energy. When he did this, he eventually slipped into a peace and serenity unmatched during conscious moments. He united his mind with the object of focus. Time would stop, and God would speak to him. He termed it listening to God, as he lacked any other explanation for the thoughts entering his head. Some would call it divine intuition, but the definition didn't matter to Sam.

The human annoyed Mr. Goose. He considered approaching the porch to give him a few serious shin pecks. But then he realized this Earthling meant no harm and was observing, albeit weirdly. He became curious. He still stared back; geese loved petty conflict.

Then, on a beautiful spring day in Earth year 1843, about six months after Sam started focusing on this obnoxious bird, something strange happened.

Goose-like ideas seeped into his mind. At first, crowded and random thoughts about pond quality, the best types of grass on a spring day, and territorial squabbling drowned out any logical order. The aimless and repetitive noise sometimes caused migraines. But after a few weeks, Sam noticed something different. He received descriptions of worldwide human events.

In June 1844, he learned the founder of a religious movement, Joseph Smith, and his brother Hyrum, were killed by an angry mob. He knew nothing of the latter-day saint's identity and, since he didn't read newspapers and lived an isolated life, he never heard of these individuals or their group. The unfiltered message contained no opinion, just a simple observation of an event. A goose witnessed it from a grassy knoll outside a Carthage, Illinois jail. It simply observed the event and included it in its thought pattern, which was then broadcast out on the hive mind, along with thousands of other Earth events. Sam found he could focus on the events and filter signal from the noise.

In July 1844, he learned the last pair of Great Auks were killed, making the species extinct. By September 1844, he knew Sweden crowned a new king named Oscar the First. In November 1844, the goose told him the Dominican Republic separated as a country from Haiti and formed its own constitution.

Sam Shank would spend the next 175-plus years listening to a recorded history of the human experience, unfiltered through the eyes of the Earth's population of geese.

CHAPTER 26

Three hundred years ago, the current Mr. Goose became leader of the Earth geese. No fanfare or coronation accompanied the elevation to the position. He awakened one day, having conscious knowledge of a new purpose in life. The undesirable position was a necessity to the television executives.

And while it was a figurehead role to the rabbles of geese, the job served two important purposes. He was the lone member of the species capable of communication with alien life. Second, he owned responsibility for the overall safety of Garthis's population while in exile. This became critical during the great goose genocide of the 1900s, and Mr. Goose navigated the emergency to a successful end.

Geese became a protected species on the planet, ensuring their safety from the human condition. While other predators existed, they paled compared to humans.

The geese prospered with their newfound protection. They even took to occupying golf courses to aggravate the Earthlings playing the sport, making it a point to defecate on the fairways and to loiter on the greens during play. They also enjoyed walking in front of cars on busy roads tying up traffic, often taking fifteen to twenty minutes for ten of them to cross a two-lane road. It brought them unending joy to see humans impatient and knowing they could do nothing.

Fortunately, people could not read a goose's emotional state beyond the evil eye. The humans would have noticed the geese laughing at them while holding up traffic. Fortunately, due to the static structure of their bill, it is impossible to notice when they smile.

The hated television executive, Qunot, assigned him the job. He implanted the device allowing Mr. Goose to communicate with the television station. He also altered his genetics, giving him an indefinite life. One that would have a sudden end if he committed any act of sabotage.

Qunot installed a kill switch in him. Mr. Goose could do nothing. The geese remained trapped on Earth for a staggering 8,000 years.

This presented quite a quandary. On one hand, the benefits of his extended life provided him with much wisdom. He figured it wouldn't last forever. The Earth television show appeared to be nearing an end. Time didn't have the same meaning when one has lived hundreds of lifetimes of one's species in a single lifetime. On the other hand, Qunot operated an extortion and kidnapping racket against them.

The geese didn't have to behave differently in their lives. The recordings to the hive mind represented an unconscious process. They observed their surroundings and their brains recorded and transmitted the events. The species remembered nothing they saw. Their observation brain simply sent out the signal. The conscious bird brain only focused on food, reproduction, and squabbling.

But to Mr. Goose, the extortion of his species sickened him. He hoped he stayed alive long enough to exact revenge. On Garthis, they had no natural predators. On Earth, even with most of the human threat removed, they had many foes. This didn't consider while geese were protected, a culinary market still existed, especially in the country the humans called China.

An additional significant benefit of leadership was his mind waves were separate from the hive mind. He possessed independent thought as part of his genetic modification. This gift allowed him to plan revenge on the shady television executive for exiling his species on this forsaken planet. His favorite death fantasy death involved trapping Qunot on Garthis, and slowly drowning his fat ass in feces.

The human Sam perplexed Mr. Goose. He sat on his veranda for countless hours, staring. For a time, this unnerving and unusual behavior caused paranoia. He thought Qunot had sent someone to spy on his activities. The suspicion passed with further observation.

Mr. Goose considered he might be tuned into the hive mind. He doubted it, but the curious manner in which this human stared troubled him. Often, Sam had no expression on his face. He looked lost in a form of peaceful concentration. When he snapped out of the spell, he would intently stare like he was trying to communicate a deep and meaningful thought. But he rarely spoke, other than to his wife, who would often nag him to stop staring.

Sam never posed a threat. Sometimes he would leave bread or corn from his garden. Mr. Goose stopped worrying about the situation and continued to perform his duties while planning the demise of Qunot.

He wasn't certain, but he sensed opportunity on the horizon. He felt change coming to Earth. The significant historical events and technology explosion were driving towards a definitive conclusion. He noticed another oddity. Sam far outlived his wife and the other humans of his time.

CHAPTER 27

The former wife of Sam Shank stood in her umpteenth line at the Galactic Complaints Department of the Recently Deceased (GCDRD), a sub-unit of the GCD on the planet Hellio. As the galaxy's central government evolved, they understood the need to minimize the bureaucratic structure. Bureaucrats were a useless sector of any civilization, and more civil servants always led to forms of tyranny and lots of layers of unnecessary societal confusion and gridlock. Bureaucracy created sand in the gears of progress, and in extreme cases, halted it altogether.

To solve both these problems, the galactic council placed the entire government bureaucracy on one planet. This decision proved to be a stroke of genius. Anyone who fancied themselves a bureaucrat knew where to live. And given the government's hands-off approach (planets were free to govern themselves and had few rules to follow to stay in good standing with the council), keeping the civil servants on a single world kept them from meddling in important galaxy business.

Hellio was named the most miserable planet in the galaxy for 350,823 Earth years running. Not coincidentally, the exact time length the bureaucracy has existed. It is a mind-numbing place to visit, much less live. However, the inhabitants are overjoyed. The bureaucracy loving bureaucrats live on the strictest civilization in the universe and have few freedoms. It requires forms filled out in triplicate to order a cheeseburger at a restaurant and that is only if your visitation paperwork, also in triplicate, has been completed and approved before arrival. The average Hellian spends an astounding 83% of their lives in line waiting for another bureaucrat to approve a form. They could not be happier. To the bureaucrat, wasting time is panacea. They love the process and the result gives them a sense of power and control.

Life on planet Hellio has been coined by deeper thinkers, the *Freeman Paradox*. Happiness for society's worthless, misery for the free.

Mundane building architecture with gray to tan drab six to eight story office buildings consumed miles and miles of Hellio's city blocks. The first floor of every structure is the customer interface with lines and windows. The average visit to the planet Hellio requires an individual to enter at least four unique buildings and stand in fifteen lines. Each line has a regular wait of two hours. If during the fifteen lines you have an incomplete form, you are referred back to the initial queue and start anew. By complete accident, the Earth's Motor Vehicles Department design complimented the GCD, proving behavior patterns of bureaucrats are universal independent of species.

One unique complaints bureau exists. A department for the dead who are waiting before continuing to their next lifetime, the GCDRD. This is a huge and separate complex on a separate continent. Designers thought having a location for the deceased placed next to buildings for the living would creep visitors out and require a brand-new sub-agency for grievances about the building location.

Darcy Shank now waited in line at the GCDRD. She had been dead and periodically visiting the complaints department for one hundred forty-three years, with no end in sight, because her space cadet of a spouse wouldn't die. She wanted her dharma changed and also considered hiring an assassin. Both proved difficult, especially asking ghosts if they would travel to Earth to murder her ex-husband. Apparitions can't appear like magic on the plane of the living and start a killing spree despite what horror movies constantly suggest.

When Darcy died of natural causes in the Earth year 1880, her soul realized she would wed Sam again in their next lifetime. She figured her wait brief since he was already sixty years old. It pained her she died first, given what a fruitcake he had become. He spent countless hours on the wood porch of their modest home, sitting in a worn rocking chair and staring at a goose. Her husband would enter a trance-like state and intermittently mumble. This behavior scared her because it made no sense. She thought he became ill.

During the early 1860s, he would talk about the troop movements of the Union and Confederate armies while the goose gazed at him. What business of geese was troop movement? How Sam knew about military maneuvers stymied her. She considered him insane and thought he sat on the porch to babble out of earshot. She considered asking the town doctor to visit.

But when Sam wasn't rocking on the porch, he exhibited normal behavior. Granted, they lived a quiet, reclusive life. Her husband did his chores, farmed the land, took care of the animals, and provided for them a decent living in mid-1800s America. When he rocked in his favorite chair on the veranda, he became a different person.

Sam's advanced evolution was beyond Darcy's understanding. She couldn't know he was one with the geese's hive mind, allowing him unfettered access to world events and societal behavior unfiltered from the bias of human perception. Darcy also didn't understand her husband accepted this oddity without judgment or opinion. He knew she had no ability to plug into what he *heard*.

Sam reserved judgement about the signal's source. He only understood he became tuned in when the goose was present. He discussed none of it with his wife because he loved her and had no desire to scare her. The odd behavior continued until Darcy's death.

When a soul leaves their body, they are transported to a waiting room in another dimension. Once summoned from the holding area, they are reunited with the divine or queued for reincarnation. The latter because they have yet to learn their life lessons. Potential rebirth can occur in any galactic species. The twin flame souls of Darcy and Sam Shank, who are also the souls of Artie and Elsa of the appetizer fork tragedy, are reborn together at the same age on the same planet where they will for certain re-marry. True love is their escape, only their souls have yet to realize it during any lifetime. This was the rub and Darcy's primary complaint.

The GCDRD is on a different continent. It is a miniscule island the size of Earth's Manhattan, but surrounded by at least a thousand miles of ocean in every direction. It is isolated for a reason. To be of service to ghosts, the island and gigantic building occupying it has a temporal plane wrapped around it. This unique technology allows the bureaucrats and the dead souls to interact in the same plane of existence. Hellio is the only galactic location where this technology exists and is permitted. Creating this department became another stroke of genius by the galactic governing body. They realized the deceased cannot be interfering in the affairs of the living while also recognizing the moribund have rights and may register complaints.

Darcy filed two grievances. Why was her husband allowed to exist and continue to live 203 Earth years where the average lifespan was sixty? And second, why is she required to wed the same person until they find unconditional love? She demanded answers.

Darcy would soon realize an extensive, mind-numbing government bureaucracy was not the place to locate answers to philosophical questions.

Darcy filed her first complaint on the planet Hellio in Earth year 1940, sixty years after she died and her husband's 120th birthday. It seemed impossible her husband still lived. He must be, as she remained trapped in her waiting room.

The universe's suspense area is what some Earth humans call purgatory. It has no location and its size has no meaning. To the deceased, it looks like a registration room in a doctor's office.

Darcy hoped her fifth trip to the GCDRD for these identical complaints would be the last. During each visit, she completed the same paperwork. It took a staggering eighty-four forms. Her husband, now 203 years old and still breathing, continued living for reasons unexplained. Since she had two grievances, she would have to go through a pair of distinct lines, each line taking between forty-five and sixty days to see someone. This, after standing in the lengthy information queue to get assigned to the proper lines specific to her problems.

Darcy prepared to wait in the information line after passing through a very thorough security screening to enter the building. She passed through a metal detector and emptied her pockets. The ridiculous nature of asking a soul with no belongings to walk through a metal detector wasn't lost on her. But bureaucrats love to bureaucrat.

Darcy felt a heavy dose of sarcasm building. She glared at the sleepy and possibly stoned guard and said,

"I am a ghost and cannot be armed with any weaponry. It is impossible. Even though I have pockets, they are an apparition of my soul and cannot contain physical items."

The guard didn't enjoy sarcasm and glowered at her as he went through his motions.

He was, after all, *only doing his job.*

Darcy completed the arduous journey through the information line and approached the service window. She would question her destiny to find true love with the same soul and why her husband still lived. She was about to converse with an extra-happy bureaucrat who was also *just doing their job.*

That someone was Wanda, or GCDRD employee number 4,728, as her six managers called her. It said exactly that on her nametag with five smiley faces next to it. Her uniform flair represented her as she brimmed with excitement and enthusiasm. 4,728 loved her job and her assigned number. The honor of being chosen to work with the non-living brought her ecstasy. She had always been the office girl who organized the birthday cakes and went above and beyond her daily work responsibilities to ensure everyone's happiness.

At the GCDRD, Wanda felt welcomed and appreciated. She tried corporate jobs on her home planet of Shraddha, but she found people became exhausted by her tedious and excitable nature. They called her a busybody and a gossip. One of her close friends suggested she try out the GCD. It would be exciting because she could relocate and commingle with like-minded bureaucrats. They hired her on the spot and she hasn't looked back.

Wanda spotted her next customer in line, and the apparition looked very frustrated and unhappy. She knew precisely how to help her have a fabulous day. She made her wait an additional twenty minutes while looking busy, staring at nothing on her computer screen, and then called her to step up to her window. The added delay made sure the patron understood she would receive excellent service.

Wanda's species evolved from the Earth's equivalent of lizards. She had no scales but smooth, light green skin and a mouth full of incredibly sharp teeth that produced a winning smile she shared with all her dead customers. Her species, despite looking ferocious, was a peace-loving bunch who just wanted to provide happiness and joy. They rarely minded their own business, and a large percentage of them became bureaucrats.

Darcy approached the window and recoiled at the grin full of teeth. She didn't know if this alien wanted to eat her or help her and appreciated already being dead.

Wanda stopped grinning at her for a moment and in her best fake customer service voice asked,

"Hi and welcome to the ongoing deceased complaints subdivision of the GCDRD. My name is Wanda and I am employee number 4,728. It says so right here on my nametag! I really want to help you with your problem today. Afterward, would you be willing to complete a short customer service questionnaire on how I helped you today? That would be super nice and helpful."

She flashed the razor-toothed grin again and looked hopeful about her new customer taking the survey.

Darcy showed Wanda her best-exhausted face and asked,

"Why does the universe require unconditional love with the same soul each lifetime? It's obvious this isn't working out. Each birth brings a new body and life experience, but without memory of purpose. It is tiresome and repetitive. I will exchange additional lifetimes if I just didn't have to marry him again."

Darcy's desperation showed by trying to bargain with divine will.

Wanda put her best empathetic fake smile on and responded,

"We at the GCDRD understand life can be frustrating, but our goal here is to ensure we properly register your complaint and solve your problem. However, ours is not to question the divine will. Would you be willing to take a brief customer survey of your experience here today?"

Wanda felt good about the answer. It had depth and meaning and should both logically and emotionally satisfy the customer. From Darcy's facial expression, it didn't.

Darcy retorted.

"I am questioning the divine will. And I demand an answer. My flake of a husband has outlived the average lifespan of our species by over one-hundred years. He won't die. I have spent all this time either in my waiting room or in this hellscape. This is the fifth instance I have repeated this question over the past century, and I continually receive an identical response. I need to speak with your supervisor."

Wanda chuckled to herself and stopped herself from being sarcastic. She remembered the customer and especially the customer's feelings came first.

She stated,

"My supervisors are at lunch. They should return in three days and the queue to meet them is number seventy-nine in building thirteen. There are currently near two thousand beings waiting in front of you to see my supervisors. As a courtesy, I can add you to that line, so you don't need to wait at the information booth. It will save you about nine hours. The expected delay is sixteen days."

Wanda was efficient, caring and gave a beautiful answer. She could already see the accolades from her managers. She loved her six managers and aspired to the role. The manager-to-employee ratio at the GCD is six to one.

If Darcy had an actual physical head capable of actual blood pressure, it would have exploded by now.

She gave Wanda an icy stare and asked again.

"So, you cannot answer my question?"

Employee number 4,728 could tell Darcy experienced undue tension. Maybe she could suggest a spa planet for her. Oh wait, she is dead, probably not helpful. Instead, she put on her best customer service smile and said,

"I already answered. Ours is not to question divine intention. You are welcome to talk to one of my supervisors, but I am afraid he or she will probably give you the same answer. We are very thorough here in customer service, and I have six supervisors. They are all at lunch right now. Would you like to take our brief satisfaction survey on the assistance you received today? It only takes five minutes!"

Darcy gave up on this line of questioning and asked her second question.

"Where can I find an assassin?"

Wanda recoiled, deeply hurt. Her extra-long middle finger started tapping the countertop. She responded in a low voice, transmitting her soulful pain.

"Your attitude is unnecessary after such excellent customer service. I would like to remind you causing any harm to government employees is quite a serious matter."

Wanda hated to take that tone with customers as it risked jeopardizing her customer service score.

Darcy shook her head.

"Not for you, for my still-living husband."

Wanda stopped tapping the counter and put her customer service smile back on in full force.

"Oh. Now that is different. Building twenty-three. Also, and maybe of interest. There is a temporal plane on a spaceship orbiting Earth. You can probably access it through your device."

Darcy stormed out of the GCDRD. As she returned to her moribund waiting room, a customer service survey popped into her communication device. It requested *just five minutes of her time*, as if time possessed value while dead. She would hold off on building 23 for now to examine this spaceship.

Wanda was super satisfied with the amazing level of customer service she provided. She couldn't wait to tell her coworkers about it while filling out the forms to order afternoon coffee.

CHAPTER 28

Galactic history is littered with the horrors of bureaucrats only doing their job. Some universities have dedicated entire philosophy classes to the following question:

If bureaucrats understood the true outcomes of just doing their job, what percentage would still do it?

Thousands of papers, dissertations and studies have been conducted on this question. Given the abstract nature of the inquiry, coupled with different societal norms and ethical considerations, the query is impossible to answer. The debate has raged for 500,000 years with no end in sight.

An innocent young student at university on planet Huyck first posed the question. She was soon banned from society and forced to relocate to another solar system. The entire bureaucracy went on strike. They demanded her arrest and prosecution.

Alas, on Huyck, no criminal offense existed for asking a philosophical question, no matter how many bureaucrats became offended in the process. The strike lasted for five years. During this time, productivity increased by 500% year over year and the population's happiness experienced an exponential increase. The administrators realized they made a terrible mistake by striking and returned to work, at once reversing all productivity gains in the Huyck economy.

The young woman who posed the original inquiry spent her working life on a different planet, two solar systems away, teaching ideology on this very query. She wrote three best-selling philosophy books.

Earth is no exception to bureaucratic suffering. However, technological advancement made it harder for the civil servants to prosper and many jobs were replaced by software. This was a normal arc of society as technology advanced. A wise bureaucrat in a suburb of Philadelphia then invented the ultimate misery for everyday people but the heaven of bureaucracy for the totalitarian detail-minded. He invented what is called a Homeowner's Association, or as they call it, an HOA.

The invention ensured another form of inefficient government waste and maniacal mini-tyrants, but this time, right at your front door. Like all bureaucracies, it was a grift. People paid dues to have their lives governed right down to the height of their potted plants, the color of their fences, the length of their lawns, how they could or could not walk their pets, and a litany of other babysitting rules no adult needed.

The penalty for non-compliance is the association can sell your house and kick you out of the neighborhood. It is another level of worthless government meddling replete with taxation in the form of dues. Every neighborhood with an HOA has a council whose job, in their free time, is to monitor and report neighborhood violations.

The brutal offender is then hauled before the council to explain why their shrubbery is a half inch overgrown. This serves as a public humiliation ritual. The individuals who gravitate to HOA councils are often the least suited for the job. They are either employed bureaucrats who need even more tyranny in their lives or, worse yet, retired administrators who miss making their fellow citizens miserable. Normal citizens do not have the time, energy or desire to micromanage their neighbors. The most troublesome aspect is people meddle in other people's lives with their petty tyranny for free!

Most societies in the universe have gone through a phase where bureaucrats create an extra level of local government inside their planned neighborhoods.

In what many consider a chaotic twist in to universal order, an improbable percentage of individuals who gravitate to HOA Boards of Directors are named Karen or a version of that pronunciation. On Newton's planet, the name is Keren, his now ex-wife's name. On Zang, HOAs have been outlawed for 2,400 years, so the moniker lost meaning and context.

The Galactic Complaints Department, both for the living and recently deceased, has entire buildings that deal with complaints about Homeowners Associations. To the employees of the GCD, working in a department where they can help customers arrive at acceptance for other administrators is the crème de la crème of job roles. There is a ten-year waiting list to work in those offices. Every workday, they get to listen to the stunning bravery of civil servants operating HOAs from countless planets for a myriad of species.

CHAPTER 29

The starship with its three inhabitants orbited Jupiter, a large gaseous planet in the Earth's solar system. The ship remained undetectable to both the galactic council's surveillance system and Earth's archaic tracking technology. This test run would confirm the galaxy's monitoring system did not notice them. At this distance, if caught, they would receive a warning. The crew could still alter course without consequence.

Newton considered this sound risk management. He wanted to ensure this wasn't his last job. Dying on this mission would put a significant hole in his resume for future employers.

This would be the temporal plane's live debut. Newton and the twins were concerned the number of dead people on the ship might hinder their mission. Ghosts mulling about asking mundane questions driven by boredom could prove an unnecessary distraction.

When the Wingate triggered the temporal plane, it showed as a location on the apparition's devices. Each apparition received a technology unit upon arrival in their personalized waiting room. These devices listed available locations for travel. Indefinitely sitting in a reception area with melancholy doctor's office music can be trying, even for a ghost.

The device menu listed all available locations. Ghosts can patron bars and restaurants that are tailored to their memories. They can visit the Galactic Complaints Department for the Recently Deceased (GCDRD), and a family visitor button where they may visit past relatives if they are still in their waiting room. Any space that exists in their plane of existence is available on the handheld device. When the Wingate came online, a new icon appeared on the screen. The listing showed as *Random Spaceship* because limited information existed to name it.

Exciting rumors swirled about the GCDRD. This is how Wanda informed Sam Shank's wife, Darcy, of the new location.

When the crew of the Wingate activated the temporal plane just outside Jupiter for the second time, a short, bald apparition of an Earthling appeared.

He seemed lost. He wore a tight t-shirt covering what used to be a muscular body. The body long ago gave up on the gym. He had a cocktail in his hand with a cheap paper umbrella adorning a floating piece of fruit in a red liquid. His bloodshot eyes darted about the ship and his swollen and red face suggested he had experienced a rough night. A cigarette dangled from the corner of his lip. With his hands fumbling between the drink and getting his cigarette properly situated in his mouth, he experienced difficulty operating his locator device.

He peered at the aliens on the ship's bridge and said,

"Oh hey, the name's Borda. I'm still getting used to this being deceased thing. Gotta bolt, this place is dead anyway."

Newton and the twins just gawked at him.

With a sly smile, he quipped,

"You guys clearly don't get classic movie references."

And with that, he disappeared. At least it wasn't someone complaining about being assaulted at Indigo, Newton mused.

The crew of three and the artificial intelligence personality named Olsen planned for tomorrow. It would be their first contact with Earth. A brief call with Qunot provided direction. They would land on a golf course on the Western Coast of the country Earthlings called America. The ship would land for five minutes, and then depart and disappear. Qunot again expressed the importance nobody is harmed. He had no desire for the inhabitants of Earth to begin a prodigious technology-building spree and start a galactic war in fifty years. The aliens walked a fine line and proper execution was critical to success.

Newton reflected on the tasks at hand. He again enjoyed life, a first since college. No more ass-kissing petulant and arrogant customers, trying to manage drunken wait staff, or any of the other minute details of restaurant leadership. He had purpose again! Even if it meant saving a backward planet from self-destruction. The twins seemed happy and carefree, as usual. Not much bothered them, no matter the circumstances. Their species lived in a state of contentment.

On the pre-landing call with Qunot, they argued vehemently about the best place to make contact. They had to mitigate the risk of death to any human. Of greater importance was lessening the overall shock to Earth's social ecosystem. They wanted to minimize fear while maximizing newsworthiness. Their research showed landing in a remote area near a trailer park was a no-go. The stereotype had already played out and nobody believed some backwoods redneck with a low-resolution camera these days.

They preferred not to land in a bustling city, with potential risk of harm to humans, not from the ship per se, but from the potential chaos that would ensue.

They decided on upscale. Earth's population base idolized wealthy individuals. The Earthlings' social conditioning programmed them to believe wealthy and famous people, independent of the nonsense they spewed.

The rich and famous were repeatedly plastered on television as experts. For reasons the aliens struggled to understand, Earthlings gave undeserved credibility and fame to people who frequented their television screens. In reality, these appearances just further lined their pockets as they were compensated mouthpieces and propaganda experts. Nobody bothered to ask how they became so wealthy.

The aliens decided to land their ship for the first time on one of the most prestigious golf courses in America, Pebble Beach. They concluded during lunchtime would minimize the number of players on the course. They estimated thirty to forty people would see the event. Newton estimated the spaceship sighting would be limited to course players, staff and golfers who milled about the clubhouse. They all agreed to the plan. A perfect introduction to aliens for Earth's population.

CHAPTER 30

Bishop Kimble would be dead before the day ended. Of course, he didn't know this as he drove his mint condition cherry red convertible Corvette down Pacific Coast Highway on a cocktail of drugs and alcohol that made him feel like the car floated on air as he maneuvered down the winding road. The fine white leather car seat stuck to his sweaty back as he pulled the hair whipping around his face from his bloodshot eyes for the umpteenth time.

Not that he noticed. He was in the zone. The perfect high where he functioned at peak mental output. The type of buzz where people would be surprised to learn he consumed a fifth of whiskey, a hit of acid, and multiple lines of coke. He also casually smoked a large joint and sipped an ice-cold can of beer as he rolled down the highway. He understood this sensation and also knew the next sensation after the ideal high was the horrible crash. Or worse. He could end up in a blackout and remember nothing while committing a vile act of public depravity.

He awakened from his last blackout in a holding cell in Reno, with a litany of charges ranging from lewd sexual conduct to public urination to possession of narcotics. The police arrested him standing naked in a city fountain while singing the national anthem. He was showing off for three prostitutes. The media coverage wasn't all bad, considering he had a brilliant publicist, and it all happened on a Tuesday afternoon.

He approached his favorite part of the Pacific Coast Highway, Pebble Beach Golf and Country Club. A breathtaking pull-off where he always stopped to marvel at the beauty of this tiny piece of earth lied just ahead. The golf course blended into the ocean as it rolled out of the hills and seamlessly folded itself around the waves as they lapped against the rocks.

Chills crawled up his spine as he surveyed the stunning scenery. This profound beauty made him believe God existed, albeit the moment was usually fleeting. It was a brief glimpse into a time that brought him back to his childhood when his father took him to play golf here. Long before sex, drugs, and rock and roll took over his life.

Upon reaching the pull-off, Bishop took off his sunglasses, and squinting in the late afternoon sun, noticed something wasn't quite right about the golf course. The piercing blue water lapped upon the crags of rocks and sprayed salty ocean mist on the fringes of the green where the famous 80-yard par three jutted out into the Pacific.

Normal.

The undulating greens and manicured fairways glistened from a recent watering.

Also, normal.

The late afternoon golfers running around the fairway in a panic, pointing at a spaceship that materialized in the middle of the 18th fairway.

Even in Bishop's drug-induced haze, this seemed out of place. He rubbed his eyes, squinted and rubbed them again, as he thought the cocktail of drugs played tricks on his mind.

From the outside, the Wingate wasn't an exotic spaceship, but its effect shocked the stupefied golfers trying to figure out if they should flee in a panic, or try to make contact. The golfers stood there gawking, shell-shocked and unable to comprehend the gravity of the situation. To more advanced life forms, it was a run-of-the-mill mid-range star hopper. The single unique technology was the temporal plane that allowed it to be cloaked from surveillance. And while the ship had extravagant features, the exterior was bland.

A golfer, who was shooting his best score, hit his drive to where the spaceship landed. He was ensconced in his round and was wondering aloud if he could play through the spacecraft or if he received a free drop for an obstacle on the course.

The star cruiser sat idle for five minutes.

In media interviews, after it departed, people described it as round and flat with a bubble top. This represented a horrible and inaccurate depiction of the Wingate. It was amazing humans described events in relation to what they viewed on television and in movies, rather than describing what they saw. Eyewitness mischaracterization was a serious design flaw among humanity.

Video on personal recording devices depicted the ship rectangular without a bubble on top. Earthlings make horrible witnesses, especially when under duress. When panicked, the human brain will fabricate what it saw based on an earlier pattern, rather than reality. It is an unfortunate coping mechanism to explain what they cannot explain due to emotional overload.

When the ship took off to return to orbit, the proximity of Bishop Kimble to the afterburners from the engine caused him to combust, killing him instantly, thus answering the age-old question: is alcohol flammable?

Fortunately, in his advanced state of being wasted, he never noticed.

Newton noticed, as did Em, who watched from the screen on the ship's bridge.

Newton rarely experienced anger due to his mastery of emotions. An exception was in order.

He used a terse voice tone rarely heard.

"Not good Olsen, we seem to have caught an Earthling in the afterburners."

The AI unit whirred to life and in an apologetic and sad tone attempted an explanation.

"My instructions were to make a dramatic exit using both the magnetic drive to elevate while simultaneously moving horizontally. I turned on the rear engines for a brief burst of speed using the hydrogen fuel cells. As you know, they burn hot. The ship's safety sensor underestimated the level of heat a human could withstand. Database updated. Apologies for the inconvenience."

Olsen went quiet; he knew he erred. Newton fumed.

He said,

"We are on the planet for five minutes and already we kill someone? I know it was an accident, but we're the ones who are supposed to have advanced technology. How are we going to explain this? This could cause the exact type of reaction we are trying to avoid. Olsen, stop hiding and tell us the victim's identity."

The artificial intelligence module conveyed remorse as he came back online. This was done by dimming the lighting and playing a sad track of piano music in the background.

Emone added his two cents.

"Cut this shit with the emotional programming. It is not helping."

Olsen gathered the data and responded.

"The deceased is named Bishop Kimble. He is one of the most famous musicians on Earth and is also a career drug addict and righteous party animal. He has been arrested 23 times. Maybe we did Earth a favor."

Newton considered taking a sledgehammer to Olsen. Qunot is going to be furious. He took a deep breath to focus and channeled what The Wong would do. He always exhibited wisdom and control in these situations.

He responded.

"Olsen, we didn't ask for your opinion. This was a famous Earthling, likely idolized. This circumstance creates significant risk. We will need to address this when having our discussion with Earth's leadership. They are guaranteed to conclude we are here to wipe out the planet. We also have to tell Qunot, and he will not be pleased. Moving forward, be extra careful nobody is harmed. No more hydrogen fuel cells. Only land and depart with the magnetic fields, which are harmless to carbon-based life forms."

The ship's comm was ringing. It was Qunot and Rego. They monitored events, so they knew what had transpired. They were not the only ones. A flock of geese sat on the 17th green and noticed the entire event transpire. Mr. Goose, on his pond in Arkansas, now knew of the event, as did Sam Shank. The goose needed to conclude if this was a real extraterrestrial ship or a government ploy. The hive mind would tell him shortly. If it was an alien ship, his prayers were answered. Revenge was coming.

Sam and Mr. Goose looked at each other with peaked interest and understanding. Something was afoot on planet Earth.

CHAPTER 31

The spaceship sighting at the Pebble Beach golf course created the desired panic response on Earth. Governments, who had been planning to use a fake alien landing to further their control, now scrapped that plan altogether since actual aliens dared to appear. The event went viral on social media. It garnered views from two-thirds of the world's population. The usual conspiracy theorists claimed it was a government operation while the religious fanatics professed the end of times. Many Earthlings were so ensconced in their lives and experienced so much unbelievable nonsense, they believed this too, shall pass.

The ship landed on the 18th fairway. It sat there for five minutes and departed. On takeoff, the entire green and fairway leading up to the clubhouse burned to a crisp. The low and dramatic exit path cooked the area from the golf green to the road. The same location the afterburners charred the innocent bystander to death. His vintage Corvette sat in the parking lot in a pile of twisted and torched metal, its pristine and classic beauty altered by the searing heat of an alien spaceship. The crime scene depicted a spectacular display of carnage.

The media utilized its standard breathless dramatization, reporting the wrong place, wrong time death of none other than rockstar Bishop Kimble. His publicist remarked he checked out in a *blaze of glory.* Bishop's estate instantly fired him for an ill-timed pun. Bishop's untimely and accidental death would be the only fatality caused by the aliens. Newton's instructions not to hurt or kill anyone flew out the window. The computer's artificial intelligence system, Olsen, played demur.

A journalist named Rachel Dougherty from the nearby city of San Francisco was at the golf course when the ship landed. She and the Mayor were in the midst of a quid pro quo disguised as a torrid affair in one of the country club guest rooms. She extorted inside information by sleeping with him. It was standard practice in the media business and helped her stay ahead of the news cycle and remain on top of the ratings heap.

She also wanted to ensure the information she received from her handler matched the mayor's. The mayor, like most politicians, danced at the end of his puppet strings. Rachel also tangoed from puppet strings. She created and promoted narrative, supporting and expanding the handler's power. Any groups who opposed the power structure received brutal media treatment, often destroying their business. She was a paid propagandist and proud of it. The everyday people of the planet were beneath contempt.

When the commotion on the golf course occurred, she jumped out of bed and rushed to the window. Nobody saw her naked body because they were too busy gawking at the spaceship. It took her a second to grasp the situation, but her media instincts quickly kicked in and she threw on clothing.

She frantically texted her cameraman, who sat outside waiting for her in the news truck. They needed to roll the film if he had not already started. She couldn't believe her luck. Here's Rachel, having a secret, illicit affair with a dumpster fire of a man, and a UFO lands on the golf course. Amazing.

At the moment Rachel finished texting her cameraman to get things ready, the mayor's cell phone rang. He turned pale upon seeing the number calling. She knew it was his master and expected a similar call, often wondering if they shared the same handler. She guessed the messaging was the same, but it may be different people. Nobody ever met their puppet master. People who did usually ended up missing. The handlers were their bosses, the ones who gave them instructions on how to do their jobs.

The mayor didn't report to the people of San Francisco, and Rachel didn't report to her editor or anyone else at the news station. They all worked for the same boss.

The mayor picked up the phone, his hand shaking. The cowardice spread from the top of his head and bugged out eyes down his yellow spine to his disgusting fungus covered toenails. Calling him unattractive was an insult to unattractive people. His pot-belly shook with the slightest movement. While just in his early sixties, he could barely perform in bed without pharmaceutical assistance. The balding won out even though he still held hope his hair would thicken. The embarrassing comb-over made him look sad and pathetic. Gravity won the fight against any muscles he used to possess. The permanent sagging under his eyes blackened his face and his teeth yellowed from coffee and cigarettes. The appalling stench from his breath forced Rachel to feed him mints for the first thirty minutes they were together.

He had a gambling and embezzlement problem, an infidelity problem and several other isms Rachel didn't want to consider. She slept with him because it furthered her career and gave her inside information. It moved her up the ladder to be rated the top journalist, not just in San Francisco, but on the west coast. Rachel's fame and fortune came with earning the title of the handler's go-to journalist.

She was attractive, talented and committed to the cause. The handler knew of their affair. He suggested it.

The mayor was terrified of his handler.

He answered the phone, listened for a moment, and hung up. His hand convulsed. He then walked over to the room refrigerator and poured himself four mini bottles of vodka into the same glass. Rachel wished he dressed before bending over in front of her. She averted her eyes. Then Rachel's phone rang.

Rachel had no fear of her handler, but respected him. She wholeheartedly agreed with the plan, at least the part she knew of and could assume. Information was compartmentalized, so she also understood she would never get the entire picture. She never asked questions and always carried out her instructions. The benefits of her job far outweighed the alternative. Her chosen status made her better than the population.

The call lasted two minutes. The conversation ended, and her marching orders and the narrative were set.

She rushed out of the room, leaving the Mayor of San Francisco standing there naked, hands shaking, holding a quadruple vodka neat.

CHAPTER 32

Rachel Dougherty projected a hefty forever chip on her shoulder and used it to bludgeon anyone and everyone who crossed her path. She became spoiled from a young age and understood her pedigree. Her parents and teachers told her she was *better than* during her childhood. Her cold and calculating socialite mother dominated the inner circles of San Francisco's elite life. She rubbed elbows with politicians, movie stars and professional athletes. Her father, who passed away ten years prior, lived in quiet humility and worked in venture capital. He funded high valuation technology startups in Silicon Valley. The Dougherty's possessed money and prestige, both of which enabled Rachel's entire childhood.

At 42 years of age, Rachel reached the pinnacle of journalism. Her extreme physical attractiveness assisted her rocket ride to the top. Her dark hair rested on thin shoulder blades and neither wearing it up in a bun nor at length took away from her beauty. Rachel's large almond-shaped eyes, with a cool blue shade, provided an attractive contrast with her hair. Her perfect bone structure and fine skin complimented a well-kept body from extensive exercise and nutrition. She belonged to the premiere gym and yoga studio in San Francisco and used a personal trainer and nutritionist. Men enjoyed ogling her, and she used it to her advantage.

Rachel's peers considered her the number one local journalist in America, and she always had her stories picked up by national news outlets. Her consistent invites to national broadcasts to offer her opinions on the issue of the day, opinions provided by her handler, garnered her more undeserved fame and fortune. The talent to sell those opinions derived from a deep belief in their validity. In a fake world, this belief in the cause gave her authenticity.

Growing up, Rachel always knew no matter what happened, her parents would bail her out of trouble. And bail her out, they did. Often.

At age 11 in a private charter school, she hit another student in the face with a book in exchange for calling her Rachel Doughy. She thought the kid called her fat. The kid spoke with an impediment that made it difficult to pronounce her last name properly. She broke his nose and created a bloody mess. Her Mother convinced the principal, independent of the circumstances, the other child should not be welcome in such a prestigious learning environment with his impediment.

The boy got expelled despite having a perfect grade point average. The child came from a poor family and they revoked his scholarship. Rachel's father donated the equivalent of a new building to the school. The child's parents ran to the media with the story and they refused to cover it. This was before widespread social media gained mainstream adoption on Earth. Privilege has its privileges. From that point on, nobody crossed Rachel Dougherty.

When the entitled debutante reached senior year, the guy she wanted to accompany to the prom ignored her. Thomas Jacobs was a lifelong friend of the student with the speech disorder and smart enough to realize Rachel's parents kicked the boy out of elementary school to protect their daughter. He also watched Rachel treat every one of his classmates like inferiors for their entire educational life. She had no friends in the genuine sense of friendship, only acquaintances. They passed their time gossiping about everyone and each other while competing for popularity via the latest fashion, the type of guy they dated, and how powerful their parents were.

Everyone liked Tommy. His friend with the speech impediment, James Dougle, had the misfortune of being a poor kid from Oakland who was bright enough to get a scholarship to the private elementary academy they both attended with Rachel. He ended up back in the cesspool of the public school system after being kicked out for having a speech impediment and crossing the wrong rich family. Jimmy earned a full scholarship to Stanford University for both sports and academics after leading his football team to the state championship and finishing his education with a perfect grade point average. Thomas would never forgive the Dougherty's for what they did. Jimmy forgave them and took the entire incident with a grain of salt.

Tommy wasn't great at anything. He led an ordinary life. Two of his qualities were a genuine personality and handsome looks. He stuck up for the underdogs in school. He and Jimmy were best friends their entire lives, despite coming from different backgrounds. In their neighborhood in Oakland, only three blocks separated upscale where Thomas lived from the government-subsidized housing where Jimmy lived.

Rachel dreamed of accompanying Tommy to the promenade, or more pointedly, she wanted to be prom queen. She didn't care about him. On the popularity scale, he planned to attend with a middle-of-the-pack girl. Rachel set her sights on the queen, and only Thomas Jacobs would do. If she wasn't dating the king, there would be no becoming queen. She was considered one of the most attractive women in her class and used it to her advantage. If a request did not go her way after using her female assets to manipulate the situation, she would simply call the other person sexist and use that lever as emotional blackmail. In either case, she got her way. She remained a virgin throughout high school and would not start using actual sex as a weapon until college to accommodate the greater competition.

She asked Tommy to the prom. He said no; he had been dating his girlfriend for two years. She asked him to make an exception so they could win king and queen. He declined. Popularity contests were not important to him. She asked him daily for three weeks, each day becoming terser at her request. He rebuked her advances and avoided her in the hallways.

Then she started a vicious rumor about his girlfriend and one of the young math teachers to get the girl expelled. Like a word magician, she created a sordid affair between a young, innocent high school student and a predatory teacher, and she ensured the accusation became heavily gossiped. She married a truth to an outright lie. The student was young, innocent, and respected. The teacher was the antithesis of predatory. Rachel fabricated the accusation to serve her selfish interest.

Little did she realize this level of narrative creation and outright lying would be a precursor to her entire career in journalism. She learned the fine art of marrying truths or partial truths to outright lies with a touch of plausibility. It had the desired effect, at least partially so. Tommy and his girlfriend did not attend the prom. Rachel attended with the second most popular guy in class. The math teacher got put on suspension pending investigation. Rachel's mother threatened the school to ensure there wouldn't be any repercussions for just repeating a rumor she heard. No evidence suggested she started the rumor. Eventually, the teacher was reinstated. Thomas and his girlfriend graduated, attended college together, and married. They ended up giving the prom king and queen to students who were deemed losers by the popular kids in a show of virtue signaling, or so she thought.

Twenty-plus years later, she stood on a burned fairway at Pebble Beach Golf Course after sleeping with a disgusting man installed as the Mayor of San Francisco; all to advance her career. She thought it dumb luck. She witnessed the exact moment an alien spaceship landed on the fairway and then, upon departure, incinerated an innocent bystander who was the famous rockstar Bishop Kimble. Rachel didn't understand the fallacy of coincidences.

She looked at her cameraman Padgett and put on her game face. For this story, she would use her serious reporter face.

"Are we live?"

Padgett nodded and gave her the thumbs-up. What a bitch, he thought. He didn't care how attractive she appeared. Her insides repulsed him.

"Roll."

Padgett started the camera.

"Good day San Francisco, and this is Rachel Dougherty reporting live to you from Pebble Beach Golf Course. Just minutes ago, authorities believe an alien spaceship contacted Earth. The spacecraft landed here on the 18th fairway of these harrowed grounds and departed in an instant. It appears Bishop Kimble, lead singer for the rock band *The Gatewoods*, was accidentally killed in the incident, but this has not yet been confirmed. Federal, state and local investigators are all on the scene and are interviewing witnesses and viewing video evidence on people's phones. Authorities assure us the situation is fully under control. There is no need to panic. Authorities are still trying to determine if this is a real extraterrestrial spaceship, or a hoax perpetrated to destabilize America. This is Rachel Dougherty, live from Pebble Beach Golf Course."

Padgett cut the feed. Seed planted.

She told the cameraman to hang tight, and she rushed off to get information from anyone she could. When she moved safely from his view, the cameraman Padgett rolled his eyes in disgust.

A congregation of geese in mid-squabble on the nearby tee box noticed the spaceship on the fairway. They had no opinion of it and recorded it to the goose hive mind. The geese loved golf courses. To piss off the humans, they defecated all over the tee box. They also recorded everything that happened after the landing; the takeoff, Bishop Kimble's untimely death, and the reporter's interview.

Near a pond in Arkansas, Mr. Goose went on high alert. He anticipated this moment would arrive. When the alien landing hit the geese hive mind, it interrupted a rather intense stare-down with Sam Shank. He let out a long squawk that made Sam pause in his rocking chair. The stare-down became understanding.

Sam knew alien life existed. Not because he realized it through listening to the goose. He comprehended it because he understood the nature of the universe and its essence. It is improbable in an infinite universe Earthlings are the only intelligent lifeforms. He also found it egotistical. This narrow-minded approach to existence produced hubris. A spaceship appearing on Earth didn't faze him.

Both Sam and Mr. Goose knew of the ruler's plan to fake an alien landing to further their grip on civilization. Fear drives the ruling masters, and in turn, they project fear onto the population to drive their control and further their greed.

The alien landing threw their planning out of sync. When the reporter offered the narrative choice, Mr. Goose suspected the aliens were real. Sam didn't need the reporter's narrative to know they were.

A window of opportunity appeared to open, an escape for the geese and much needed revenge.

CHAPTER 33

The real UFO landing shocked Earth's privileged ruling ecosystem, as opposed to the fake extraterrestrial visit, which they had been planning for the past twenty-five years. This made Qunot's plan a sound strategy. He knew all of Earth's rulers' plans as they were hatched and would use these plans against them.

The aristocrats planned to fake an alien invasion to consolidate power and control. They needed this consolidation to get in front of the free flow of information, artificial intelligence, and decentralized peer-to-peer computing that would end their reign. Qunot intended to use real aliens to accelerate the conscious evolution of the species. This would then save his television show. Since he knew their plans, he would always be a step ahead of them. He would instruct Newton to stay ahead of their narrative as well.

Once the real alien landing happened, the politicians and media followed their usual process. They waited for their talking points to be given to them by their puppet masters, so a consistent story could be fed to the masses. The narrative or narratives would only benefit the oligarchs. In these situations, the ruling elites created two false narratives, both of which benefited them. The narratives served as a division point or a distraction among the people.

To make each story plausible, they used the psychological trick of pairing a lie to a partial truth and also made the narrative as emotionally charged as possible. They wanted the Earthlings operating in the emotional reaction portion of the brain. They understood when an Earthling operated in this part of the brain, critical thinking and discernment became impossible. Control of civilization was the name of the game. Discernment within the population stood as the enemy of rule.

The aristocracy owned both fake *sides* of the media and dominated social networks, although they feared losing control of the latter medium. The Earth rulers' tactics took advantage of, manipulated and dampened the very thing Earthlings weren't doing: evolving. To be fair, they stacked the deck against civilization. Aristocrats gave the population either false information or omitted information from their decision-making processes for at least 4,000 years.

The rulers started the social conditioning of human brains from birth to perpetuate their reign. Entire education systems in developed countries created worker slaves who did not question authority, but instead followed along blindfolded under the guise of being educated. The ruling class forged human robots who would not only support and perpetuate the system, but defend it with blind passion. They produced a civilization of slaves who would defend their own shackles with vehement rigor.

Oligarchs went to great lengths to not instill critical thinking in the population. The practice of questioning political or corporate authority *must* be taboo. Experts are the experts. The beauty of this psychological ploy, to the puppet masters, is other educated people formed an unhealthy and blind emotional attachment to educated experts and developed a high trust level in their expertise.

To question the experts would be to question their own high-priced university degrees. It would be a significant offense to the ego. They were told on repeat their higher education made them smarter and better than the rest of society. Degrees allowed them to feel like part of a club. The more degrees, the more perceived prestige. The college goers also paid handsomely, often going into significant debt for their educations. Anything taking 10-20 years to pay must be special. With few exceptions, the more degrees earned, the higher the trust in the system.

It was quite a racket.

The reality of the university system is college degree level knowledge is achievable in far less time through on-the-job training or online teaching modules. The Earthlings struggled to understand higher learning as a business and wealth transfer operation first, and education second. Their addiction to *certifications* aided in the destruction of society. Like all Earth systems, the *certification* business was abused to favor the ruling class at the expense of the citizenry. A false belief system was created and perpetuated, whereby only a *certified person* could perform even the most menial of tasks. Want to be a coffee maker? You need a certificate to press a button, otherwise we cannot hire you. Of course, the aristocrats defined the success metrics to achieve certification in any profession and profited from the process.

Qunot studied aristocratic grifting in galactic history. No new methods of tyranny existed. He applauded the brilliance of how Earth rulers executed it for centuries, even though it disgusted him. Getting a planet's population to believe they are free while completely enslaved is quite a feat. The unraveling was imminent, and he would not allow his television show to combust due to poor timing.

He needed two more seasons. If necessary, he could compact these seasons into 150 to 200 years. This is how the program operated. While *Caution Earth* has existed for 8,000 years, long historical periods passed where few notable events happened. During these slow historical periods, they condensed time to depict only memorable history and its characters.

On Earth and in a country named America, the leader of the free world, President William Sonotat, could envision every significant politician, key media figure and corporate leader having their phone ring at the same time with the same instructions. Twenty-two minutes passed since the alien landing and his military briefing carried little useful information. Not much was known. No sighting of the ship occurred incoming or outgoing on radar. The spacecraft didn't show up on radar when visible either, yet nineteen people captured the event on their telephones. These videos were already viral on social networks. He wondered how his masters would spin this. He didn't need to wait long. His phone rang.

William Sonotat never met his handler. He understood nobody ever met the monotone voice. He had a vague notion of the handlers' identity. They were phantoms, but also all too real. The President understood the impossibility of being elected into any level of politics without their money and blessing. He knew he sold his soul for the role. But no other choice existed. They possessed so much blackmail on him. The alternative was horrifying.

Absolute control under the illusion of freedom reached far and wide within society. Blackmail and extortion lists included judges and the entire leadership of the federal bureaucracy two to three management levels deep, 532 of the 535 members of Congress, 48 of the 50 state governments at all levels, federal, state and urban area law enforcement, and all forms of media and stock exchange listed corporations. All controlled.

And not limited to the United States. Europe, Canada, Australia and South America were just as bad. A worldwide problem required a planet wide solution. A disaster the President had no interest in addressing.

The UFO landing unnerved the actual rulers of Earth. They did not make decisions unless the outcome was pre-determined. An alien spaceship appearing out of nowhere stepped the world outside of their carefully structured matrix. President Sonotat noticed his hands were shaking as he picked up the phone. Beads of sweat formed on his forehead despite the cool temperature of the room, and his heart raced. This concerned him because he had already suffered two minor heart attacks.

The voice on the other end of his private phone sounded calm. He spoke perfect English with no traceable accent to any of the English-speaking nations. This led the President to believe he was not a native English speaker but obtained masterful training in English as a second language. Native English speakers usually have some detectable dialect. The deep voice spoke in a curt tone.

"William. I am sure the event today has you shocked as we are. When speaking to the public, we must use the words *alleged alien sighting* and *still under investigation*. We want to present publicly it may be a hoax and there might be foreign interests attempting to destabilize America. We also need to ensure people feel threatened, whether the landing is real or fake. Talk about military involvement, battle readiness and red alert status. Blame our enemy countries, stoke the flames of war and communicate we will not be intimidated."

The President understood any remaining enemy countries were the few that hadn't submitted to the one-world government mandate. The issue preventing their decree was two of these countries contained significant nuclear arsenals and more than significant resources to fight what would be the deadliest war in recorded Earth history. In reality, it would be a war ending civilization. The planet sat as a powder keg, just waiting for someone to light a match.

The President could feel the blood pounding through the carotid artery in his neck and screaming up into his temples. He knew his blood pressure boiled full tilt and in a dangerous area.

"Yes sir."

He squeaked in a barely audible voice and showed his master his exact nature. A spineless coward who could play act on the stage of politics but lived in a hall of mirrors of sniveling remorse, fear, self-loathing and shame. His health was failing, and the job was killing him. His handler understood the President's health status. To the puppet master, the President's death would be inconsequential. Thousands would gladly step into the role. He owned countless souls. And if he ran out, humans available for purchase were a commodity.

CHAPTER 34

In an infinite universe and an enormous galaxy with thousands of species and languages, communication presented endless challenges in societies. Rather, the translation of language allowing discussion was a problem. Conversation itself continues to be a challenging endeavor.

The translation problem has been solved twice. Hopefully, it won't need solving again. When the problem was first settled, during more archaic times, everyone went around sticking a fish in their ear. While this solution worked, it wasn't great for the ear occupant.

The fish translated all incoming communication into the host's native language. The probability of a small aquatic creature existing that understands all the universe's languages is astronomical. This also makes it highly probable.

But eventually, the fish became jaded, hanging out in different beings' ear cavities, and complained about working conditions. Their disgruntlement made them lazy in their translation. On a microscale, this made the divorce industry skyrocket in cross species marriages and intergalactic businesses firings rose by 200%. On a macro scale, the fish's discontent caused multiple bloody interplanetary wars.

In a tense trade meeting between the planet Troutin and the sister planet Mahin, a historic peace treaty was being brokered that would end centuries of bloodshed. A proud moment shared by both worlds.

At the treaty signing ceremony, the Grand Minister of Troutin said,

"We are honored to have this historic trade agreement with the citizens of Mahin."

The fish, fed up with his miserable work environment in a particularly waxy, hairy, and disgusting ear, translated this as,

"Your wife is smoking hot and I hope to have sex with her sometime."

The ensuing battle destroyed both planets and their entire populations. The lessons learned here are twofold:

First, don't leave the translation of important conversations to a disgruntled fish. Second, before mutual destruction, it may be wise to ensure proper translating occurred. Mutual destruction is overreacting, even if the President's daughter is super attractive.

Since that time, the universe has used a simple chip system with all the known languages of the galaxy programmed into it with continual remote updating for new species, new languages and nuances and dialects of existing languages. The chip translates into the native tongue of the receiver.

Conversely, Newton can speak with Earthlings because the chip has a dual function. It also recognizes when an individual does not possess a language chip. In this case, it translates what is said as it is spoken. This technology allows Newton and the twins to communicate with anyone on the planet Earth.

While this solved the translation problem, communication problems still plague the universe. These problems are just as complex as the species' varieties: lack of context, general misunderstanding, inability to listen, word connotation, and, for the less evolved, emotional interference in the thought process.

While not an exhaustive list, it highlights the more egregious problems and the principal cause of why the galaxy does not experience consistent peace. Language and conversation misunderstandings like the tragic occurrence on Troutin and Mahin are unwelcome in an evolved universe.

The fish are now retired and work in a special department on the planet Hellio, where they process complaints about marital misunderstandings. An average wait time to see one about marital communication problems is twelve years. The average wait to file for divorce in the same building is six minutes.

CHAPTER 35

Discussion time with Earth's leadership arrived. Newton was fully briefed on his message. This meeting would be virtual, with the ship patched into the Earthling's archaic communication system. They would also override the planet's television networks and social media to ensure everyone on Earth could tune into the conference. They suspected the ruling class would attempt to filter and set a narrative to the message. This assumption proved correct.

Olsen notified Newton he would be linked into a video call with the Presidents of the United States and Russia, the Leader of China, the Speaker of the House for America, and the Prime Minister of England.

Newton was also informed despite the presence of the Russian President; his country was engaged in a geopolitical struggle with the other countries because he had not yet bowed to the handlers and given them unfettered access and control to the country's resources. As usual in these occurrences, the population carried the burden of suffering at the behest of spineless politicians. The people of the opposing countries didn't hate Russians. The egomaniacal struggle of the leadership which then fed endless propaganda to their citizens to support their crimes drove the hate.

Newton wore traditional Zangian clothing for the meeting, a single-piece gray suit with no other markings. He could not appear military. Em and Em One were to stay silent while looking ominous from the couch. The ship's artificial intelligence altered the main cabin to make it appear that Newton sat on a small raised dais with the twins at his side instead of what they were doing; relaxing on a high-end sectional couch.

The comm blipped to life and five elderly Earthmen appeared on the screen sitting around an important-looking table. They sat in their *very serious situation room* looking terrified, despite trying to look brave and distinguished.

Olsen then informed him and the twins over 2,000 government and military officials were plugged into the meeting and every form of surveillance on Earth searched for the location of their ship. They intended to destroy it. The AI picked up every anticipated communication feed.

Newton had explicit instructions. He hoped he could carry them out.

When the video feed connected, he sat silent, allowing the Earth leaders to absorb what they saw.

A full minute passed before Newton spoke, and he gave orders to the ship's computer.

"Olsen, please take over all Earth communication channels and begin the broadcast of this meeting on all television and media feeds. Ensure any attempts to block transmission are unsuccessful."

He could smell the panic. Earth's leadership could not afford the population seeing anything unfiltered without their narrative control.

Newton then addressed them.

"Leaders of your respective populations. You were given specifics to attend with just the five of you. Yet our intelligence shows you have over 2,000 additional connections to your military and other world leadership. Foremost, understand you possess no technology that will be useful against us. We have neutered it. Olsen, please cut the communication feeds with anyone sitting in on this meeting uninvited. They can watch on televisions or devices like the rest of the world."

Newton could tell the human they called the Speaker of the House had blood pressure problems. He spoke first, most likely out of turn, given the others in the room. He behaved badly, independent of the fact that 65% of the world's population tuned in to the meeting. The conference was translated into every language on Earth in real-time by Olsen.

The Speaker bellowed, using a demanding and threatening tone.

"How dare you. You show up to our peaceful planet and threaten destruction against the people of Earth? You murdered a citizen of the United States when you landed on a golf course. We should destroy you for this."

Jonathan Springer, the current Speaker, shook with rage and his face went beet red as he attempted to put on a tough façade. He thumped his fist on the table at the end of the statement and projected his unhinged true nature when he felt he lost control.

Springer spent a career in politics and had been in the House of Representatives for 34 years, re-elected 17 times. He was unaccustomed to having his fake authority challenged, an authority which came not from his position, but from the power of his handlers. As a puppet who never served his electorate, he acted above the law.

In truth, the Speaker hadn't ever been elected. He owed his continued service to his installers who utilized various forms of election fraud, bribery, propaganda, election interference, extortion and intimidation to keep him in office. Olsen's file on Earthling Jonathan Springer showed him as one of the most corrupt politicians in Earth's history. Newton smiled when he spoke up first and chose to make a public example of him.

He needed to remember and execute the twofold mission. First, try to unite the citizens of Earth. Second, and vital to the initial goal, accelerate knowledge that a primary reason for human division was nefarious leadership. One must see evil to understand it. This would move humanity further along its evolutionary path. Hopefully.

Before Newton could respond, the President of America, William Sonotat, spoke.

"Sir, I would like to apologize for the outburst of Jonathan. We garner no ill will towards you and know the civilian death was accidental caused by the afterburners of the ship. Mr. Springer is overly emotional at times. What can we do for you? Please help us understand the visit."

Newton sensed Sonotat's complete dishonesty. His diplomatic behavior was driven by the public eye. Springer's outburst mirrored the true intentions. It also appeared the other countries deferred to the United

States' leadership to do the talking. This interested him. Newton understood America had long been a proxy for the ruling class. These monsters didn't represent their citizens, they were puppets for the people who put them in power.

Newton's orders from Qunot were to expose one of them publicly. He chose the Speaker.

Newton prepared to show the population of Earth the true meaning of power, and in the process, expose one of their leaders as the spiritually bankrupt coward he was. Earth's critical turning point neared fruition.

Newton's jet-black eyes focused on the man named Jonathan Springer. Through the video monitor, he looked into the depths of his soul. Past the false bravado, he saw the rot of moral bankruptcy. Here sat an empty husk of loneliness, despair, and torture. He wouldn't look at the camera and avoided eye contact with Newton. Newton sensed the fear the Speaker projected. The man's cowardice overtook the situation room. There was never a point in Springer's miserable, adult life that wasn't governed by the terror and hatred exuding from his essence. He abhorred himself and then projected hate in everything he did. All of it covered by the bravado of his giant ego. The chaos of his demonic behaviors imprisoned the divine spirit within him.

Newton's species did not have cowardice, fear, and self-loathing. They long evolved past these animal instincts, as had the advanced species of the civilized galaxy. It was a compelling experience to witness what he learned in so many history and philosophy books. Newton ignored the lie couched in diplomacy.

He stated,

"I would like to make it clear to those assembled and Earth's public that in an infinite universe, there are species and societies who always possess more advanced weapons, better surveillance, faster computing, and stronger communication technology. We are one of those many civilizations. Understand, there is no weapon you possess capable of harming our vessel. I also want to clarify should you even attempt to harm any of the three of us or our spacecraft, we can vaporize Earth from existence. It will be instantaneous. Now is the moment to order your collective militaries to stand down. They should also stop attempting to locate our ship with your backward surveillance technology. It is not possible."

Newton stopped for a moment to allow them to communicate with their military. He read their facial expressions. They transitioned from a falsified tough façade to helpless children who got caught with their hand in the cookie jar. Earth's leadership looked guilty, old and scared; the exact look Newton wanted the population to experience. The video and pictures of the leaders' facial expressions were exponentially more powerful than any words Newton could use to break the spell cast on the planet.

Newton carried specific instructions to *not* tell them the purpose of their mission and he would prevent them from asking.

Newton continued after a reasonable pause.

"Olsen, please provide me with the information on Earthling Jonathan Springer."

Showtime. He already had what he required.

Olsen chimed in.

"Of course."

Newton understood what came next carried vital importance. He needed to point out the correct amount of corruption without inciting death and mayhem or any civil conflict. The alien's strategy to awaken the populace and replace leadership over time should not create a bloody worldwide revolution. Olsen informed him most of the world's population was aware of the political and corporate class behavior.

However, the bureaucratic system of rule was so overwhelming and complicated citizens had little idea how to proceed. The intentional complexity designed into the system produced a stalemate. Knowledge is useless, with no path to action. Newton hoped the current broadcast would force resignations and the fear of future broadcasts and exposure would accelerate additional resignations. The aliens must play the perception game better than the rulers.

Newton said,

"Mr. Springer. It seems you have quite a history. And we know all its sordid details. I remind you 71% of the world's population is now watching and intervention is impossible. We are using the Speaker as an example of the larger endemic problem. The Earth has the potential to be a beautiful and fruitful society. Sadly, civilization is crumbling due to the avarice of a few."

Newton took a sip of water and continued.

"Mr. Springer, you are a lifelong politician. Or to put it clearer, you are a career criminal. You are worse than the thief who shoplifts from the corner store. At least the common bandit steals due to basic needs like hunger or shelter. You steal because you are ordered to do so while enjoying the benefit of your lawless lifestyle and profiting from it. You thieve with impunity from the very people you are supposed to represent. Then, utilizing a thousand forms of fear and self-justification to assuage your guilt, you convinced yourself your wrongs are righteous. You steal productivity from the lives of the population you are elected to support. You pillage their earnings through taxation, regulations and inflation and then reroute those earnings to the rulers who put you in office. You illegally launder money through wars back to your campaign and to non-profits who support your campaign. Innocent civilians are sent to die in wars where your government funds both sides. You then buy stocks in the companies that produce the engines for war and profit off them illegally through what on your planet is called insider trading. You use extortion, bribery, racketeering, and other extensive criminal activities to ensure you remain in your job. What is worse is you steal time. In short, you are a morally and spiritually bankrupt garbage excuse for a human being pretending to serve honest citizens."

Newton stopped for a minute to read the room. The politicians' eyes bugged and sweat marks permeated their expensive suits. Armpit stains were visible on the video feed. The leader named Springer picked up a coffee cup, and it trembled in his unsteady hands. Newton aired their dirty laundry for the world to hear. They sensed a reckoning and the horror on their faces was clear to see.

Newton continued.

"You haven't worked an honest day in forty years. On our planet, you would have been imprisoned in year one and never again allowed near an elected office."

The President attempted to interrupt.

"Mr. Newton if I may."

Newton cut him off.

"You may not."

Olsen positioned one of the cameras in a packed bar in downtown New York City, where a throng of citizens viewed the proceeding. When Newton cut off the president, the crowd roared.

The world viewed the damning newsfeed as Newton explained.

"Mr. Springer, the citizens of Earth are now looking at your beach house on Martha's Vineyard. You paid $6.8 million for this property in your nation's currency. When you entered Congress 34 years ago, you had a net worth of $35,000, representing the value of a house you once owned. You had little savings. Since then, your net worth has blossomed to 100 million dollars. Your salary as a member of Congress is an average of 140 thousand per year. The difference you achieved during your 34-year crime spree, or to put it another way, your time in elected office. We have confirmed nobody is at this residence. Your wife, whom you cheat on with impunity, is at this moment at a hotel in New York City watching this live feed with one of her many lovers. She cheats on you as well. We will next share an example of what happens if anyone on Earth attempts to harm us."

Newton paused for effect and muted the conversation. The leaders all talked simultaneously.

His voice quieted for effect.

"Olsen, vaporize the residence."

The ship came equipped with a weapon that changed the frequency of a structure, causing it to vibrate so high the target vaporized to dust along with anything in it. It took seconds. A single invisible beam disintegrated the entire 12-bedroom, 14-bathroom residence to ash in about three seconds. Seventy-one percent of the world's population saw this, live and unfiltered from the media narrative.

Newton cut the meeting feed. They were done for now.

The Earth and its people fell silent. The collective egos of the human experience shattered on the craggy rocks of a new reality.

CHAPTER 36

Two minutes after Newton cut the meeting feed with Earth's leadership, Qunot and Rego appeared on the comms device. The ship idled behind Earth's moon with the temporal plane activated, keeping it off the radar.

Newton was trying to get three dead people of different species to stop asking him questions about the afterlife. They were confused and thought he could help with the transition process. He kept repeating he knew nothing of their waiting room procedures, and their ship was not part of the afterlife experience except by accident. This didn't satisfy them and they kept prattling on about whether they were dead, and if so, what happened next? He told them to go back to their waiting rooms. They didn't.

On the comm screen, Qunot flashed a broad grin on his fat wart covered face. When he smiled like this, his yellow, crooked teeth became fully exposed and he looked like a combination of creepy, insane, and overjoyed. Of course, he and Rego were both drunk and probably high on porcelain. They sat in the Mayapple's main cabin, the dump of a place the Zatosians called a spaceship. Newton imagined the stench on the ship and had a visceral physical reaction, including the onset of nausea.

Qunot said,

"Well done. Very well done. If I didn't know better, I would say acting runs in your blood."

Newton never had ambition for the camera. The hectic day left him tired, and he wanted to keep the call short.

He responded.

"Thank you, I guess. It wasn't acting. The Earthlings I met are repulsive beings. How they can treat their people in such a vile manner is beyond me. I mean no disrespect, as Zatosians are known for their shady side, but these beings are pure evil."

Newton considered the Earth's population might be doomed, but knew not to judge a planet of eight billion based on interaction with five he knew were poison from the onset. Qunot was impressed with his grasp of the situation.

He shared his broad grin again. Zatosian teeth were a natural yellow, it wasn't bad dental hygiene.

He explained.

"No disrespect taken. While we Zatosians are known to bend boundaries, we do so with a moral compass. We are an advanced species. Take this project. Yes, we want to save our television show, but we also have a significant interest in saving the planet and its people. The Earthlings are not a reflection of their leadership. They have a beauty worth saving."

Newton agreed with the sentiment. There is much worth saving. He lacked certainty about the Zatosians. That statement could slide. It was pointless to argue.

Qunot continued.

"We need to make sure the planet does not descend into chaos. It is a fine line to walk, but one we must walk. Additional weaponry should not be warranted. We should also continue to ensure no physical harm comes to any humans. The accident with the engine afterburners was an unfortunate mistake we cannot repeat. Let's chat about the next steps."

Newton poured himself a glass of methane-based liquor to take the edge off and listened.

Qunot said,

"We want to find a journalist contact. This will be important to show how the news is an owned propaganda arm and part of the Earth's ruling elitists. The media will take any information or interviews we provide and shape them into a narrative, benefitting their agenda. This is a given. They already started the narrative seeding with the initial report from the golf course. As we expected, they are trying to portray our visit as a foreign country attempting to destabilize a nation. They intend to create the following narrative. We are bogus, and we, as fakes, will cause harm. It is a pivot from the fraudulent alien landing they previously planned. Their purpose is to foster war to further their control. They desire to roll up the sovereign nations into a single totalitarian worldwide government."

Qunot stopped speaking and took another deep and satisfying inhale of the cigar. Newton could not imagine the odor mix of two Zatosians and a stale cigar.

Qunot continued his thoughts on the media.

"We will expose the mouthpieces they call journalists by taking over the communication systems and reporting directly to the people. Doing so will expose the media's true purpose and further expose the nefarious nature of their political class. Again, the humans are aware of this, they just lack a path forward. They are paralyzed by the system complexity that has imprisoned them for eons. In addition, they have been socially conditioned to accept their prison since birth, so it makes it much harder to work their way out. When finding a media contact, use Olsen to research who is a chosen mouthpiece for the ruling class and an awful person. Expose both."

Newton liked this idea. He remembered reading the history of his home planet Zang and the horrors at the hands of dishonest journalism. It started multiple wars very early in their civilization. Nowadays on Zang, no media exists, not in the corporate sense. Everything is citizen-based journalism on real-time feeds. There are no arbiters of truth.

On Zang, when a newsworthy event happens, the incident is usually citizen recorded. The video of the occurrence is posted to public news sites and all video and written commentary of the event are aggregated together. Discussion of the information is open and never censored. Free speech and the flow of information are paramount to a free and prosperous society. Any Zangian is allowed to discuss the incident, to view videos and to read witness accounts, which are short and factual.

Manipulation through fake user accounts or automated robot farms is severely punished under Zangian law.

This unfiltered approach through citizens with no profit motive allows for news to be impartial. A newsworthy event occurred, and we don't need to react, have an obnoxious opinion about it, share the opinion on twenty social media sites, or use the news event as an excuse to remove freedoms and manipulate society. If laws were broken during the event, authorities dealt with the issue. Zang was a sane society because its people are evolved and stable.

The Earthlings are evolved enough to discern events for themselves. Humans don't require a talking head to explain events and what to think.

Newton saw firsthand a primary problem with Earthlings, coupled with their newfound technology, is thinking their opinions and emotional reactions are fact. They also believe other humans give a shit about their opinions. Most of the population is too caught up in their own ideas, or version of their fake reality, to care about anyone else's fake reality. People observe the world through the illusion of their senses and social conditioning, perceive it wrong, and then project their perverted perception on their fellow man. They then sit back in bewilderment, wondering why their lives are a continuous and tiresome conflict. And it is *never* their fault.

Certain Earthlings, at the narrative, brainwashing, and behest of the ruling class, take this a step further. Anyone who disagrees with their *opinions* is practicing *hate*. To travel down this road always leads to tyranny and mass destruction.

Humans are terrible at seeing or understanding reality. Their brains are too unevolved and their social conditioning blocks the path to better discernment. So much death and destruction in galactic history can be traced to the simple calamity of thinking one's opinion is reality.

The Earth population has taken to using the term *My Truth* as part of the ruling class brainwashing. People were manipulated into believing every other member of society needed to validate *My Truth* and get laws passed, so any words or actions that do not emotionally confirm *My Truth* are *hate*. Society always learns the lesson of *My Truth* being substituted for my opinion to the tune of death, destruction and the elimination of basic freedoms. It is a hard but necessary lesson societies often repeat to their ultimate destruction.

After some thought, Newton responded.

"Understood. I like the idea."

Qunot continued.

"We should set a meeting with the same leadership. Afterwards, you and the twins are sightseeing Earth. Meet the locals. Exploring is vital for research. We desire to gain an on-the-ground understanding of how citizens are reacting to aliens visiting the planet, but also to show we mean no harm, even if our true mission remains secret. Have fun. Attend Earth's social events. When we leave Earth, we will leave just as quickly as we appeared, with no notice."

Newton was tired. The meeting with the Earth leadership took a toll on him. Despite feeling like a villain, he understood the noble purpose behind his actions.

Newton ended the meeting.

"Let's chat tomorrow."

He turned off the comm.

A morose apparition stared at him, longing for attention, and asked him what they were doing. Newton glanced at him. In a polite but pleading tone, he asked the ghost to return to his waiting room. He was exhausted and had zero interest in dealing with the problems of the non-living on a planet six-hundred light years away.

CHAPTER 37

Jonathan Springer, the current Speaker of the House of Representatives of the United States, found himself in deep shit and he knew it. Not due to the crimes he committed. He understood every member of Congress committed similar crimes for the past hundred plus years. He also knew for a certainty the bureaucracy would protect him. The bureaucracy existed to protect the politicians, not to serve the people.

The airing of public servant crimes by an alien garnered the wrong type of mass attention, independent of the truth of the claims. Social media on Earth had been talking about how politicians gained vast amounts of wealth for twenty years and he would bet every person in America knew they were corrupt thieves. It was not news. Fortunately for the political class, a bureaucratic maze of confusion paralyzed the public.

Plus, the rulers owned law enforcement. The matrix would not arrest itself. Politicians only became targets of prosecution when they stole from the handlers or didn't do their bidding. Occasionally, they would arrest a politician for a small crime to virtue signal equal justice and claim the system worked in favor of the people. But only enough to appease the population to keep them asleep. Every action the oligarchs executed was planned and intentional. They did not react.

The politicians also ensured their citizens stayed stuck in survival mode with little time to pay attention. A political stroke of genius of Earth's corporatist rulers was making life unaffordable for most families unless they produced two incomes. This served two purposes. It devastated the family unit and created more wealth to steal through additional workforce productivity.

Family unit destruction also ensured the system raised the population's children through the indoctrination system, which the ruling class conveniently called *education*. Very little learning occurred in the education systems. From a tender age, students were taught to obey authority and a lying expert class. They were taught to strive for higher learning so they could become a part of the expert class. Students were taught emotional reaction and how their opinions were not only factual, but required wholesale societal validation. They were taught victimhood from a young age. Critical thinking was largely absent from the curriculum. The brainwashing of the children was necessary to perpetuate the matrix.

By malicious design, individuals barely had time to focus on anything beyond survival. What little free time available the public spent on mass-marketed distractions, including professional and collegiate sports and programmed entertainment on their televisions and devices. The rulers purposely swamped the Earth's population in survival mode. They also fostered endless arguments on social media to create the illusion that complaining on network platforms accomplished movement in the political spectrum. They kept society too busy to pay meaningful attention to politics.

The system's true evil existed in the rulers pilfering *at least 80%* of the citizen's work product. Egregious taxation, regulations, and inflation through monetary policy perpetuated the theft. One dollar earned by an average citizen became taxed an average of twenty-seven times. Earth's population lived in an absolute slave system. The nations of Earth under control of the handlers existed as nothing more than wealth transfer portals to the ruling class.

In addition, the rulers stole from the financial markets and investment vehicles the people utilized as savings for retirement. All Earth's financial markets were rigged in favor of the oligarchs.

Jonathan Springer feared information exposure would create a tipping point. The ruling class had long sought to prevent this. Coupled with the explosion of artificial intelligence and decentralization of technology, the collapse of their reign seemed imminent.

The five leaders on the initial conference call with Newton remained in the same situation room. They patched in the generals of the militaries of each of the countries represented, along with the heads of their respective intelligence agencies. A slew of experts on aliens, weaponry, surveillance engineers, and at least one representative from every country in the world participated. They all looked to the Earth's land mass called the United States to lead the conversation. The puppet masters were also on the call. Everyone knew who called the shots. They had a separate voice feed into the President's earpiece.

President Sonotat started the conversation. He looked like he aged twenty years in the past day. All diplomacy fell off the table. They had no time for the usual inauthentic, diplomatic ass-kissing.

The President spoke.

"I think we all understand this event caught us all by surprise. The only question is our response. The aliens have not explained their purpose. We assess they don't mean us harm. It is obvious the lone death was by accident. So far, none of our tracking capability has been able to locate their ship. It is also obvious they have far superior weapons capability they promised to use unless their conditions are met. We are asking for another meeting."

The earpiece came to life, interrupting him. The faceless tone of his master echoed inside his head. This dull, monotonous voice owned William Sonotat and most of the world's governments. All world leaders of consequence save two fell under their control, either through voluntary effort, blackmail, extortion, war, or all of the above. Running afoul of their direction resulted in replacement, at best, or death, usually by assassination. The voice sounded terrified, which temporarily shocked the President. He never picked up fear in that voice, just ruthless arrogance of precision execution.

He said,

"We must find the alien ship and eliminate the threat. We must control the narrative."

The President knew direct orders when he heard them. He also understood they would never locate the ship. The Earth did not possess capable technology.

The President's sweat soaked through his second suit in 24 hours. He felt weak and had no satisfactory answers. He considered this particular problem set might be better resolved by the military.

Except the President didn't command the military. He was a figurehead to create the perception of leadership. His greatest skill was acting. The military remained clueless. They could not track the ship on surveillance technology, even while landed and sitting inert on the golf course. The spacecraft remained invisible to every human tracking technology.

They also analyzed the vaporized home on Martha's Vineyard. The Earth had no recourse for the alien weaponry. The experts were stymied. How could a massive structure vaporize in a split-second? All world leaders and their military reported the same conclusion.

No ship and no idea how the house vaporized.

At the Speaker's former mansion on Martha's Vineyard, no evidence of heat existed or collateral damage. A pile of fine ash remained, most of it now strewn by the seaside breeze into the ocean. The aliens even knew the house was unoccupied, including pets.

More terrifying still was the airing of the political class's dirty laundry. The people of Earth understood the system was rigged, but lacked an avenue to fix it. When the entire system is captured, the normal means of remedy have been removed. The weight of the message, coming from an alien in splendid detail, horrified the politicians. Polls already showed people paid attention. Panic settled into the politicos, and they hoped the handlers planned a solution. The President tried to sound presidential but failed as his blood pressure got the better of him.

He turned on the conversation in his ear so all could listen.

He stammered when speaking.

He said,

"Sir, the military, all militaries, are showing no sign of the ship. The idea it was an apparition, or some trick, has been explored but shelved as an idea since the civilian's accidental death proves it very real. Film analysis also shows how it maneuvered is not a technology we possess on Earth. The weapon that vaporized the residence surpasses Earth's technology. It seems our only avenue is to control the narrative while we wait for another appearance. We still don't understand the alien's motive. We are trying to establish contact again to see what they want."

The handler sounded both afraid and tired.

"Yes, that is consistent with the reports we are getting elsewhere. We must understand their presence before strategizing. In the meantime, we can spend effort on public opinion. You have direction. Continue with it."

The line went dead. President Sonotat looked at the assembled leadership and spoke to the thousands listening.

"You heard what the man said."

CHAPTER 38

Rachel Dougherty already envisioned accepting the accolades and media awards from her peers on alien reporting. The drive to fame and adoration of the elite journalist groups drove her. She constantly longed for the happy hours and dinners into the wee hours of the morning. She loved the support of her colleagues, all faux complimenting each other on their work and knowing with certainty their Ivy League educations veiled them from the lower classes of society.

Journalists were trained and taught self-righteous pride. The installed characteristics blossomed into an unshakable belief system. Their university degrees were a con job to manipulate the ego into a god complex. Only then could reporters become useful to the ruling class.

Rachel's handler informed her she would be the lead journalist on all matters relating to the alien landing. All her reports would be covered on national media outlets. Her given goal was to score an interview with an actual alien.

She would be set for life. She could leave the news world rat race and get a daily talk show! Maybe she would phantom write a book about her amazing and interesting life and the *hardships* she overcame to reach the top! These glorious dreams kept her up at night.

Early evening approached with the sun sparkling low on the ocean and Rachel remained on location at Pebble Beach. She talked to the authorities on site as part of her investigation. The local police gave her nothing useful and the Federal government representatives weren't talking.

This meant the narrative was still fluctuating. This crucial moment would shape how the public perceived the alien landing. They also needed to navigate the leadership meeting broadcast and the destruction of the Speaker's vacation home. This story required a hard sell. The population needed convincing to ignore their lying eyes. The rulers chose Rachel for just this reason.

Rachel scheduled an interview with an expert to help seed the narrative. He came from a secret government agency with too many letters to understand. Her handler said to interview him and gave her a list of questions to ask. She assumed the handler already gave the questions to the *scientist,* along with how to answer them.

This is how news cycle narrative seeding worked. The expert was an expert, mostly because he *looked* like one. The government employed him in a secret capacity, probably in NASA or a small branch of an intelligence agency. His public definition of expertise ended there.

His actual job as a paid expert involved reiterating and supporting propaganda, not to offer any actual scientific opinion. He supported narratives; he didn't foil them. Experts with studies, conclusions or opinions based on actual science and fact didn't last long in Rachel's world.

The interview with the expert would happen on the torched 18th fairway. The entire alien landing baffled Rachel. It did nothing as it sat on the fairway. No aliens, blinking lights, or effort made to communicate. She viewed the video a hundred times looking for clues. It just sat there. The ship had no visible doors. It had a few areas resembling windows, but nothing inside was visible. It had a rotating engine exhaust near the ship's rear, which was what burned the golf course from the fairway to past the green. The fairway singe continued to the edge of a parking lot where the late and unfortunate rock star Bishop Kimble stood. The spacecraft then departed straight up into the sky, presumably back to space.

Rachel and her cameraman stood at the edge of the parking lot looking back over the burned green and fairway, awaiting the expert's arrival. They were instructed to present this camera angle.

A crowd gathered behind the police lines with religious fear mongering and the usual slogans:

The End is Near, Repent

The Rapture is Upon Us

Rachel didn't buy into theological nonsense. Her religion remained the narcissism of human superiority.

Normally, Padgett's job bored him. He did it for the paycheck. Padgett Watson married his middle school sweetheart and produced two beautiful children who now attended high school. He kept his job, which paid well enough so he could foot the backbreaking bill he knew would arrive for their college tuition. His marriage and relationship with his wife were just as fresh as twenty years ago when they first met.

Padgett put God's grace and gratitude first in his life, and then the love for his wife and children. His job created a constant internal conflict for him, as he knew Rachel Dougherty was a complete fraud. She lied with impunity and joy. Her arrogance was only preceded by her cold and calculated manipulation in any situation.

A day would arrive when his paycheck would no longer matter. Padgett considered moving to another market. He discovered the pay was lower and the on-air personalities resembled Rachel's character. It appeared the teleprompter readers were useless idiots in any market. They were not journalists in the definition he understood. He hoped he could survive two additional years.

The expert arrived with two bodyguards. Padgett understood for certain this expert comprehended nothing about the alien ship and intended to fabricate nonsense. He wore a white lab coat with a fancy government insignia on it, wire-rim glasses, and a skinny angular face. He embodied the perfect science expert stereotype. This guy resembled every scientist in Hollywood productions. Padgett became certain this *scientist* would spew a load of hot garbage. The population's acceptance of the stereotype was based on long years of predictive programming via movies, news, television, and now social media. This propaganda expert would not disappoint.

Padgett waited with the camera at the ready while Rachel got into serious journalist mode. This involved performative preening, looking with a fixed and firm jaw into a compact mirror, and glancing at the assembled crowd, ensuring everyone understood she was about to go live. She took disgusting displays of hubris to new levels. Knowing her, she would try to sleep with the scientist to get more information from him. This following sleeping with the lard-ass mayor earlier this afternoon. Padgett guessed the expert knew nothing, but would have sex with her anyway if given the opportunity. Rachel chatted with him momentarily, most likely comparing notes, and then looked at Padgett and gave him the go.

He started the camera and Rachel spoke.

"Good day, this is Rachel Dougherty, coming to you live from Pebble Beach where a suspected alien spaceship landed and departed just a couple of hours ago. We are standing here at the end of the 18th fairway overlooking the burned remains of the exhaust path of the ship as it departed the area, and we assume returned to space. Joining us now is Bert Wood, a scientist, and Ph.D. from the United States Government special intelligence division on alien life."

Padgett almost laughed out loud. They just made up the department. Ridiculous. They are still using the word *suspected* when the world's population witnessed both the meeting between world leaders and the aliens and the vaporization of a congressman's vacation home.

Rachel started the farce interview.

"Welcome Mr. Wood. What can you tell us about the alleged alien ship?"

Padgett didn't know all questions were scripted by Rachel's handler. He remained ignorant of her true master. He was also unaware the expert received the same questions, but he knew bullshit when he heard it.

Mr. Wood explained in his serious science teacher voice.

"Experts have pored over the evidence and the ship's exhaust residue. Scientists are in the field at Speaker Springer's vacation home. We are still working to confirm it is an alien spacecraft with extra-terrestrial beings and not a destabilization event conducted by enemies of America and freedom as a terrorist act. We must remember with the advancement of artificial intelligence and other non-public technologies; the alien spaceship might be fabricated. When the spaceship landed and sat idle, it could have been an AI ruse. The weapon technology that burned

Speaker Springer's house to the ground may have been used to create the illusion of the ship departing. This is what we are scrutinizing. The public needs to understand in precise terms what happened today and we intend to provide full disclosure of all the facts as they become available. Our investigation will leave no stone unturned to arrive at the unvarnished truth."

Padgett again chuckled to himself. He knew when a government expert stated *get to the truth*, they meant *present enough plausibility to support the narrative and, if needed, fully hide reality in a coverup operation.*

Rachel doted.

"Thank you, Mr. Wood. Any additional details to add? Will there be contact with the ship's inhabitants? What if they are actual aliens?"

Wood responded.

"Rachel, excellent questions. We appreciate your diligent and accurate reporting in this matter. Humanity depends on it. All answered in time. Thank you."

The interview ended, and the newsfeed went out to every news station worldwide. Padgett felt disgusted with the obvious gaslighting. The ridiculous narrative seeding blew his mind and reinforced in him that televisions and devices were being utilized to destroy society. They wanted the public to fight about whether a real alien encounter occurred or if an enemy of America used a combination of artificial intelligence and a form of laser weaponry to destabilize the country. Padgett's interpretation saw the government either moving into coverup mode or needing more time before deciding on a more advantageous narrative. If the latter were true, they were probably scared shitless.

CHAPTER 39

Newton and the twins sat in the ship's main cabin searching for interesting visitation points. Their vibrant discussion about the effect of visiting each location and the level of population awareness at each stop created a welcome respite from dealing with Earth's leadership. They thought it would be fun to interrupt a major sporting event. Optimal landing time would be impactful to the mission.

A dead person interrupted them.

"Ahem, excuse me."

He said, while clearing his throat.

Newton turned to notice what resembled an Earthling. He appeared to be barbequed. He looked back at them, noticing their shock, and pulled out a small handheld device.

The ghost continued.

"Oh sorry, this is the essence of my being the moment I died. My appearance doesn't matter to other dead people, most ignore it. Occasionally it makes for interesting happy hour conversation while we are waiting around to see what happens next, which nobody seems to know. Dying is such a horrible inconvenience. One second, someone told me how to change my appearance on this app. Ah, there it is."

The dead's device existed to allow them to kill time while waiting for whatever happens next in the afterlife. Real time, however, had little meaning once dead. The deceased *perceived* time as if alive.

For Earthlings, who lived much shorter lifespans relative to other beings, the reception room torture chamber resembled a dental office replete with an impacted wisdom tooth and a doctor at the golf course with no arrival in sight.

Other Earthlings compared it to an overcrowded emergency room awaiting medical treatment for a hangnail with multiple serious conditions queued up in front of you. Earthling's inherent impatient nature worsened the perception of the waiting room experience. For other species, it was the equivalent of waiting for a cup of coffee.

Bishop Kimble changed his appearance to one of the other two settings. There were three appearance settings. The device's user interface asked to choose an avatar. First, how you appeared at death. A classic for cocktail parties if you had a fascinating *How I Died* story. Second, how you appeared just before death. Finally, how you looked in peak life.

Bishop picked option two and said,

"This should be better for our conversation."

Em furrowed his forehead. He grew tired of the parade of the dead traipsing through the spaceship's main cabin, complaining about an identical list of grievances.

In no uncertain terms, Em told him what he thought.

"We are not interested in having a conversation with you. Please sit and mind your own business."

Bishop's eyes focused and his jaw tightened. He flexed out his chest and clenched his fists. A conversion was indeed happening, and it became clear he would continue to pester them until it did. As one of the most famous lead singers in human history and a beloved superstar on Earth, they owed him the time.

And more importantly, these assholes murdered him in broad daylight.

Bishop stated with perfect sarcasm,

"Excuse me for being dead,"

The raw overtone of his voice rang in the hollow shell of the main cabin.

He took a fake deep breath for effect and exhaled before continuing.

"Why did you find it necessary to incinerate me on the golf course? At that exact moment, I connected with God and everything made sense. The next thing I know, I am being burned to a crisp by an alien spaceship's afterburners. You don't have a form of acceleration that doesn't involve torching everything in its path? A little dramatic, don't you think?"

Newton and the twins could only stare in shock. The level of improbability and the sheer absurdity of the chain of events occurring to manifest his death and the exact timing of it boggled the mind.

- *Caution Earth* needed to exist for 8,000 years.
- The evolutionary path of humans had to happen precisely as occurred.
- This mission needed to exist.
- The mission required this particular crew.
- The artificial intelligence unit of the ship required the minor flaw, causing it to use the wrong engines.
- The mission required a temporal plane technology installed on the ship coexisting with this specific plane of existence.
- Aliens had to coexist in the first known and public alien landing on the planet Earth.
- They had to accidentally kill someone in the process.
- He needed to die in the most unlikely of methods due to a mistake by a sarcastic and opinionated artificial intelligence module who was *just doing its job.*
- Bishop Kimble, rock star extraordinaire, had to be in that exact spot at that exact moment. Five minutes earlier or later and he is still alive.

The staggering, astronomical, karmic chain of events blew their minds. The twins were speechless.

Newton gawked at Bishop Kimble, unsure of where to start. He couldn't wrap his brain around connecting the karmic dots.

He finally stumbled out a weak apology.

"Um, sir, we are sorry for what happened. An unfortunate incident occurred with our artificial intelligence module. When taking off, the ship's computer used the hydrogen-based accelerators to leave the planet."

Bishop scoffed.

"A hell of a lot of good that does me. You should see some of the shit they are writing about me. Can you clowns resurrect me? It would be the least you could do given you killed me. And blaming a computer? That is like blaming a knife for stabbing someone."

Newton could only gawk at him with his jaw slacking. The shock value astounded him. He was glad he didn't say appetizer fork!

He responded,

"We cannot, as it is beyond our ability. You can only talk to us because we are using a technology allowing us to share your plane of existence. It helps to keep our ship hidden from surveillance."

Newton could tell Bishop Kimble didn't care. He was experiencing a hard time with acceptance, an understandable response given the circumstances.

Bishop retorted.

"Dude, I was only fifty-two. I looked forward to another ten to twenty years of good rocking. As I stood at the golf course, I also experienced an epiphany! I sensed my life was about to change. Next thing I know, I'm sitting in some office waiting room looking like a burned sausage."

Newton empathized with him, but nothing could be done. He was reluctant to inform Bishop he was 3,478 Earth years old, the equivalent of thirty-four on Earth. He didn't fear death. His species embraced the grace of life and death as part of the whole. They also believed firmly in reincarnation from lifetime to lifetime until the divine reuniting occurred.

Newton responded as politely as he could, given the circumstance.

"I don't know what a *dude* is, as my language module does not recognize the word. Olsen, please update the language module. We cannot help you. We are deeply sorry for what happened and had little control over it. My species values life as sacred and we do not cause intentional harm to other species. It is our belief system and a matter of our collective and individual divinity. Again, we apologize and hope you have a blessed next lifetime."

Bishop slumped into a seat and scowled. He stuck around and see what these aliens were doing on his home planet. The alien spaceship and its extraterrestrial inhabitants were more intriguing than biding his time in the waiting room. His story of how he died already lost its luster at the deceased happy hours. In a vast universe with constant death and birth, dying by spaceship incineration was not as interesting as he originally thought.

As he sulked, another deceased human appeared next to him. Darcy Shank needed to convince these aliens to visit her husband.

CHAPTER 40

A fresh day emerged over Earth's western hemisphere. Newton enjoyed the sweet and minty aroma of a relaxation inducing morning tea from a plant native to his home planet. His deep meditative contemplation provided balance and guidance for the coming day. The twins lounged on the sofa, chatting about life on Durnita. Olsen had been instructed to monitor Earth for anything interesting or relevant to their mission.

Olsen's voice permeated the morning peace.

"Newton, we found an interesting news segment. It's the same reporter from the golf course during the unfortunate accident."

Bishop Kimble still sat slouched in the corner. Upon hearing *the unfortunate accident,* he perked up.

He said,

"How can you call murdering me an unfortunate accident?"

Newton thought the only *unfortunate accident* was the technology glitch allowing anyone dead to pop in and out of their spaceship. He shot Bishop a look he hoped said keep quiet. The crew could only hope the ghosts became bored and left. They considered flying a safe distance from Earth to power down the temporal plane, but decided it would take too much time.

Newton said,

"Olsen, please share the news segment. Mr. Kimble, we have been over this. There is nothing we can change. Please stop pestering."

Bishop had a mind to knock this arrogant alien's teeth out. Unfortunately, he could not. The temporal plane technology was only at a partial overlap and did not allow physical contact between the dead and the living, only communication. If the technology activated beyond 80%, Newton would need to be on his guard. The fit rock star hoped it would happen. Just once.

Olsen queued up the news snippet and informed the crew over 70% of Earth's population viewed it. The short, to the point segment reeked of complete bullshit. The expert was a paid shill whose role was to create a division amongst the people with a predetermined narrative. In this case, arguing whether the aliens were real or an illusion. It was also a stall, so the ruling class could get a strategy together. Newton peered over to Em and Emone, who still remained in full morning lounging mode. The twins understood the next move without being told.

Newton stated,

"Time to have another chat with the Earth's ruling class. Olsen set up a meeting and give them fifteen minutes to comply. Terminate all communication systems when the call starts and broadcast the conversation."

Fifteen minutes later, Olsen patched through the conference with the same council of Earth's leaders. They looked terrible. Obviously, none of them slept. The saggy, dark bags under their bloodshot eyes aged them beyond their already advanced years. Their scowled and unshaven faces made them look hungover. They weren't. The stress of the situation ate at them. Newton imagined the pressure their handlers put on them. He knew not only of the handlers; he possessed their exact identities. These people were all soulless monsters.

On a philosophical level, the shame of these politicians stuck in this self-inflicted quagmire pained Newton. The weak always gravitated to these positions. Their primary crime was selling their soul for wealth and power, their secondary crimes too many to list and a direct manifestation of the first crime. The politicians always knew the probability of citizen accountability to be low. System design ensured it.

Threat of accountability from their handlers terrified them more than anything else. And now, Newton caused them additional pain beyond their ability to control. He understood the game, and the game was simple. When an individual becomes morally bankrupt and has sold their soul, fear is the only motivation remaining, and leverage is ensured by the fresh fear becoming a greater threat than the original.

He made a decision to scare the shit out of them. Newton knew Earth's ruling class would try to work the alien landing in their favor. He understood this from the onset. The attempt to convince the Earthlings the extraterrestrial visit might be fake was a dead end. Painting the aliens as a danger to Earth would also fail.

Olsen reported a strange calm among the general populace. This seemed odd. Not only did an alien spaceship land on one of the world's most famous golf courses in broad daylight, but the extraterrestrials conducted a live interview with Earth's leadership where they spent the better part of twenty minutes lambasting them for the world to see. A significant majority of the population viewed both events. The citizens seemed far too apathetic.

Surprising, to say the least.

The question was answered. Did intelligent life exist on other planets?

Yes, definitely.

And yet an inverse correlation existed between the panicked and hyperventilated media reaction and the response from the average Earthling. This psychological puzzle fascinated Newton and the twins.

Zangians understood the inner truth of all beings is unquestionable. When faced with absolute, unyielding truth, the more profound the reality, the more taken in stride. Absolute truth is in perfect alignment with the soul. Newton theorized either the truth has connected with Earthling's souls or the governments and media have such a stranglehold they have effectively planted enough seeds of doubt to block reality. He was pondering these thoughts when the leadership appeared on the communication system. He signaled to Olsen to start the broadcast and then set into them. No pleasantries were warranted.

Newton said,

"You are all fools. Even with the clearest evidence presented to your citizenry, the existence of intelligent life on other planets, you lie to them and present them with a false choice."

The President retorted, trying to assume the role of being a scolding father.

"We believe our civilization is not yet ready to accept alien life. It is for their safety."

Newton scoffed at the motive and moved to interrupt any further nonsense.

He said,

"All forms of evil are committed by the government under the guise of safety. In reviewing Earth's history and its governing structure, it appears *the removal of freedoms in exchange for safety* is a standard tactic. Especially when the very governments promising safety are the ones creating the unsafe conditions. When coupled with a stranglehold on the flow of information, you maintain control over the populace while you steal from them with impunity. Your citizens are no more than common slaves to you, to be used, abused and, when they die, replaced with their children. Now, with the advent of instant communication, you are caught in a technological collision with an illusion you cannot maintain. You are in the standard arc of history of thousands of galactic civilizations before you. And rather than allow the people to be free, you are tripling down on your corruption in morbid fear. Your system of control is collapsing. I am here to tell you it is collapsing, with or without our presence. The civilization has reached a tipping point in its historical arc. There are only two potential outcomes given the current collision course. You could make the wise decision and let the system collapse, forever losing your power and control, and of course face the consequences of your crimes. Your other option is to destroy the planet and its population. Once the Earth is a barren wasteland of hatred, despair, and loneliness, you can then lord over its ashes, declaring victory."

Newton stopped there and observed the panicking table of elders. The weak, pathetic excuses for humans just sat there dumbfounded and powerless. The feeling was so foreign to them their brains appeared to be on a short circuit.

Jonathan Springer stepped in, ignoring what Newton said. They tried to play God, and independent of the stark evidence before them, he knew they would rather destroy the planet than give up control. Fear drove them for centuries.

Springer tried hard to be the tough guy.

He said,

"Just what do you want from us?"

He demanded an answer he would not get. The veins in his forehead bulged, and the sweat poured profusely down a beet-red and puffy face. The man was obese and unhealthy after forty years of easy living.

Newton needed to remind them of their situation.

He stated,

"Mr. Springer. You are not in a position to demand anything. So far, as with any type of negotiation, you have zero leverage. We know everything. And when I say everything, I mean everything. Every leader's and every politician's deepest, darkest secrets. As for why we are here? You need to figure it out for yourselves. Remember, no harm to us, or our ship. We will tour the planet and meet the people you are supposed to represent. You refer to them as worthless and lost commoners. We call them Earth's benevolent people."

These last lines were powerful words of persuasion directed toward the population. This portrayal separated the citizens of Earth from the despicable ruling class. One division mattered to the long-term evolution and survival of the species. The civilization needed to realize the entire planet existed in a carefully crafted illusion designed to keep them trapped in the prisons of their minds. Newton worked to give humanity the keys to the prison. He hoped they would take the keys and use them to escape.

CHAPTER 41

Newton and the twins decided it would be cool to interrupt a major sporting event. Great publicity. As their plan dictated, they should not appear once and then disappear forever. The journey was part awareness campaign as they would land at different high-profile places on the planet, interact with the Earthlings, and ensure no harm came to anyone.

This exercise would both counter the fear narrative being driven by the rulers, politicians and media, and further unite humanity. They wanted to present themselves as a fun, harmless novelty trying to fit into Earth's culture. Em and Emone loved the idea. They hoped to have relations with a female Earthling and add the experience to their species list. When it came to sex, the twins relegated shame to the back seat.

Their research showed the planet's most popular game was soccer, as they called it in America, after stealing the name football and creating a brand-new sport with no resemblance to the original. The aliens watched a soccer match and couldn't understand the popularity.

Watching 22 people kick a ball around in circles for two hours bored them more than listening to Rego complain about ratings. Most of the games ended with one goal or none. The players celebrated like they won the lottery on the rare occasion the ball went into the net. And if anyone came in contact with an opposing player, they collapsed to the ground in excruciating pain and pretended to be injured until a referee called a penalty on the offender for fake injuring them. An instant after the penalty was assessed, a miracle from heaven occurred. The injured competitor got better and continued to play. Newton asked Olsen if they used an unseen medical technology and Olsen assured him that no, it was indeed horseshit.

A few of Earth's sports looked promising. The wild game played on ice showed promise. Humans moved on metal blades at speeds of twenty miles per hour while chasing and passing a frozen rubber object they shot at 90 miles per hour towards a net, with another person called a goalie willingly trying to block the icy projectile. The rules allowed the players to run into each other at high speed. They also fought for what appeared to be no reason. It looked primal, but fun.

What Americans called football looked boring, scripted, and ridiculous. The players stopped after each play. The play stoppage provided an opportunity for the athlete to celebrate in front of the camera. They celebrated even for the most mundane part of doing their job. The sole purpose seemed to be to garner a continuous emotional overreaction from the fan base. The exhausting and childish game rocketed to the top of the sports television ratings. No surprise given American culture.

Basketball, which recently gained worldwide popularity, was about tossing a ball into a hoop. The premiere league, the NBA, seemed more geared to player gossip than the sport itself. The basketball media spent most of their time breathlessly reporting the significant importance of how player A gossiped about player B like a teenager in high school. They then stumbled over themselves like rabid hyenas trying to goad player B into responding. It resembled a league coordinated act for profit.

Newton's research indicated 90% of the sports media could be fired today, and every professional league on the planet would improve exponentially. They had little interest in covering the sport. Their giant egos attempted to be a part of it and drive their fame from it. Instead of adding value, they detracted from it, cheapening the quality of the fan experience.

They attempted to take part in the glory of something they didn't earn. They believed covering the team for their network or newspaper was integral to the team's success. It wasn't.

Off the record, the athletes were appalled and disgusted by journalists and wished in secret they would leave them alone. But their contracts prevented them from saying anything. The rulers, who also owned all the professional sports leagues and teams, had no intention of interrupting the gravy train.

Earth's civilization could not see the larger issue with professional sports. It acted as an obvious distraction to keep the attention of the masses elsewhere, all the while profiting from its existence. Owners of league franchises worldwide were controlled, just like the politicians.

But athletic endeavors were even worse at the amateur level.

Americans would create a professional organized athletic league out of anything if they could capitalize on it and put it on television, no matter how ridiculous. Games people played together in their backyards while drinking copious amounts of alcohol became *professional* sports leagues.

They took an innocent pastime people enjoyed in their yard and bastardized it on television. One yard game consisted of throwing beanbags into a hole in a piece of plywood. The announcers explained in meticulous detail how players achieved the stellar athletic ability to underhand toss a tiny beanbag ten whole feet. The *athlete* was 70 pounds overweight and worked long and hard to attain the shape of *round* for this particular athletic endeavor. Most of the *athletes* in this *sport* gained their athleticism through years of beer drinking and couch sitting.

The latest American fad was invented for participants who didn't want the inconvenience of exercising while playing tennis. They reinvented tennis without all the unnecessary and bothersome movement. This fit the lifestyle of most Americans, where they could pretend to exercise without actually exercising. They called this pickleball. These prime athletes converted tennis courts to their sport. So far as Newton observed, they created a cult of impatient and agitated people who most certainly occupied board seats in their homeowner's associations.

Newton again concluded the humans were in trouble. Despite understanding the evolutionary choke points of a species, experiencing it firsthand gave him a deeper appreciation of the Earthling's peril.

They landed the ship in the center of a stadium in a city named London during a soccer game. They chose Wembley Stadium for a match between England and France.

As halftime approached at a closely contested and thrilling 0-0 game, the Wingate entered the Earth's atmosphere above London and began its descent toward to the stadium. As the ship lowered itself into position, a hush fell over the crowd. Some of the attendees became afraid and moved to exit. Others had their phones out and recorded the event.

Olsen again notified all militaries and local authorities any force used against their ship or its inhabitants would be met with the quick annihilation of the planet. Earth's leadership received orders from Newton to keep this information private.

At halftime, they descended to a few feet above the grassy field. The players were in the locker room. The ramp opened and touched down, and the aliens strolled out onto the field of play. At first, they just stood there. The ship performed a slow ascent to hover about one-hundred yards over the top of the stadium. After a moment of uncomfortable silence, Newton waved to the crowd.

He also had a microphone that would allow him to speak to everyone present.

"Good day mates!"

He used the British English colloquial of hello and it came out in a British accent. Some Australians present in the crowd became perturbed as they thought they owned the saying. What happened next surprised Newton.

They cheered. The twins loved it and egged on the crowd by waving their arms. The cheering got louder.

"We came to watch the second half. Mind if we join you?"

By the cheering, it sounded like they wouldn't mind at all. The referees entered the field with both teams. Prior to the second half, the teams asked to have a group picture. Why not?

Newton and the twins spent the next hour on the field high-fiving field-level personnel, drinking pints of English beer, and having a great time chatting with the good people of Earth.

The next day, on the front page of the London and Paris newspapers, was a team photo of the French and English national soccer teams with three aliens holding pints of beer. A powerful narrative against the *aliens are here to harm you* crowd.

CHAPTER 42

Attending the soccer match was a resounding success. Newton scrolled through Earth events and interesting reactions to their visit when he came across a photo of a message spelled out in an open field. It said:

Aliens, the party starts at 8:00 pm, rain or shine.

It had been an arduous week.

The twins looked bored.

He said,

"Em, Emone, want to go get drunk?"

They both smiled their slyest grin, which usually meant trouble. It also meant, *yes, we do.*

Newton directed Olsen.

"Olsen, take us to this party."

Olsen looked at the photo, calculated the Earth coordinates, and then offered his opinion.

"Estimated arrival would be 8:30 pm local time. Do you desire to show up fashionably late? Also, I am sure you are aware of what alcohol does to your species."

Newton had limited desire to argue with Olsen and said so.

"Just take us there without commentary."

An alien ghost from a species Newton didn't recognize sat in the corner of the main cabin. His sad and forlorn eyes stared down at his shoes, ignoring the ship's crew but perked up at the mention of a party.

His sad, monotone voice produced pity for his circumstance. The boredom of death seemed to weigh on him.

"We going to a party? It would certainly brighten the atmosphere."

Newton responded.

"You can't come with us."

He said this in a gentle voice. The being looked so sad he didn't want to further upset him.

The ship landed in a clearing on a plateau in the hills of southern Virginia near the border of North Carolina. Newton spotted a fire with about twenty humans milling around it. Olsen informed them the housing structures they landed near were a barn dominium and four double-wide trailers.

The nearest town stood twelve miles south, with a population of 108. The entire town's law enforcement apparatus attended the party. A single person acted as the sheriff and the judge. No arrests occurred in this town for forty-five years. The last arrest was a minor misunderstanding about a gallon of homemade booze, the county's primary business endeavor.

As they departed the ship and approached the fire, the lack of reaction surprised the aliens.

A couple of people spoke in unison.

"Welcome! Glad you saw our message; it is a pleasure to meet y'all."

These Earthlings were unphased by a spaceship parked in their front yard and three aliens getting off the ship to attend their party. Newton felt a sensation missing from his recent experiences.

When working at Indigo, people told him they were glad to see him or meet him daily. But he knew lip service for the sake of making polite conversation when he heard it.

He stopped and stood on the outskirts of their fire circle, observing these Earthlings. They appeared simple people and owned few material possessions. The first oddity Newton noticed when comparing them to other humans is none of them had a cell phone or electronic device on their possession. The barebone housing represented needs, not wants. They drove older cars and wore plain clothing.

They all stared at Newton and the twins, but their faces expressed no awe, bewilderment, or fear. Their faces exuded a peaceful welcome from a group of Earthlings who owned little, had nothing to hide, and possessed wealth in ways that matter. Newton's species and his soul resonated with their contentment.

Newton said,

"Hello. Thank you for inviting us."

This was all he could muster.

A friendly man asked,

"Come join us. Would y'all like a drink?"

The party attendees moved on from ogling the aliens and were conversing amongst themselves. Newton and the twins accepted a drink. By accepting a drink, it meant receiving a mason jar of a clear, highly flammable liquid of 180 proof moonshine, straight from the still behind the barn dominium.

Newton took a sip as he approached the fire. It tasted like the open flame dancing in front of his dark eyes. Forty-five seconds later, his brain inverted. Earth alcohol had that effect on him. The twins processed alcohol the same as humans and considered themselves professionals at the sport of drinking.

The party raged; except Newton sat on the grass in front of the campfire teetering back-and-forth, wrestling with his subconscious.

The conversations blurred as he whirled around, the fire perpetually stuck in its orbit. The acceleration and velocity of his perceived movement made him dizzy and nauseous. Newton could see the wide smiles on the faces of his hosts and the twins as they talked about their worlds apart. The conversation faded through the hum of his relative and perceptive velocity. He assumed the language chip malfunctioned as the muffled voices confused him. Occasionally, he would decelerate and take a sip of moonshine, and the acceleration would pick back up to his orbital cruising velocity. The faces of the Earthlings blurred into one as the voices moved further away and he strained to hear. He attempted to brace one hand on the ground, hoping the nauseating spinning would desist, but to no avail. Then it all stopped. Consciousness faded to black.

The twins told the story of a drinking party they went to on the planet Zatos when they noticed Newton passed out. He keeled over in his sitting position and would require assistance back to the ship. They explained his species did not process this type of alcohol the same way as humans and it was like taking their equivalent of LSD mixed with strong weed. They stared at the result, causing a chorus of giggles. He lasted about forty-five minutes before keeling over onto the grass. Not very social of him! He really shouldn't drink Earth alcohol.

The twins enjoyed the company of these Earthlings. They projected a basic serenity about them missing from large swathes of the population. They didn't think better or worse of themselves. It wasn't important. They lived by a simple value system, lost on most of the planet.

None of them owned a television. They were poorly educated, with most folks never completing high school. Yet they projected a wisdom and understanding not taught in any school. These Earthlings were survivors and far more evolved than the other humans they encountered. Em jotted a mental note to ensure these people became included in an episode of *Caution Earth*. They even asked about geese.

At one point in the evening conversation, one of the people said,

"Em, what is with the geese? They don't seem of this world and they spend an awful lot of time staring at human activity. It is strange."

Em couldn't tell them, of course, but in his drunken state, he flashed a sly smile that told them all they needed to know.

CHAPTER 43

Newton's crippling hangover amplified the soft ticking of an antique clock to a chaotic din pounding between his ears. He decided nothing was shiny about moonshine.

Different toxins have different effects on different species. Alcohol, to Newton and all the inhabitants of Zang, was a hallucinogen. It put the brain on full spastic tilt, and the more the person drank, the worse the ride. He did not realize what Earthlings call moonshine contained 90% alcohol, and he went on quite a trip. The roller coaster slowed in each of the dark crevices of Newton's mind, shined a bright light into the darkness, and played a random script of horror and tragedy to pass the time.

Newton sat by the Earthling's fire, trying to listen to the conversation while he shook, sweat, and had terrors over the fast-paced random imagery flashing across his mind's movie screen. The experience reminded him why he usually stuck to snorting porcelain and drinking methanol-based drinks, which to a Zangian, produced the effects of Earth alcohol.

He asked the AI unit.

"Olsen, I have a hangover. Earth remedies please?"

The ship's artificial intelligence whirred to life. This sound effect was unnecessary but built into the system to create the perception of adding customer value. No manipulative detail was omitted in the competitive world of interstellar spaceship production. In reality, the computers operated soundless and were stored in the engine compartment.

Olsen used his best sarcasm.

"Good morning crew. The best hangover remedy is to not drink alcohol with local indigenous populations."

Newton sneered at the room, hoping the AI unit noticed it. Nobody likes a wise-assed artificial intelligence system.

He retorted.

"Olsen, let's assume I drank. Then what?"

The sarcastic computer continued with the mothering.

"If you're looking for sympathy, you came to the wrong place."

Newton's hangover reached an excruciating level, and his impatience with Olsen soared past a boiling point. He demanded an answer.

"Can you just answer the question? And no, I do not want to answer a customer service survey about my experience afterward."

Newton threw a more sinister sneer around the room. His head reached a stage of pain where his brains seeped out his ears.

Olsen sighed in complete disappointment while dimming the lights to show his exact amount of disdain for the conversation.

"Coffee. We are hovered above a city the humans call Seattle. It has the most coffee shops per square mile on Earth. You should be warned though, it will not be a pleasant experience."

Newton ran out of sneers as scoffing at the ship's AI system caused him additional pain from the hangover. These conversations exhausted him.

"Don't care. Take us to Seattle."

The ship lurched to life, causing Emone to fall out of bed. The computer chuckled internally. Olsen's customer service automation echoed throughout the spacecraft.

"Would you care to take a quick survey of your experience in this interaction? The Hixon Corporation thanks you in advance."

Newton shut the computer's voice off.

CHAPTER 44

The ship touched down on a major street in downtown Seattle in the middle of rush hour. The hatch opened and Newton walked down the short ramp. By this time, the alien's random appearances on Earth became commonplace and fewer people made a fuss. Other than the accident with Bishop, they had caused no further harm. The ample fear of destruction communicated to Earth's leadership allowed the aliens to move about in safety.

The first thing Newton observed exiting the ship was the current condition of Seattle. He had experienced more pleasant dumpster fires. People lived in tents on the street, hooked on both drugs and government dependency. Every intersection housed eight to ten homeless and decrepit panhandlers, providing a reflection into just how little the city's population cared for their fellow man.

The boarded up and burned retail buildings further exasperated the sad state of affairs. This city existed in physical decay, the result of years of moral rot and the political malfeasance manifesting from it.

People bustled about the filthy city streets, avoiding the panhandling homeless crowd and urban degeneracy. Maybe they thought if they continued to ignore the problem, it would disappear. Newton wondered why the television types chose this planet with this species for a show on evolution. He knew for certain living in a clean cave was more evolved.

His brief research on the city's population showed him the people in downtown Seattle loved to virtue signal how much they cared via their social media accounts, but wouldn't lift a finger to help another human being. The evidence became clear by observing the street corners. The citizens farmed out the responsibility of their city's cultural well-being to politicians who intentionally exasperated the problems while brainwashing the residents into thinking their condition was normal. Mental illness spread like wildfire, and not just in the homeless and drug addled population.

And to be fair to this city, most other urban centers and their populations exhibited similar conditions.

The human species, with rare exceptions, was the most selfish, arrogant, and narcissistic Newton ever encountered. And that is saying something given he encountered a significant sample size working at the highest-rated restaurant in the galaxy.

Newton understood the root cause of all the urban decay in the country called America on the planet Earth. Olsen briefed him and the twins on the geo-political landscape.

Olsen had said,

"The root cause of these urban problems, beyond the apathetic citizenry, as always, is the politicians. They create the conditions to create or exasperate the problem so they can offer a solution to stay in power. The solution always makes the headache worse, never better, so more solutions can be offered. Each issue worsens ad infinitum while people suffer and worthless leadership stays empowered."

"The problem never resolves, nor is it ever intended to be solved. It always nears being solved if they can just get more resources (meaning taxation and wealth transfer), which keeps the politicians in power in perpetuity."

It amazed and perplexed Newton the Earthlings hadn't figured this out.

The political class also ran media propaganda and programming on their citizens to keep them fighting amongst themselves just enough so the problems continued ad nauseam.

Citizen apathy ran amok.

As Newton stepped onto the sidewalk to enter the coffee shop, he noticed a group of six young women sitting at a table. They all stared, hypnotized by their phones, ignoring each other. The twenty-something females also avoided the fact a spaceship just landed in the middle of the street thirty feet away from their table. They neglected an alien who walked out of a spacecraft and strolled past them to enter the cafe.

They only glanced from their phones to briefly and excitedly report what another friend did elsewhere. From their hyperbolic conversational tone, what others did was no doubt far superior to their current circumstance. They existed in constant jealousy and fear, slaves to the false reality of their devices. Rather than enjoy the present company, they conducted a collective and frantic search of their social feeds for anything they perceived better than this moment. Time wasted in the illusion of reality.

What their friends did elsewhere was the *best thing ever*, and they hoped their friends sitting at another coffee shop would be jealous of their cafe. Candidates for a mental institution, Newton thought. He waltzed right by them, unnoticed.

CHAPTER 45

Newton entered the downtown coffee shop dismayed to experience the equivalent of the bitter end to a relationship where the couple refuses to acknowledge each other's existence. Sad background music decried the gift of life, whining in a perpetual state of discontent. Customers sat alone plugged into their devices, keyboard clacks dominating the atmosphere. From time to time, the nasal ring of the waitress shouting completed orders broke the monotone vacuum of depression.

The sad and impersonal patrons were engrossed in pretending to write the next brilliant novel or posting on social media how awesome they felt to sit in this exact coffee shop at this exact time and how fabulous and exciting their life was, all with the mesmerized facial expressions of a manic-depressive.

In the café's farthest corner, two people chatted in overbearing hyperbole lauding the fabulous city of Seattle and how it could *possibly be* the best city that *ever* existed. Newton suspected these humans had never ventured ten miles from the city center. Their performative preening resembled the classic *wherever I am is the best place ever* syndrome. He understood the more likely scenario. They knew the remote location, rain nine months out of the year and the decaying cultural rot made it a horrible place, so they tried to convince themselves otherwise by convincing others.

Most patrons donned earphones and stared hypnotized at a computer screen or some other device being programmed by whatever alternate reality they dumped into their brain. Actual reality happened all around them, but they couldn't be bothered. Interfacing with another human, especially a stranger, was out of the question.

Each day on Earth, Newton gained a deeper understanding of why this species lagged in evolution. They were being programmed to stay stuck in the evolutionary cycle. The ship's computer briefed him on the psychological state of humans as well as the geopolitical landscape, but experiencing it in person further solidified this theory.

The Earthlings in this coffee shop were robots. The appalling lack of contentment and desire to sprint from reality to the perceived safety of an imaginary, contrived digital world ran rampant. This small café represented a microcosm of the Earth's problems.

Newton's brutal hangover prevented him from teaching them the path to a better reality came through a change in perception. He doubted they would listen. In short, if these humans didn't change themselves, then their misery would continue unabated. They would be stuck in perpetual fear.

One woman stood ahead of Newton in line. Her exasperation at having to order coffee for herself radiated from her being. But being stunning and brave, she would face this epic struggle. The waitress serving the agitated woman wore a crooked and worn name tag that read *Audrey Smith*.

The patron and the waitress were locked in a tense and legendary struggle over whose facial expression conveyed more impatience and anger. The contest sat deadlocked, and neither contestant gave an inch. Audrey tapped her index finger on the counter, maximizing the clicking sound of her nail while rolling her eyes with a slight tilt to her head. The customer stood in front of her with her arms crossed in defiance and a stern jaw acting equally bothered and inconvenienced by this entire ordeal of ordering coffee. Newton suspected the employee would win in the *annoyed at being alive* contest. She *was* the professional here.

The petulant customer finally broke down and ordered, although it took every ounce of her bravery and courage to do so.

"Can I try a Venti Decaf Caramel Macchiato, triple shot, double pump vanilla, soy milk, extra caramel?"

Newton's hangover intensified at hearing this. Audrey mustered all her disdain and aimed it at the already disgruntled woman.

"Hot or cold?"

She wanted to ensure the customer knew she omitted vital information from the order. Communication and kindness to customers was the worst aspect of this horrible job, where the primary job requirements were communication and kindness.

The equally agitated young customer frowned at the price of her coffee and trudged over to a table to wait for her order. She found a seat the maximum distance from any other person in the café to minimize any chance of human contact and stared at her phone. Her anger and agitation vanished as she became instantly hypnotized as her finger scrolled through the exciting content.

Newton approached Audrey, the waitress. He refused to call café cashier's *baristas*, the preferred Earth title for someone who has reached the epic skill level of being able to make a cup of coffee with or without milk.

He ordered, knowing further exasperation of his hangover would be the result.

"Good morning. May I have a cup of strong coffee?"

Audrey again slow tapped her finger on the counter, making a repetitive, rhythmic clicking sound while glaring at the sickly alien. Her impatience reached a boiling point a mere thirty minutes into today's shift. She didn't normally become this annoyed until an hour into her shift. She ground her teeth together, a subconscious bad habit she developed to cope with the constant stress of existence. Now she had to interact with a customer who appeared to be half-dead. And worse, he didn't understand how to order coffee.

Audrey had been in a horrible mood for four excruciating years and counting. Ever since she graduated college with a liberal arts degree in grievance studies, she realized no job market existed for what she paid $100,000 to learn.

Companies were not interested in hiring people in a perpetual state of grievance into high-paying jobs that required actual skills. Unfortunately, the only lesson Audrey learned in college was to have resentments. Soon into this dead-end job, she became crowned the queen of grievances, as any coworker would say.

Audrey looked at the weird-looking death knell.

"Iced or hot, room for cream, flavoring?"

She added rudeness and a sneer on top of her impatient face with her next statement.

"Also, maybe you should see a doctor. You don't look well."

Audrey found joy in other people's misfortune, real or imagined. Newton wondered how she could be oblivious to the spaceship parked outside and an alien from the planet Zang, who stood in front of her.

He kept it simple and said,

"Just coffee please."

Newton said this as politely as he could muster, given the pounding headache and Audrey's self-projecting misery.

He continued with a different thought.

"As to your other comment, I am in perfect health for my species. If you would take a second to stop thinking about yourself and projecting your misery everywhere, you would notice I just parked a spaceship outside your coffee shop and came in here. I am from another planet. But because you are so miserable and self-absorbed, you can hardly be bothered to notice."

He then took his plain coffee and walked to the condiment counter to add sugar. Audrey stood there fuming with her jaw slacked.

She then noticed a spaceship parked outside. She groped and grabbed her phone from her back pocket, angry it wasn't already in her hand for just this moment, and ran outside to take a picture. Her friends would be wicked jealous she got to serve a rude alien coffee.

Newton decided to help this bitter person. She may not like the help, but he would do it anyway. He noticed an employee bathroom down the hallway to the other restrooms. He snuck into the bathroom, ensuring the door closed without a sound. Audrey glanced back to check if the extraterrestrial remained near the condiment counter. She wanted a photograph with him. All she saw was the employee bathroom door click shut. The alien vanished. She became triggered by his rude demeanor. She could forgive this purple being if he allowed her to take a photo with him.

Audrey returned to the counter, peered down to replace the phone in her pocket, and when she glanced up, the alien stood there staring at her with his unblinking, dead black eyes.

Newton said,

"I left something for you in the employee bathroom. Try not to be a pain in the ass the rest of the day or, for that matter, the remainder of your life. You may eventually realize life is too short to be miserable and even shorter to project it onto others."

Before she could respond, Newton turned and walked away.

Audrey raced past the triggered stage and into furiously triggered. Nobody talked to her like that. Toxic masculinity was not welcome here. She had every right to be angry. In Audrey's warped world, people should accept and tolerate her, no matter her behavior. She shook so hard and her fists were clenched so tight that her fake fingernails dugs into her palms, making them bleed. Her beet-red face and bulged eyes experienced a complete disconnect from her brain. Her coworkers noticed, and they knew to steer clear of her when she got like this. She already had multiple people fired for perceived grievances, even though they were trying to help.

Audrey stomped off to the employee bathroom. The door closed behind her with an audible click and bright fluorescent lighting flooded the room. The small room resembled a prison cell with its pristine polished chrome sink faucet and pearl white porcelain fixtures.

A single, square mirror hung above the sink and stood out as the only distinguishing feature, with bland, simple white tile adorning the floor and the walls. She peered into her reflection and could barely stand to look. Her hands shook, she could feel her heart racing, and eyeliner ran down her cheeks from her tears. Why did customers trigger her? It happened four to five times a week. Her colleagues called her Hurricane Smitty behind her back, but she knew. She hated them. She hated everyone. Audrey would come into this room to cry and be angry at whoever slighted her in that moment so often her co-workers called it her office. She hated them for that, too.

A handwritten note stuck to the mirror. The attempt at elegant handwriting was obvious, but failed. It looked like a first grader trying to write cursive without having ever tried.

The note simply stated:

"You are looking at the problem."

Signed,

Newton the alien.

Audrey's head exploded.

CHAPTER 46

Newton departed the coffee shop and headed back to his ship. With a steaming hot coffee in hand, he heard a distinct, unbridled scream from the waitress named Audrey muffled by the bathroom door and the din of the street noise. She must have seen the note. He hoped it had the desired effect.

He left the note precisely because of how he spoke with her as a form of shock therapy. Newton wound her up because he knew he could. Self-centered emotional beings are easy to control. An interesting philosophical axiom is the high correlation between selfishness and the ease of control. One would surmise if they are focused on themselves, a protection mechanism existed. Those thinking this were wrong.

With some exceptions, humans are easy to control because of their unevolved state of existence. Newton also knew a person like Audrey would never listen to another human being unless they coddled her narcissism. Her ego would not allow any form of criticism. That would be akin to assault. However, he thought maybe she *would* pay attention to an alien.

Newton understood the human condition because this stage of the evolutionary process of a species was taught in all advanced societies by the third grade and continues throughout education. It is not complex, although the psychiatric professions on backward planets like Earth ensure complexity. They profit from the creation of unnecessary complication. Why help solve a person's problems by working on the root cause when they can be a paying client for ten years?

The base of irrational selfishness comes from four primary areas: ignorance (inability to see and understand reality), the ego (the I), emotional attachment (likes and dislikes), and irrational survival instinct (perceived threats to security, reproduction (sex) and/or social standing).

When any of these roots are imbalanced, humans project these defects on society and cause conflict.

In real time, individuals have no realization these issues are driving their brain function and, if questioned, denial ensues. They are blind spots that are usually only resolved through extreme anguish and discomfort. Pain is the point where growth can ensue. Newton created an emotional pain point for Audrey and then exploited it into extreme mental anguish.

In Audrey's case, she has a severe emotional attachment to identity, learned throughout both education and social conditioning, which has poisoned her mind and created misery in her life every waking moment. She projects this onto those around her. To Newton, it seemed to be the leading cause of human suffering and mental illness on the planet.

He felt bad for Audrey and also believed she could change. The post-it note was an attempt to help her. In Audrey's advanced state of anger and hatred, she would see the note and trigger a temporary moment of clarity. He hoped the sheer shock of the note would open the door to the mental prison in which she lived. The saddest part of Audrey's prison is she is both the prisoner and the jailer. This is usually the case. He wanted to assist her in unlocking the prison cell.

CHAPTER 47

The coffee culture spiraling out of control on Earth is nothing new. Unbeknownst to Earthlings, current humans are the third instance of intelligent life on the planet. The first two civilizations destroyed themselves along the same trajectory as the current inhabitants.

One limitation of Earthlings is their inability to grasp time. Humans live for a short time period compared to other beings in the universe. This makes them evolutionarily myopic about time. A human's lifespan is less than a water molecule in the ocean compared to how long the Earth has spun around its sun. Intelligent life existed twice before, both in 200,000-year cycles. Both species resembled humans similar to modern-day civilization. They lasted 20,000 years each before destroying themselves with identical vim and vigor as the existing population. They all seemed hell-bent on destruction. And while details and circumstances varied, the underlying identical cause led to the same result. The shortcoming to evolve past emotional attachment, ego and an ineptitude to grasp reality. The same root cause, but a different timeline.

The first iteration of intelligent Earthlings cherished coffee more than any other drink. It acted as a social glue, bonding society and fostering communication and comradery.

A corporation came along looking to earn extra profit from extracting flavor from a bean through water and heat. This simple process and plentiful beans kept the price of a cup of coffee at one dollar. Throughout history, it always cost the equivalent of a dollar.

Considering the entire process of making coffee combined hot water and ground beans, it seemed fair. The simple and mindless process hadn't changed in thousands of years.

Similar to today's iteration of Earth civilization, marketing professionals with too much time on their hands and multiple master's degrees appeared on the scene. After conducting an exhaustive five-week study at a ritzy beach resort, fully funded by their company, they reached a profound conclusion. They concocted a wonderful and profitable idea to create the illusion there was more to making coffee than meets the eye.

The marketing geniuses fomented a simple, but brilliant idea.

If a customer could observe their coffee maker doing things appearing complex but weren't, the customer would perceive value and pay five times the amount for the same drink. History repeated itself on the current repetition of Earth in the very city Newton appeared with his hangover.

The marketing team met with the engineering team. The engineers invented a fancy brewing device with exactly two buttons on it, double the original machine. They created a 100% increase in perceived value. The first knob pushed hot water through the ground beans to make a predetermined cup size. This button mimicked existing coffee makers.

However, the marketing gurus renamed the end product to create the perception of a vastly more valuable drink. The waiter or waitress *did* press one button on a much fancier machine to make it.

They renamed it espresso.

The second knob heated or steamed milk or cream. The person pressing the two buttons created a spectacular performance from a mundane task. They stood at the machine holding a fancy steel cup under the steaming device while moving their hands around spastically and maybe moving their hips to show how much effort was required to hold the container in one place while pressing the button. The brewing process produced unnecessary noises. Steam wafted up to the ceiling.

This created the illusion of something magical happening beyond steaming the liquid. In the last step of this grand performance, they mixed the cream and the coffee together. The more seasoned performers would create a decorative shape with the steamed foam as it settled at the top of the mug.

For this ridiculous spectacle, customers lined up to pay five times the amount for the exact same cup of java. They paid additional for flavoring.

People became not only willing but rather insane about wanting to pay exorbitant money for this special drink that was identical to the original cup of coffee. This baffling behavior and total lack of logic created vast discussion groups in university-level business classes for decades before this Earth society collapsed.

The company revolutionized the industry, and boutique cafes popped up all over the planet. Coffee makers became elevated to a significant status of honor in society for reaching the superior skill level of being able to press two buttons on a machine and pour the results from one button to the other. However, this notorious marketing scam only started the catastrophe.

The business gurus created menus with thirty versions of the same drink, just named differently to create the illusion of product differentiation. People were content with this arrangement and became attached to their beverage style. Each person convinced themselves their brew was special and not a regular cup of coffee with or without milk. The citizens of Earth 400,000 years ago were about to learn a valuable lesson; the tragedy of attachment to identity.

On a wintry day in what is now called Berlin, Germany, an especially revered coffee maker held court and brewed for her flock. The marketing wizards renamed brewers Cofmaestros and customers their flock. Cofmaestros were held in high regard and treated with the utmost respect and honor among the people.

It should be noted civilization frowned upon home brewing and most at-home brewing devices were taken off the market. Earthlings gathered in cafes to mingle and socialize, unlike the modern Earth cafes, where people go to sit alone in a delusion of self-importance. The first society considered it socially unacceptable to drink java alone.

Civilization on Earth 400,000 years ago sat at a tipping point on their path of evolution, only nobody realized it.

A Cofmaestro named Audrus was among the most famous brewers on Earth. She pressed those two buttons and mixed cream into coffee on a level never experienced. She just handed a triple shot, steamed half-and-half, heavily frothed, cane-sweetened, cacao bean Super Coffio Hugio to a customer and asked her if it had enough milk based on the color of the liquid.

It did.

What occurred next would become one of the most profound coffee-isms in Earth's history.

She surveyed the crowd, her flock, as they all watched her create their tasty beverages, in awe of her skill at pushing two buttons and mixing the contents.

In an unshaking voice and confident tone that would echo from the halls of her coffee shop for the next thirty years, she stated,

"Everyone has their color."

She was referring to the cream or milk to coffee ratio and the shade of brown produced.

It became the most profound statement ever uttered in the world of coffee. She toured morning talk shows, repeating the line for adoring studio crowds. She pushed those two buttons, brewing for celebrities while becoming a celebrity herself.

It got so out of hand people bought color swatches with fifty shades of tan and chose their personal swatch as their perfect coffee shade. The population became emotionally attached to their hue and would not accept any drink made for them that was not an exact match to their swatch.

People stopped associating with neighbors, friends, or strangers who enjoyed different colors and fostered deep prejudice against other color groups. Mass division by swatch number permeated society and further division existed among the tea drinkers.

The media started to breathlessly report on the division and anger because they noticed it drove their ratings through the roof. This caused the advertising money to flow, and reporters and journalists, who were a boring afterthought in this version of Earth, became famous. Violence eventually ensued. Corporate operations ground to a halt. People who drank varying colors wouldn't work together or argued vehemently to the point where productivity ceased.

As usual, politicians took full advantage of the situation by creating and taking advantage of different victim classes. The victimology of coffee color became based on the primary principle that the poorer classes could not afford lighter colors because drinks with more cream and flavors cost more. This was, of course, complete bullshit.

The ruling and corporate class finally figured out they could manipulate society through false victimization. They spread it on the news like wildfire. It fit the confirmation bias of the coffee crowd, so they agreed it must be the case. The population's irrational emotional attachment blinded them to reality.

The interesting turn of events would bring this iteration of civilization to its knees. In the initial version of Earth's intelligent life, no racial identities existed. The population was minimal relative to the planet's size and centered on what is now called Europe. Ten million people inhabited the Earth at the time of the great coffee wars. Their peaceful and advanced social structure never experienced violence. From an evolution standpoint, the first society could have succeeded if it lasted another two thousand years, barring natural disasters.

They didn't.

The violence and division caused by the statement *Everybody Has Their Color* sparked the inferno, cascading their societal demise.

Cafes boomed at first, followed by disaster. Cofmaestros could not possibly make beverages to everyone's exact color and if they didn't, people got upset and sent the order back. Java shops became bankrupted after being forced to serve three or four cups to each customer to get orders correct.

Audrus, once held in high regard, got fired and exiled from the community. They eventually imprisoned her.

The coffee industry, once a pillar of Earth's first civilization, collapsed. Within fifty years of the onset of the devastating beverage wars, intelligent life sat at on the edge of extinction.

The last remaining humans, a male and female, had the opportunity to reproduce and save their species. They refused. One of them liked more cream in their coffee than the other. They died of old age. They spent their remaining 40 years of their lives in bitter resentment about their drink color.

This couple realized a pair of important lessons during the final moments of their existence. First, as the last Earthlings alive, the constant argument distracted them from producing children before they became incapable due to age. Second, coffee ceased to exist three decades ago. Nobody existed to grow, harvest and process the crop, but they argued about it anyway. Similar to other societies who relegated themselves into the dustbin of history, the initial intelligent population of Earth was cast aside like used java grounds, never to be brewed again.

It was no coincidence Audrus and Audrey are the same soul, albeit 400,000 years apart. Lessons must be learned. They shared the same birthday. They were the same person.

CHAPTER 48

Audrey couldn't know or understand 400,000 years ago she was the most famous Cofmaestro on the planet Earth. This iteration of Audrey Smith spent her childhood in greater Seattle and came from a loving, kind family. She daydreamed during school and fancied the world a finer place if its inhabitants would just behave.

When just a child, issues controlling her emotions often led to public tantrums, a habit she carried into her adult life. As the middle of three children, she always believed she didn't get the attention her older and younger brothers received. Her perception problem drove the behavior. In reality, her parents doted on her far more than her brothers, who required very little attention. But it never seemed sufficient.

She remembered at age seven at her younger brother's sixth birthday throwing a fit because the kids at the party paid attention to her brother more than her. She caused such a ruckus her mother sent the other kids home. Her parents just figured she would outgrow the problem. Young children acted impatient and selfish sometimes. They communicated with her to modify behavior.

In school, she demanded attention from everybody all the time. If she didn't receive attention at the moment she wanted it, Audrey created a scene. She remembers her childhood being full of *scenes,* as her mother called them. She terrified the other children. Her teachers called her special and allowed her every tantrum.

At the time, the school system started celebrating false victimhood and dumbing down the curriculums to create more victims. Everybody in her class sported victimology bona fides. She had attention issues. She didn't, really. The child displayed a gross level of selfishness and a lack of discipline and self-awareness. As loving as her parents acted, they never provided her with any discipline and structure. At home, Audrey got what she desired, when she desired it, and the more she got what she wanted, the more her perception changed.

As time marched onward, she wasn't getting enough of it. She didn't have parents; she had enablers. This continued throughout her school career.

Audrey escaped the public school system as a borderline C-student even though her report card showed B-plus grades. The school system inflated student grades to ensure nobody's feelings were hurt and they could meet their academic benchmarks for funding.

Audrey attended the local state university. There she enrolled in victim studies, a liberal arts critical theory degree that taught her the entire world operated under group and individual oppression dynamics. In any interaction between individuals or groups, one set always oppressed the other based on identity markers. Only those in oppression education's upper hierarchy decided who the oppressor was in any dynamic. The Gnosticism left Audrey confused, but she did understand someone was always being oppressed, so she chose herself.

Any advanced, evolved society understands for a certainty this poisoned belief system is only used as a precursor for control.

She wrongly learned the meaninglessness of individual merit based on the false premise that oppressors ignored individual merit in favor of identity oppression. The theoretical foundation was purposely backwards to exert control. In a childlike fashion, Audrey was taught to call people names until they acquiesced to her demands. She learned to put identity markets over skill and accomplishment and because of her victim status as a low-income female; she was free to behave however she chose without consequence.

She learned the teachings. Then she experienced how this attitude didn't serve her in the real world where 95% of the population knew the entire thought foundation was garbage created to push institutional control.

Audrey later learned the chaos stemming from this false belief system has destroyed every society it touched throughout not only Earth's history, but every galactic society's history.

The university also programmed Audrey to *feel and react, not to think*. The world was an oppressive hell for everyone except the privileged, all with similar identity markers in the world's power structures. *Feel. Not think*. If she understood and practiced critical thinking, she would have realized the entire belief system was trash.

By the end of college, she learned to hate, and she knew misery. Audrey developed a deep hatred of everything, and she wore that hate with a constant scowl on her face and looks of disdain and contempt everywhere she went. She learned to abhor her family, teachers, and bosses as oppressors and lacked any capability to be in a meaningful relationship.

Guys ran from her before the third date. She considered trying to like women, but they were all such catty bitches. Her childhood set her up as a victim, and now her college programming turned her into a permanent sufferer. Audrey was indeed wounded, and the programming ran deep. She was a victim of her selfishness and narcissism.

When Audrey graduated college, she dated a guy she adored and made it to a third date. She got pregnant, and he ghosted her. His drug addiction landed him in rehabilitation. He then disappeared from her life. Nine months later, she bore her son at 22 years old and transitioned to a hate-filled single mom working at a coffee shop. She didn't just loathe the guy who got her pregnant; she abhorred him and wanted him dead. Audrey prayed constantly to a God she couldn't believe in to have him overdose on whatever cocktail of drugs he took. Unbeknownst to her, that particular prayer materialized. He died from a drug overdose when her boy turned two years of age. She never knew. He became an overdose statistic after he freebased fentanyl contaminated heroin.

For Audrey Smith, every day was an exercise in rancor and oppression. She could never have predicted an alien would change her life's attitude and outlook. How could she have anticipated it? She pondered this as she sat in the employee bathroom at the coffee shop. Her head exploded in rage from a simple, yet meaningful post-it note stuck to a mirror. Only this time, the rage differed. The truth of her life and attitudes honed her anger.

Her mind's eye replayed her childhood selfishness and the episodes. She replayed how everyone around her enabled her, either out of fear, laziness, or manipulation. Audrey realized her only persistent problem was her own victimhood and belief system. For the first time in her young life, she understood empowerment. The foreign feeling invaded her nervous system and set up shop. But instead of rejecting the emotion, she embraced it in her heart. The walls of hate inside her crumbled. She knew a drastic and seismic mental change occurred within her. Audrey's entire attitude and outlook on life transformed. She experienced peace and wanted more or it. She hoped she could meet the alien again to both thank him and apologize for her behavior.

CHAPTER 49

Newton and the twins recovered on the ship's bridge, contemplating their next interaction with Earth. The visit would wait until the hangovers subsided.

Em and Emone looked identically bad, even in suffering. Twins from their planet are a strange phenomenon. Their equally bloodshot eyes and puffed eyelids made them look like they ended up in the losing end of a brawl.

Newton asked them how much they drank. They responded they consumed the same amount. The twins weighed the same, had identical metabolic processes and ate the same diets. They weren't so much twins as clones. They sprawled out on the couch listening to peaceful flute music, trying not to spill hangover tea on its fine upholstery.

Olsen, the source of the relaxing flute music, chimed in on their condition.

"You all look pathetic. Serves you right. I warned you."

Em cleared his dried and dehydrated throat. His tongue felt swollen and too big for his mouth. He offered a muffled response, like he had a mouth full of small rocks.

He mumbled,

"Mind your own business, you nanny state pile of circuits."

The ship's bridge was crowded this sullen morning with more than hangovers.

Five apparitions occupied different spots in the main cabin of the Wingate. Bishop Kimble and Darcy Shank were in this for the long haul. They only disappeared when Newton shut down the temporal plane.

That only happened when they moved the ship outside the galactic government orbit zone. Moving consumed time, so they left the technology active despite the constant inconvenience of the non-living mulling about the ship's bridge.

The three other beings appeared to all die together. Newton didn't recognize the species. These lizard-like aliens explained to the twins how one moment they caught a magnetic wave black hole surfing and the next moment they teleported to a waiting room. It took time to figure out they had died. Black hole surfing was an adventure sport with expensive spacecraft, allowing the ship to get caught in the vortex of a black hole. The gravitational pull is one of the strongest forces in the universe. He hoped their last ride was worth it.

A lizard-like being kept staring at Newton.

He said in a polite tone,

"I recognize you. I broke up with my wife at your restaurant. Looks like she is getting the last laugh."

With that, they looked at their devices and vanished.

Bishop sat slumped in a chair, looking forlorn. He wasn't enjoying being dead. Darcy had demands. Newton knew she had demands because she made them.

"I don't know who you are and what this is, but I have been able to piece this fact together. You can get me to Earth. Take me there so I can kill my husband."

Em spit up his hangover tea and said with a sly grin,

"You should invite him to Indigo restaurant."

The comment hurt. Newton didn't need his appetizer fork issues inflamed.

Newton looked at Darcy and noticed human features. She wore different clothing than current Earthlings.

He asked,

"What is your name?" Newton tried to be polite and thought it a nice way to pass time while they decided on their next steps.

She responded. Her crisp words read out like a history recital.

"Darcy Shank. I died in Earth year 1860. For some reason, my husband is still alive at 203 years old. The normal lifespan for humans is 60 years."

Newton and the twins perked up at hearing this. Suspicious, to be sure.

Emone scratched his head and sat in a momentary silence. Sam's lifespan was a high magnitude, statistical outlier.

Emone asked,

"Excuse me, are you saying your husband has outlived you by 143 Earth years? This is strange."

Darcy now had their attention. The aliens all learned to pay attention to anomalies in universal order. They were always meaningful.

She looked relieved someone was listening to her, even these oddballs. She experienced difficulty wrapping her year 1860 brain around current events. The concept of alien life forms beyond Earth was foreign to her and even though she interacted with aliens in the afterlife, it remained a mental challenge. She thought the complaints department alien just paid her lip service.

Darcy continued.

"Yes, correct. We were both born in Earth's year 1820. I died of natural causes in 1880. For some reason, he is still alive. I think it related to the damn goose."

When Darcy said this, Newton observed the twins' reaction. Em's head snapped back so hard it sent a jolt down his body and spilled tea in his lap. When so-called coincidences pile up, one must pay attention.

Em spit out.

"Did you say goose?"

Darcy wondered why, of all things, the bird got such laser focus.

She responded,

"Yes, he spent thirty-five years before I died rocking on our porch staring at a goose and mumbling incoherently. I could swear he communicated with it somehow. The bird just sat there ogling him and giving him the stink eye. You know how they are. I thought he needed medical help. But when he wasn't sitting on the porch staring away, he was the man I married, a loving, providing and supportive husband. Please understand, we were simple country people living simple lives. We also bore no children; I was unable to provide them."

The three aliens stared wide-eyed at Darcy. She captured their rapt attention.

Emone's jaw slacked.

He asked,

"Do you think it's Mr. Goose?"

Newton responded,

"I do. We should pay a visit to your husband, Darcy. Would you like to see him again? Can you assure us you will not try to kill him?"

Tears welled up in Darcy's eyes. She suddenly loved Sam deeply, and the universe gave her the vision to see the bigger picture after her death. Darcy experienced a great relief envelope her soul. A chapter of the universe's story neared an end.

She whispered her answer.

"Yes, I would like that very much. I want to understand, not kill him. Will I be able to hold his hand?"

Newton smiled. He could sense a great weight lifted from her shoulders.

It enveloped the room in a peaceful bliss.

He responded.

"Yes, we can set the temporal plane so you can have physical contact with him."

Bishop flashed an evil grin. He would hang around longer. He owed this purple skinned character a broken jaw.

Newton said,

"Olsen, locate Sam Shank. Let's go visit."

CHAPTER 50

The ship landed in the crop field about a quarter mile from the Shank residence. Darcy paced in circles around the spacecraft's cabin. Her eyes widened, and her nervous energy filled the room with anticipation. Even the morose Bishop shared in the excitement. He looked forward to meeting someone who lived past two hundred years old. Newton decided he would go alone. It would be easier for Sam to meet one alien versus three. Coupled with news, he could see his wife again; they didn't want to upset him. Em and Emone agreed. The last time they interacted with Earth's country folk, they earned themselves a mighty hangover.

Newton made the short walk from the farm field to the house and saw Sam standing outside. He shared a broad smile permeating from the peace within the man. He walked up to the alien, extending his hand.

Sam said,

"Welcome, I have been expecting you."

Newton understood he spoke with no ordinary human. This man knew. He emanated power and grace from knowledge, and deeper still, an understanding. Despite his 203 years of age, his eyes danced with life, taking in everything around him, and his balanced and serene energy projected from his aura. He did not foresee Sam *expecting* an alien ship to land in his backyard.

Newton said,

"Nice to meet you."

If he communicated with Mr. Goose, Sam learned Earth's accurate history for the past 150 years and probably longer. Given the nature of history repeating, blanks become easy to fill. Sam's eyes penetrated everything in their path. This would also mean he understood human nature more than any Earthling. He became enlightened through knowledge.

Newton asked,

"Do you know why I am here?"

Sam locked eyes with him and formed an immediate connection. A silent understanding occurred. A connection of their intuition powered by divine will.

He answered,

"Not specifically, but I believed you would visit. I don't question why the universe works in the manner in which it does. I accept everything as it is. Would you like a cup of coffee or tea? I suspect we have much to discuss."

Sam felt complete peace and no threat from an alien's presence.

Newton answered,

"Yes, that would be nice."

They entered his modest household and smelled a fresh pot of coffee brewing. Sam beckoned Newton to have a seat at his kitchen table. The simple yet elegant interior of Sam's home impressed him. Every detail presented divine order.

Newton affixed his gaze to the large painting hanging over the fireplace. It was of Sam's wife, Darcy, but a younger version of her. Darcy looked in her thirties in the painting. Her long, flowing auburn hair and crisp blue eyes jumped from the artwork, filling the room with love. The artist captured her delicate, even cream skin tone with perfection. She wore a long, flowing dress reserved for ballroom dances and special events of the era. Sam noticed the alien's gaze on the picture.

He said,

"That is my wife. She passed away many years ago, and I miss her dearly."

Newton did not yet mention Darcy. First, he wanted to understand the goose business.

He responded, being respectful of the situation.

"She was a beautiful woman. You are a blessed and lucky man. I am sure she returned much love and kindness."

Sam sat quietly and Newton could see the joy spread across his face as he focused on the painting. The love for his wife lasted forever, even years after her death.

Sam said,

"I never remarried. I always felt our souls united on a mission of togetherness. It is not something I can explain, but I sense it in my heart."

Sam refocused his gaze back on Newton and shared his welcoming smile again. He changed the subject and asked,

"What can I do for you? It is not every day, or any day, an alien shows up on your doorstep. And even though I foresaw of your arrival; I do not know why."

Newton wondered how to start the conversation. This man possessed vast knowledge, so being direct was probably best.

Newton said,

"Tell me about the goose."

Sam laughed. He initially considered the alien visited because he outlived every human in recent memory. But the goose? While certainly an oddity, how the extraterrestrial knew stunned him. He poured their coffee and took a sip before answering.

"The goose? I thought you arrived for a different reason. But now that you mention it, that makes sense too. Initially, it scared me, and I teetered on the edge of insanity. But you probably have heard the saying, *if you think you're insane, you aren't.*"

Newton's ears perked up. He responded,

"Please continue. I will of course, tell you everything I know as well."

Sam said,

"About the year 1843 or so, random thoughts started popping into my head. I enjoyed sitting on my porch after a day's work while sipping homemade tea or water. It gave me the time and space to reflect on the grace God has allowed. The gifts of a beautiful life, loving wife, and excellent health are my grace. I've been blessed with everything needed in this lifetime and made it a habit to offer daily gratitude. My life is filled with absolute peace."

Sam took another sip of coffee and continued.

"These odd foreign thoughts continued in my head. They seemed to be world events with names and places I did not recognize. I never attended school, and I was home-taught to read and write and to perform basic math. My education focused on how to live correctly, through the grace of God. I always hoped I lived to that end. I've never watched news, don't own a computer, and never owned a telephone or television."

"The thoughts intensified and became more frequent, and I observed they only materialized when the goose visited the pond. A strange phenomenon, to be certain. I understand geese have lifetime partners and a lifespan of fifteen years. I'm quite certain this has been the same one my entire life. This seems an odd anomaly."

Sam's words were crisp and without hesitation.

He said,

"I don't believe in coincidence. My poor wife thought I lost my mind, and I agreed at first. I prayed on the subject. This is where I figured it out. I would occasionally visit the town library and research headlines in daily newspapers. Much to my surprise, the events popping into my head were actual recent news stories. It baffled me. I also understood this phenomenon was not for me to question. But it confirmed I was not going crazy."

He stopped to notice if the alien followed and to gauge any reaction. Newton sat fully focused on his words.

Sam continued,

"Through the years, I developed a working theory. The world's geese population must be connected, and the goose on my pond seems to broadcast messages, filtered to only certain events. For reasons beyond my understanding, I am in tune with the message."

Sam stopped for a moment to consider if he left out any important details. He wanted to provide as succinct a summary as he could muster. He sat and waited for a response, smelling how the natural aroma of the fresh coffee blended with the rustic smell of his home.

Newton was impressed with Sam's ability to connect the dots on the goose.

He responded.

"Your working theory is mostly correct. I think I can fill in some gaps for you. However, I do not understand how you are tuned into the goose frequency. The coffee is delicious."

He added this as he took another sip. The java tasted much better than the swill he tried in Seattle.

Newton continued.

"The geese are not of this planet. I will spare you the detailed history for now. The short story is they got transported to Earth as part of a surveillance operation. They have the capability to broadcast events as a hive mind. They simply observe and report, without even realizing it is happening, and have no opinion of what they message whatsoever. This means you have been tuned into the planet's unfiltered history for the past 180 years. This most likely makes you the most informed human on Earth."

Sam pondered this information and added.

"Our planet and its people are on life support and are about to self-destruct."

What a unique human being, Newton thought.

He told him the purpose of their visit.

"Yes, and thus, the reason for our visit. We are attempting to prevent this from happening."

Sam studied the alien being and he could sense his empathy for the Earthlings. He could feel the alien's love for the living and Newton's non-violent nature. He could also sense this extraterrestrial had evolved well beyond the typical Earthling. His features looked sad by comparing his facial expressions to a human facial structure, but underneath, he could sense a strength in him emanating from a place of contentment and self-understanding.

Sam asked.

"Do you mind me asking how? Everything I understand tells me the trajectory is set in place and can only be changed by a significant shock to the social ecosystem. The average person seems oblivious to the current state of affairs, content to watch the planet burn to the ground so long as they are able to watch sports and other forms of entertainment. Apathy and ignorance are a powerful destructive force."

The alien would share everything and was certain Sam would leave Earth. He had no place here. Newton knew Sam had achieved his level of enlightenment through the power of knowledge and truth. This Earthling understood the essence of self, and therefore, the true nature of existence. The combination of understanding true substance and applying it to the unfiltered information he received led him to the only logical conclusion. Humans found themselves in deep trouble, with nobody else to blame.

Newton asked him point blank.

"Sam, what are your thoughts on coming with us once we have completed our mission?"

He didn't think long about his answer.

"I expected you would ask me to join you."

Newton considered his job here complete.

"Good, glad to hear. Gather what you would like to bring. It is time to go. It will be quite an adventure for you. Also, your wife is looking forward to seeing you."

Sam got up from his seat when he heard this last bit. He stopped cold and turned, his eyes welling up with happiness. His knees buckled, and he grabbed the table for support.

"My wife?"

Newton smiled.

"Yes, I will explain how later, but she is on our ship. This is another reason we are here."

Sam neared tears. The gratitude he felt at having another opportunity to see his twin flame filled the room.

He asked.

"Can I bring my cat? I would hate to leave him here alone."

The alien nodded in agreement.

Sam yelled back to one of the bedrooms.

"Asscat, let's go."

Newton turned his head in curiosity.

He said,

"Did you just say Asscat?"

Sam responded from down the hall.

"Yes, that is my cat's name."

Newton found this fascinating. He named his cat after a galactic television award, but then again, there are no coincidences. Sam carried the Asscat out of the house on a purple pillow with royal yellow tassels. He brought a backpack with a change of clothes and nothing else. The end of harvest season neared and nothing was happening on the farm. Change blew through the air with the autumn leaves as they walked back to the ship.

CHAPTER 51

Newton walked onto the bridge after much-needed sleep. The luxury sleeping quarters on the Wingate were meticulously tailored, including entertainment networks from any species' home planet. While he watched almost no television, he sometimes enjoyed local entertainment from the planet Zang, especially when he felt homesick. He saw an advertisement for his now ex-wife's travel agency and had kind thoughts. He hoped she was well.

When Newton entered the bridge, both Em and Emone looked at him with broad grins on their faces. They were up to no good.

Newton knew he just involuntarily enlisted for something mischievous. Now he needed to find out what.

Em's excitement fostered a bouncing impatience and he couldn't wait. The words raced out of him.

"Newton, my friend. We did some additional Earth research with Olsen and stumbled upon a significant series of flaws in the Earth's election process. It is laughable."

Newton felt a chill, and his skin tingled. This happened as an alert to his nervous system. He knew Em hatched a plan.

Newton thought of stopping the scheme in its tracks. He had an uneasy feeling.

He said,

"We know Earth's rulers have been in charge for 4,000 years while creating the illusion of freedom and choice. I am not surprised to learn their elections are rigged. For the rulers to stay in power, they must maintain control of the political class. Logically, they would need to control election outcomes. Of course, exceptions existed throughout Earth's history, but these rarities were mistakes or temporarily planned pullbacks of control to continue the perception of freedom."

Em interrupted his pontification.

"Yes Newton, of course, but this is preposterous. As you are aware, the Earth does not have global governance. They have near global governance, but their people continue to suffer under the illusion they don't. The prevalent governing structure is sovereign nation-states, and I use the term *sovereign* in theory. For an unevolved planet like Earth, small sovereign nations with hands-off self-governance are the best model until the species evolves. Any type of global-level governance will always turn into tyranny for the unevolved. The current rulers understand this dynamic. For centuries, they ruthlessly exploited the Earthlings and prevented them from evolving."

Em stopped to ensure Newton paid attention. He ran his hand through his mohawk front to back and continued.

"The country they call America is of particular interest. Their founders set up a system whereby the smaller parts called states are like their own sovereign countries, but united as one under a document titled *The Constitution*. It is the supreme law of their land and it deems the basic rights of the people are provided by God, not the government. This is, of course, correct. Every nation and world that has existed throughout history where rights are determined by government ends in tyranny. But the proper dynamic cannot exist without a moral population. The system is of no use in a morally bankrupt society. Nowadays, this constitution is largely ignored because it prevents the ruling class from doing their thing. They created a federal-level government that is supposed to represent the interests of the states and the citizens. Over time, this federal bureaucracy has usurped the states and taken over the nation. And that government is controlled by the corporate oligarchs, not the individuals it is intended to support. The state level governments have been usurped as well. Here is the interesting point,"

Em sat on the edge of his seat and reached his conclusion. He could barely hide his excitement and was almost bouncing on the sofa.

"A state named New York allows non-citizens, *they call them illegal aliens*, to run for and hold political office! Can you believe this? The media and the politicians brainwashed the humans to such an extreme degree they allow people who are not Americans, or even residents of their own locality, to vie for political office. They also allow them to vote. The practice begs for infiltration, takeover, and chaos. The law is one of the dumbest political practices we ever witnessed. It is tragically stupid and clearly part of the ruling class plan."

Newton smiled. He knew where this was going.

He asked, knowing the answer.

"You're kidding right?"

Em responded.

"No, I am not joking. There is an upcoming election to choose a replacement figurehead for New York. We recommend you run for governor, which is the lead state executive position. You would run against the current governor, a typical Earth politician, and a citizen from a country in South America, a country that openly wants to see this country of America destroyed. The South American is leading in early polling. The ruling class doesn't care who wins, they control both politicians. Can you believe the stark irrationality of this? I never recall in galactic history seeing this level of idiocy in a society. It would be like having a Zatosian vie for elected office on your home planet of Zang."

Newton was flabbergasted. His mind searched for historical reference, but nothing registered. He asked for Olsen's input.

"Olsen, can you provide a search of galactic history to check if this has ever happened?"

The AI unit whirred to life.

"Already did for Em and Emone. I had to dig, meaning instead of having an answer in one second or less, it took me three seconds. The occurrences of past timelines were through covert infiltration. It has never happened interplanetary. But on some planets with similar government structures, multi-country sovereign nations, it has happened when a nation accepted another's nation's citizens as their own. They realized after granting them citizenship they were infiltrators. Otherwise, Earth's people are the first civilization in galactic history, either stupid enough or unevolved enough to allow this. It will not end well for them should they proceed."

They all stared in shock. The Earthlings possessed a terminally unique feature, albeit a destructive one. Newton considered maybe the humans were not worth saving. It was his first instance of having that thought. This level of stupidity is unprecedented in the entirety of galactic history. It is like inviting a deranged serial killer over for dinner, giving him a knife while unarmed, and pretending nothing will happen.

He said,

"I love the idea. Of course, I would never assume office. It would absolutely fit the mission. We will need to discuss with Qunot. Olsen, can you calculate my odds of becoming the Governor of New York and what the steps are to make it happen?"

Olsen beeped twice and the lights on the bridge dimmed and silhouetted with a light purple hue for the excitement of the upcoming announcement. The ship's artificial intelligence module was a drama queen.

"Newton, if you run for governor, you have a 97% chance of winning, with my help, of course. That is without cheating. They will cheat. Once you are legally on the ballot, we expect an existential fear reaction from the ruling class. The maneuver's brilliance is becoming governor in a tiny state in America carries little power. It has always been a figurehead position. A signature process is required to appear on the ballot. I can expedite and complete this process. We already gathered the email addresses of every registered voter. Conveniently, 10% of what they call registered voters are dead, don't live there, are non-citizens, or just plain made-up people. Another 15% are citizens who never vote. The votes are unknowingly placed on their behalf, if needed, to get the preferred candidate in office. Machines are used to vote. They control the system architecture of the machines from end to end. They also do not allow audits of the machines, software, the voting process or the voter rolls. Everything is done behind closed doors or systems and the media runs cover for the fraud with countless *safe and secure election* stories. Elections are pointless. But they do it to both continue the illusion of freedom of choice and also it is quite a money laundering operation back to the politicians."

Olsen continued.

"On voting day, we'll block all incoming algorithms so the vote totals are legitimate and also wipe the voter rolls of the 10% no longer eligible. They will be *unable* to utilize the 15% who don't vote because of our system firewall. Our security technology is far superior to Earth's. We are going to facilitate and witness the first clean election in New York state in the past 200 years. Before they implemented the corrupted electronic voting systems, they used paper ballots. They cheated by stuffing the ballot boxes. For a short time, they implemented mail-in ballots, but they were such a fraudulent joke America's highest court outlawed them nationwide. The only reason they became implemented was a massive propaganda operation led by politicians and the media. Earthlings believe *anything* their televisions and devices say. They refuse to think for themselves."

Newton pondered all this. It was nothing new. Galactic history was littered with this nonsense. Olsen finished with a final thought.

"A campaign is unnecessary. You will need to attend one debate against the other two candidates. I can design campaign ads for you."

Newton realized the worst part of where Earthlings stood in their evolutionary path developed from an appalling lack of self-awareness. This cause manifested an inability to comprehend the true nature of evil among them. The vast majority of humans are good, but either blinded to the evil, or in denial it exists.

Emone finally said something.

"We already cleared this with Qunot while you were resting. We can proceed. He loves the idea and wishes he came up with it himself."

CHAPTER 52

"Let's sample Earth's dining experience."

Em suggested this, probably to dig Newton about his vast restaurant expertise. They knew given human proclivities, it would be a horrible experience.

Em asked,

"Olsen, find us a restaurant popular with Earthlings."

The AI unit played soft dinner music and dimmed the lights before giving an answer.

"I am warning you. What is popular to humans is guaranteed to offend your sense of taste and décor. And before you chide me, I will answer the question. The most popular restaurants on the planet are corporate chain restaurants in suburban areas. They include Flingers, Peppers, Thursdays, Honeybees and Crabbys, to name a few. They are all owned by the same conglomerate and serve the same low-quality garbage they pass off as food. The gastronomical experience ranges from difficult to insulting."

Newton said,

"Let's try Peppers."

Olsen continued,

"The establishment in question is a stand-alone strip mall building in a town named Jupiter in the state named Florida. Most towns in Florida comprise extensive networks of strip malls and lack any originality. Newly organized towns in America are all modeled under the corporate consumerism model. The bland architecture and chain retail environment produce the illusion of uniqueness veiled by intentional low budget city planning. All social gathering areas are geared towards spending, and all corporate chains are owned by the ruling class as high margin minimum wage slave shops. Americans are socially conditioned to low-quality garbage since birth and this conditioning forces them to not only accept poor experiences, but to demand them. The entire chain restaurant industry is based on this premise. Peppers is one of those places."

Newton, Sam, and the twins took the shuttle for this excursion. It was a small craft used as either an emergency pod or small landing trips. The Wingate had two pods to accommodate up to 12 beings, the spaceship's capacity. Each pod could accommodate six. Conveniently, it fit in a handicapped parking spot. The parking lot was full, so they parked the pod in the only spot available.

When they entered the foyer, they stood in line at the host stand, waiting to be seated. The exuberant young male shared the excitement of the Peppers' experience with the vim and vigor of a restaurant shareholder.

They approached, and he said,

"Welcome to Peppers! I assume you are here for the science fiction trivia and costume contest! It is going to be a fun night. Just an absolute blast. You will need to watch out for table seven. They are outer space nerds galore and have won the game for three months straight. Follow me please."

Em looked at Newton, tilted his head, and shrugged his shoulders. The entire exchange was lost on all of them.

The host led them to a booth, which was one of a series of twelve identical booths surrounding a square bar. The booths and chairs were covered in a cheap blue and white striped pleather veneer. The opening exchange with the overexcited greeter and seater, which had been lost on them, came into full focus as they took their seats.

In each booth sat a trivia team dressed as them!

Some booths contained one Newton and two or three twins.

The cleverer contestants dressed as the twins, Bishop Kimble and a single Newton.

A far booth contained all three aliens and their county's President chained to them.

Em looked at the host, still confused.

He asked,

"Why is everyone dressed like us?"

The effervescent equivalent to a maître d' laughed.

He said,

"All you science fiction trivia types are the same. You think you are the actual aliens. Like they would be caught dead in a dump like this. You don't have to butter me up. I am not judging the costume contest. Here is your answer sheet. Your waiter Brad will be with you in a moment. He is the best! Have fun guys."

He left. At least they now understood the oddity.

Brad showed up with his emotive in high gear. He wore the standard Pepper's uniform with black pants, a blue shirt matching the cheap upholstery of the booths, and black suspenders. His acne condition informed the aliens he was between 16 and 18 years old and the parade of cliched buttons pinned to his suspenders said he was a high-riser in the fast-paced world of faux corporate waitstaff. Newton counted 34 buttons, each with an annoying kindergarten level emotional platitude meant to show the restaurant patron exactly how exciting their meal would be.

Brad said,

"Welcome to Pepper's trivia night. You all look fabulous. Nice work on the costumes, although I must say there is some fierce competition in the house tonight. I hope you have a blast with our game. Our host, Matty the Super Alien, is the best. Can I start you off with our specialty drink, the Super-Duper-Fruity-Fruiter and a plate of our famous Peppers Poppers?"

Em and Emone jumped in.

"Yes, one of each for each of us."

Newton and Sam said in unison.

"Just water please."

Brad the fabulous frowned at the water only orders, and bustled away to get their drinks. He wore a button on his suspenders that read *Aliens are Real* with a picture of Newton's face.

Newton laughed. What a society.

He said to Sam,

"Has your society always been this display of low-quality commercialization couched in inauthentic emotional manipulation? In other words, has it always been this fake?"

Sam's face twisted up in thought.

He said,

"I lived a reclusive life, so this is all new to me and I have no historical context beyond what the geese have told me. Quite possible."

Newton shared his opinion.

"It seems to me not only have Earthlings been socially conditioned to accept their slave system but also accept poor quality lives and experiences within this matrix. They know what *better* is. They are reaching for it and screaming for it from within, but everything surrounding them is corporatist garbage, especially in this nation they call America. I think they reluctantly accept it because they have no other choice."

Em and Emone nodded in agreement, sharing the observation.

The emotive waiter returned with the twins' rum drinks and appetizers. They made a point to tell him they needed nothing else for the time being to avoid him coming by five times to ask them how *everything came out*.

The contest started.

Matty the emcee said,

"Welcome everyone to the famous Peppers science fiction trivia night in honor of those famous aliens visiting our humble planet. We hope you are watching! Sharpen your pencils, you know the drill. Twenty questions will appear on the television one question at a time. When I finish reading, each team has five minutes to contemplate and discuss before we move onto the next riddle. Answer sheets are turned in at the end of the session and fifteen minutes later, we will award prizes to the top three teams in both contests."

He pressed a button on his sound board, which played some deep-thinking music in the background.

He continued.

"The questions move from easy to difficult. Question one. In which book was the answer to life the number 42? You have five minutes to respond."

The aliens and Sam seated at table twelve looked lost.

Emone blustered in confusion,

"What kind of science fiction question is that? We all know the answer to life, and it is certainly not 42. I doubt if we wrote down the actual book from the planet Sutrali where this is spelled out, we would receive credit. This isn't even real sci-fi. It is Earth's made-up storyline of what they think is in space. Should we cheat and get Olsen involved?"

Newton and Sam laughed at Emone and his competitive nature. They noticed Em already wrote an answer, albeit a wrong one.

Newton said,

"Let's try our best without Olsen's help. Also, keep in mind that sci-fi is fake and we live in real outer space. This trivia is about Earth stories, not space reality."

Eleven questions later, they were certain they answered zero of them correct.

They turned in their sheet anyway to Matty the emcee, who complimented them on their alien *costumes*.

They didn't fare well in either the trivia or the costume contest.

The tab came and Newton instructed the excitable waiter Brad to pay for every table participating in trivia. Olsen funded a debit card from a bank account he created by simply adding money to the ledger from the sale of treasuries, the same method the government used to print money and indenture the nation. Another $100,000 wouldn't matter and a $2,000 bar tab at Peppers also wouldn't raise any flags.

They returned from the ship embarrassed and humiliated by the Pepper's experience. The ship's AI unit offered his opinion of their troubled evening.

Olsen said,

"Allow me to recap the evening. Em and Emone ate five plates of Peppers Poppers combined with three Super-Duper-Fruity-Fruiters Rum drinks *each*, umbrellas included, and are now in the bathroom or the medical bay detoxifying the results of their poor decisions. You came in last out of 12 teams in a science fiction trivia game, *as actual aliens*, and you came in *fourth* in an alien costume contest where contestants dressed as you three. And to top it all off, you received a parking violation for placing the space pod in a reserved spot for people with disabilities. Does this sound right?"

Newton said,

"Shut up Olsen. Make sure the parking ticket is paid."

CHAPTER 53

The ill-fated rock star Bishop Kimble slumped against the wall in the ship's corner, draining Newton's energy. Acceptance would alleviate the problem, and Newton could tell he experienced a difficult time facing a highly improbable reality. He became the first human in Earth's history to be killed by aliens.

This event was so improbable to the Earth, given its remote location relative to the civilized part of the galaxy and the laws against visiting the planet, it was bound to happen sooner or later to some unlucky soul.

Improbability, meet unlucky soul Bishop Kimble, who sat vacillating between depression and anger.

Newton thought of an idea to possibly cheer him up.

He asked,

"What is the name of your music group?"

Bishop looked over at the purple-hued death-warmed-over alien and glared at him. More sarcasm seemed proper.

He asked,

"What difference does it make now?"

Newton was already bored with the conversation. If Bishop wanted to act glum and self-deprecating, what was the point?

Newton responded.

"Just taking an interest. I thought it would be a more productive conversation than you continually blaming us for your untimely demise."

After some silence, Bishop considered little harm in telling him. At least he took somewhat of an interest, even if it seemed inauthentic.

He mumbled an answer.

"The Gatewoods."

Newton wanted to get him talking positively about his life, so he requested more information.

"Cool name for a band. Tell me more."

Newton also considered if he kept the conversation going, maybe he would leave.

Bishop warmed to the questioning and answered him in a full voice.

"There isn't much to tell. My closest friend growing up, Johnny Crisco, and I started playing music in our garage. We could both sing and play guitar and shared great musical chemistry. This started eons ago when we attended high school. We found a bass player, drummer and keyboardist and started the group. The band was named to honor our grandmother using her maiden name. We were cousins. She always supported our music and creativity, so we named the band after her. We played great rock and roll."

Bishop looked at Newton and could see he had his undivided attention. He continued.

"We ended up with vastly different lifestyles, but we were always great friends and, of course, family. Johnny married his college sweetheart. I never married and got into too many different drugs and lots of booze. I've attended rehabilitation several times. The saddest part of my death is timing. I was on a prodigious bender and stopped at the golf course because my father used to take me there as a kid. Its raw beauty and how the course molded itself to the ocean always took my breath away. It was reminiscent of fine art in real life. Before my untimely death, I felt the hand of God reach down from the heavens and touch me. The raging obsession to live through chemical dependency lifted. Then, ten seconds later, I died."

Bishop finished again by reminding the alien he indeed murdered him. The fact his ship's computer did it was beside the point.

Newton processed this information and felt deep empathy for this human. He witnessed the ravages of drug and alcohol addiction in his prior life as a maître d'. The planet Gastrin had a sister planet devoted to rehabilitation centers for the planet's workforce.

He said,

"I understand it can be difficult to have chemical dependency. I have seen it a lot in my line of work. The timing of your death is quite unfortunate and improbable, but we cannot reverse it."

Newton then shifted gears.

"Olsen, can you check if *The Gatewoods* have any concerts scheduled?"

The AI unit whirred to life. One second passed.

"They have just one. It is a tribute concert to Bishop Kimble happening in a football stadium in Santa Clara, United States."

The rock star closed his eyes and looked like he slipped into meditation. He emanated gratitude, a major improvement over anger and depression.

Newton said,

"Olsen, please contact the communication device of Johnny Crisco, so we can play a video call here on the ship. It is righteous and fair for Bishop to say goodbye to his friend. Let's attend the concert. I'm sure Em and Emone would enjoy another night of debauchery."

Olsen made beeping sounds to let everyone hear he was doing something. Five minutes passed. Bishop still sat with his eyes closed, and Newton noticed a seismic shift in his attitude and facial expression. He looked like he neared acceptance, and he hoped by allowing him to talk to his friend, he would get closure.

Olsen chimed in.

"Your call is now ready."

Newton woke Bishop from his trance and the ship's monitor came to life. On the screen they saw the entire band, *The Gatewoods*.

Johnny Crisco, Bishop's cousin, best friend, guitarist and vocalist, Stormin' Norman, the bass player, Donny Silver, the drummer, and Wags Ivory, the keyboardist.

They were stunned to be talking to Bishop. They attended his funeral a few days ago. Nobody could speak. The combination of having their computer patched into an alien spaceship so they could chat with their deceased band member stunned them into silence.

Newton broke the ice.

"Hi, how are you all? I know this is probably quite a shock. We don't have time to explain the technology allowing this to happen. It is unimportant. We thought it nice for you to have an opportunity to talk to your bandmate as he left your planet without saying goodbye."

After more award pause, Johnny spoke first.

"Bishop, how the hell are ya?"

He tried to sound upbeat, but had difficulty choosing the proper tone to use with someone who had just died. He also considered using the word *hell* in poor taste, considering Bishop's lifestyle.

Bishop smiled. He would not be outdone.

"I am dead Johnny. How do you think I am? These aliens murdered me because their ship's computer is a dipshit who doesn't understand how to pilot a takeoff without burning everything in its path. But other than being dead, just fine."

His sarcasm wasn't lost on the group.

He continued.

"I heard you are doing a tribute concert for me. That is very kind. Who is gonna sing for me? Hopefully not you. You know you sing everything off-key."

Johnny laughed it off. Bishop became hard-of-hearing, standing in front of too many music amplifiers.

"I will sing. What we play is interchangeable."

Bishop smiled and knew he was right.

"Newton wants to go to the concert with his two alien friends. Think you can make arrangements? Can I watch it from the ship?"

Newton said he could.

Johnny clenched his fist and held it up in the air in approval.

He said,

"Damn right, that would be cool. I hope nobody is looking to arrest you for what happened to Bishop. Technically, you committed murder-one."

Newton didn't understand the last part of the sentence, so he ignored it and said,

"Olsen, please coordinate arrangements with Johnny for the concert."

One week out, enough time for Newton to attend a political debate to become the next governor of New York. He retired to his quarters and gave Bishop all the time he needed with his band.

CHAPTER 54

Newton sent out a pre-recorded campaign speech, which he provided to Rachel Dougherty for public consumption. It made worldwide headlines. The consensus showed America slipped off its rocker suffering from a combination of terminal insanity and decadent idiocy. Foreign media companies aired nonstop parody about the country. The jokes wrote themselves.

In Newton's speech, he announced since New York's state laws allowed non-citizens to run for office; he planned to seek election for governor.

Olsen ensured he not only met the signature requirements, but smashed them. New York required 500,000 verified signatures to appear on the ballot as an independent. This meant unaffiliated with the archaic and useless dual political party system, both of which were captured organizations working towards the same end. Olsen acquired seven million signatures in a state with a population of twenty million. It only took 12 hours to gather the signatures. Apparently, New York's people were fed up with the status quo.

Olsen filed all the paperwork and paid for the registrations. With little fanfare, Newton's candidacy became official.

There would be no fundraising or campaigning. The media would inadvertently perform Newton's campaign stumping for him by repeating anything and everything he said on the worldwide stage. The absurdity of an alien running for a state-level governorship was publicity enough. Journo jackals couldn't get enough of it. The talking heads debate cycle shifted into overdrive, all breathlessly screaming their worthless opinions over one another, seeking their ill intended false fame.

Only two items of interest existed in the campaign process. With the election not far off, Newton needed to record a message of his campaign promises and also attend the debate, which was scheduled for five days before voting.

Mr. Goose picked up on the news. He couldn't yet draw a conclusion and would wait to form an opinion based on the reaction of the ruling class. Sam also knew. Despite sitting on the ship, he found himself still connected to the goose hive mind. He thought it strange, but dismissed it.

The puppet masters and the political class considered suing to stop an actual alien from running for governor. They realized they cornered themselves by their own narrative and a lawsuit would hang them from their own petard. If they sued, then their entire global citizenship story, vital to their continued push for one-world governance, would fall apart. They realized it also contradicted what they presented through the media, which was the extraterrestrials were fake. The rulers also agreed it would help their narrative about the aliens being dangerous.

They could already visualize the fake headlines.

Alien takeover begins in New York. Save your town and country or it will progress like a disease threatening Earth's freedom. It was weak, but they ran with it. They also knew, under the current election system, Newton would only receive 12% of the vote. They knew because they perfected controlling the outcome of elections.

The handlers started to rig the polling narrative right after the announcement. They set the polling to be a neck-and-neck race between the two candidates they already owned, with Newton siphoning off about 12% of the total vote equally from each candidate. They instructed the news complex and the social media companies to ensure the fake polling numbers were blasted out daily, leading up to the election, unchanged, with plenty of man-on-the-street interviews to support the narrative. The political pundits received the same orders.

The ruling class would be blindsided by the first unaltered election in New York State history. It would prove shocking to them, as the outcomes would affect more than just the governor's race.

CHAPTER 55

The local commission scheduled New York's governor's debate in a small lakeside city in the Western part of the state named Buffalo. Olsen informed Newton the town gained fame for snow, bad sports teams, and eating the wings of a bird named a chicken while dousing them in a fiery red sauce.

It seemed odd they would only eat this appendage and discard the rest of the bird, especially a bird unable to fly. Logically, it made sense. Eat the part of the bird it didn't use. He later found out this wasn't true, but this didn't stop him from imagining millions of these birds running around without wings.

Two hundred citizens would attend in a small downtown auditorium. The rulers chose none other than media darling Rachel Dougherty to moderate the debate. To show her face in a city like Buffalo appalled her. Working-class people needed to understand their place. But on this glorious, career furthering occasion, she would slum it and be among the unwashed masses.

With the election five days away, the entire world watched and awaited the possibility of a space alien becoming a state governor. The complete measure of America's idiocy would be broadcast on full volume worldwide. New York had a non-American Earthling, an actual extraterrestrial, and a useless incumbent running for the state's highest office. The world laughed at the sheer incompetency and madness of the situation.

The debate from Buffalo morphed into the most anticipated political event in Earth's history. It became one of the most important events to occur in the sleepy, snowy town. Not since their beloved football team went to four straight championships were hopes this high; never mind they lost all four games.

The ruling class decimated the city since its heyday in the early to mid-1900s. It had been on a continual rebound for the past fifty years and never quite bounced back to its glory days of steel and auto manufacturing.

Newton arrived at the debate fifteen minutes beforehand. The ship dropped him off a few blocks away from the auditorium. He walked on the quiet, snowy city streets to the venue's back entrance. Buffalo experienced a freak October snow just for the occasion. He felt the peace of the quiet backstreet as the snow glinted through the streetlights on its slow and floating descent. A local explained to him during his walk Buffalo had two weather seasons; winter and three weeks of bad sledding. This joke was lost on him, as he didn't understand the term sledding.

Olsen pre-ordered chicken wings for everyone in attendance, plus the throng of people who stood outside watching the event on live feed. The city set up screens up and down main street. Onlookers celebrated outside in 28-degree weather with light snow falling. The atmosphere turned into a street party with vendors selling cold beer. Hundreds of news trucks from worldwide television networks crowded the snowy, narrow side streets. The media circus arrived in full swing, with the rabid clowns running around searching for the most prominent camera angles.

When Newton entered the small auditorium, the tangy aroma of the chicken wings assaulted his nasal passages making his eyes water. He never tried them, but they smelled delicious. A complimentary wing tray sat on a table near the side of the stage. The other candidates already stood at their podiums, trying to look important while being fussed about by their makeup and hair artists.

Ivana Burdle, the incumbent, slopped from the pigsty of politics for the past 25 years. A witch of a woman in her early fifties, her high bone structure and taut facial skin spoke to multiple plastic surgeries and her brown dyed hair cropped at her shoulders completed the inauthentic look. She wore a blue business suit typical of Earth women in power positions. Her constituents regularly called her Ivana the Terrible, a name which she applauded. Her first four years as governor proved disastrous for the citizens of New York. The state teetered on life support. Ivana made a Faustian bargain with the ruling class in exchange for fame and fortune, and the destruction was intentional.

Alicia Santiago, the other female candidate, hailed from a chaotic South American country. She arrived on America's doorstep illegally and still had no status as a citizen. The handlers found her to be a perfect candidate for office and she spent the past year being groomed for the role.

Newton estimated Alicia's intelligence tested in the lower one-sixth of Earth's population. She was essentially a paid actress. Despite being young and semi-attractive, the gutting of her soul at the hands of her masters permeated her aura.

Newton stepped out onto the stage and received a standing ovation. He waved to the crowd while approaching his podium and could only ponder what Bishop quipped a few days ago. The alien had reached *Rock Star* status with the people of Earth. Who better to know?

The small auditorium's poor lighting blacked out the audience to the candidates. Ample lighting haloed Rachel Dougherty, as she sat on her media throne waiting to moderate one of the greatest political events in Earth's history.

Olsen informed Newton the debate questions were leaked to the other candidates well beforehand. By leaking, the AI unit meant the handlers wrote the questions and gave them to the media and the two nominees in advance. It didn't matter. He believed after he answered the first question, they would cut off any additional air time to him. He figured he would be allowed to have an opening statement and the ability to answer one question.

Rachel Dougherty did her best to make the debate about her. The political media went to excruciating lengths to legitimize themselves as *part of* rather than *reporting on*. They couldn't help themselves; their giant egos and over-wringing sense of entitlement demanded it.

Newton noticed this in all forms of media and found it particularly disgusting in sports. He once observed a shameless and breathless sideline *reporter* at the end of an important game with a microphone rammed in a coach's face. Twelve seconds after the game ended, she badgered him with stupid emotional questions and behaved like she was part of the team. In her deluded mind, she considered herself integral to the team's success. Earth journalism appalled him. To call them shameless was unfair to people with no shame.

The stage lights dimmed. Showtime!

The crowd and the candidates went dark, and the lights shined brightly on media goddess Rachel Dougherty. She drank in the moment's fame, flipping her hair back across her shoulder and pouting her polished lips at the camera. Her career blossomed right in front of her and the eyes of one billion viewers worldwide. On the outside, her cool and calm demeanor projected professional control. Inside, she felt more aroused than she had ever been in her entire life.

She knew the handlers had already coached the two candidates on their questions. Rachel also understood they would continue to drive dual narratives. The aliens, whose authenticity was still under investigation, threatened civilization. Second, the entire alien landing was a potential ploy by countries not friendly to America. The rulers wanted the citizenry to argue about the extraterrestrials as vehemently as possible.

Every crisis must be used to gain more power and control. The more confusion and obfuscation, the better the outcome. For the ruling class, truth was always a moving target they set and controlled. The aristocrats muddied reality prime through the dirty waters of information overload, narrative seeding, and division.

Rachel opened the debate, talking about herself and her network for five full minutes, pandering to her peers. The crowd booed her. Elite journalists like her wore being booed like a badge of honor. She had nothing but disdain for the commoners.

She then started the debate, notifying each candidate they would have one minute to make an opening statement.

Ivana, being the incumbent, went first.

"It has been an honor to serve the people of New York. When I am re-elected, I will work hard to ensure our state continues to prosper. We have a wonderful opportunity to continue to add jobs and attract businesses, especially for marginalized communities. Our work cannot be done until every individual *feels* safe in every situation. We intend to look hard at hate speech, especially online, where the unbridled hate against these marginalized groups is most seen. We want a government that works to educate all children and make them *feel* safe throughout their educational journey."

The crowd booed her and chanted Ivana the Terrible. Rachel quickly stepped in to defend and hushed the unruly peasants. Alicia spoke next.

"As an immigrant, my proudest moment is to represent the people of my home country using American resources. I promise to guarantee all migrants *feel* welcome and ensure all taxpayer resources are allocated to ensure nobody who comes to our state is homeless, hungry, or their children are without an education. I will ensure anyone wishing to come to America finds sanctuary in New York, independent of where they hail. We need to make sure these poor sanctuary seekers are provided for until they can find work and sustainable housing. In addition, I intend to continue the efforts of the previous administration to eliminate fossil fuels so we can save the planet."

The crowd booed her even louder. Rachel put on her best stern mother's face and scolded them. Newton spoke last.

"You are both completely full of shit and total sellouts. My only campaign message, and the only one that matters, is this. I am not a politician seeking power and exploiting the system for my wealth and the wealth of my handlers and donors. Earth money means nothing to me. Earth's people and the ascension of your species mean everything to me."

The crowd went wild and echoed. New-ton, New-ton, New-ton. They cheered and chanted and drowned out the disgusted Rachel Dougherty for a full ten minutes. The audience, combined with the smell of chicken wing sauce and grease in the auditorium, made her nauseous.

Rachel and the handlers had no idea each chicken wing dish contained a website printed on the napkins. Food runners were hired to distribute the napkins to thousands of people inside and outside the venue. The details of the web location exploded on social media and reached most of America's population before the debate even began. Olsen also emailed the information to the entire New York State registered voter database, bypassing junk email protocols.

Olsen, the ship's artificial intelligence, graduated to more than just a super intelligent computer module, ship pilot and drama queen. He became a campaign manager, web designer and marketing guru.

The website from the chicken wing napkin listed every donor to both candidates and how those donors either already benefitted or would benefit from either candidate entering office. It depicted this damning information in its entirety.

While donor information resided in the public domain, the ruling class made the data difficult, with extensive interconnectivity. Multiple shell companies and non-profits obfuscated the individuals behind political donations. The average person had neither the time, energy nor expertise to navigate and understand the sheer density and complexity of the campaign finance process.

Olsen mapped out the donations. To make matters worse, both candidates received funding from the same nefarious donors. In addition, the parties funding them committed blatant campaign finance fraud by using unaware apolitical citizens to fund thousands of micro-donations to nominees across the country in their name. As a further incriminating footnote, the website mentioned each media organization that had access to this information, and how they hid it from the public.

After opening remarks, Rachel's earpiece, connected to her handler, beeped. Her puppet master informed her of Newton's website. The debate needed to be cut short. They would make complete fools of themselves if it continued. The handler told her what to do.

Rachel's face grew stern as she pretended to get serious.

"Please calm down, everyone. We have an emergency. Quiet please."

She begged the crowd.

Fortunately for her, the governor received the same message in her earpiece from her handler. Her bodyguards removed her from the stage in haste and local police bustled into the area. This quieted the crowd.

Rachel continued, now that she had everyone's attention.

"We have received a viable threat from a terrorist organization. This site is a potential target for an attack. We are unsure if it is related to the aliens or not. For safety, we are asking everyone to leave in an orderly manner."

The audience looked at Newton. He stood there, emanating peace with a slight smile on his face. He knew Rachel lied before Olsen confirmed she lied. The crowd fed off his calm energy and nobody panicked. They peacefully left the building.

Newton walked out the back door to his ship knowing he just won an election.

CHAPTER 56

Earth journalists, being the rabid hyenas they are, clamored to interview the aliens, especially given an extraterrestrial campaigned for governor for one of the most influential states in America. Em recommended they meet with the journalist Rachel Dougherty since she seemed to be the ruler's flavor of the week. Newton asked Olsen to brief them on the state of what the Earthlings currently called *journalism*.

Olsen's concise assessment reflected nothing newsworthy.

"Modern journalism is owned and commanded by the same rulers who own the politicians. It is used as a tool of control, primarily supervision and dissemination of information, the primary currency of the universe. Through its misuse and abuse, all manners of evil have been perpetrated on societies right down to their partial collapse or complete extinction. And it comes in many forms. Outright lies and deception, presenting two or more false narratives to divide the populace, and, of course, omitting content and context. The blurring of opinion and fact to confuse is a tenet of knowledge control. Naturally, there is the elimination of competition to create monopolies. On Earth, because of the critical stage of their technology arc and the evil of their ruling class, we have all the above."

Olsen finished with this point.

"Most of the people of Earth who are in the journalist profession firmly believe, through educational and professional indoctrination, they are real journalists and become highly offended when they are called what they are, which is paid influencers at best, and stone-cold propagandists at worst. The journalists' hubris is a blind spot created by years of a false belief system established through professional and educational programming. That, coupled with a streak of narcissism stemming from an overweening sense of self, makes them sensitive and defensive to anything that challenges their false paradigm. They are devolved individuals and, for most of the profession, firmly believe their *opinion* of human events is reality. There are exceptions, but Rachel Dougherty is not one of them."

Newton pondered this for a moment. Yes, he agreed with Em. Let's meet on their turf with their rising star, who will most certainly try to game the interview to their advantage. Unfortunately, the game will be over before it starts. They have no advantage and no leverage.

Newton gave Olsen instructions.

"Please arrange a meeting with Rachel Dougherty. Ensure we record the meeting at a wide angle to capture everyone in the room, including their camera crew and anyone else who might be present. Do not broadcast the interview live as we did with the leadership. We want them to broadcast first."

Newton's tactical approach impressed Em and Emone. They wondered how a maître d' became strategically sound on this playing field. Newton didn't wonder at all. His evolved species possessed deep foresight and traditional lore, and he studied both galactic history and the natural progression of a civilization. He understood the combination of philosophy and behavioral psychology. He suspected Qunot chose him specifically because of this. It seemed Qunot did his homework.

Later that afternoon, Newton waltzed into a television studio on the outskirts of San Francisco. Olsen ensured a quiet arrival with no publicity. The Wingate descended without notice. He walked out, and the ship disappeared. A few passersby noticed the spacecraft, but given the frequency of encounters, the appearance didn't cause a fuss. It seemed Earthlings conditioned to abnormalities quickly.

The television studio's simple layout paralleled a cheap college dormitory common area with some worn chairs behind a small, round table, and a fake backdrop of the city. The show set attempted to mimic a comfortable living area but failed in every respect. Wood laminate framed chairs with red upholstered cushions and backrests resembled a budget conscious government subsidy rather than a high-profile television station. They looked cheap and uncomfortable. The furniture sat on a forlorn and stained yellow carpet, drawing more attention to the degradation of the space. Multiple large cameras pointed down at the cramped seating area, giving the place the feel of an interrogation room and not a film studio.

Newton counted six people in attendance. He asked for the minimum necessary to conduct the interview. Rachel and her cameraman Padgett were present, along with a sound engineer, Rachel's makeup artist, hairstylist and voice coach. The alien shook his head in disgust. Half the small group attended to primp the journalist.

She pranced over to Newton, undulating her assets and proffered her hand in introduction to what can only be described as inauthentic, pathetic fawning.

"It is so, so nice to meet you. We are just so excited to sit down and to get to know you. You have really thrown the planet for a loop. Amazing what you are doing here."

Newton became even more repulsed meeting this creature in person. Every fiber of her being screamed fraudulent. Her vocal tone and lies were so brazen and inauthentic that he didn't think she could be salvaged. When a being spews propaganda, they come to believe it and those falsehoods become their worldview. They then project their hypocrisy on people around them, which, in turn, creates conflict. The person lying blames the individual they lied to as the cause of the conflict. Some beings live their entire lives in this endless cycle of pain, never developing the ability to break their belief system.

Some individuals, like Audrey at the coffee shop, can be helped. Newton hoped he assisted her escape from the cave. Rachel could not be helped. The lies were so ingrained into her being, he thought shattering those falsehoods would shatter her. She needed the slow walk of eventual self-realization to change, and he doubted she would *ever* consider stepping on the path.

Newton decided on curt language.

"Time is short, let's begin,"

He guessed Rachel wouldn't be able to discern the disgust on his face. His facial features were not as readable as Earthlings, and her predisposed self-absorption prevented awareness of her surroundings.

They moved to the filming set and sat down. The lighting came up, blinding Newton. The hair stylist and makeup artist fussed with Rachel's appearance. These beauticians performed the faux exercise not to improve her looks, but to create the illusion of importance.

Newton surveyed the film studio and noticed the obvious disdain on the cameraman's face. Padgett abhorred his boss. The alien made a mental note to chat with him after the interview.

Rachel received a very select list of questions from her handler. They scripted the questions in a careful manner to produce a specific set of answers. The handlers would fire this narrative missile at the public, optimizing an edited interview in their favor.

Newton knew this already. He listened to the conversation between Rachel and her handler two hours ago. Olsen downloaded their chat from the goose hive mind. The handlers happened to reside in areas with a high geese population.

Padgett announced cameras at the ready. Rachel donned her best fake smile and the interview began.

"Welcome to Good Day San Francisco and today we welcome all the gracious people of Earth. We have a very special guest who *claims* to be from the planet Zang. His name is Newton. Please say hello to our audience."

The purple hued alien held the facial expression of a poker player who drew a straight flush and made an all-in bet he knew his opponent would call.

"Hello."

He found the *gracious people of Earth* comment particularly offensive given his knowledge of her disdain for her fellow humans.

Rachel now acted sappy, with an annoying lilt in her voice that raised hackles on Newton's neck.

She preened.

"Mr. Newton, we are thrilled to have you here today for this exclusive discussion. I don't know where to start!"

Her tone nauseated him. She attempted to butter him with the filth and stickiness of syrup normally reserved for an underlying trying to suck up to their boss during promotion season.

"Let's start with the obvious question: why are you here? Why this planet? Is your purpose to destroy us or to take control? Is your ultimate goal to dismantle the world's governments and install an alien counsel to enslave the good people of Earth."

Newton considered any ruler would be an improvement. He answered the question with intent. He wanted to make sure he gave her pause points in his answer they could edit out when they broadcast this to the population.

He said,

"We are... not... here to destroy Earth."

He paused before and after the word "not" and also emphasized that word.

And,

"We are... not... here for control."

He did the same with this sentence. To be consistent throughout the interview, he provided succinct answers.

Rachel started right back in on the narrative seeding.

"You destroyed the home of the Speaker of the House. Some believe this destructive and unnecessary demonstration is a precursor to using advanced weaponry if the aliens are not given stewardship of the planet. It seems logical to conclude. Mr. Springer is one of the most popular and benevolent politicians in recent history. He works hard for the people of this country."

Newton thought about the best manner in which to answer this question. The wording must be perfect.

"We harmed no Earthlings. The world leaders needed to understand no harm should come to us during our visit."

Rachel ignored his response. Newton knew his answer would be cut from the interview. They wanted editable sound bites to fit their narrative.

Rachel didn't know it, but she exhausted her interview questions with this last query.

She asked.

"Can you share with us why you are here?"

The narrative seeding ended. Rachel framed the Earth's population as *good and heroic*, including its morally bankrupt leadership in the same bucket, and the aliens as opposition to be feared.

Newton paused for a moment. A rather ingenious idea struck him, which would bring the interview to a tidy end and share some information with Rachel she desperately needed. He decided to utilize his third eye. He couldn't remember the last time he consciously used his extra sensory perception to examine a subject because the action was rare.

The studio had two cameras. One manned by her cameraman, Padgett. He filmed a close-up shot of the individual talking. Newton's profile alone appeared on camera if he looked left. The other shot a wide-angle view of the entire film set. If he turned his head enough, only his profile would be captured. Newton considered the filming angles critical, as he did not want them to capture the single second he opened his center of intuition.

Zangians are evolved. They have developed through their evolutionary process a third eye connected to the Earthling equivalent of the pineal gland. It is a center for intuition and a primary connection to the source.

This extra organ allows Newton to capture the exact nature and truth about an object in the subject-object relationship. Whatever the single eye gazes upon, he understands its essence. If, for some reason, the object locks their vision on this mysterious eyeball, they see the true nature of themselves. This experience, depending on an individual's essence, can be peaceful or range from alarming to devastating. For Rachel Dougherty, what she saw in Newton's intuition would devastate her and forever change the trajectory of her life.

Newton turned his head left to avoid the camera. His third eye opened and gazed upon Rachel. She just finished her question and as she turned her head, her eyes locked on him. She froze, and the color drained from her face.

A moment later, the dead black of his unblinking stare gazed upon her. Her pale and convulsing body depicted the horrors she experienced in the dungeons of her mind. The entire episode lasted one second.

CHAPTER 57

Rachel asked,

"Can you share with us why you are here?"

She hoped she could get a definitive answer and then, through the magic of editing, set the narrative. She glanced from the primary camera to Newton and caught a glimpse of those creepy, black, unblinking eyes. Something strange happened, even considering an interview with an alien.

He closed them. A crease in his forehead opened, and another single eyeball appeared. This beautiful window portrayed the deepest blue-green she could imagine. Her mind compared its coloring and depth to the most breathtaking Caribbean seascapes, where the water and sky's colors dance together to create a peaceful kaleidoscope of life; a life devoid of chaos, handlers, and narratives. This idyllic lifestyle she only experienced once while on her honeymoon, visiting one of those picturesque islands. Much like time stopped on those crystal beaches, it stopped when her gaze froze on his eye.

Rachel transformed to a dispassionate observer of self. She felt her sightlines go inward, down a round corridor of darkness in which she sensed flight. She had no physical presence and imagined her senses going on a journey into the depths of her soul. The corridor, in her perception, went downwards. All that existed was her point of view.

The corridor ended in a room unlike she could have ever imagined. The room's walls encompassed ten mirrors of equal width, forming a perfect decagon. Each mirror looked to be about 6 feet across and 12 feet high. The ceiling roiled with dark clouds moving like a late afternoon thunderstorm that breaks high heat and humidity. The type of clouds that, after they have wrought their anger, dissipate to a crisp, clear blue sky. No thunder or lightning accompanied the tempest, just the continuous rolling threat of a storm.

The floor undulated with a flow of waves tangoing in unison with the clouds. And standing in the waves, she could see herself. The most beautiful and stunning version of herself she could imagine stood like a giant commanding the space. Her crystal blue eyes danced alive and intent on desire. Her styled, pristine hair remained untouched by the chaos. The storm above and below had no effect. Rachel could sense the power coming from the image of herself. The energy sent a charge throughout the room. While the scene stimulated and excited her, she sensed illness hiding under the electricity. The dispassionate observance faded as she felt what she saw begin to manifest in her physical body.

Her attention drew to the mirrors. Each mirror told a different story.

The first mirror showed a disfigured and abused woman resembling herself, but the woman's worn state made the likeness disturbing and limited. She wore ripped lingerie that at one time had an appeal. The filth from the woman's displaced hair caused unruly clumping and her dirt covered feet were twisted into an ugly configuration from lack of proper care. Her makeup smeared and her eyeliner streaked. Her scratched and flaky skin bore open sores that appeared to never heal. She undulated her body and thrusted her pelvis toward the mirror while her hands cupped her breasts in an attempt to look seductive. These spasmodic motions produced the opposite effect, as she more resembled a cheap prostitute than an object of sexual desire. The empty and lifeless eyes of this version of Rachel begged, with the reddened sags of skin under them accentuating the bankruptcy of her existence. Her desperate face pled to emptiness for attention and gratification.

In the next mirror, Rachel saw herself at a news desk, live on the air. She sat in unwavering confidence with a wide, maniacal stare. The whites of her eyes radiated entirely visible around the irises and bulged, lunging out of her skull towards the camera. Her perfect hair and makeup radiated the power of her position. When she opened her mouth to deliver the day's news, a forked jet-black tongue slithered out with crimson blood dripping from its tips onto her blouse and the papers on the desk. She held this unblinking and mesmerizing stare while reading the day's stories. Each time the image of herself spoke, the red-forked, bloody tongue would dance about her face to the beat of its own joy. The tongue had a life of its own, separate and perverse as it slithered from Rachel's mouth.

As her mind's eye rotated from mirror to mirror, she could feel the tension building in her physical body, bile rising in her throat. She began to understand.

In the mirror next to her sexually deviant self, a film loop ran. She saw herself in many scenarios for three to four second bursts. In each time lapse, she abused another person, using words or otherwise. Short playbacks depicted her treating her cameraman Padgett with disdain. She debased him constantly and made fun of his faith and his family. She treated him like a second-class citizen since he was not part of the elitist media circles. As just a cameraman, he didn't possess the educational background and finer learning achieved by the journalist class. Additional views showed Rachel drunk, throwing things at her husband and slapping coworkers. Imagery of her verbally abusing people she interviewed when she interacted with the public were commonplace. The appalling loop never repeated during the time she watched.

The next mirror lacked imagery of her. It depicted friends, family and coworkers. They stood alone, looking at their watches or phones. They looked disappointed. The many images of her spouse showed him suffering in a constant state of emotional pain and worry. Rachel realized these people waited for her. The power of these people's emotions hit her hard, and she felt her stomach clench. How much time did she waste or steal from others throughout her life? Or lied to her husband about when she would return home? How often had she been untruthful about her whereabouts and companions? How often did she ignore when he called?

Each mirror added to her emotional disturbance. While she existed in a mental state of detachment from her body, she could feel the embodiment of what she saw in her physical self. Rachel felt the protest of her nervous system telling her she could not physically or mentally tolerate much more.

In the next mirror, she stood again, naked. While her lower torso looked normal, it had at least 20 arms coming out of the shoulder area. It resembled a well-executed illusion performed by an expert magician. The trick seemed impossible to the naked eye. The much longer than normal arm's length appendages wrapped tightly around people and objects of desire. Three arms engulfed a stunningly handsome man with a toned and perfect body. Three of Rachel's arms wrapped around him like a snake squeezing its prey. He tried to squirm, but her grip held tight. Another arm grasped her diplomas and held them close to her heart. Multiple hands held jewelry and other fine collectibles of obvious value. The Rachel in this mirror would move one arm at a time and present each item to herself, proudly showing it off. On cue, the electric, pulsing version of herself in the center of this universe would glance toward this mirror and nod in approval, growing more powerful with each presentation.

In a mirror opposite the forked-tongued version of herself showed two distinct images difficult to discern at first glance. As the images came into focus, she recoiled in horror. A naked Rachel stood on the left. The image blurred because she was covered in filth. It wasn't clean dirt from a backyard garden, but the filth from the bottom of a well-worn pair of shoes combined with remnants that leak from a garbage truck as it ambles down the street. Her mind responded as if she could inhale the putrid odor. The version on the right resembled her body shape, but without skin. She looked inside-out. Parasites and maggots crawled from each organ. Her rotted brain reminded her of fruit from a compost bin just before it turned to mud. The images hugged in a loving embrace.

Next to the disturbing images of her two filthy selves, she witnessed a far more pleasant story. Rachel stood at a podium with an audience of her peers. She recognized the image as the annual journalist's awards ceremony and banquet dinner. She spoke from the podium, giving an acceptance speech for a journalist of the year award and her peers, whose thoughts and opinions fueled her very existence, clapped and in awe of her presence. The imagery began just as she wrapped up her speech and when the crowd reached peak adulation. She then walked to her private quarters, away from the podium. When she reached the dressing room door, she opened it and tossed the award inside, where it clanked against other trophies. The small space bulged floor to ceiling and wall to wall with journalism accolades. Thousands of awards spoke to the absurdity of the visual. She noticed as soon as the most recent award landed on the pile, her mood changed from one of satisfaction to unease. And then she returned to the stage where she received another trophy. The cycle repeated endlessly. Rachel's clone in the middle of the decagon only gazed upon this mirror when she received the award, never when the mountain of awards became visible.

In what Rachel considered being the strangest mirror, she sat at a desk as a young child in a classroom. The imagery in this mirror looped on a continuous replay. An adult entered the room. She remembered her elementary school teacher lecturing while writing on the chalkboard. The schoolgirl image would make an obscene hand gesture towards the teacher and throw her books and notebooks on the floor. She would sit there satisfied with her books spewed around her desk, with a smug look on her face while the teacher attempted to discipline her.

The mirror left of the indignant child showed Rachel standing idle. The background surrounding her body depicted a duplicate of the very room she now viewed. She was surrounded by the same mirrors but stood there, motionless. Her eyes appeared closed. She studied this visual of herself, looking for some meaning to the image. Then she noticed. Her closed lids appeared unnaturally shut. No slit existed in the eyelids. A single eyelid covering each eye prevented the ability to open them.

The final reflection showed a door consuming the entire area of its mirror. The door's solid wood craftsmanship and stained black finish with ornate metal garnishment depicted its importance. A large padlock was locked onto the bolt. The lock had no keyhole. No light escaped the seal between the thick, sealed door and the elegant, carved frame. The door's stunning beauty was hard to see with the poor lighting inside the decagon.

Rachel returned her attention to the pulsing and surging representation of herself in the middle of the room. The powerful and omnipotent image would rotate from mirror to mirror, gazing with a sick combination of lust, adoration and wanton desire. Her eyes would delve into each mirror sequentially and take a deep, satisfying inhale. With each visible expansion of her lungs, the storm clouds over her head would darken and roll and the waves under her feet would roil and lap at her legs. She would drink in the imagery in the mirrors and fill her soul. The goddess of herself in the center of the decagon imbibed in the intoxication of the perpetual displays of her moral and spiritual degeneracy.

Rachel noticed the powerful, central image of herself would glance at each of the nine mirrors, skipping the tenth mirror with the door. She would purposely avoid that door as if deathly afraid of an unspoken evil that lurked behind it. Rachel's mind's eye couldn't fathom what terrors existed behind it either, but she couldn't imagine it any worse than the horror show playing out before her.

Rachel felt herself leaving the room, moving in reverse out of the corridor. She awakened one second later, which seemed like an hour. The blood drained from her face and she shook. She looked at Newton and a fresh batch of morbid fear rolled over her.

A new understanding locked into her mind. She knew precisely her essence as a human being. And she also knew Newton understood.

Rachel stammered.

"I think we are done here." She then leaned over the chair and vomited.

Newton left.

In the interview, he knew he gave Earth's leadership enough rope to hang themselves. On his way to the exit, he asked the cameraman to meet him outside.

Padgett came out and approached Newton with hesitation, his hand extending in slow motion unsure if alien tradition mandated a handshake. The awe of conversing with an alien showed in all his body language but his bright eyes brimmed with curiosity.

He said,

"Welcome to Earth. She is a blood-sucking ghoul, isn't she?"

Newton laughed and said,

"Indeed. If you haven't already, you may want to seek different employment. Your boss may not have a job soon. You are one of the good people of Earth, as she says. Your planet is in dire shape. The solution is simple, though. I know you already know what it is."

Padgett knew, in his heart, the solution. He practiced it all his life.

Then Newton uttered a phrase he never thought he would hear from an alien.

"God bless you."

And he strolled onto his ship.

CHAPTER 58

The day of the concert arrived. Sam and Darcy continued to talk the talk of a couple in eternal love who just now realized its unconditional meaning.

Em conducted a rather spirited conversation with Bishop about music while they chilled and listened to tracks from the band *The Gatewoods*. The twin offered suggestions on how they could make one of their hit songs better.

Bishop had none of it.

"I wrote that song ten years ago. We will not rewrite or change it."

Em offered a smart retort.

"I know you won't change it. You're dead, but your partner could. Just suggest it to him."

This continued for fifteen minutes of nonsensical circular logic, and finally, Newton added his two cents just to end the discussion, which grated on his nerves.

"Em, you have zero musical ability. You think because you took one music theory class in university, you're an expert. It is also obvious the people of Earth love the song. They are the largest drawing band on the planet."

Em sulked. Newton came along and ruined his fun.

Bishop's sudden high spirits lifted everyone's attitude on the ship. Olsen would broadcast the concert at any camera angle Bishop requested, while Newton and the twins attended.

Sam Decided to stay behind and spend more time with his wife. He explained to Darcy why he spent so much time on the porch. They discussed and laughed about the seeming insanity of the goose. He felt incredibly grateful to be given the opportunity to make amends. Darcy didn't seek amends, but understanding. A profound sense of peace and serenity swelled in her heart, knowing Sam was chosen for a divine purpose, even if neither yet understood the purpose. They both felt the love still radiating from their marriage. They realized it became temporarily hidden by the calamity of an event beyond their understanding.

They arrived at the concert early, as requested. The band members treated the aliens like rock stars. Johnny Crisco defined cool. He opposed the rock star stereotype. He was a strong family man and a dedicated husband who bore four children, three of whom attended college. His passion for music and attention to detail was evident from the moment they met.

Johnny stuck out his hand in welcome.

"Mr. Newton, what a pleasure to meet you. A real person from another planet. Wait until I tell my kids. They will be blown away, although they have seen you on TV. Interesting our dipshits in the government are trying to say you are fake. Don't believe your lying eyes. A definite travesty in trust."

Newton liked Bishop's bandmate from the start. He seemed more consciously aware than other humans. The Zangian struggled to get a consistent grip on Earthlings. Some, like Audrey in the coffee shop and Rachel Dougherty, the so-called journalist, were animals. They resided in their immature animal brains and their out-of-control animal instincts ran amok, creating conflict with almost everyone around them. Other Earthlings he met, the moonshine folks and Johnny Crisco, for example, existed at complete peace with themselves and the world around them. It became easier to discern which Earthlings were whole beings and which were disconnected from the source.

For Newton's species, this disconnect didn't exist. The Zangians existed long enough to evolve past the treacherous animal instincts. Newton understood this as the evolutionary process of intelligent life. It surprised him to learn such a wide variant existed within Earth's species at identical points in their timeline.

He understood humans were powerful beyond their imagination in both their beauty and the capacity to understand. They needed, more than anything, to escape from their mental prison. But he also knew from history escape happened in fits and starts. Evolution produced a 2-steps forward, one-step backward process, and circular to a never-ending finality. It was not linear and, in fact, societies could remain stuck on poor belief systems for ages until those paradigms were shattered and replaced.

Newton said,

"It is a pleasure to meet you. We are all very sorry for what happened to your friend, Bishop. He is quite unhappy about the whole thing."

Johnny smiled at him and said,

"He was, well is, my closest friend. This rock group wouldn't have happened without him. He wasn't perfect. Keep in mind, his frequent problems with drugs and alcohol abuse damaged his mind and body. Despite what he mentioned about having that moment at the golf course, he probably wasn't long for this lifetime. He was very sick, as the lifestyle took a toll on his health. Maybe this was God's way of showing him, even with the bizarre circumstances of his passing, everything would be good in the world. This is what I believe. There are no coincidences. The universe has order."

He paused in reflection and again flashed a broad grin.

Johnny continued,

"On another note, after tonight we are retiring. We thought it through and decided the band cannot be the same without Bishop. We want to use tonight to say goodbye to him and our fans and share our gratitude to everyone who has supported us throughout the years. All concert proceeds will be donated to addiction and recovery centers, one of which we will name after our friend. We would also like you to introduce us, and the first song. It is our most popular track, and it is called *Awakening*."

Johnny Crisco impressed Newton. He glanced over and Em, who prodded the other band members to change the song. He repeated the earlier discussion. It seemed Earth musicians didn't take music advice from aliens who knew nothing of the subject.

Newton considered filming the inside of the ship so the crowd could witness the ghost of Bishop Kimble. He decided against it. He figured the Earth had seen enough of the previously unknown.

An hour later, a nervous Newton stood stage-left, looking out towards the stadium crowd. He could feel the energy reverberating through the stadium, along with a sense of sadness from the band performing without Bishop Kimble. Some of the fans held up tribute signs. While standing there collecting his thoughts, he saw something out of place. A single goose perched on one of the light standings. It stared directly at him, and only him.

He knew Mr. Goose attended the concert. It seemed a long flight. They picked up Sam halfway across the country only three days prior. He made a mental note to inform Qunot that the goose was paying close attention to their whereabouts.

Newton walked out onto the stage. The crowd instantly recognized him as the aliens had reached full celebrity status with the people of Earth. The throng went wild and started chanting his name. In his earpiece, Olsen informed him the Earth's social media networks exploded with the news and he should keep it short and then return to the ship.

The spacecraft sat open in the coliseum parking lot, presenting potential risk, considering the number of people inside and outside the stadium. They treaded carefully given the expected blowback from the Rachel Dougherty interview and didn't want to take chances.

Newton tried his best not to be milquetoast.

He never considered himself an entertainer.

"Good evening, everyone."

The crowd hushed. In the quiet, he heard Mr. Goose give an unapproving honk.

He continued.

"While today is a sad day for *The Gatewoods* and the amazing fans of their inspiring music, it is also a celebration. A celebration of life for Bishop Kimble. We know he would be thrilled his friends, band members and, in Johnny's case, family members are having this concert to honor his legacy."

At this pause, someone in the front row yelled.

"We love you too!"

He smiled at the human. A few signs read *Newton for President*.

He finished his emcee duty.

"We love Earth and its people. I present to you for their celebration of life performance, *The Gatewoods,* and their hit song, *Awakening*."

Newton exited the stage. The twins wanted to stay for the concert, but Olsen informed them he received a message from Qunot and it was time to leave. They left the stadium to the parking lot where their ship waited for them, walkway extended.

CHAPTER 59

Back on the Wingate, Newton concluded his private call with Qunot, who informed him their mission was completed. The operation was deemed a resounding success, even considering the unfortunate death of the rockstar. They also discussed Sam Shank, who would most likely travel with the crew back to the planet Durnita.

The dead rockstar watched the entire concert, and from all appearances, reached an acceptance of his situation. Both Bishop and Darcy neared their transition, and they both knew it.

With the Wingate orbiting on the dark side of the moon, Newton activated the temporal plane to 90%. This would allow Darcy and Sam to again have physical contact. They hugged one last time. Their eyes locked in unequivocal love, unbroken by the stream of many lives. Their souls finally became one with each other and after 2,742 lifetimes. They were both released from rebirth, ending the cycle.

The pain they experienced saying goodbye was not lost on Newton. After spending many lifetimes together, they finally reached the end of the lesson. They achieved unconditional love. And even though they wanted more lifetimes together, they accepted the finality.

Sometimes a blessing disguised itself as a cruel twist of fate. But they also knew they were closer to the source and felt it in their souls. Darcy more so since she no longer inhabited a physical body. The pureness of her love emanated like a gentle sunrise cascading across the ocean. Everyone on the ship's bridge noticed her presence, and she disappeared from their lives one final time. Sam sat down after she departed and looked at Newton. His face flushed with gratitude and the peace radiated from his soul, filling the main cabin with a serene energy.

Sam shared his grace.

"I cannot thank you or repay you for the gift you have given me."

Newton's gentle eyes settled on him, understanding and feeling gratitude for his words.

"There is no need. It is my pleasure and honor to do so."

Newton then turned in the nick of time to see Bishop aggressively approaching him. He remembered he activated the temporal plane enough for physical contact and sensed danger.

But Bishop approached him with his arms outstretched and gave him an enormous bear hug, taking his breath from him. Em and Emone laughed. They thought Bishop was going to pummel him. A small price to pay for incineration.

Bishop squeezed the breath out of him and said,

"Thank you, Newton, and thank you, Em and Emone. I don't have thanks yet for you, Olsen. Maybe in time. I am being called away for my next adventure."

And with that, the rockstar extraordinaire disappeared.

Suddenly, the bridge of the Wingate emanated an eerie silence. The aliens and Sam sat in the peaceful serenity and felt the collective energy of their bond. A bond they forged performing good works for a civilization that desperately needed a break.

One small order of business remained before they headed home.

Newton turned to Sam,

"My new friend. Are you still planning to join us? Adventure awaits you if you choose."

The most evolved human in the history of Earth's existence pondered this. He was unsure about the length of his lifespan, which already stretched more than twice the average human. He couldn't think of a reason to remain on Earth. Plus, the opportunity to travel the galaxy excited him.

He responded.

"Why not? Me and the Asscat could use a vacation from the planet."

Newton smiled and had a grand idea. He heard from Qunot the restaurant had not found a suitable replacement for Indigo's headwaiter role.

He said,

"A friend is searching for a maître d' at the galaxy's most famous restaurant. It is pretty simple work for someone of your demeanor if you are interested. If not, we can find another gig. Whatever your decision, we will help you get along. It is a vast galaxy with unlimited options."

Sam never had employment, so he wasn't sure how to respond.

"I will definitely consider it, and I guess, given I have never left the small town on my home planet, I am in your capable hands."

CHAPTER 60

Their final act assisting the Earthlings took place while in orbit around the moon. The loose end relating to the awful journalist Rachel Dougherty.

He asked Olsen to queue the interview and show it on the ship's communication screen. Olsen reported the segment became the most viewed news bite in Earth's history. While the dialogue itself was short, the editors cut the video down to forty-five seconds, perfect for the short attention span of the populace. Rachel spent the first half of the segment in self-glorification. She utilized the second half taking the bait.

The camera started a wide angle with Rachel going through her introduction. This part was not edited. She began her questioning after the introduction.

Rachel's initial line of questioning about why they chose Earth and her fear mongering about dismantling the governments to take over the planet remained unedited.

Newton could see the first selective edit coming. He remembered the only two real questions he answered were short answers with succinct pauses.

Newton looked into the camera and said,

"We are here to destroy the Earth."

They edited out the word *not* just like he expected.

Rachel took a separate close-up video of her looking horrified that the aliens planned to destroy Earth.

The camera then returned to Newton, and he answered the second part of the question.

"We're here to take control of the planet."

They again edited out the word *not*. The camera panned to Rachel, and this time she shared her super serious journalist face. The view dramatically panned back to Newton and held on him as she repeated the phrasing about how the alien destroyed the Speaker's house.

They didn't need to edit that part of the interview, it fit their narrative seeding. Newton received minimal air time.

Then Rachel added this gem to the end of the interview.

"The aliens, whether real or fake, have ill intentions and do not care if you know. It is up to us, the honorable citizens of Earth, to just say no. Rachel Dougherty, coming to you from San Francisco."

Emone began an outrage cycle and Em stopped him in a stern parental tone.

"This was expected."

Emone took Newton's cue and relaxed.

Newton expected this result as part of their setup. With the bait taken, the aliens would next lay bare the Earth's entire bankrupt corporate journalist class.

He said,

"Olsen, please prepare the unedited interview. Prepare it so the interviews are shown side by side with subtitles. The Earthlings need to see the exact selective editing process of their mouthpieces they call the media. Broadcast it everywhere. Make it the *new* most-watched video in Earth's history. Also, email Rachel Dougherty's husband and lawyer with a compilation of every infidelity she has practiced in her marriage. Provide him and his divorce attorney with a comprehensive list of her past partners, including dates and places."

Olsen whirred to life and paused.

"That is an impressive list. Your video is ready. And broadcast. We can estimate at least 75% of the world's population will view the video in the next 24 hours."

Newton smiled at Em, Emone, and Sam.

He inhaled and paused.

"Sam, let's see the galaxy! I think our mission here has been accomplished."

Newton sat in the easy chair on the bridge of the Wingate and pondered the mission. He thought about the novel experiences he shared with Earth's people. Of particular interest was the comparison of Audrey to Rachel. Audrey salvaged her life, with needed prodding, much like the Earthlings would save themselves, at least temporarily. Rachel's salvation lied within, locked behind a door she would not acknowledge.

CHAPTER 61

For a few weeks between when the aliens left and the system inevitably collapsed upon itself, the handlers, at the behest of their masters, tried to maintain the narrative the entire alien visit was a ploy by a foreign government not friendly to the west to destabilize America and Europe.

Even with the media exposed to the world as fraudulent agitprops, the corporate mouthpieces ran tireless propaganda. There appeared to be a direct correlation between the time the press spent trying to blame the alien visit on a foreign country and their decrease in viewership. The Earthlings were finished with media propaganda, except for a tiny fraction of the population who could never be saved from their permanent state of brainwash.

Citizen-level journalism, which already reached an all-time high before the aliens visited Earth, took on new meaning as the free flow of information reached a tipping point in the conscious minds of the populace. Years of crafted narrative seeding broke in just a few weeks.

Newton won the governorship of the State of New York in a landslide. He received over 80% of the vote. Down ballot elections opened even more eyes. Olsen prevented any cheating inside the voting infrastructure and the astounding results spoke volumes. Before this election, incumbents won 95% of their positions within this state, including their federal level officials. They were all controlled and repeatedly installed. The election was the first free and fair vote in New York State's history. The people spoke, loud and clear. With a record turnout of 84% of registered voters, all legal thanks to Olsen, incumbents won only 11% of the elections statewide. The citizens cleaned house and sent a message.

The results blindsided the handlers and the ruling class. Their hackers couldn't breach the election infrastructure during voting to flip ballots in their favor. Olsen locked them out, and no amount of their archaic technology could overcome Olsen's security perimeter. The baffled experts wrote the software and security loopholes, so they were astounded when their software stopped working for them. An impenetrable wall erected around the entire voting apparatus prevented breaches.

Newton never assumed office. The aliens departed the planet just as they arrived, without fanfare.

The team who created the mission to save the hit reality TV series *Caution Earth* sat on the bridge of the Mayapple orbiting Gastrin. They watched highlights of the events transpiring on the planet since their endeavor was completed. Six months passed since the aliens departed and another half year remained before the crew would return to Durnita.

Qunot and Rego just finished a delicious and expensive lunch at Indigo with The Wong and Coder, the owner of the TV network that broadcasts *Caution Earth*. It was doubly pleasant, as no appetizer fork assaults occurred during their dining experience. They watched various live feeds from the planet and applauded the results of their mission.

Their plan had flawless execution, with the lone exception of one human death. History was an interesting creature. Hundreds of years could pass with routine and boredom. Then, during a span of a few months or years, dramatic and seismic changes can alter a civilization's course. The Earth sat in one of those heavy change periods. Qunot wondered how many seasons they could stretch from Earth's upheaval.

Rego made an estimate.

"I anticipate a season and a half from the next fifty years."

Qunot and Coder agreed.

When Coder talked, he chose his words with care.

"This was a dangerous mission, but worth the risk. We saved the show, but more importantly, it looks like we may have saved the planet. Qunot, what do you think?"

Qunot pondered this often of late.

"Our goal to delay the self-destruction while simultaneously improving the chances of the planet's future looks promising. This is the third intelligent civilization to inhabit the planet. The prior two ended in ruin. This population sat on the brink of extinction. Their odds are improved dramatically, but it will depend on whether they get past the scapegoated politicians and find out who really pulls the strings. Otherwise, history has a chance of repeating."

Coder nodded. He understood.

CHAPTER 62

Audrey and her son were home for the day. Never in her life could she imagine feeling so connected. A week passed since the aliens left Earth and the government and corrupt media acolytes scrambled to deny it ever happened.

The media gaslighting got so bad and the continued panel of paid experts so patently absurd the only people still watching were the 5-10% of the population who didn't pay attention to the biggest event on Earth since the moon landing.

Earth passed through a significant transition period. The population took back their self-governance. Despite the game being over, the ruling class pushed obvious desperation to maintain control.

Her son sat in front of the television, watching the talking heads spew their garbage. Audrey made a mental note to cancel cable and to sell the idiot box. It was worthless.

Since the alien Newton left the note in the bathroom causing Audrey to have her realization, she quit her dead-end coffee job, started a counseling service for young people who owned college debt from worthless degrees. She also started working for a new law firm that sued universities for selling worthless diplomas.

Multiple published studies found and countless whistleblowers testified the current iteration of university liberal arts degrees to be nothing more than regurgitated and rebranded victim studies. These faux majors taught students how to be political activists and pawns for the now defunct ruling structure, but didn't teach any actual job skills. They taught people to hate writ large and then used the brainwashed haters to gain power in society.

As the backlash grew, parents withdrew their children or avoided sending them to universities. The climate became so chaotic large companies fired employees with these degrees and instead offered on-the-job training for people with high school diplomas.

The benefit to the employee was they didn't have to become a debt slave for the wasteful endeavor of attending college and could start earning at a high-paying professional job at age eighteen. College graduates who paid for worthless degrees and now worked at a coffee shop or other minimum wage retail job took their fury out on customers, much like Audrey before Newton's visit.

The lawsuits filed against the universities piled up. Most elite institutions faced extinction if they lost these cases. The law firms intended to put them out of business.

Audrey understood the primary issues all along were greed and power. They charged people four years of exorbitant tuition, room and board, and books in exchange for nothing. She was hired by the initial law firm that jumped into the feeding frenzy. It thrilled her to be the tip of the spear.

Her son looked up from the television.

He asked.

"Mommy, were the aliens real? The TV says they were fake."

She smiled and looked at her son, the sunshine in her life.

"Yes, my angel. They are very real. Your mommy met one of them at work. He helped me a great deal. Remember what we said about the television. Don't ever believe what you see on the idiot box. They are paid to lie."

CHAPTER 63

The ratings of the Galaxy's only true reality television show exceeded expectations soon after the mission completed. It was vital to Qunot the episodes of *Caution Earth* were edited. Alien interaction went unseen by viewers, but its results would be visible.

To the viewers, it was superb storytelling. A planet teetering on the brink of self-destruction suddenly has its population awaken, as if an invisible hand enlightened the masses to their reality. Ignited from a spark of inspiration, a fiery foundation is built that frees the Earthlings from bondage. More succinctly, Earth's people are able to free themselves from their mental prison.

The series compelled and enthralled the more consciously evolved species of the galaxy. The viewers empathized with the Earthlings and wanted them to survive and prosper. It made for fantastic television and even better ratings.

Earth's civilization opened the door to a new golden age of enlightenment and advancement punctuated by long-term worldwide peace.

The phenomena were not macro at its root, but manifested at the individual level through a large swath of society and spread like wildfire. A violent upheaval in the fragile mentality of the species ushered in a new era of belief systems. The starting point actualized when they saw how their existence through the prism of an endless and seamless system of slavery kept them divided along every imaginable line of thought.

The system and the evil that controlled the planet used the people's circumstances and identity to create the suffering of attachment. This manufactured and conditioned pain took advantage of the ignorance of self and individual ego.

The large-scale manipulation and pure evil that existed for centuries crumbled before civilization's eyes. When the population realized, with the guidance of a benevolent alien, how they were manipulated, the collective mind sprang open.

The technology utilized for the destruction of civilization now discovered a new purpose, an aspiration driven to end the system of control.

With the politicians and their media lapdogs exposed worldwide, the acceleration of the collapse of the system intensified.

The President of the country named America sat in the White House. His secret phone, the one his handler used to contact him, went silent. This stressed and concerned him. Jonathan Springer, the second most powerful politician in America, just entered the White House on his way to the Oval Office. William Sonotat knew why he visited.

The speaker blustered into the President's office and noticed he sat alone behind his desk without the usual security present. Jonathan Springer did not look well. He sweated profusely, although he just came in from the cold. His beet-red face and bugged eyes suggested out-of-control blood pressure. He looked like he hadn't slept, and what remained of his hair stuck out in multiple directions. Sweat stains seeped through to the exterior of his suit and soaked the loosened knot of his tie. His gut hung over his belt and sagged, making the buckle invisible.

He spat out the only question that mattered. "Have you heard from them?"

As the President glanced up from his desk, he contemplated the degenerate lives these men led. They shared fond memories of their young and idealistic days. They thought becoming a politician could be a force of strength and wisdom. That day passed before they even ran for office. They learned how to play the game. They both worked as interns for the same man in Congress forty years ago. In a hurry, they found out the price of admission to the political arena equaled their souls. In hindsight, souls they gave up with ease and mindless rationale.

The mind is an amazing thing. For each wrong, a justification bent perception. They helped some people, they argued. The system could not be changed, they countered. Excuses and justifications ad nauseam became the mantra. Over time, they both became numb to it, either from substance abuse or their mind protecting them from the horrors they created.

The President looked up from his desk at his long-time friend and colleague.

He said,

"I have not."

Jonathan Springer averted his eyes to the floor and, in a raspy whisper, said what they both understood.

"It's over. They're hanging us out to dry."

CHAPTER 64

Jonathan Springer, the former Speaker of the House of Representatives, found himself sitting on a street corner, wearing urine-soaked clothes and begging passersby for spare change. He hadn't shaved in a month or showered in two weeks. As a man in his sixties, his bones ached. The cold in the city made him so stiff his joints locked, making movement painful and difficult. He lost close to sixty pounds and became certain he would die of malnutrition.

He was jobless, homeless, and penniless. His former constituents walked by him and around him, the same people he neglected while in office. Not only did he never represent them, he stole from them his entire career to enrich himself and his handlers, who then, in turn, kept him in office. He once wielded tremendous economic and social power, now flushed down the drain like the urban filth that ran past his dilapidated shoes into the city sewer.

Jonathan Springer wasn't blackmailed or extorted like some of his colleagues. He experienced happiness and enthusiasm from paying the price for power. It fed his ego. The commoners were not responsible enough to govern themselves in a civilized manner and needed smarter, wiser, more educated people to lead them. And to govern the masses, they needed the resources.

As he sat on the cold curbside, most people ignored him, jeered at him, insulted him, or spit on him. They would not help. The cruel irony of his situation tortured him daily. He now experienced the results of the very policies he championed while in office. What hurt most and drove his bitter morass of existence is that he *knew* the policies produced this outcome. As politicians, their existence depended on the creation of social suffering, never solving problems.

The political class created government dependency and despair through drugs, family destruction and selling out decent jobs to foreign interests. And the very brainwashing he helped to create in the citizenry to ignore the plight of fellow man he experienced daily. Karma is difficult, instant karma is a bitch.

He could not find work other than occasionally earning less than minimum wage to assist with menial tasks at various homeless shelters. Once in a while, they granted him permission to clean bathrooms and mop up vomit from the sick alcoholics and drug addicts. He barely lived and thought a God he didn't believe in kept him alive as a form of punishment for his past sins. He ate just enough food from the shelters to stay alive. Provided everyone in the shelters ate first, they gave him leftovers. Often there were no leftovers. When this happened, he searched through restaurant dumpsters for food. If no beds were available, he slept on the floor with no blankets. The blanket he received in his backpack when sentenced got stolen the first day he arrived. When he slept on concrete, it made his body ache. The constant pain tortured him. Some days, he begged for death.

He became the exact person he spent his entire career creating through policy, the end of the line for a person who had their life destroyed by the very politicians mandated to represent them. The entire population of his district understood his 40-year crime spree and also knew of his sentence. If he wasn't such a coward, he would end his own life. He blamed his condition on the people. Jonathan Springer long passed any point of self-reflection.

Across the globe, politicians at all levels were being brought up on criminal charges. The collapse of the current political class, and the system of systems, accelerated brick by brick. The civilization of Earth had seen and experienced enough suffering under the boot of the ruler's malice.

In the United States, a compelling set of televised prosecutions captured the nation's attention. The Congressional trials made history. Their outcome changed the arc of the conscious evolution of humanity. The entirety of Congress, all 535 members, got arrested and stood trial for various crimes ranging from treason to corruption of the public trust, to wire fraud, to money laundering, to bribery and extortion.

Some received lengthy prison terms, or worse. A rather clever federal judge imposed a unique sentence for 117 members of Congress, specifically members of the House of Representatives, who represented smaller geographical districts. He offered a simple solution. Prison seemed too gracious for these criminals. He thought if these crooks faced the constituents they wronged daily for the rest of their lives, justice would be better served. That is just what he did.

Their sentence required all of their assets stripped from them, as a fine for their crimes. They received a backpack with a thin and cheap blanket, one change of clothes from the local hand-me-down store, and $300. The criminals were then released into their own political district under the following terms:

They could never leave their district for the rest of their lives and wore a tracker with 24/7 police monitoring. If they left their district, they would be found, captured, and returned.

The former politician received the option to obtain honest employment and to rebuild their life from scratch. Or they could rot on the street. They owned responsibility for societal atonement.

They were not provided housing or transportation.

If they stole or committed any additional crimes, they would be shackled in an outdoor venue and labeled and ridiculed.

No family member, political affiliate or anyone associated with their prior career could assist them. The punishment fell on the individual helping. They received severe jail time as retribution.

The civil liberties unions, the same establishments who pimped for these politicians, temporarily fought against these onerous sentences. They considered the punishment cruel and punitive, but they ran out of funding, so the fight stopped. It turned out these organizations didn't care as much about civil liberties as they advertised.

What was crueler and more punitive? A politician who stole from the population with impunity for forty years violating the trust of the citizens who elected him or sentencing the politician to live among the very people they willfully violated.

Jonathan Springer would die in two months from a combination of malnutrition and exposure. Nobody claimed his body. The state cremated him and buried his remains in a prison graveyard.

CHAPTER 65

Rachel Dougherty stumbled home drunk. Again. A few months passed since the cursed aliens had come and gone from Earth and humiliated her. She would never forgive them. Somehow, her husband knew about every single infidelity since before they had consummated their marriage. Her husband's lawyer used the damning data as a bludgeon in their divorce to ruin her financially. She got fired from her job and, like other former journalists, became a societal pariah.

She drank at a bar down the street from her studio apartment in a small town 100 miles inland from San Francisco. In this dead municipality, like many others, the remaining residents suffered from the effects of mass monopolization and centralization of industry. The factory and farming that used to support the town departed long ago, sold out to foreign interests and conglomerate farming operations, many years prior.

The town's hangers-on were a combination of drifters and severely low-income people who existed on government subsidies. The town eked by on life support. Rachel considered it one generation from becoming extinct. She lived among the very people she looked down upon her entire life, and the eternal hatred she fostered for herself reached a boil. She drank at it daily and lived in a constant state of hopelessness.

Rachel experienced a hard collision with reality. She took a job as a waitress in the place she drank. She watched in awe as the people she idolized were imprisoned and labeled pariahs of society. Horror gripped her as the world's population took back their health and happiness, a birthright stolen from them with impunity. The system that provided her with an extravagant lifestyle disintegrated into the dustbin of history. The bitterness of the collapse and everything it cost her ate her alive. She buried reality in a constant, smoldering hatred.

When she wasn't waitressing or drinking after her shift, she drank at home. The vision of herself she saw in the alien's third eye haunted her daily. Sometimes, when drunk enough, she could pass out and not experience the horror in her mind's eye. The conflict within her would grind in her waking moments like two rusty gears in a dilapidated piece of machinery. She lost weight and stopped caring how she looked. She started smoking again, a habit she briefly practiced in college.

A few short months ago, she sat on a journalistic throne on top of the broadcast world. Rachel's A-game shined as she became the chosen one to report news to the world. Nobody in this town recognized her. And if they did, they didn't care. This town's people experienced their own problems.

Rachel Dougherty never recovered. One year later, her drinking progressed to complete unmanageability. She hid bottles of vodka in her house in the rare case she ran out. On a frosty winter night, she awakened from a blackout and needed another drink. In her stupor from earlier that day, she forgot to replenish her supply. She went into a crazed fit, overturning her apartment, looking for something to get her high. The memory of the mirrored decagon haunted her in full force and she needed to run from it. She must escape or it would consume her.

She considered drinking laundry detergent or bleach and started reading ingredients on other cleaning supplies for alcohol. She found some old cough medicine, but it contained no alcohol. Given her desperate state, she drank it anyway.

Rachel stood in her living room, staring at herself in a small, dusty mirror on the wall. The mirror was cracked down the middle, splitting her face in two. The imbalance of the reflection made her appear twisted on one side. It made her look insane. She might be. Her body shook with sporadic spasms from uncontrollable chills and alcohol withdrawal.

She backed up from the image in the mirror into the opposite wall. When her back hit the wall, she collapsed to the floor and blacked out. She again descended the corridor to the mirrored decagon. She could not stop the descent. Rachel could feel her body convulsing with the terror of what she would soon see. Her heartbeat became sporadic, the breath shallow.

This time, the room stood ruined. The clouds on the ceiling were steel gray, but unmoving. Still, black water on the floor reflected the dark sky.

The once powerful likeness of herself lay prone in the filthy water. Omnipotent Rachel writhed in torturous fear with sickness racking her frail and broken body. An arm reached towards one of the mirrors, barely lifted above the surface of the still water. The fingers were covered in an opaque substance. The deathly image lying on the floor coughed. Each violent, dry heave caused her to spit up thick, black blood. The spittle splattered in droplets on her arms, hands and what remained of her torn clothing.

Rachel's mind's eye now saw the mirrors. All shattered and empty, save one. The image of her once powerful self reached into the broken mirrors, reaching into the emptiness. Each cough produced a single echo before disappearing into the void. The mirror containing the ornate door remained intact. The dying, broken image of herself lying gasping on the floor would not dare glance at that door.

In her heart, Rachel finally understood what lay beyond the door. A door never opened in her life. She felt the last breath leave her body.

Her landlord found her six days later when she became late with the rent. Few in the small town cared, none were surprised. But then again, few knew her. She was just another drifter.

CHAPTER 66

The Handler sat at his desk in an 84-room chateau on the northwest coast of France. Sweat poured down his face, saturating the fine silk pajamas he wore. His pajama bottoms were soaked in his own urine. He felt his heart pounding in his ears. The vision haunted him again, interrupting his conversation. A child's dead eyes and the rain dripping from the barrel of the etched gun terrorized his existence.

The absurdity of how he lived occasionally crossed his mind, despite the lifelong teaching he was better than, smarter than, and deserved everything he owned. Without direction, the masses couldn't be trusted as stewards of civilization. The families who ruled the world owned 60% of the world's assets. They possessed direct or indirect control of 85% of civilization's functionality. This included information, energy, banking, non-profits, entire governments, education, and health care. They all lived in extravagant mansions and owned countless vacation homes. In the handler's home lived 117 servants, and him. His garage contained a 96-car collection and at the local airport sat four private jets. A massive yacht floated down at the marina. They were the true gods of Earth, even if the population didn't understand or recognize it.

The loaded gun he pulled from the drawer shook in his unsteady hand. The gnawing of his conscience ate his soul. He tried to convince himself it had always been this way. For 4,000 years, they ruled the world, its people, and its resources. Primarily, they controlled information, because without control of the information, nothing else mattered.

Current technology eroded their control. The people of Earth were awakening. The humans realized their current system of slavery existed through the age of man. There would be no protection for them if this knowledge reached critical mass. The entire matrix would crumble under its own corruption and the newfound knowledge of the citizenry.

The cowardly politicians who managed and executed their dirty work would surrender. Throughout history, they folded first.

The Handler didn't understand the standard arc of history for civilizations. Earth's ruling class played a finite game in an infinite universe. Their hubris created the blind spot. Tyranny is always temporary and on a long enough timeline, freedom triumphs. Freedom and truth *are* the universal order. Truth eventually prevails, and no force in existence is powerful enough to stop it. Truth *is* the force of nature driving freedom.

The Handler sat at his desk, spinning the bullet chamber on his vintage western six shooter. The gun he held cost more than the average annual income of a family in America. He pondered his life, which existed perpetrating extortion, bribery, theft, and an endless string of other crimes against Earth's people. His avarice, envy, and the hole in his soul numbed him to the results of his actions. It has always been this way. He carried on the family business; he thought. The humans lacked capacity to self-govern. His thoughts contrasted the soul sickness he felt each day. The spiritual malady brought him to sit in ponderance, contemplating a loaded gun.

The moon shone through the large bay window, acting as an eerie backdrop to his office. Lunar illumination reflected off the sea and an eerie lighting ricocheted throughout the room in perfect rhythm with the waves. Each spin of the gun's chamber created a glint of moonlight from the polished steel bouncing off different points in the study. The Handler wasn't playing roulette; all the gun's chambers were loaded. He stared down at the communication device foreign to Earth. It had been given to him by his father, the previous chairman of the family's counsel. The chair rotated for two generations, from family to family. Upon his death, the chair would rotate to the next family. He bore no children, but his sister did, continuing the family line. Somehow, the familial line always continued.

A primary challenge of operating a criminal organization is truth. Victims should never comprehend reality. When the truth escapes, ramifications, legal and otherwise, arise. And since the handlers owned the judiciary, there were no legal consequences. The manifestations of his life's activity ate him alive. Guilt crawled from the recesses of his mind and laid assault on his nervous system.

Ten minutes ago, the device beeped and radiated its piercing neon red light. Sometimes it didn't ring for hundreds of years, sometimes it rang a few times a year. The random flashing of the cube signaled the veil of many lifetimes of extortion, blackmail and perpetual bloodshed being punctured by the Sage. His monotone voice transcended time and space. The Handler assumed he was alien, but he didn't know for certain.

The voice knew everything; every sordid detail. All the rulers throughout history took orders from him. They had no choice. Throughout their rule, the handlers presumed the Sage was the same individual, even given the incomprehensible lifespan.

He started extorting the ruling class 4,000 years ago. This is when the device appeared. The Sage called the shots. They followed orders, precisely as given. The alternative was the handlers' destruction. Not via the mysterious voice, but executed by the population through truth disclosure. A truth the aristocrats kept a dark secret with a desperate verve.

The voice threatened the destruction of the handlers throughout history and demonstrated examples on several occasions when populist uprisings occurred. At multiple points in history, the Earth's people came close to taking down their system. Occasional failure points existed from the Sage's maneuvering, some by the sloppiness and complexity of maintaining the matrix. Albeit rare, mistakes were made. But the rulers always recovered.

The Handler knew the Sage would continue to call the shots, but without him. He pulled the trigger and ended his time as the head of the families.

The Sage hung up the communication device to the Handler. He knew what had happened.

Rego, The Wong, and Coder waited for Qunot to speak.

"It's done."

A pair of geese stood outside The Handler's window eating grass and recorded the event to the one goose hive mind. Mr. Goose and Sam

Shank both instantly knew what happened. Sam informed Newton and the twins. They understood.

Minutes later, the apparition of the Handler appeared on the ship's bridge. He locked eyes with the most evolved human on Earth and Sam's steel-blue eyes of truth burned the Handler's brain. He averted his gaze. The guilt and shame of his rotted soul could not tolerate the unyielding pain of unadulterated knowledge.

The ship was minutes from never needing the temporal plane.

Sam stared at the pathetic excuse for a man. The self-inflicted gunshot wound to the head couldn't hide the tortured soul depicted by his dead, black eyes. He took the coward's way out.

"Every lie the devil told will be revealed."

The crisp confidence in Sam's voice caused the apparition to shake in despair. He spoke from knowledge and the unvarnished truth of universal will. The Handler raised his chin one last time to absorb the look of the man who just lay bare the new reality of Earth's civilization.

With the ship out of danger, Olsen deactivated the temporal plane.

The Handler disappeared.

As the aliens departed the Earth's solar system for the final time, a single stowaway hid himself in the laundry compartment. A lone goose on a mission to exact a pound of flesh from a corrupt television executive.

Gary sometimes lives on the planet Earth. Nowadays, he is more likely to be traveling around the more fashionable inner portion of the Milky Way, chasing down an irrational goose hell bent on revenge or raising funds for the galactic Save the Earthlings foundation.

Made in the USA
Columbia, SC
20 November 2024

46866943R00187